Praise for the novels of

Mary Alice Monroe

"An inspirational tale of redemption."
—*Publishers Weekly* on *Swimming Lessons*

"Monroe makes her characters so believable,
the reader can almost hear them breathing....
Readers who enjoy such fine southern voices as Pat Conroy
will add the talented Monroe to their list of favorites."
—*Booklist* on *Sweetgrass*

"*Skyward* is a soaring, passionate story of loneliness and pain
and the simple ability of love to heal and transcend both.
Mary Alice Monroe's voice is as strong and true
as the great birds of prey of whom she writes."
—*New York Times* bestselling author Anne Rivers Siddons

"With each new book, Mary Alice Monroe continues to
cement her growing reputation as an author of power and depth.
The Beach House is filled with the agony of past mistakes,
present pain and hope for a brighter future."
—*RT Book Reviews*

"Monroe writes with a crisp precision and narrative energy that
will keep [readers] turning the pages. Her talent for infusing her
characters with warmth and vitality and her ability to spin a tale
with emotional depth will earn her a broad spectrum of readers,
particularly fans of Barbara Delinsky and Nora Roberts."
—*Publishers Weekly* on *The Four Seasons*

Skyward

Mary Alice Monroe

MIRA®

MIRA®

Recycling programs
for this product may
not exist in your area.

ISBN-13: 978-0-7783-2997-8

SKYWARD

For questions and comments about the quality of this book please contact us
at Customer_eCare@Harlequin.ca.

www.MIRABooks.com

Printed in U.S.A.

First Printing: July 2003
10 9 8 7 6 5 4 3 2 1

This book is dedicated to
Jim Elliott, Jemima Parry-Jones, Grace Gaspar,
Stacy Hughes, Franci Krawcke, Mary Pringle
and to all my fellow volunteers at the
South Carolina Center for Birds of Prey

And to dedicated professionals and volunteers
across the country—and the world—
who dedicate their time to help preserve and protect
the magnificent birds of prey.

CONTRETEMPS

Though the world's dark heart
brought me here,
where time was hiding
in the unleashed sea,
I will stay in this fragile place
of broken trees and wounded birds
that teach me patience as I watch
them fill the bared branches
like clusters of singing leaves.

I will follow
a passing flock of plovers,
who think faster than we can see
when they suddenly turn
and flash their snowy undersides
in one bright act
of collected caring consciousness.

They must have heard a warning
in the lost language
of the river wind.

But the silent merlin—
in pursuit
disarmed, confused, and angry—
cackles at his lazy gods.

I see the breath
of another god, moving
beneath still wings
of the osprey and the eagle
in flight. I see
countless angels, rising from the river
with open hands
and upturned palms
to hold the wings in place
as the animals glide over
this sanctuary
and pull the sky
back into the universe.

—Marjory Wentworth

__Birds of Prey__ (also known as raptors) have characteristics that distinguish them from other birds. A bird of prey has a sharp, hooked beak for tearing food, sharp, curved talons, powerful feet for killing its prey and binocular vision. Thirty-eight species of raptors are found in the geographic limits of the United States and Canada. These species are divided into categories: buteos, accipiters, falcons, harriers, kites, eagles, ospreys and owls.

1

A BRISK, WINTRY WIND WHISTLED ALONG THE South Carolina coast. It rattled the ice-tipped, yellowed spartina grass and rolled a thick, steely gray fog in from the sea. The old black man paused in his walk and cocked his ear toward the sky. He heard the whispers of change in the wind. Hunching his shoulders, he turned the collar of his threadbare woolen jacket high up to the brim of his fedora, then dug his hands deep into his pockets. He resumed walking, but he kept his eyes skyward.

The old man had walked nearly half a mile when he heard a high, plaintive whistle over the wind's song. He stopped abruptly, rigid with expectation, staring out at the heavy shroud that hovered over the wetlands. It was a still morning; the pale night moon lingered in the dusty sky. Suddenly, a magnificent white-crested eagle broke through the mist. Its broad, plank-straight wings stretched wide as it soared over the water.

"There you be!" he muttered with deep satisfaction. Bringing his large, gnarled hands to cup his mouth, he whistled sharp and clear, mimicking the birdcall.

The bald eagle circled wide, flapping its powerful wings with a majesty reserved for royalty. The great bird took a lap around the marsh before deigning to return the call.

The effect was not lost on the old man. Heartened, he rushed his hands to his mouth and whistled again, louder and more insistently. This time, the eagle banked, then flew unwaveringly toward him.

This was the moment Harris Henderson relished. He squinted and let his gaze slowly traverse the wide, open meadow encircled by tall, leggy pines. The grasses were crisp and the ground was hard with the early morning frost. In only one day's time, winter had blustered into the Lowcountry, plummeting temperatures from balmy to freezing. He took a long, deep breath, feeling the moist chill go straight to his lungs. The morning air carried the scent of burning wood—cedar, he thought—so strong he could almost taste it.

Turning his head, he gazed upon the sleek red-tailed hawk held firm against his chest by his thick leather gloves. Maggie Mims, a robust woman with hair almost the same color red as the hawk's tail, looked up at him with eyes sparkling with excitement.

She gave a curt nod.

Harris moved his gloved hands so that his left wrapped around the hawk's wings and the right maintained a firm hold of the hawk's feet. Instantly, the hawk's dark gaze sharpened, her mouth opened and she jerked her wings hard for freedom.

"So, you're eager to be off," he said in a low voice.

He waited patiently for the bird to calm itself, all the while looking on with admiration. She was a beautiful specimen, creamy breasted with a dark bellyband and the brick-red tail feathers that gave the species its name. Red-taileds were superb hunters, "the black warriors" J. J. Audubon had called them. It was hard to believe, looking at her sleek, healthy form, that she'd been brought into the clinic with gunshot wounds a mere two months earlier. "Well, it won't be long now."

The bird cocked its head at the sound of his voice, glaring, ferocious—the right attitude for survival. Every instinct in its body was on alert for flight. Harris could feel the bird's anticipation in his own veins.

In this brief moment before flight, Harris sought to merge spirits with the bird. He'd read stories of shamans who practiced this ancient art, myths of Indians whose spirits soared with eagles, tales that he'd heard spoken of only in passing or in jest. Though he'd tell this to no one, deep down he'd always believed that at the core of legends and myths lay a kernel of truth. There *were* individuals who communicated at some visceral level with birds. He knew it. Witnessed it.

And it was his private pain that he was not one of them. Although highly skilled, he didn't possess the rare instinct— the gift—of connection. The art of truly flying the birds.

The closest he came to it was at liftoff. The seconds when the bird's wings stretched out and he heard the *whup-whup* of their flapping and felt the quick fluttering of air against his cheek as the bird flew fearlessly into the wind. At that stolen moment in time he caught an exhilarating glimpse of what it might be like to fly, to feel the lift, then the air glide over him like water.

"Ready?" asked Maggie.

Sensing freedom at hand, the red-tailed tightened its talons on his arm. The brisk wind gusted, riffling the feathers on its head. She didn't flinch. Her eyes were focused. A faint stream of breath clouded the air like steam as her chest rose and fell. The moment had come.

"Okay, my beauty," he said softly to the hawk. "Let's send you home."

With a lift of his arm, he let his hands go. Instantly the talons released their grip. Wings fluttered, stirring the air. Harris released a sigh as the hawk took flight.

Up, up, the red-tailed climbed. Harris tracked the bird, assessing her strength and looking for any tipping, which would indicate the broken wing hadn't completely healed. The margin for survival was very slim in the wild. A raptor had to be one hundred percent to successfully hunt. There was nothing tentative about this bird's flying, however, and Harris felt a bone-deep satisfaction that their work at the rehabilitation center had been successful.

This bird, number 1985, was successfully released to the wild.

"We're not s'posed to hunt in there."

Brady Simmons pointed the business end of his .22 caliber rifle toward the No Hunting sign posted on the gnarled bark of a bare-leafed live oak. "It says right here, see?" he said, careful to make it more question than statement.

His father rubbed his bristled jaw and drawled, "I don't see no sign."

"Billy Trumplin's dad says we could get in big trouble if we hunt in there. 'Specially birds. It ain't even the season."

Roy Simmons slowly turned his head, narrowing his eyes as he focused on his eldest son. His voice was low but lethal. "You tellin' me what to do now, boy?"

Brady took a step back. "N-no, sir."

The spark in his father's eyes banked as he acknowledged the respect. "Our family's been huntin' this here land longer than anyone can remember. There ain't nothing wrong with takin' a little of what's there for the takin'." He hoisted his rifle. "Besides, we ain't here for sport. We're here to put food on the table. And I'll be dog damned if some tree hugger's gonna up and tell me I can't."

Brady gave a curt nod and kept an eye on his father's balled fists. The stench of stale whiskey on his father's breath kept the boy mute with fear and contempt.

His father reached out to rip the sign from the tree bark and throw it on the ground.

Brady's face was a portrait of teenage apathy as he watched his father grind the muddy heel of his boot on the federal sign. *What a jerk,* he thought. He was sick of hearing his father grouse about land that had been "stolen" from the people. How could someone steal what wasn't theirs in the first place? Besides, what did he care about the land and who owned it? All he wanted was to get as far away from this hellhole as he could.

Satisfied, his father turned and pushed into the federally protected land. "Well, come on, then," he said over his shoulder. "Don't lag behind."

The woods were still dark in the dank hush of early morning. The crush of Brady's boots in the layers of frosted, composting leaves sounded violent in the quiet forest. There were lots of loblolly pines, growing thin and so close together it would be easy to get lost if one didn't know the territory. Brady always preferred the longleaf pine and the way its long needles stirred in the breeze. There was something regal about them, the way they stood ten stories tall, six feet around and straight-backed—the kings of the pine forest. He liked them even if his father hated them, calling them nothing better than wood weeds on account of the fact that the fire-resistant bark was no good for firewood. He'd heard him tell of a time when longleafs used to dominate the woods, back before the buzzsaws did their work. Brady would like to have seen that.

As he walked around the clustered trunks, he noticed how the light of the rising sun dappled through the leaves, making the melting frost sparkle like diamonds. In the thick branches over his head, he could hear fox squirrels chattering and, farther off, a red-cockaded woodpecker hammering into the sapwood.

"Quit draggin' your feet back there! If you didn't stay up all night with that rowdy bunch of no-counts you call friends you wouldn't be so damned worthless in the mornin'. Took a bomb to get you outta that bed this morning. I *told* you we was goin' huntin' this mornin'."

Brady spit out the sour taste of his breakfast of cold biscuits and jerky, then picked up his pace behind the bulky, wide-shouldered man in the camouflage jacket. At least it would be the last thing he'd hear from the old man for a while, he thought. From here on in, he'd be telling him what to do in hissed whispers and jabs with his index finger so as not to spook the game.

Roy Simmons never asked his son where he might think was a good place to hunt or even what game he'd like to go after. Brady felt little more than a lackey behind the skilled huntsman who knew better than most where to find the first buck of the season, or a fertile oyster bed, or where to flush out birds. That's what they were after this morning. Some pheasant, or maybe quail…something special to put on the Christmas dinner table tomorrow.

Most of the food on their table came from what his daddy hunted or fished. It was pretty much a hand-to-mouth existence for the family of seven. His mama did all she could with whatever his father brought home, but he never seemed satisfied. And lately, with the neighboring land just made into a national preserve, places to hunt were hard to come by. More and more folks were after what little game was left. Roy Simmons had to hunt longer and smarter to bring less to the table, even as his young were growing bigger and eating more.

He preferred hunting alone, but for the past few days since school was out for the holiday he'd dragged Brady, the eldest son, along on his early-morning hunting trips. They'd come up empty-handed each time. It being the holiday, the stakes were higher. Every day Brady saw his father's desperation turn to anger. As he followed the pounding footfall of his father, Brady hoped he wouldn't take that anger out on him.

Brady and his father walked without luck for more than an hour into the Francis Marion National Forest, miles from the small spread of ramshackle house and barn that his family called home. The scrap of land was deeded to his great-grandfather back when this place on earth was considered nowhere. Now the sprawl from Charleston was spreading its tentacles their way, causing environmentalists to scoop up whatever they could as protected land. Their scrubby bit of earth was a small speck of private land bordered by thousands of acres of national forest, what his daddy smugly called "the thorn in the ass of the feds."

"You think maybe we should head back?" he asked, foot weary.

"We're not going back without we get somethin' for dinner."

Brady silently groaned. His eyelids were drooping and his toes were cold in his boots as he silently kept up. He hated being forced to get up early in the morning. He hated being stuck in these godforsaken woods, hungry and tired, when all he wanted to do was go back to his warm bed, even if he did have to share the room with his brother and the dog. And though he'd never admit it to his father, he hated hunting. It was boring and pointless, like most things in his life.

At last they came to where the flat woodlands opened up to a wide expanse of open marshland. His father stopped here, his shotgun hanging from his arm, to survey the landscape with an eagle eye.

A brisk wind was blowing in from the ocean, stinging Brady's cheeks with crisp freshness and waking him to the beauty of the eastern sky. He lowered his rifle in quiet awe. The dawn had already declared itself. Pink streaks softly shadowed a pearly blue sky, but an approaching armada of low-lying gray clouds and fog stretched threatening fingers across the horizon.

"Look! There!" His father jabbed his side and pointed.

"Where?"

"There. Over that stretch of marsh. At nine o'clock."

Brady turned his head to see an enormous black bird soaring on a great expanse of wing. The beauty of the sight was awesome.

"Go on, son. Take the shot!"

Frozen with shock that his father was actually offering him the rare opportunity to take the shot, Brady fumbled as he raised the barrel, losing precious seconds.

"Hurry up! You'll lose it."

I ain't gonna lose it, he thought to himself, aware that actually speaking the words could cause him to lose his train on the bird. He could hear the blood roar in his ears, and excitement thrummed in his veins as he brought his eye to the scope.

"It's bankin'," his father said. "Comin' right for you."

"I can't see it!"

"It went back into the fog. Don't matter. Wait for him. Be cocked and ready."

Brady eased off the safety, put his right forefinger on the trigger and placed his site squarely on the spot he figured the bird would emerge. He tried to calm himself, to take slow breaths and make certain he got the shot. His father wouldn't give him a second chance.

Okay, where are you? One…two…three… Suddenly, out from the fog, the bird emerged—right where Brady figured it would. Oh, yeah, it was a big bird. A real big bird. He told himself to take it slow and careful as he trailed the soaring bird and focused. His finger applied pressure. He held his breath.

Brady released his breath with the curse, lowering his rifle. "I can't shoot. It's an eagle."

"A what? Goddamn… That's all that's left in these goddamn government woods." Roy shook his head and mumbled a curse. "They won't let us hunt nowhere or shoot nothin' no more. Look up there! It's comin' straight for us. Bold as can be, knowin' we can't shoot. Probably gonna steal some decent farmer's chickens. Well, hell. Go on, son. Take it."

"*What?* I can't. It's against the law."

"What's the law got to do with my god-given right to hunt like my father and my father before him? I'm tellin' you, that bird is the enemy, you hear me?"

"That bird ain't done nothing."

"I'm not playin' with you, boy." He looked his son in the eyes with steely rage and said in a low, threatening voice, "You're either with me on this or against me."

Brady hesitated.

His father muttered with disgust that he was as weak as a woman, bringing his own shotgun to his shoulder.

Brady felt his chest constrict and brought his eye back to the scope of his rifle and his finger to the trigger. Life with his father had always been an endless, agonizing series of tests.

Was he with his father, or against him? In that moment, one that seemed to linger in the air without regard for time or judgment, Brady knew that, whatever action he took, his life was going to change forever.

The old man smiled from ear to ear in elation at the magnificent sight of seven feet of wingspan riding a thermal. The Good Lord sure knew what he was doing when he made the eagle, he thought to himself. Powerful wings, a razor-sharp beak and talons as long and sharp as tiger claws. And the way she flew… It was like she knew she was queen of the skies. There weren't no creature more beautiful in the whole world, he thought.

He whistled again and reached into the pouch hanging from his side to pull out a wide-mouth bass he'd brought just for this bird. He knew she was busy with her nest, knew she was hungry.

"Well, come on and get yourself some bittle," he told the bird as he raised the fish high into the air. He whistled again, loud and clear, wiggled the outstretched fish and began walking through the field. She saw it. He could tell by the way she was circling.

Suddenly, the unmistakable thundering of gunshot shattered the morning's peace. The old man stumbled. His arms jerked outstretched, dropping the fish to the field. He watched with helpless horror as the eagle's great wings fluttered against the bruise-colored sky. His breath choked in his throat as the bird seemed to hang in the air. Then the wings crumpled and the eagle dropped like a stone to the earth.

His cry of anguish mingled with the shrieking wind that streaked across the wetlands, whisking away the old man's hat to reveal a head of snowy white hair. Spurred forward, he took off at a stiff-legged gait across the frosted fields straight for the fallen bird.

Buteos: The Soaring Hawks. Buteos are medium-to-large hawks with broad wings and a short tail. Although slow flyers, they excel in soaring and hunt on the wing. They are a diverse group with a wide range of habitats and prey. Buteos include red-tailed hawks, red-shouldered hawks, broad-winged hawks, Swainson's hawks, rough-legged hawks and ferruginous hawks.

2

HARRIS STOOD IN THE BRISK WIND WATCHING the sky until the tiny speck of brown that was the hawk disappeared from view. Scanning the horizon, there wasn't another hawk in sight; only a broad-winged vulture coasted over the treetops.

He could remember his grandfather telling him of the days when he could walk a mile through a country field like this one and see every kind of hawk: sharp-shinned, Cooper's, red-tailed and red-shouldered, kestrel and harrier—though his grandfather called those small but quick birds "marsh hawks." Harris was no older than five when his grandfather began walking the fields with him. His grandfather would pause, point to the sky and ask, "What's that?" Harris would shout out an answer with boyish confidence and never feel rebuked when his grandfather, more often than not, gently corrected him. Those walks were some of the most memorable in his life and fired a lifelong devotion to birds of prey. His grandfather had loved raptors, hawks especially, and taught him that identifying a hawk in the air was not as much a skill as it was an art. Color of plumage wasn't a key, as it was in smaller birds. He was a shrewd and patient teacher, instructing Harris to take his time to read the subtle signs—the cant of a wing, the speed of the flap—and to trust his intuitive sense of how a bird appeared in flight before making his call. By the time his grandfather passed away Harris was only twelve years of age, but he could unerringly spot and name a raptor from a distance.

Harris was born in the early 1960s, a decade that recognized the devastation DDT brought to the environment. Since his boyhood he'd worked to help rebuild the birds of prey population from near extinction. They still had a long way to go before the skies would be as filled with raptors as his grandfather remembered, but they were on the right track. Each time he released a bird back to the wild he felt his entire being stir with hope.

"Harris!"

He reluctantly turned from the sky to see a young, black, teenage girl neatly dressed in jeans and fleece trotting toward him from the edge of the open meadow. He waved an arm in silent acknowledgment, then cast a final glance toward the sky. The hawk was long gone. Beyond the circle of meadow, the fog was closing in.

"Mr. Henderson?" the girl called again, breathless from her run. "I'm supposed to tell you that Sherry needs you back at the clinic right away. Someone's brought in a bird that's been shot."

Harris cursed softly.

"I'll take this one," Maggie said, bending to pick up the gear. "Aren't you supposed to take Marion Christmas shopping? That little darling's been talking about nothing else all week."

He nodded with acknowledgment as he helped gather the gear. His five-year-old daughter had woken him at dawn that morning, already dressed in her best pants and sweater, her hair haphazardly pulled back with a pink plastic headband. She was so excited about their holiday outing that she only nibbled at her breakfast, preferring to drink several glasses of orange juice that kept her running back and forth from the bathroom. He chuckled quietly as he walked, recalling how he'd asked if she had a valve open in her plumbing. His last view before leaving the house was of Marion's forlorn face staring back at him from the front window. He'd waved and called out that he'd be back soon, but she hadn't smiled. He'd had to go to release the hawk, but the memory still tugged at his heartstrings.

"You haven't bought a thing for that child yet, have you?" Maggie asked in response to his long silence. They'd walked across the field to the truck and she was regarding him skeptically. When he didn't reply she added, "Good Lord, Harris. Do you even have a Christmas tree up?"

"Yep. The tree's up and it's even got lights on it, so don't you worry, Mother Maggie," he said with a teasing grin, and was pleased to see her face soften in response. Once Maggie got going, it was hard to derail her. "Marion and I amble into town every Christmas Eve, just the two of us, and she gets to pick out something special. It's kind of our ritual."

"Ritual?" Maggie looked at him disbelievingly. "Come on, Henderson, you can't fool me. I've known you too long. You're a hermit who'd never leave the woods if you didn't have to, and this so-called ritual is your excuse for not having to face going into stores more than you absolutely have to." She was nearly as tall as he was and her green eyes were

fiery as they bore into his. "No more excuses today. You go
on and leave that bird to me and give that poor child a Merry
Christmas."

Harris held up his hands in mock defeat. "All right, all
right, I'll go. You can take this one."

"But Sherry said she needs *you,* Harris," the young girl interrupted. "It's an eagle. She said for you to hurry." The cold
wind puckered the volunteer's lips but her brown eyes were
soft with worry.

Harris gave Maggie a knowing look and took off at a trot
for his truck parked at the edge of the field. He treated all
kinds of raptors at the center: hawks, owls, ospreys and falcons. But it was the eagle that he had the greatest affinity for.
In his opinion, no other raptor could compare with the eagle's grace and power. And it was that very power that made
them so dangerous to handle. Unlike substantial Maggie,
Sherry was older and as small and delicate as a peregrine falcon. And though just as clever and quick, she didn't have the
physical strength to handle eagles. When an injured one was
brought in, Harris took the call.

Silenced by duty, Maggie jumped into the cab beside him.
The gravel flew as his wheels dug in and he took off down
the dirt road. The bird-flying field was only a short drive
down the main road from the Coastal Carolina Center for
Birds of Prey. He parked his truck at the house and trotted
through the small tangle of trees straight toward the small
white frame house mounted on cinder blocks that was the
clinic. Immediately, he spotted Sherry Dodds, his senior volunteer, in full leather protective gear hovering uncertainly
near a tall, slender black man with snowy white hair. Harris's
eyes fell to the man's arms and his step faltered.

Maggie grasped his arm tight. "Oh, my God…"

Harris swallowed hard. He couldn't believe what he was

seeing. The old man carried a full-size bald eagle in his bare arms. That eagle's talons could rip apart the man's thin coat and arms, and its razor-sharp beak could slash his face with the speed of a bullet.

"Slow down," Harris said to Maggie as they approached. They didn't want to startle the eagle. It seemed to be in shock, not moving a muscle save for its glaring yellow eyes that followed their approach with typical intensity.

"Thank God you're here," Sherry exclaimed, straining to keep her voice down. It was rare to see her flustered. "This man...he just walked in here with the eagle...in his arms! I got the gloves out, but with him holding it like that, unprotected... I didn't know what to do!"

Harris nodded curtly. He understood too well the dangers. The old man was holding on to the eagle's feet with one hand, which was good, but he cradled the bird too damn close to his chest and face.

Sherry slipped out of the leather chest protector and long gloves and handed them to Harris, keeping her eyes on the bird all the while. As he stuck his arms into the protective gear, Harris assessed the bird with an experienced eye. It was a very large eagle, with shiny plumage, obviously healthy before the gunshot wounds. The white head feathers marked it as an adult, at least five years of age.

"Excuse me, sir. But you the doctor?" the old man asked. His long, weathered face was heavily creased with age and worry. He had a distinguished bearing, dressed almost entirely in faded black, yet he cradled the bird in his arms and large, gnarled hands as tenderly as a nursemaid with a baby. Harris figured he was either a fearless old coot or just plain ignorant to the danger he'd put himself into. At least he had the sense to keep a firm grip on the talons.

"Yes, but don't talk. The sound of human voices is distress-

ing to wild birds, and right now we don't want to do anything unnecessary to rile this ol' boy."

"Girl."

Harris narrowed his eyes. From the size of the bird, the
old man was likely right. "I've got to get that eagle out of
your arms. Now, I want you to listen carefully. I'm going to
approach the bird and get a firm grip on its talons with these
gloves. When I say go, I mean just that. You let go of the
bird and get away as fast as you can. Understand?"

"You think Santee's gonna hurt me?" he asked. The old
man shook his head slightly. "No, she ain't. She knows me."

"*Knows* you?"

He nodded solemnly. "I be the one that called her. She
was coming straight to me when someone shot her from the
sky. I tracked her and found her lying on the ground. Alive,
praise Jesus! I heard about you folks here. How you help the
birds. I'm grateful you were somewheres I could walk to."

"You *walked* the bird here?"

"Came down the big road, straight as the crow flies."

"How far did you come?"

"Not far. That way, back yonder a few miles, maybe. But
it was slow going through the marsh."

He almost laughed at the absurdity of it all. "How long
have you been carrying that eagle?"

"Since after sunup."

It was already almost nine. That meant the eagle had been
wounded for hours. Harris shifted his gaze to the eagle. The
large bird continued to stare at him, not lethargically or with
head dangling, as one would expect from a bird in shock,
but with an unnerving calm. Yet only shock could explain
its nonresponsiveness—and shock was a killer. He had to act
quickly to save the eagle's life. He cast a worried glance at

Sherry, who had returned wearing another set of long leather gloves. She was waiting, hands in the ready.

"The bird's in shock," he told her.

"I figured. I've got the body wrap and dex ready."

He took a deep breath to squelch the flicker of anxiety in his chest. He met the old man's steady gaze. He seemed to have no fear at all. "Okay, then…ready?"

"Yes, sir."

With slow, deliberate movements, Harris moved his gloved hands to get a secure grip on the feather-coated legs. "I've got her. Let go."

When the old man retracted his hands, the bird flinched its enormous talons and squirmed in Harris's grip. In a flash, Harris cupped his free hand under and around the wings, then lifted the bird from the old man's arms. Even with shot in its wings, the eagle had surprising strength as it flexed its talons and jerked to escape during the transfer. Harris's experience quickly brought the bird under control.

Once stilled, however, its breathing grew more labored and its mouth gaped with stress. Sherry moved to place a light towel over the eagle's head.

"What for you did that?" the old man asked.

"It helps reduce stress," she replied.

"You're a lucky man," Harris said, exhaling with relief. "If this bird wasn't in shock, you could be in the hospital yourself. Never forget these are wild creatures. Don't make the mistake of trusting them."

"Trust ain't never a mistake," the old man replied.

The man's gaze held him with the same unnerving intensity of the eagle's. Harris abruptly turned to the two women standing close by. "Can you get the intake information from this gentleman?"

"Will do," Maggie replied, stepping forward.

Harris turned again to the old man. "We're grateful you brought the eagle to us. I'm taking it into surgery now. You can give your name and phone number to Maggie and we'll call you once we know how things turn out. Thanks again for taking the trouble to bring the bird in." He moved toward the treatment room, dismissing him.

"I'll wait."

"We don't have a waiting area," Maggie replied kindly. "Don't worry. We'll call you right after surgery. It could take hours."

"No matter. I'll just wait outside."

Maggie looked questioningly at Harris. His eyes flashed with annoyance, but he didn't have time to argue the point. "He can wait in my office," he said briskly, then turned and carried the eagle indoors.

The sun was beginning its descent by the time Harris's duties in surgery were completed. It had been an unusually busy day. Two barred owls and a black vulture had also been admitted, all with head traumas from being hit by cars—a result of the heavy holiday traffic. After surgery, the birds were placed in the critical-care unit, a small, narrow room off the treatment room comprised of two long shelves holding two rows of kennels. Each kennel was draped with a cloth for darkness and quiet. Stress in captivity was a killer for wild birds, and at the center they did everything possible to minimize it.

Before closing up, Harris went to check the eagle one more time. In the darkness of her large kennel, she lay on her side, groggy from the anesthesia. She was hurt pretty badly with pellet wounds, some of them lodged where they could still cause trouble. There was also head trauma from the fall. Whether she'd be able to hunt again remained to be seen.

He ran his hands through his hair as he stepped from the treatment room, then let them slip down to rub the small of his back. His muscles ached from the hours of standing bent over the treatment table. He wanted nothing more than to strip from his dirty flannel shirt and jeans, kick off his hiking boots, shower, grab a bite to eat and collapse. The phone was blissfully silent and he was ready to call it a day. Yawning, he stopped short when he spotted the old black man still sitting in his office, elbows on his knees and his long, gnarled fingers worrying the brim of his hat. The man leapt to his feet when Harris walked in.

"How is she?"

"Amazingly good for a bird that just had a bucket of buck-shot taken from its wings. It was slow, tedious work." He shook his head. "But I've got to tell you, despite several punctures of lead shot, not a bone was broken. It's pretty damn unbelievable. I'd have thought there'd be at least one break. This was one lucky bird."

"Praise Jesus!" the man replied.

"I think Dr. Henderson had a little to do with it, too," Sherry chimed in good-naturedly as she followed Harris into the office. She'd tucked her salt-and-pepper hair into a knit cap and was stuffing her arms into her parka en route to the sign-out sheet.

"No doubt, no doubt. And I'm grateful. Don't know ex-actly how to repay you for your kindness. While I was sitting here, I was thinking…I might could do some work around the place. I saw a few spots that could use a good carpenter. And I'm a good carpenter."

"You don't have to do anything," Sherry blurted out as she rushed by. "That's what we're here for, you know. To help injured birds."

"But this ain't just any bird. This be *my* bird."

Sherry paused her hurried exit to look at Harris. He read in her eyes the same question running through his own mind. Eagles were a threatened species protected by the United States government. No one could own an eagle or possess it in any way. Even at the birds of prey center they were restricted to keep an eagle for only ninety days without federal permission for an extension.

"Excuse me, but I didn't catch your name," Harris said.

"The name's Elijah. Elijah Cooper," he said, straightening and extending his hand with an almost courtly manner. "But most folks call me Lijah."

Harris shook the offered hand. It was surprisingly large and strong.

"Well, Lijah, a Merry Christmas to you," Sherry interrupted as she swept by them. Her eyes were sparkling behind her glasses with anticipation of the holidays. "You too, you ol' humbug," she said to Harris with a brief but heartfelt hug. Then with a softer tone, "I left a little something for you and Marion under your tree."

"You didn't have to." He was always surprised and deeply touched by the many kindnesses the women at the center showed to him and his daughter. It was as though they had some silent pact between them to keep a close eye on the motherless home.

"Of course I did. I won't be in tomorrow at all, remember. Neither will Maggie. But I'll be here all the earlier on the twenty-sixth."

"We'll be fine. You just have a wonderful Christmas with your family. And drive carefully. The snow's still coming down."

"Don't worry about me. You just make sure you give that little girl of yours some time tomorrow. The birds will be fine for one day," she called as she hurried down the hall, eager to be home.

Harris turned back to Elijah, who stood waiting with a patient smile on his face as though he had nowhere to hurry off to on this snowy Christmas Eve. Harris usually didn't like talking to strangers or engaging in social chitchat, but there was something compelling about the man's serenity.

"Lijah, I don't mean to keep you any longer, but there's something I don't understand."

He cocked his head and his dark eyes glowed with interest.

"How is the eagle *your* bird?" Harris asked. "Do you keep it somewhere?"

"Keep it? You mean like in a cage?" Long lines crinkled the edges of his eyes, joining the multitude of others as he shook his head and chuckled. "No, sir. Nobody can keep an eagle. First off, it ain't legal. Second most, it ain't right. They noble creatures, meant to be free."

"Then how is it that this bird is *yours?*"

"I figure you can say she adopted me." When Harris's brows knit in confusion, Lijah explained, "See, years back, when she was still in her black feathers, she flew low, right by me. You know how they be… She just glided in, curious like, then she perched on a low branch not ten yards in front of me. She sat there watching me. I reckon it was only for a few minutes or so, but it seemed like a long time we stayed there, studying each other." He shook his head and smiled at some thought he meant to keep private because he simply shrugged. "Ever since, we just sort of looked out for each other. I call her Santee, after the river where I first seen her."

Harris stared at the old man, unsure of what to make of the story. He'd never heard such a fantastical tale before, but he couldn't discredit what he'd seen with his own eyes. Lijah had, after all, walked to the birds of prey center with the eagle held in his bare arms.

"Tell me what happened this morning."

"Well, sir, I was walking along the big road early this morning, looking for her. I'd parked my car a ways back, knowing she has a nest not too far from here. I knew she'd be showing up to hunt sooner or later. And then, there she was. So I called her."

"You called her?"

"Mmm-hmm. Like this." He raised his hands to his mouth, then stopped and shook his head with a rueful smile. "No, best not. She'd hear it and try to come."

Harris could barely restrain the wonder from his face. "You call and the eagle comes to you?"

"That's right. Like I said, we look out for each other. And she knows I'd brung her something good to eat. Anyway, this morning I called to her like I always do. She was banking in a nice loop, coming for me." His expression darkened. "Then them gunshots rang out. They shot her down." His cheeks stiffened in anguish. "What kind of man would do something like that? Why would anybody shoot such a fine creature of God?"

"I don't know," he replied soberly. It was a question he'd asked himself every time he pulled pellets from a bird. "Did you happen to see who shot the bird?"

Lijah paused while his face clouded with mixed emotions. "Yes, sir, I did. Leastways, I caught sight of two men with guns back in the woods when I went to fetch Santee. They were standing right where the sound of the gunshot came from so it was most likely them. But I didn't approach them or ask them nothing. Things being the way they were." He shook his head and his eyes flashed. "But it was them, most likely."

"You should report it to the police."

"I called them already. The woman let me use the phone and they came by while you was in surgery. We talked a bit, I told them what I know, then they left."

"Good. I hope they catch the bastards."

Lijah's lips pursed in thought. "You did say you pulled buckshot out of Santee? Not a bullet?"

"That's right. A mother lode of it. Why?"

"No reason. Just curious."

"Another thing. This eagle—" He paused and smiled briefly, conceding the name. "Santee. She has a brood patch. Did you say she had a nest somewhere near here?"

"Yes, sir. Not too far away. They're good parents, Santee and Pee Dee—I named 'em after the rivers. It's the second year they bred in that nest. Had two babies last time. That's what brings me this far north, you see. I be from St. Helena, but I been following them to check out the nest. Sometimes I camp, sometimes I stay with friends. It's a hike, but I don't stay long. Santee likes to nest up here. I figure it most likely be where she was born."

"Most likely. It's still early in the season. She may not have laid her eggs yet."

"Can't tell you that. Only just arrived myself. I been watching them, though. They been busy up there."

Harris weighed the lecture building in his mind about how humans needed to keep away from raptor nests so as not to disturb them, but decided against it. This man seemed pretty knowledgeable, and at the moment, he needed his help.

"Could you show me where this nest is?"

Lijah rubbed his jaw with his brow creased, then said with hesitation, "I suppose I could."

"Lijah, it's going to be hard for that male to incubate any young that may have hatched. Damn near impossible, in fact. We'll have to watch the nest carefully, in case he abandons it."

"I intend to."

"Maybe if we…"

Harris's attention was diverted by a gentle tug on his trousers. Looking down, he saw the sweet, pale face of his five-year-old daughter. Marion's hair was pulled back into an elastic that was slipping off center. The clothes he'd seen her in that morning were now slightly soiled and a smudge of grape jelly lingered at the corner of her pouting lips.

"Daddy?"

His face softened at the sight of her. "Yes, baby?"

"Are we gonna go shopping yet?" she asked in a soft whine.

Shopping. Christmas Eve. Dusk. All these realities hit him like a bucket of cold water dumped down his back. How could he have forgotten the outing? It was always this way with him. He'd get so caught up in his work he'd lose track of time and anything else that was on his calendar.

His daughter's eyes were filled with childish expectation and longing and Maggie's admonitions played again in his mind. He swung his head around to look out the window. It was only four o'clock but already the sky was dark. A few flakes floated in the dim light outside the door, but nothing to be worried about. He had to make good on his promise. If he hurried, they'd be in town and back before too late.

"Why, sure, honey," he replied, tousling her hair, sending the elastic flying. "Just give me a minute to close things up here." He looked again at the old man, who had already reached out to grab his hat.

"I best be going," he told Harris. "It's Christmas and looks like you've got an evening planned."

"We do. Heck of a night to hit the roads, though, isn't it. Can I drop you somewhere?"

"No, sir. Thank you but I'll find my own way."

"But didn't you say you walked here?"

"I did. But don't pay me mind. My friends live a short way down the road."

"But the closest house is a long walk through the woods. I insist. Let me drive you."

Lijah shook his head and began heading toward the door. "I been sitting here all day. My legs'll enjoy the stretch. Thanks again for tending to my bird. I'll stop by tomorrow, if you don't mind. Just to see how she is." Before leaving, he bent his snowy white head and smiled warmly at Marion. "Merry Christmas to you, little missy."

Marion smiled shyly and ducked behind her father's legs.

"We'll talk again. I'd like to go to that nest," Harris said.

Lijah nodded, then left, quietly closing the door behind him.

Harris stared after him a moment. The man left a lingering impression. With a sigh, he peeked out the window at the smattering of faint snowflakes dancing in the gray-blue afternoon. Placing his arm around his daughter's slim shoulders, he bent close to her ear.

"Will you look at that?" he asked. "It's been a long time since I last saw snow for Christmas right here in South Carolina. In fact," he said, squeezing her close, "I'll bet this is the first time you've seen snow at all. Guess it'll help ol' Santa."

"You told me there's no such thing as Santa."

His brows rose. "I did, huh?"

She nodded her head.

Even though he never encouraged belief in such things as fairies, Santa and the Easter Bunny, he believed firmly in the magic and beauty found in the wilds of nature and human nature alike. Life was full of hard realities, like people putting buckshot into an eagle for sport. And though he was dog-tired and hungry, at least for tonight he'd do what he could to keep the magic alive.

Harris felt blinded by the fluorescent lights as he strolled into the Wal-Mart store with Marion in tow. There was so much stuff everywhere. Who could need so many things? Bright red bows, gold tinsel and moving Santas seemed to jump out at him from the shelves. Compared to the silence of the woods, the loud and persistent Christmas music was grating to his ears. He squeezed his daughter's hand and fought the urge to walk faster through the aisles. Other shoppers racing through the store brushed clumsily as they passed in a buying frenzy. He couldn't wait to get back outdoors.

"Daddy, I'm thirsty." Marion's face peeked out from the hood of her pink parka, a hand-me-down from one of Maggie's girls. It was too small; Marion's shoulders were squeezed and the cuffs were inching up her forearms. He thought of buying her a new coat, since they were already here, then thought again. Money was tight and it wasn't cold for that long in South Carolina. He figured this parka would make do awhile longer.

"You had a drink before we left the house and another at the gas station. You can't be thirsty again."

"But I *am*. Can I have some of that?" she asked, pointing to some icy blue swirling mixture for sale at the snack bar.

"Maybe later."

Marion dragged tiredly on his arm and whined, "I'm thirsty *now*, Daddy."

Her tone was insistent, drawing his attention from the aisles of toys. On closer inspection her face appeared flushed and her eyes glassy. Come to think of it, she'd downed those glasses of juice this morning as if she were dying of thirst. He wondered if she could be coming down with something.

"I'll tell you what," he said, bending over to speak gently. "Let's pick out your present first and then, if you feel up to it, we'll go someplace real special for our Christmas Eve dinner. You can get anything you want then. How's that sound?"

"Okay," she replied with lackluster, casting a final longing glance at the drink machine.

It was his fault they'd had such a late start, but he couldn't help feeling disappointed. He'd hoped she might be a little excited by their special outing instead of dragging her feet and complaining. When they reached the doll section, he spread out his arm grandly and said with the enthusiasm of a carnival barker, "Look, Marion! Have you ever seen so many dolls in one place? And you can pick any which one you want for Christmas. Go on! Any one at all."

Marion let go of his hand and shuffled close to the row of dolls, staring dully at them with her arms dropped to her sides. There was no squeal of delight or so much as an ooh of anticipation.

He sighed and lowered himself to her level. "What's wrong, honey?"

She shrugged.

"But you said you wanted a doll for Christmas."

She shook her head no.

"Oh," he replied, perplexed. Then, regrouping, "Well, that's okay. You don't have to get one."

At least he hadn't gone out and bought one, he thought to himself. Kids changed their minds all the time, didn't they?

"There are lots of toys here. Games, stuffed animals, sports stuff... Hey, how about a bike?"

She turned to look at him, her eyes forlorn. "Daddy, you know what I want for Christmas."

On her pale, thin face he saw the yearning of a lonely child. It near broke his heart. Marion wasn't by nature a whiner or a complainer. In fact, she rarely asked for anything for herself. He wrapped his arm around her and rested her against his knee as he racked his brain for what to say.

"Honey, you know I can't get you your mama for Christmas. We talked about this. That's just silly."

"No, it isn't silly." Her lower lip shot out in a pout.

"I know, I'm sorry. Why don't you pick out a doll that looks like Mama? Won't that be fine? Look at those over there. They're very pretty, just like her."

When she looked up at him with those large, trusting blue eyes, she looked so much like her mother that his heart wrenched. He kissed her tender cheek. "Go on, now."

With a resigned sigh, Marion turned and looked again at the row of dolls. After some thought, she raised her arm and pointed toward a Barbie doll dressed in a neon pink ball gown littered with colored glitter. Harris thought it was the gaudiest doll on the shelf—and sadly appropriate. Fannie did like bright colors. He shifted his weight and reached for the chosen Barbie doll.

"That's a fine choice, honey! It's real pretty. What are you going to call her?" He held his breath, hoping she wouldn't name the doll Fannie after her mother.

Marion scrunched her face in deliberation, then announced, "Lulu."

He smiled. "Perfect. Now, you stay put and have fun looking at these dolls while I go buy her," he told her. "Don't go anywhere. Promise? Daddy'll be right back. Okay?"

When she nodded he hurried to the checkout line with the Barbie doll in his hands. He wasn't the only one doing last-minute shopping, but only two checkout registers were open so the lines were long. He took his place, all the while anxiously looking over his shoulder to keep an eye on Marion in the toy aisle. The line seemed to move to the same slow pace of "White Christmas" blaring from the speakers. He longed for the quiet peace of his home in the woods and tapped his fingers on the box. Nearing the counter, he picked through the selections of last-minute Christmas items: decorated sugar cookies, a plush red Christmas stocking filled with candy, a small stuffed reindeer and wrapping paper with ribbon. When at last it was his turn, he set his parcels on the belt, pulled a few bills from the worn leather wallet and gave them to the cashier. He fingered the remaining bills in his wallet, mentally tallying up the bill and figuring the cost of dinner.

It was times like these he wondered if he'd made the right choice to dedicate his life to saving birds. Most biologists connected with wildlife conservation understood from the get-go that the job required long hours and endless dedication. They loved their work, couldn't imagine doing anything else, but the job took its toll on their personal lives, not to mention their bankbooks. He sighed. Putting his wallet back into his pocket, he knew his answer would be yes.

When he looked up again, he saw a minor commotion over at the toy aisle. A few people were bending over something on the floor.

"Marion!" he blurted out, and took off at a run. He pushed through the small cluster of people to find his daughter lying on the floor ashen-faced with her eyes rolled back, jerking uncontrollably. His heart rate zoomed. Kneeling, he scooped his little girl in his arms and began loosening her hood and jacket with shaky fingers.

"She just fell down, like she fainted!" an elderly woman exclaimed. "I saw her."

A slight trickle of blood oozed from her mouth. Had she bitten her tongue? He tried to wedge open her mouth but her teeth were clamped tight. His mind fought through a horrifying panic as he tried to diagnose Marion's problem. Epilepsy? Fever? He felt choked and his hands shook. This wasn't some hawk or an eagle. This was his daughter and he didn't know what to do.

He looked up at the wall of onlookers, eyes wild, and shouted, "Will someone call an ambulance?"

Accipiters: The Woodland Darters. Accipiters are agile, determined hunters. Their shorter, rounder wings and long tails are adapted for the quick bursts of speed and weaving through branches and brush needed to hunt other birds. Accipiters include sharp-shinned hawks, Cooper's hawks and goshawks.

3

HARRIS NEVER REALIZED HOW MERE WEEKS could change an entire life. In less than a month's time, his hard-won routine was turned upside down. There were times that he could almost hear the gods laughing at his hubris for believing he'd had everything in control.

Still, he was lucky. He knew that, too. Things could always be worse, had been worse.

He stood in the main room of the small Cape Cod house watching his daughter as she lay peacefully on the sofa. She was enveloped in a cocoon of pillows and wrapped in an old yellow-and-brown afghan. Clutched to her chest was the ever-present doll, Gaudy Lulu. Marion's blue eyes, fringed with pale lashes, stared fixedly at the cartoons on the television. Her wispy blond hair curled behind gently pointed ears that protruded a tad too far. A smattering of faint freckles bloomed over an upturned nose.

To look at her now, she appeared like any other normal five-year-old girl watching television.

But she wasn't.

Marion had juvenile diabetes.

Diabetes. He still couldn't reconcile it in his mind. When the doctor had given him the diagnosis that night in the hospital, he'd felt the floor open up to swallow him. He'd stood staring back at the doctor, mouth agape. Of all the possibilities that had spun madly in his worry-crazed mind while pacing in the hospital waiting room, diabetes had never occurred to him. Sure, he knew a little about the disease. Diabetes meant there was too much sugar in the body. People with diabetes needed insulin. But these were adult people, not little children. Not five-year-olds who had never had a serious illness before.

But later, once he began reading about the disease, he recognized all the symptoms that had been there all along if only he'd really paid attention. The excessive thirst, increased urination, weight loss, irritability—they were all warning signs of Type 1 diabetes, the rarest and most severe form of the disease.

That was when the guilt set in. A gnawing, insidious, ever-present self-loathing that he could have let her condition get so bad that her sugar dropped low enough to cause convulsions. He felt like the world's worst and most pathetic father.

Only he didn't have time for guilt. Living with diabetes was all-consuming. Nothing was easy. He couldn't even make Marion a snack without worrying about what calories she was taking in and watching for reactions. For the first time since becoming a father, Harris was afraid to take care of his own child.

He looked again at his daughter curled up on the couch

watching TV. How sweet and innocent she appeared. And how deceiving it was. He shook his head, took a deep breath and braced himself for what was coming.

"Marion? It's time to do the test."

Instantly, all sweetness fled from her face as she jackknifed her knees to her chest, locking her arms tight around them. "No!" she shouted.

"Come on, honey. You know we've got to do this."

"No!"

Harris released a ragged sigh. So, it was going to be another fight. As he walked toward her, she backed up against the armrest and cowered in the corner of the sofa, her hands up, nails out, to ward him off. She looked just like one of the wild, terrified birds when he reached to grab them—all glaring eyes and talons ready to attack.

As with his birds, he moved toward her in slow strides, murmuring assurances in low tones. Then, swiftly, he grabbed hold. Marion reacted instantly, shrieking and kicking at him as viciously as any wild bird.

"No! I don't wanna. No, no, no!"

Her screams ricocheted from the walls to reverberate in his head. She was an amazingly strong child for such a skinny thing—and wily. When he tried to pick her up, her legs sprang straight out and she began kicking and pummeling with bunched fists even as she began sliding from the sofa.

"What in heaven's name is going on in here?"

Harris recognized Maggie's voice over the shrieks. So did Marion. She paused for just a second, then renewed her fight with even more vigor. He tightened his grip as she tried to wriggle away.

"Oh, no you don't," he said to his daughter as he hoisted her back up onto the sofa.

"It sounds like you're committing bloody murder in here," said Maggie, entering the house.

"That'd be easier than this," he said over his shoulder. "I've got to prick her finger for a blood sample. Ouch! Marion, stop kicking me."

Maggie chuckled and came forward. "It might help if you took off her shoes."

"Be my guest."

Maggie reached out and, with the same skill she employed with birds, quickly took hold of Marion's feet and in seconds had both shoes removed. She kept her grip on Marion's legs. This seemed to make Marion even madder and she tried all the harder to kick and wiggle her way free, her face turning beet red.

"Lord, she's stronger than a great horned owl."

"She bites like one, too. Quick, grab hold of her left hand."

Once Maggie took hold of her hand, Marion's screams heightened in pitch to near hysteria.

"She's holding her breath. Quick!"

Harris wiped the sweat from his brow with his elbow, took aim, quickly pricked the finger, then with split-second timing, dabbed the test strip against the bright red drop of blood on her fingertip.

"Got it," he said with triumph.

The fight seemed to flee from Marion's little body as she exhaled a defiant cry, then slumped, defeated and sobbing, against the pillows.

"There's got to be an easier way," Maggie said, checking her arm for bruises.

"If there is, I'd like to know what it is." He reached over to pat his daughter's head but she slapped his hand away.

"I hate you!" she cried, scrambling from the sofa and run-

ning off to her bedroom like someone escaping an inqui-
sition.

Harris ran his hand through his hair when the bedroom
door slammed shut between them.

Maggie raised her eyes to heaven. "How often do you
have to do this?"

"I have to check the blood sugar six times a day, then I get
to give her a shot of insulin three times a day. At least. That's
six to nine pokes with a needle each day."

"Lord have mercy."

"Yeah. Mercy on me. She tried being brave at first, now
it's just total war."

"I hate to say it, but it looks like you're losing."

His face fell. "That's the problem. I can't lose. Her life de-
pends on it." He reached for the container, checked the test
strip against the model, then set it down on the table, satisfied with the result.

"The first week home I screwed up and didn't check her
blood. She was carrying on like this, so I thought I could
skip just one. Next thing I knew she was weak and sweaty
and her hands started shaking. Thank God for glucose tab-
lets. But I can tell you, it scared the hell out of me."

"But she's all right now. That's what matters."

"You're right. And I'm going to keep her all right." He
glanced up at her, the better to gauge her reaction to his
news. "I've hired someone to live in and take care of Marion
full-time."

Maggie's eyes widened. "Live in? Here? But, Harris, this
house is so small. Where will she sleep?"

"She can have my room. I'll bunk in my office."

"You'll find that awfully cramped. And I'm not talking
about just the layout of furniture."

"Maybe. But it'll have to do. At least for now." When

Maggie opened her mouth to voice another objection, Harris held up his palm. "It's all arranged, Maggie. I placed an ad in the paper and she's agreed to come. Please. I don't need a lecture. Right now, I need support. Marion and I both do."

Maggie's mouth clamped tight against the torrent of words. She nodded her head, then leaned forward to wrap her ample arms around him in a hug of support. In the five years that they'd worked side by side, they'd shared a need for peace and quiet on the job. When they spoke, it was in spurts, mostly about the patient birds and what tasks needed doing. Though Maggie was the mother hen of the organization and gave opinions often and loudly, rarely did she probe into his personal life. Important bits of information they announced plainly, more like bulletins. *Bob's been laid off. Marion's got the flu. The kids are home from school today. The washing machine's on the fritz again.* Their loyalty and friendship was deep, and though not discussed, it was never questioned.

"You just call if you need me," she said.

"I always do."

Harris knocked lightly on Marion's bedroom door. There was no reply. He put his ear to the door, relieved to hear silence instead of the hiccupping sobs and mutterings of how mean her daddy was. He opened the door slowly, lest she be asleep. He stuck his head in to see her lying on her bed playing with Gaudy Lulu. Her head darted up when she heard him, her blue eyes widening with surprise, then quickly changing to a scowl.

"May I come in?"

"No."

"Well, I'm coming in, anyway." He walked to her side, picking up dirty clothes from the floor en route, and sat on the bed beside her. "So, do you still hate me?"

She pouted, stroking the doll's hair. "I hate the shots."

"I know you do. But you need the shots for your diabetes."

"I hate 'betes."

His smile was bittersweet. Harris leaned over to kiss the soft hair on the top of her head. "Ah, my favorite perfume," he said, inhaling the scent of her.

"I'm not wearing perfume, Daddy," she replied as she always did when he said this to her. It was a little game they played and her response told him the storm was over.

"I'd like to talk to you for a minute."

She kept her eyes on the doll while she maneuvered the tight bodice of the pearly gown over the doll's impressive breasts. He waited patiently for her to finish the snap at the tiny waist and set the doll aside. When she raised her eyes to him, he began in a calm voice.

"We have a problem. Or, rather, I have a problem. I'm not doing a very good job taking care of you."

Marion's eyes rounded in surprise. Clearly she'd not expected this.

"You need someone who can give you your medicine and watch over your diet."

"*You* can do that."

He shook his head. "No, I can't. We both know it's not working out."

"I won't kick—"

"Honey, it's not just that. Well, it *is,* in part," he said teasingly, wrapping an arm around her and tucking her close. Marion rested her head against his chest. "I work long hours. I'm gone a lot. You need someone to keep an eye on you all the time."

"Why can't Maggie take care of me?"

"Maggie works at the clinic, honey. With the birds."

"How come the birds get everything?" she asked, sitting up to face him with a scowl on her face. "*I'm* sick now, too."

Harris wondered at the level of resentment she had to feel to make that comparison. "The birds are my job, honey. But you're my heart."

That seemed to appease her somewhat. She sighed raggedly and leaned back against her father's chest. "You mean I'm going to get a new baby-sitter, right? Like Katie?"

"Sort of. You know how Katie went home to her own house every night? Well, I've hired a lady to stay here with us."

"You mean, she's going to live here? In our house?"

"Yes."

Marion turned in his arms to look into his face. Her own was alert with interest. "Is she gonna be like a *mother?*"

"Heavens no," he said with a light chuckle. Then, seeing the light dim in her eyes, he said more tenderly, "Well, maybe a little. She'll read to you, cook your meals and help you get dressed in the morning. Most important, she'll make sure you get your medicine."

"You mean my shots?"

"Yep. Those, too."

Marion scrunched up her face. "I don't want her to come. She's *not* my mama. This is *our* house."

"Hold on, now. That's not the right attitude. It's her job to help you and it's your job to be cooperative. You have to help us take care of you." He reached into his shirt pocket to pull out a folded white paper. He opened it and held it up to the bedside light.

"I put an ad in the newspaper and I got a few replies. Miss Majors is the one I chose to be your caretaker," he replied.

"She's a nurse, so she knows a lot about diabetes and how to take care of you. A lot better than I can."

"I want *you* to do it." Her voice was more frightened than belligerent.

"Would you like me to read her letter?"

"I don't care."

Harris cleared his throat and began to read.

Dear Mr. Henderson,

I am replying to your ad for child care in the Charleston Post and Courier. The ad was very timely as I've just arrived in town and am looking for a position. I am from Rutland, Vermont, where I worked for the past decade as a pediatric nurse.

You are probably wondering why I would seek out a position in child care instead of nursing. I have had offers. Please rest assured that I have not lost my license or committed some violation or crime. You will find my complete résumé attached, along with multiple references. Please contact them if you feel the need. I know I would if it were my child.

To be frank, I have worked for many years in an emergency room and I feel the need for a respite from my career. I moved to the south for a change in climate as well as a change in lifestyle. When I saw your ad, it seemed a perfect solution. I am very familiar with the treatment of juvenile diabetes and welcome the chance to care for one child rather than many.

If you are agreeable, and if my credentials meet your standards, I can take the position as caretaker for your daughter immediately for the term of one year.

Naturally, we should allow for one month's trial period, after which one or the other of us can cancel the arrangement without penalty or blame.

I look forward to meeting both you and Marion. Tell her that I love to read and play games, that I know lots of card tricks and that I'm curious to learn what she likes to do, too.

Most sincerely,

Ella Elizabeth Majors, R.N.

Harris sat in the resulting quiet looking at the letter in his hands. He'd read the letter a dozen times since receiving it a week earlier. He'd been very impressed with her résumé and every person he'd telephoned on her long list of references only had the highest words of praise for her abilities. They'd said she was bright, clean and neat, punctual, efficient, responsible. All qualities that made her a first-rate nurse. There was nothing, however, about how well she played with children, or whether she could cook, or even if she was kind.

But once again, Harris counted himself lucky. He'd requested some medical knowledge in his ad but he hadn't expected a nurse. The personnel director of the hospital had assured him that Ella Majors had no skeletons in her closet when he'd asked what her reason was for leaving. In closing, the woman's voice had lowered and she'd made one comment that lingered in his mind.

Sometimes, a nurse in the emergency room just sees one too many children die.

He wondered as he folded the letter back up if that was the case for Miss Majors. If it was, he thought, cringing at the memory of the gut-wrenching fear he'd felt while waiting for Marion in the emergency room, he certainly could understand the woman's need for a break.

"Is that all, Daddy?"

He nodded, tucking the letter back in his pocket. "Yep, that's it. Except, of course, she's coming. I expect she'll be here by lunchtime tomorrow." *Please God...* "So, what do you think?"

"I dunno," she said with a shrug. "Is she pretty?"

He smiled at the child's question. "I have no idea."

Marion yawned wide and blinked sleepily. "Okay. I just hope she doesn't smell bad."

He laughed out loud and squeezed his daughter with affection. "I sure hope so, too."

Later that night, after Marion was asleep, Harris walked around the mews of the resident raptors, then strolled through the medical pens where the injured birds were housed. It was his customary evening walk and the birds knew him—his looks and movements—so they were not flustered by his presence. Likewise, he was soothed by their quiet acceptance. In contrast to the quiet of the pens, outside in the plush cover of the surrounding trees, the little southern screech owls were trilling and wailing, wildly searching for mates.

He stopped outside the medical pens to check the three ospreys currently in Med 8. With that black band across their eyes, he'd always thought ospreys looked like dashing Zorros as they soared through the sky. Only they weren't bandits at all. They were fish hawks, skilled fishermen that neither begged for nor stole their food. One of the ospreys was breathing in wheezy pants that rocked his body, a sign of possible lung infection. Harris made a mental note to take him out for treatment in the morning. With that decision, his tour of the grounds was completed. He turned and began his trek home, his mind free to struggle with his decision to bring Miss Ella Elizabeth Majors into his home.

He was as wary and testy as any bird at having a stranger enter his territory. It was far different to hire someone for a job at the neutral ground of an office than it was to bring someone into one's home, into one's daily routine. This allowed entry at an intimate level. How was he, someone who eschewed company, going to handle such an intrusion?

She'd written in her letter that she'd stay one year. That meant twelve months, fifty-two weeks, three hundred and sixty-five days of togetherness. He hoped in that space of time he'd be able to get a grip on the diabetes situation. Then he'd only have to endure her presence for that finite amount of time. He could put up with that, for Marion's sake.

He could only afford one year, anyway. Miss Majors was taking a minimum salary, a lucky break for him. But even that small salary would eat up every penny in his savings account, and then some. Somehow, he'd make do. He'd always managed in the past, hadn't he? Even with Fannie's bills.

Fannie. He paused to run his hand through his hair and take a deep breath. Other than his mother, she was the only woman he'd lived with in his life. And if that was any indication of what that experience was like, he would pass, thanks very much. Lord, if this Miss Majors was anything like Fannie...

He shook his head, surprised at the way his adrenaline was pumping even at the thought. There was no way she could be like Fannie. There was only one like her...

He'd made the decision to bring Miss Ella Elizabeth Majors into his sanctuary. He'd see it through. Even if the very thought of it made his breath come as wheezy and as fast as the osprey's.

★ ★ ★

Early the next morning, Harris followed Lijah to the site of Santee's nest. They trudged in a companionable silence through miles of silt and mud along the Wando River. Harris's long legs could traverse a rough landscape at a clipped pace. He paused twice during the long trek, thinking perhaps the older man might need a rest. Lijah, however, wasn't even winded. It was a cold, damp morning and most of the South Carolina reptiles and amphibians were nestled in a quiet, dark place, waiting for the warm sunshine of spring. Here and there, however, they'd spy a shiny black salamander burrowed in a pile of moist, composting leaves, no doubt waiting for a meal of earthworms and grubs. They reveled in the brisk wintry air, breeding and laying their gelatinous egg packets that would emerge as tadpoles months later.

At last the two men reached a cluster of ancient, proud longleaf pines that towered into the sky. Countless smaller trees and shrubs clustered around the bases of the giants like children holding on to the hems of aunts. Lijah reached out and pointed.

"That'll be it."

Harris craned his neck to gaze up at the conical nest. It was massive, more than six feet in diameter, comprised of large sticks knitted together, deep in a vertical fork of the tree. Sitting beside the nest like a lone sentinel was the eagle. He glared at them, as though daring them to come closer.

"He's still sitting by the nest," Harris said. "Poor guy."

"He sat on those eggs for the longest time. I knew he'd have a hard time of it without Santee. Did what I could to help. Brung him fish most every day. I'd whistle to let him know I was here, then set the fish right at the bottom of the tree. Once he knew it was me, he'd come on down, grab a fish, then go right back up to the eggs. I was hopeful." He shook his head.

"Don't take it too hard, Lijah. It's just the way of things. It takes two adults to incubate the eggs."

"But Pee Dee… He kept with the nest. He didn't give up."

"Even when the father makes a valiant effort, he eventually has to leave the eggs from time to time to feed. The odds were against him. It's just too cold to leave those eggs exposed. Sometimes, if he's lucky, a male will find a new mate who will help incubate and raise the young as her own. But that's rare."

"It's a real shame."

"That it is. I feel for him."

Something in his voice must have alerted Lijah, because he turned his attention from the nest to look at Harris. "You mean, on account you taking care of your young one alone, too?"

Harris drew in a long breath and placed his hands on his hips. It was rare for Harris to speak openly to others. He found the act of confiding personal information painful and often wondered why others seemed to do it freely. But the old man's sincerity and disarming warmth thawed his icy hesitance. Or, it might just have been some private longing for advice from a father he'd never had.

"Marion's mother left me soon after she was born. Fannie was a beautiful woman, but flighty. She had…problems. But she gave me Marion, and for that I'll always be grateful to her. I never for one moment regretted having my daughter."

"'Course not."

"I do the best that I can for her. I've provided a decent home. I see that she's warm, fed and has enough clothes. I'm

gone a lot, but I've always had someone to look out for her."
He shrugged, hearing the plea for understanding in his own
voice. "It's hard. They count on me at the clinic to treat the
injured birds that come in day after day. Then there are the
resident birds to look after, and their training. That alone
requires hours of my time. On top of all that, I'm always
seeking donations, doing fundraisers, sending out mailings,
anything I can to keep the center afloat. I have to bring
home food to the nest, too, so to speak."

He looked up at the eagle sitting alone among the cluster
of tree limbs. The nest beside him loomed empty and desolate.

"I rationalized how busy I was, how I had so much to get
done." His lips tightened. "But when I look back on those
days, those weeks, before her illness, if I'm honest, I see how
I wasn't paying attention. Sure I put the food on the table
and paid the baby-sitters, but I wasn't really watching. If I
had been, I would have seen her symptoms, seen that she was
thirsty or losing weight. Seen that she was looking poorly.
I'm her father. I should have seen. My daughter had to have
convulsions before I noticed. What the hell kind of a father
was I?" He paused. "So yeah. I do feel for that eagle up
there. You think Pee Dee failed? I failed."

He wanted Lijah to agree with him, to tell him that he
was a bad father, guilty as charged. Maybe then the voice in
his head that whispered those words over and over would be
silenced.

Lijah only nodded to indicate he'd heard. After a moment,
he looked across the wetlands. "Son, it's a fair way back," he
said. "I'll walk with you."

They walked shoulder to shoulder through the mud, back
toward home. The sun was rising higher into an azure sky,
promising a clear day. Without preamble, Lijah began to sing.

His rich baritone rose up from his chest and poured out over
the wetlands like a fresh morning breeze that spirits away
the darkness. He sang a Gullah spiritual, one that Harris had
heard long ago, perhaps in his childhood along the Edisto
River.

> I look down duh road, en duh road so lonesome,
> Lawd, I got tuh walk down dat lonesome road.
> En I look down duh road, en duh road so lonesome,
> Lawd, I got tuh walk down dat lonesome road.

***Owls: Hunters of the Night.** Owls are nocturnal raptors adapted for hunting at night. Fringed feathers allow for soundless flight and larger eyes and ears aid auditory hunting. Owls rest during the day, but at dusk they come alive, ready to hunt. South Carolina owls include great horned owls, barred owls, Eastern screech owls and barn owls.*

4

HIGHWAY 17, A LONG STRETCH OF FOUR-LANE divided highway, took Ella Elizabeth Majors toward what she'd hoped would be the beginning of something new in her life. She wasn't looking for magic. She wasn't looking for love. What she was looking for, at the very least, was a rest stop between where she'd been and where she was heading.

The open map lying on the passenger seat of her modest four-door sedan informed her that the highway dated back to the colonial days when it was called King's Highway. Red-coats, "Swamp Fox" Francis Marion, slaves and planters had all traveled up and down this roadbed once upon a time.

But it was all new to her. She'd arrived in Charleston a month earlier, and though she'd moved to the South to stay, she was as yet a Yankee tourist—and would be for another twenty years, if the guidebooks she'd read were true.

Ella liked to drive and was accustomed to long journeys

alone along highways and winding roads. In her home state of Vermont, she'd driven through deep snow and acres of mud, driven through periods of ecstasy and despair, driven in a glassy-eyed stupor after double shifts in the emergency room. She'd driven in the pinks and yellows of dawn when only the dairy farmers waved from the fields, and she'd driven in the primordial darkness of night on a county road when she saw little but the yellow eyes of raccoons as they scampered across her line of vision.

Yet even her experienced knuckles had whitened on the steering wheel as she crossed over Charleston's narrow Cooper River Bridge and saw an enormous tanker the size of several football fields ease its way beneath her with seemingly inches to spare. A few minutes and several Hail Marys later, she was over the bridge and following the highway down a long, straight stretch through Mount Pleasant, where shops and strip malls crowded both sides and traffic was slow but polite. As she traveled farther north, the tentacles of the city's growth thinned. Clusters of stores gave way to a few showy entrances of gated communities, occasional rickety wooden roadside stands where sweetgrass baskets were sold by descendants of slaves, some gas stations and, here and there, small homes barely visible behind foliage.

Less than an hour after leaving the bridge, the road began to curve, the traffic whittled down to a few vehicles and vast tracts of pinewoods bordered both sides of the road. She breathed deeply, more at home in the open space. The flat landscape was different from the cragged, green mountains of Vermont. Here, the blue sky stretched uninterrupted over broad vistas of marsh and, beyond, the glistening blue of water. Above the treetops, the ubiquitous vulture tipped its wings as it circled.

It was hard to believe that only a month earlier she'd

packed up her sedan and made the drive from the Green Mountain State to the Lowcountry. In the few weeks since she'd arrived in Charleston, she'd stayed at a hotel and interviewed for several nursing positions. There was a shortage of nurses in the city and hospitals were clamoring to have her.

But the plain truth was, she couldn't go back to work at a hospital. Not yet. Ella's heart was bled dry. Her very soul was parched, and her instincts told her to find an oasis quick or she'd wither up forever.

That was when she'd found the ad in the newspaper. It was a small ad, barely catching her notice. Someone needed full-time help caring for a child with diabetes. Some medical knowledge was preferred. That drew her in. But it was the phrase *We need someone who cares* that made Ella circle the ad and call the number. She wasn't the type to believe in miracles, but she wasn't about to deny fate.

So here she was again, with all she owned crammed in the back of her sedan, driving toward a new destination. This time to a rural town called Awendaw, a short ways north of Charleston. When she'd left Vermont, her aunts had told her to have a fine adventure. Choosing to live as a nanny in a private home that she'd never seen certainly qualified as an adventure in her book. She'd thought it best not to write her maiden aunts about her latest decision, however, lest they flutter with worry like two old hens. Truth was, her own heart was jumping in her chest each time she wondered if the child would like her, if the family was friendly and whether or not the house would be clean.

After a dozen or so more miles she began paying attention to the mile markers, then slowed to turn off Highway 17 onto a narrow, gravel-strewn road that seemed to lead to nowhere. She stopped, adjusted her eyeglasses, checked her written directions, then craned her neck as she searched the area. There was no sign or mailbox to indicate where she was.

She gazed warily down the road, then pressed the gas and drove twenty yards farther, her tires crunching in the gravel. She came to a stop before a wide metal gate that crossed the road. And sitting on it, not the least flustered that her car had driven within a foot of the gate, was a plump white rooster that stared haughtily at her over its yellow beak. She chuckled. This just *had* to be the Coastal Carolina Center for Birds of Prey.

She opened the car door and put out a foot. "Hey, there!" she called.

The rooster watched her with dark, shining eyes and without so much as a shake from its bright red wattle.

"Okay, old boy. Have it your way." She was well acquainted with the stubbornness of roosters, having lived with them for most of her childhood. She drove slowly closer to the gate, sure that at any moment the rooster would fly off, squawking.

It didn't happen. The bird sat unflinchingly as she walked straight up to the gate and lifted the heavy chain from it. Then it hitched a ride as she swung open the gate and walked it along its arc across the road. After she drove the car through, the whole scene repeated itself as she closed the gate back again. Driving away, she saw the white rooster in her rearview mirror, still sitting, still staring impassively. Ella laughed out loud, liking the bird's spirit enormously.

Passing the gate and its mysterious guardian, it felt as if she was entering another world. Here, the impersonal highway gave way to a narrow gravel road bordered by a jungle of pines, live oaks and choking clusters of chinaberry. Taking it at a crawl, Ella rolled down the window, letting the cool, moist air permeate the stale cabin of her car. It was January

in the Lowcountry, yet she didn't need more than a fleece
jacket. She didn't even need gloves or a hat. Yet, for the first
time since leaving Vermont, she felt a twinge of homesickness. These southern trees had to compete with sand and
marsh for bits of scrubby soil to exist and their leaves were
paler and scrappier compared to their northern cousins. Still,
she was surrounded by the familiar smell of grass, moss, mold
and damp earth. Songbirds called in the trees. Her senses
came alive, awakening dormant memories under her skin.

She followed the curving road to a clearing in the woods
where a few cars were parked. She stopped here and got out
to stretch her legs and look around. Beyond a barrier of leaf-
less trees, she caught a glimpse of a pod of small wood structures. Up front and closer, and a bit larger than the others,
was a Cape Cod house.

She crossed her arms and studied the white clapboard
house nestled snug between two enormous longleaf pines,
rather like a scene from a Japanese woodblock print. At first
glance, the little house made a welcoming impression with
its long, narrow veranda, the low-slung roof above it and a
solid base of red brick. The porch pillars stood as straight as a
spinster's back and white smoke curled from a blunt chimney,
filling the air with the delicious scent of cedar. But the house
was weathered gray in spots and the surrounding yard barely
held back the wilderness. On the porch, two handsome twig
chairs, iron garden tools, all-weather boots and a wooden
barrel filled with scrap wood lent the house that shabby-chic,
comfortable feel of a home truly lived in.

It was a man's house, she thought.

Leaving her bags in the car, she removed her eyeglasses
and gathered her long brown hair into a clasp, even as she
gathered her courage. If all went well, she thought, smoothing the wrinkles from her long khaki skirt, this little house

nestled in these woods would be her home for the next twelve months. She would become intimately involved with the family within those walls, help a child adapt to the life-style of a diabetic and, if she was lucky, in the process she might regain a measure of joy and purpose in her own life, as well. Straightening her shoulders, she walked across the scrubby yard, with each step hoping that the people who lived in this house were decent and kind. She climbed the six red-brick stairs, relieved to see that the porch was well swept and tidy. A small index card was taped to the door.

Please knock. Doorbell broken.

From somewhere in the trees she heard the song of a mockingbird, and from inside, the canned voice of the tele-vision. Reaching out to knock, she smiled at the normalcy of everything. She didn't wait more than a minute before the door swung open.

A slender girl about five years of age with flyaway hair hung on the door and stared at her with cornflower-blue eyes narrowed in speculation.

Ella smiled and said, "Hello there. You must be Marion."

The child didn't reply.

"I'm Ella. I've come to see you."

The child released the door and blurted, "You're not pretty."

A short laugh burst from Ella's mouth. "No. No, I'm not. But I'm bright. And that's ever so much better."

The child glared at her, uncertain of what to say next.

Behind her, a man came forward from the shadowy hall to fill the doorway. Ella sucked in her breath and straight-ened her shoulders, filled with anxiety. He stepped into the light and met her gaze. He was tall and lanky, what her aunts would call a long, cool drink of water. She guessed him to be somewhere in his late thirties, but it was hard to tell with men. Most important, he appeared clean and mannerly. She almost sighed aloud with relief.

"Hello. I'm Harris Henderson," he said, extending his hand. "You must be Miss Majors. Please, come in."

She took his hand briefly. It was warm with long, slender fingers. The cuff of his white shirt was frayed. "Yes, I am."

"I see you've found your way. A lot of people miss the turn."

"The directions were fine. Thank you." She dragged her gaze to meet his, clasping her hands before her. He had a pleasing-enough face, even handsome, and it touched her that he went to the trouble to put on a freshly ironed shirt and tie for their first meeting. But it was his eyes that arrested her. They were blue, like Marion's, but without all her distrust. Rather, his were wide spaced and wary. She suspected he was as nervous of this first meeting as she.

"You've met Marion," he said, rubbing his palms together.

Ella smiled at the child, not the least dismayed that she didn't smile back. "Oh, yes."

"It's cold out there today," he said, closing the door behind her.

"I don't find it cold. Where I come from, this weather would be considered positively balmy for January."

"Vermont, is that right?"

"That's right. South central. I'm from a small town called Wallingford, but I've been living in Rutland for several years now. That's where the hospital was, you see."

"Right. A long way to come."

"Ayah, it is. I wanted a change and started with climate. I had to go a ways from Vermont to find a palm tree." She smiled tentatively.

He nodded noncommittally and rubbed his hands again. "Would you like some coffee? Or do you prefer tea?"

"Coffee would be great, thank you. With milk, please."

"Make yourself at home. I've got some freshly made. It'll only be a moment."

While he went for the coffee, Ella unclasped her hands and looked around the room. The low ceilings, dark wood paneling and thick red curtains gave it a heavy feel. At the far end near the kitchen sat a round wood table surrounded with four hardwood chairs. A few more mismatched chairs and a sagging sofa clustered before a stone fireplace that dominated the eastern wall. Inserted into this, like an afterthought, was a black iron stove. There were dramatic framed photographs of large birds in flight on the walls, and several wood shelves overflowing with books took up the rest of the space. It was a small, compact room and the wood-burning stove was doing its job, for the house was warm and cozy. She removed her fleece jacket, aware that Marion was watching her every move.

"Where do you sleep?" she asked her with enthusiasm.

Marion's curiosity apparently got the better of her resentment because she walked over to open a door on the side wall. Ella followed, fingers crossed, peeking her head through the doorway. A narrow hall divided the small house in two. Directly opposite the hall door was a yellow-tiled bathroom. It was spacious but spare, with a tub that stood on clawed feet. The towels hanging on the metal rail were mismatched, but he'd made the effort to supply new bars of soap for the bath and sink. It was, from what she could see, the *only* bathroom.

"That's where Daddy sleeps," Marion said, pointing.

Through the partially opened door Ella saw a black iron bed covered with a bright white matelasse coverlet that looked brand-new. She turned her head to look down the opposite end of the hall at a closed door. "What's in there?"

"Daddy's office."

"I see. And where do you sleep?"

Marion pointed up. "It used to be the attic. But Daddy made it *my* room. It's pink. That's my favorite color. There's a stair in the back, by the kitchen."

"Is there a room for me up there?"

"No-o-o," she drawled, looking at her as if she was crazy to ask. "There's only my bed up there. And a closet where Daddy puts all his stuff."

"Ah, I see."

Did she, she wondered? The house was much smaller than she'd imagined it would be and there didn't seem to be any other rooms. She chewed her lip, seized with a sudden fear that she'd misunderstood Mr. Henderson's job description.

"Coffee?" Harris called, stepping into the room carrying a tray from the kitchen.

She settled herself on a hard chair by the warm stove. He'd thoughtfully put leftover holiday gingerbread cookies and chunks of cheese on crackers on a plate along with a blue pottery pitcher filled with milk. He poured a glass of it for Marion and set a few chunks of cheese on a napkin before her. She quickly gobbled them up. Ella took a sip from her mug, glad to have something to do with her hands in the awkward silence. The coffee was good and strong, not that black water some people made. Restored, she waited until he was settled on the sofa with his coffee before speaking.

"Mr. Henderson," she began, sitting straight in her chair. "Allow me to get right to the point. This *is* a live-in situation, isn't it?"

He hesitated with his mug close to his lips. He placed it back on the table and put his hands on his knees. "Yes." A faint blush colored his cheeks as he chose his words. "I realize that the house is small. Not too small, I hope. It might be a bit cramped at first, but once the weather warms, I figured...well, there's a small cabin by the pond. There's no heat, you see. But come spring, I could move there. And use the outdoor shower."

"Oh, I'm sure the house will be fine," she replied hastily, relieved that she hadn't misunderstood. "But... Mr. Henderson, which is to be my room?"

Understanding dawned on his features and he brightened. "I guess I should have showed you that right away. I gave you the main bedroom. It's the largest and it has a nice view of the pond. I put a little television in there, too. And a small rolltop desk. I thought, well, I figured you'd want some privacy."

"I hate to put you out."

"It's no problem. There's a bed in my study for me. I'll sleep fine there, and besides, I'm at the clinic most hours, anyway."

Ella was enormously relieved. It would be cramped, indeed, but manageable.

She saw Marion eyeing the cookies. Ella reached out to place a few more crackers and cheese on the child's plate. These she ate without argument. Ella made a mental note to toss away all the gingerbread cookies, cakes and other sugary items that might tempt a five-year-old.

"Can you tell me about Marion's diabetes," Ella began. "What are her current insulin levels?"

Harris wiped his mouth with the napkin. "Marion," he said, turning to his daughter, "why don't you go in your room to play for a while. Miss Majors and I need to talk."

"Do I have to?"

"She can stay," Ella added.

"I think we should be alone to discuss this," he replied firmly.

"It's healthy for Marion to be a part of this discussion. She might have questions of her own."

"I don't think she has any questions."

"No? After all, the disease is happening to her."

He paused, and she wasn't blind to his growing annoyance "I don't want her to be afraid of the disease," he said with finality.

"She might already have fears that need listening to."

The two adults stared at each other, each recognizing the stubborn strength in the other.

Harris turned again to his daughter. "Marion, do you want to hear this or do you want to play in your room?" His tone clearly was trying to persuade her to play.

"I wanna stay," she replied without a moment's hesitation, settling farther back into the sofa with a smug gleam in her eye.

Harris pursed his lips, his eyes flashing his irritation, but conceded.

It was hardly a victory, thought Ella, since there was no real battle, yet it established her position in the house. She couldn't possibly stay if he was going to dictate her job. The house may be strange and new, but managing a diabetic child was her field.

They moved into a lengthy discussion of Marion's diabetes, during which Ella noticed that, though the child picked at a scab and looked at the ceiling, she was listening intently. Ella had experience with children of all ages who had diabetes. Though they all reacted differently according to their personalities and level of maturity, they had one thing in common. They each wanted to know what was going on in their own bodies, and most of all, they wanted to know how many shots they needed to take each day.

"Would you like to take a walk and look around before it gets dark?" Harris asked after they were through.

"When did Marion last have her blood checked?"

Ella saw Marion tuck her legs in close and her face grow mutinous. Harris's face visibly paled.

"I checked it before you arrived," he replied.

Ella looked at her watch. "There's been lots of nervous excitement since then. Let's give it a look-see before we go out."

Harris cast a wary look at his daughter. Ella saw this—and how Marion watched and waited for it. On cue, Marion began to howl like a banshee, kicking and screaming. Harris went toward her, but Ella stuck out her arm, warding him off. She stood abruptly and slammed her hands on her hips.

"That will be quite enough of that, young lady," she said in a voice loud enough to be heard over the wails. "I will be testing you four, five, six times a day, and I'll be giving you your shots, too. Every day. That's my job and…Marion, listen to me." She moved quickly to grasp hold of the child's shoulders and lift her to a sitting position. She held tight, ignoring the pummeling.

"Marion!" she said louder, in a command.

Marion sucked in her breath, silent for a second.

Ella rushed, "There's nothing to be afraid of. I'm a nurse. I know exactly what to do and I'm good at this. Really, I've given lots of shots to hundreds of children."

"But it hurts."

"It will hurt a little, I know, but not that much if you sit still. And pretty soon, you *will* get used to it. I promise."

Ella spoke quickly, while she had the child's attention. "I want to show you something. I have a special little tool." She looked over her shoulder at Harris, who stood with his arms by his sides, waiting to assist. "Could you bring my purse over here? Quickly, please."

Marion was still crouched in the corner of the sofa, but her screaming at least had ceased. She watched warily as Ella dug into her purse.

"What's that?" she asked with panic when Ella pulled out a little plastic box.

"It's a kind of magic box that will prick your finger so fast you'll just be surprised, that's all." She held it in the palm of her hand and was pleased to see Marion lean closer to inspect it. She knew the child wouldn't see the needle.

"But first, come with me. Oh, don't balk, you silly goose. We're just going to wash your hands. Come along." Without waiting for her to agree, Ella took Marion's hand and half dragged her to the bathroom. She looked over her shoulder and mouthed "test strip" to Harris. He nodded his understanding and went to fetch them. While she rubbed soap onto Marion's hand, she surveyed the bathroom. An effort had been made to keep the tile and sink decent, but it was a far cry from hospital clean.

"Okay, now let's check those nails." While she looked at the short nails she milked the finger she planned to prick. "Hmm…I see we'll have to clip those little nails later. Maybe paint them, too. Pink? Isn't that your favorite color?"

Marion brightened, distracted.

"Now rinse," Ella said, waiting for Marion to turn her back before slipping the lancet box from her pocket. She raised her brows at Harris and he nodded, holding up the test strip.

"All ready? Inspection time!" She took hold of the hands. "Very good job, Marion. Nice nails, too. Okay, then, let's do it, shall we?" Before Marion had time to go into her fight mode, Ella brought the box up and with a quick, precise movement pricked the side of her fingertip and swooped in with the test strip.

Marion's mouth popped open in a gasp, but she was too stunned to cry.

"All done!" Ella knew it was the sight of the needles that frightened children most. Looking up at Harris, she was amused to see that his expression wasn't that different from his daughter's. She handed him the test strip to check with the meter.

"She's good to go," he replied with obvious relief.

"I think we're ready for that walk now, aren't we?" She took Marion's hand again, squeezing it gently. Just as quickly, Marion yanked her hand away and made a face at her, full of reproach. Ella let the snub slip by. She couldn't blame the child for being miffed. After all, Ella had just outmanipulated her. "Marion, will you lead the way?"

They strolled at a child's pace through the grounds. The mantle of dark was falling, and as she walked through the shifting shadows and shapes of early night, Ella felt again the strong sense of place she'd experienced when she first passed the gate with its watchful gatekeeper. This strange place was a sanctuary in a harried world. She felt safe here in the cocoon of trees and wondered as she passed a pen of owls that stared back at her with their wise and all-knowing eyes if perhaps coincidence and destiny were intertwined, after all. If perhaps her long journey to this small outpost of healing was written in the stars.

She followed Harris around a cluster of shadowed trees to a few wood structures of various sizes and shapes.

"It's late and the diurnal birds are settled so we'd better not disturb them. I'm afraid this will have to be an abbreviated tour tonight. Over there," he said, pointing to an L-shaped white house with a low-slung roof, "is the clinic where we treat and house the critically injured birds. We only take in birds of prey, though we sometimes get a wood stork we just can't say no to."

"And the crows, Daddy."

"Yes, we have two crows," he conceded, smiling at the child. "Marion likes the crows."

"There's a baby crow," she said.

"We try to keep Marion away from the birds," he said, in such a way that Ella understood this was part of her new duties. "It's dangerous and she might disturb them."

"I saw a rooster at the gate," Ella said. "That's not exactly a bird of prey, either."

"Him!" Harris said with a laugh. "We don't know where he came from. He just showed up one day and never left. We think he roosts in one of the pines and comes down to scrounge for insects. I toss feed his way, too, especially now that it's winter. He's quite a character. Very vigilant. We've grown pretty fond of him."

"What's his name?"

"We don't name the birds. It gives the wrong impression. We feel we need to reinforce that they're wild creatures, not our pets."

"Cherokee has a name," Marion said.

He shrugged. "See? Children catch you lying all the time. She's right. Some of the birds do have names, but only the resident birds, those that won't be set free for one reason or another. Sometimes they come to us with names already and, frankly, with them living here year-round, it's easier for us to remember names than numbers."

He began walking again, pointing toward a series of smaller pens grouped together in pods. "Over there is where the resident birds live. We can see them tomorrow. And over there," he said, pointing to larger wooden structures to the right, "are pens for rehabilitation."

They walked in that direction as Harris talked on about how the birds were moved from place to place based on their stage of rehabilitation. They began in the critical-care kennels in the clinic and, if they survived, they were moved to the larger pens in the medical unit, then finally to the flight pen where they could exercise and test their hunting ability with live mice.

"This is the final checkpoint to determine if the bird is fit to be released," he said when they reached the long, narrow flight pen. It was screened with the same heavy black wire mesh and framed in wood. "It's too small. We hope to build a bigger one soon. Maybe two, if we're lucky. That would give the larger birds a chance to really test their wings. So, that's about it," he said by way of conclusion. "Our goals here at the center are to observe, heal and release."

As he looked over the grounds she saw in his eyes the pride and satisfaction he felt at having achieved this much. Ella was also keeping an eye on Marion as she meandered along at their sides. What was it like to grow up surrounded by all these wild and ferocious raptors, she wondered, then made a mental note to discuss safety issues with Harris.

He moved closer to the flight pen, bending at the waist to see between the slats. "Look at them back there. Red-tailed hawks. They're fit and ready to go. I'm hoping to release them soon."

She squinted, trying to focus in the dimming light. Perched at the far wall, the three hawks were an impressive group, robust and muscular, much larger than they appeared flying in the sky. The hawks glared at them menacingly.

"I think they know they're being spied on," said Ella.

"Count on it," he replied. Then, catching sight of something over her shoulder, he said, "Hold on a minute. There's something I need to check on." He hurried off to meet a woman volunteer who appeared carrying a tray of fish and mice on her way to the medical pens.

"Mmm…dinnertime!" Marion said with a giggle.

Ella wasn't squeamish, but she made a fake shudder to play along. "I hope that's not for us."

"It is!" Marion giggled harder, putting her hand up to her mouth.

Enjoying their first friendly exchange, Ella gave a look that said, *you dickens!* She went too far, because immediately the smile faded from Marion's face and the wariness returned.

Around them, the day's light was fading fast. Looking at her watch, Ella was surprised to see that they'd been walking for half an hour. She looked again at Marion. The child leaned against the wall and had a tired, hangdog expression, which, in a diabetic child, could signal much more than fatigue.

Harris talked on with the volunteer, apparently about some problem with an osprey. His hands gesticulated in the air as he spoke. Ella wondered how he could be so attentive to the needs of the birds yet be blind to the signals his daughter was giving? The birds weren't the only ones needing their dinner.

"I'm getting hungry," she said with decision to Marion. "How about you?"

She nodded, scratching her head lethargically.

"Let's you and I see what's planned for dinner." She reached out her hand and was gratified when the child took it. "Do you think we might find something in your refrigerator other than mice?"

To her horror, mice were exactly what she found.

Ella opened the fridge to find a container of milk, a carton of eggs, a half loaf of bread and myriad condiments. There was also a large Rubbermaid plastic bin. Curious, she bent closer to open it. The seal burped, releasing a pungent odor as she removed the lid.

"Oh!" The lid fell to the floor as Ella slapped her hand to her mouth with a shriek.

She stood panting before the fridge, her eyes wide with disbelief. Inside the container were dozens of dead mice, black, white and bloody, packed high to the rim. Seeing mice outside on a tray for the birds was one thing. But here in the refrigerator next to a wrapped package of butcher's meat was another thing entirely.

"Is everything all right?" Harris asked, entering the house. His voice was winded, as though he'd come running. "I heard you shriek."

"There are mice in the fridge!" she exclaimed, standing in front of it and pointing accusingly.

"I know."

"You know?"

"I put them there."

"Well, that's not right! It's…it's totally unacceptable."

"I didn't think nurses were so squeamish."

"Squeamish? Squeamish?" she repeated, her voice rising. "I can think of a thousand reasons why dozens of bloody, dead mice should not be in the family refrigerator that have nothing to do with being squeamish." She moved her hand to her forehead, catching her breath. After a minute, her lips twitched and she said, "But let me tell you that one top reason is that they are an absolute appetite killer."

He reached up to scratch behind his ear, holding back a grin. "I guess they are at that. I sometimes keep the overflow in this fridge when the one at the clinic is full. But I didn't mean for you to cook tonight. You're our guest. I have steaks thawing."

Her stomach turned at the thought of eating any meat that came from that fridge. "Marion needed to eat," she explained. "I thought I'd fix up something quick."

His face reflected understanding, even approval. "I'll get the grill started."

"Mr. Henderson," she called out, halting his retreat. "Please, before you do anything else, could you take these mice out of here? It really isn't sanitary. And…" She gathered her courage. "It's not my business how you manage things at the clinic, but as this will be *my* workplace, I simply cannot have dead animals in my refrigerator."

He paused to consider, then nodded and came to retrieve the offending container. Marion was leaning against the sofa in the next room, watching with keen interest.

"Thank you," Ella said with heartfelt sincerity as he took the bin. Then, wanting to be helpful, "Is there anything I can help make for dinner?"

"No. I'll do it. Like I said, you're a guest."

"But I'm not. I don't like sitting around uselessly and Marion should eat as soon as possible. Why don't I season the steaks while you start the grill? And I could make a salad. I see fixings."

"You certainly are a go-getter," he replied in a flat tone that she couldn't decide was complimentary or critical. "All right, I'll leave it to you, then. It's your kitchen from here on out. I'll just get rid of these and start the grill."

Later that night, Ella sat on the edge of her bed staring out at the night from her open window. Her long hair flowed loose down her back and ruffled in the occasional breeze. The night was nippy and she'd opened the window to hear the hooting of courting owls. Harris had explained over dinner that it was the mating season for owls. He'd told her how at dusk, when the rest of the bird world was settling in, the owls were just waking up, becoming active and vocalizing.

Harris. She'd been pleased to find that her employer was an appealing, well-mannered man. Yet she'd not been prepared for her reaction to him. The attraction hit her hard and caused her heart to beat so fast in her chest that when he was near her she had to wrap her arms around herself to try to still it, sure he might hear its thundering. At this moment he was lying in his bed down the hall from her and she was painfully aware of every noise she made in this small bedroom, exquisitely aware of his nearness.

Ella wrapped her robe tight around her neck and leaned forward while listening intently to the melodious series of low hoots. The melancholy cries moved in a synchronized manner from one pen to another. Occasionally, an owl from the trees answered the calls. Over and over, east to west, calling and answering, the mysterious, erotic song circled her in the night.

She closed her eyes and put her face to the chilled, moist breeze. The ghostly moon shone overhead, and it felt to her as though it opened up her chest and drew out her neatly folded and stored memories like so many antique linens and gowns being removed and aired from a dusty trunk. They hung, suspended, around her in the mist, leaving her feeling empty and lonely. Love sang all around her, and she sat, utterly alone, on her bed.

As usual.

Ella was thirty-five years old. She could say that to anyone who asked without stuttering, blushing or trying to fudge a year or two. For fifteen years, Ella had worked as a pediatric nurse with all the tenacity and devotion that was in her nature to give. On the eve of her last birthday, Ella had, in typical practical manner, made herself a cup of tea, lit a fire in her fireplace and, while staring at the flames, laid out her realities as neatly as sums on a ledger.

She was a plain woman with a good education and solid job prospects. She hadn't had a date in eighteen months, a boyfriend in four years, and her romantic prospects weren't rosy. She'd told herself that it was time to face the likelihood of a life lived alone.

The reality was not so much frightening as it was chilling. While she stared at the embers, her private dream of a family of her own thinned and dissipated like the wisps of smoke that curled from an old fire grown cold.

On that birthday evening spent alone, she'd dragged herself up from the edge of despair to arrive at a decision. She couldn't change her lot in life, but she could alter its course. Her life *would* have meaning, success and joy. If she couldn't dedicate herself to a family and children of her own, then she would dedicate herself to her career and the children placed in her care.

And, she'd determined as she shivered in the bitterness of a Vermont winter's night, she would at least be warm.

The next morning she'd pulled out maps and chosen only those cities that were near sandy beaches and palm trees. A big medical hospital was a must, a theater and good music would be nice, and museums a big plus. Number one on the list, however, was a balmy climate. It didn't seem to her to be an unreasonable demand and she'd set her mind to it. Just after the Christmas wreaths and boughs were hung around the inn, she'd packed her Toyota Camry with everything she could squeeze into it, kissed her weeping aunts goodbye and driven south to begin her new life by the New Year in sunny Charleston.

On the long drive, she'd blindly passed the landscape. Her mind was too occupied wildly wondering what awaited her at the end of the long journey. Her imagination played with all manner of possibilities. But never, not even at her most creative high, did she consider that she'd have raptors as neighbors and live in a teensy house with a single bathroom she'd be sharing with a stubborn man and his recalcitrant daughter.

She chuckled at the perversity of fate, then rose to close the window tight. Shivering, she slipped from her robe and climbed under the heavy down quilt. It took a few minutes to warm her chilled body. She tucked her arms close to her chest and rubbed her feet together. Soon, the cocoon of warmth softened her muscles and her breathing grew rhythmic. Closing her eyes, she could still hear through the closed window the soft lullaby of the owls' love songs circling her. It was a melancholy song, rich with longing. This time, her heart responded.

Before falling asleep, just when her heavy lids began to seal, she thought she heard the rich baritone of a man's voice join the owls in song.

Feathers are marvels of evolutionary adaptation. They are some of the strongest and lightest structures formed of living tissue and do more than merely help birds fly. When fluffed up, feathers form dead air spaces that act as insulators against the bitter cold. When pressed tightly against the body, they help to expel excessive heat. All birds periodically shed their old feathers and replace them with new. This is known as a molt.

5

ELLA AWOKE AS THE PINK LIGHT OF DAWN HERALDED a cacophony of bird chirping outside her window. Not the melancholy love songs of owls or the piercing cry of raptors, but the squabbling and squawking of jays and mockingbirds in the surrounding woods. She brought the edge of her comforter closer to her chin and cuddled deeper in its warmth. Suddenly, her eyes sprang open. With a burst of clarity, she recalled where she was.

My Lord, what time was it? She pushed back the covers and the chilly, dank air hit her like a cold shower.

Grabbing for her watch, she saw that it was not even half past six. The air had that bitter, dank cold that told her the fire had gone out. She shivered and reached for her robe from the bottom of the bed where she'd tossed it the night before. While slipping her arms through the sleeves she crossed the icy floor on bare feet and peeked through a small opening in the window curtains.

Outside, the morning sky held that rosy, misty softness of an awakening day. Enchanted, she pulled back the curtain for a better view. The pastoral scene of a small black-bottomed pond tucked away by vivid green pinewoods was one she hadn't noticed on her arrival. A small smile tugged at her lips. She was pleased at the prospect of such a charming view each morning. A one-room cabin with a tin roof perched on a small rise beside the pond. It was probably the very cabin Harris had offered to sleep in, once the weather turned warm. Very sweet-looking, she thought as she let the curtain fall from her fingers. She began to turn away when, from the corner of her eye, she saw a blur of movement by the cabin.

She yanked back the curtain again and bent close to the glass to peer out. It wasn't her imagination.... A lean black man carrying a small bundle under his arm slipped from the cabin in a furtive manner, then hurried out of sight.

Her mouth slipped open in surprise. Could anyone be sleeping in that cold cabin? she wondered. In this weather? There wasn't any telltale sign of smoke from a chimney and icicles formed at the corners of the roof. It had to be freezing in there, she thought, shivering at the nippiness in the house. It was all very suspicious, and she decided she'd best mention it to Mr. Henderson at breakfast.

"A man in the cabin? Are you sure?" Harris asked her as he studied the plate of bacon before him. Three thick strips of bacon, blackened at the edges and pink in the middle, were drowning in a puddle of grease.

"Of course I'm sure," Ella replied, standing at his side, re-filling his coffee. "You don't think I'm making this up, do you?"

"No, no of course not. It's just that…" He returned the bacon to the plate and reached for the toast. This, too, was burnt to a crisp at the edges. "A tall man, you say? Slender? Black?"

Ella cringed inwardly at seeing him scrape the burnt edges from the toast. He had a sleepy look about him with his tousled hair and heavy-lidded eyes. He looked so boyish she had to stop herself from calling out "Eat up!" the way her aunts had when she was growing up and fiddling with the food on her plate.

"That'll be him," she replied.

Harris set his elbows on the table. "Lijah," he concluded before slathering the blackened toast with jam.

Ella felt another swift flush of embarrassment at the sorry breakfast and quickly returned to the kitchen and poured herself a fortifying second cup of coffee. She'd already been up for hours. The first one up, she'd showered quickly in the single bathroom, then dressed in jeans and a thick navy sweater in record time. The house felt strange to her and she'd fought off a sudden attack of homesickness and doubt as to why she'd ever left home in the first place. But she marshaled her will, focused on the task at hand, then went in search of a broom and dustpan. She'd found a butcher's-style apron hanging on a hook in the kitchen and the broom behind the kitchen door. Tools in hand, she went directly to the woodstove. As she'd suspected, the stove had long since gone cold to the touch.

Woodburning stoves were commonplace in Vermont and in no time she'd swept the ashes, dumped them outdoors and revved up a good fire with wood she found in a basket on the front porch. Then, after washing her hands, she thought it high time to make better acquaintance with the kitchen. The north was in her blood, after all, and a chill in the morning air energized her.

Now, looking around the kitchen, Ella thought again how it really was a pathetic little room. Everything was out of proportion. The miniature Roper stove was so small she'd bet it had been pulled into service from a camper. In contrast, the porcelain farm sink was deliciously enormous. It stuck far out from the narrow, dark green Formica counter like a full-term belly on a thin woman. It would be fine for washing big pots and produce, and she wondered if Marion hadn't bathed in it a few times over the years. There was also the tiny refrigerator—sans mice—an ancient toaster with a dangerously frayed cord and beautiful hand-hewn wood cabinets that looked so heavy she hoped the wall wouldn't collapse under their weight. All in all, a challenge to even the most capable cook—which she was not.

Ella sighed, hoping she'd find a few good cookbooks in the bookshelves to steer her through the ordeal. She was about to add a dollop of milk to her coffee but stopped, seeing how little was left in the jug. She thought Marion would likely want some when she awoke, and with a resigned sigh she put the remaining milk in the fridge. Frowning at her cup of jet-black coffee, she joined Harris at the table.

"We need milk," she said, taking a seat.

"I'll go shopping today."

"No need. I can go, once you tell me where the nearest grocer is. I'm good at directions, as you can tell," she added with a slight smile. "We'll need to work out some kind of system for shopping. A budget and all. I expect you'll give me a weekly allowance?"

"If that works best for you."

He wasn't much of a talker, but he was trying to be amenable. "I got up early and took a look around. I made out a list of things we need," she said, pulling a sheet of paper from her apron pocket. In two tidy columns, she'd started to list all manner of groceries, sundries and cleaning supplies she'd need to get the job started. In fact, she could feel the caffeine racing through her veins and couldn't wait to roll up her sleeves. She very much wanted to make a good start.

"Of course, I want to ask you what kind of meals you and Marion prefer, and what kind of things you hate, like onions, peppers, that sort of thing. You're not allergic to anything?"

"No, but Marion's not great with vegetables. Especially not okra."

She laughed. "I wouldn't know an okra from a collard green, anyway."

"Oh."

Ella thought it sounded more of a groan than a comment. She tapped her fingers on the rim of her cup before setting it down and folding her hands on the table. "Mr. Henderson, I suppose now's the time to tell you I'm not the best cook."

He looked up with a worried expression.

"It's just that I grew up with my aunts, you see," she hurried to explain. "They own an inn and they just love to cook. My aunt Eudora is a master chef. She can make a béarnaise sauce that would send you swooning. And her desserts!" Ella rolled her eyes. "Not to be believed, all made with fresh Vermont cream and butter.

"Aunt Rhoda is a baker. She has no interest in anything but breads, rolls, cakes, pies and the most delicate pastries. She always smells of sweet flour and has these big strong hands that can knead out a kink in your shoulders as readily as a glob of dough. They received a four-star rating from Fodor's," she added with pride.

Harris was now looking at her with an air of hopefulness. Realizing what he was thinking, Ella shook her head and smiled sheepishly. "So, you see, there was nothing left for me to do but clean up after them. *That's* what I'm good at. Cleaning. Really, I know more household hints than Heloise and my specialty is getting rid of germs. I'm organized, too. Even as a little girl I could take charge of the pantry, and let me tell you, I ran a tight ship at the hospital." She glanced around the room, narrowing her eyes in speculation. "And I can see I've got my work cut out for me."

"But, you *do* know how to cook?" Concern deepened the creases in his long forehead.

"Sort of," she confessed. "After all, I've lived on my own for years." She refrained from telling him that, other than the hospital cafeteria, she existed mainly on food that came out of boxes, the freezer or from care packages from the aunts. "My aunts taught me the rudiments, of course. I mean, I can boil water and I know what *bake* and *fry* mean. I figure with a good cookbook, how hard can it be?"

Harris looked at the congealed, undercooked bacon on the plate like a condemned man.

"This Lijah," she asked, eager to go back to the earlier subject. "Does he work here?"

"He's the fellow I was telling you about. The one who carried that eagle in his bare arms? Had to be him coming out of the cabin, that cagey old coot," he added, the affection in his eyes belying the scold in his tone.

"You didn't know he was there?"

Harris shook his head. "He's a strange man, decent and hardworking, but it's an unusual situation. He lives in St. Helena, but he followed this eagle north to its nesting area. They have this…relationship, I guess you'd call it." He paused, recollecting the night he came upon Lijah standing outside Santee's pen, anxiously peering in. "It's a rare and beautiful thing to witness, actually. He says he'll stay only as long as his eagle does. I doubt he expected to stay this long. Then again, he didn't expect for his eagle to get shot, either. I'm not sure where he's staying, or even how to reach him, for that matter. When I asked him about it, he just said, 'I do all right.' I accepted that and let him be. He's Gullah."

Ella shook her head, not understanding what that meant.

He leaned back in his chair, stretching long legs in jeans under the table. "Gullah is both a local culture and a language descended from enslaved Africans. I guess you could say it's a legacy that was born during the slave trade, flourished on the plantations and, because of the isolation of the Sea Islands, survives to today. You see evidence of the culture all throughout the Lowcountry. The sweetgrass baskets, hoppin' John, music." He smiled with recollection. "Every once in a while I hear Lijah slip into Gullah when he's talking to the birds—especially that eagle he likes to think is his. I can't understand most of what he's saying, but I'll be damned if the birds don't." He shook his head, chuckling softly at the memory. "They sit and listen like children with a bedtime story."

"Does he come around often?"

"Ever since he brought that eagle in he's been volunteering his time here at the clinic most every day. He does odd jobs—carpentry, fixing perches, general maintenance. There doesn't seem to be anything he can't build or fix. We're damn lucky to have him, truth be known." He frowned at his plate. "But I can't have him sleeping in the cabin."

"Why not? It's a perfectly nice living space."

"For one thing, there's no heat. It's freezing out there."

"Couldn't we get a heat source for him?"

"Probably," he allowed. "But that's not the point. The cabin was constructed for fair weather only. We often have students and interns come in the summer, and the cabin is where we put them up. I can't be having the volunteers sleeping here."

"And you have no idea where he's staying while he's here?"

"No. And quite frankly, I don't think it's really any of my business to look into the private lives of my volunteers. They come here to give their time and energy to help these birds. I don't pay them. Some stick around for a long time, others get bored, or figure it wasn't what they'd thought it would be, or just get busy and drop away." He paused. "But Lijah, he's one of the dedicated ones. At first I had to point out where the supplies were and what had to be done, but pretty soon he just seemed to find out for himself what needed to be done and did it. People like that are hard to find. I'll hate to lose him."

"So don't lose him."

"You don't understand. He's made it clear, he's only temporary."

"But if he's as good as you say, surely you can find an agreeable arrangement? Perhaps you can offer him a job?"

He steepled his fingers and stared at them. "Miss Majors, I have my own way of doing things."

"Well, you really should find out if he needs a place to stay. There's not a hotel or motel for miles. Does he even have enough food?"

"I'll handle it," he said, effectively cutting off her questions. He reached for his coffee, taking a long sip as he ruminated the problem.

Ella picked up her own coffee cup and debated in her mind whether or not she was overstepping her bounds by pursuing this. She felt certain that she was starting to antagonize him again, even though she'd promised herself she'd start off on the right foot this morning. She looked at him through the rising steam of her coffee. He was staring into the distance, the rigid set to his jaw giving clue to his personality.

"I realize my job is to tend to Marion in this house. And I don't mean to interfere with what goes on at the clinic next door." She took a deep breath. "But you simply can't turn your back and pretend we didn't see anything. What if that poor man hasn't anywhere to go? He can't sleep in that cabin another night without heat, that's for sure and certain. It's just not right. Why, it was so cold in *here* this morning I could see my breath. Imagine what it must've been like in there last night?"

"Sorry about the fire," he said quickly. "I don't usually let it go out."

"No matter. I'm accustomed to woodburning stoves. I'll check it at night before bed from now on. And sweep the ashes in the morning." She saw him about to object and added with finality, "It's my job, Mr. Henderson."

He studied her face for several moments and she felt he was taking her full measure. "You like to have things your way, don't you, Miss Majors?"

"And you don't?"

He set down his cup and looked at her with an expression of exasperation. He didn't reply. Instead, he tucked in his legs and rose from the table. Ella remained sitting straight-shouldered in her chair, looking at him and wondering how the two of them were ever going to abide being in the same house for a year.

"Thanks for breakfast," he said without a hint of sarcasm. "It's been a real long time since I woke up to the smell of coffee I didn't make myself."

Her shoulders softened. "You're welcome."

He walked to the door, where he grabbed a thick navy-blue peacoat from the wall hook. "Marion likes to sleep late sometimes," he said, pulling his arms through the sleeves. Then, pulling up his collar close to his ears, he added, "I'll be back in a few hours to settle the budget with you."

He spoke in declarative sentences and she worried that she'd annoyed him. She thought back to the morning long ago when she'd told the local pastor of her church—after his stirring sermon about original sin—that she couldn't believe in a God that would send poor little unbaptized children to a horrid nowhere place called Limbo. So either the pastor was wrong or she was giving up coming to his church. She was nine at the time and distinctly remembered wagging her finger at the pastor as she spoke. Her aunt Eudora had studied her with pale gray eyes more sad than critical behind wire-rimmed glasses and said, "Child, when will you learn to curb your tongue?" Ella never had learned, and this facet of her personality was both her strength and a curse.

"I'll be ready to discuss the budget whenever you are," she replied. "Oh, and Mr. Henderson…" she said, catching him before he turned away.

He stood with one hand on the door and a look of uncertainty on his face.

She looked at the untouched plate of bacon. "I'll try to do better with the cooking."

His smile came reluctantly, but when it blossomed, it transformed his face, lighting up his pale blue eyes like a sunny blue sky against white clouds.

"Miss Majors," he said, seemingly moved enough to venture a small confidence.

Ella waited expectantly. The words seemed pried from his mouth.

"I *care* about my volunteers. They're good people, just private individuals going out of their way to help. All I can offer them in return for all the work they do here is to work as hard or harder than they do and to respect their reasons for being here. We come from different places but we're all bound together by our common love of raptors. We count on one another." He opened the door, paused, then added before leaving, "And right now, I'm off to find out what's what with Elijah Cooper."

Harris found Elijah in the weighing room, bent over the worktable. It hadn't occurred to him until now how often he found the old man in this room, hard at work, so early in the morning. Now, stepping in the cozy warmth of the handsome one-room building, he understood. It was a fine little room. Neat rows of hanging leather bird-handling gloves and hoods hung on hooks beside organized charts on the walls, a weigh scale and spare perches. A long wooden table sat under a wide plate-glass window overlooking the resident bird mews, and in its deep drawers he knew he'd find the bells, swivels, leashes and other equipment of falconry. It made perfect sense that a man who loved raptors as he did would feel at home in this space.

The old man turned to look over his shoulder when Harris entered. "Morning, Harris. Sleep well?"

"Well enough," he replied, closing the door behind him. "What's that you're busy with?"

Lijah returned to his work. "Oh, just cutting jesses. Thought I'd start off slow this morning, since I'm fixing to stretch AstroTurf on the perches later. That's one mean job, but someone's got to do it. And looks like that someone be me." His chuckle seemed to rumble low in his chest.

"Much appreciated," Harris said, drawing closer. He watched as Lijah cut a few strips of light, tough leather to make into jesses, the slender straps that were secured to the birds' legs. These looked to be about the right size for a peregrine.

"Here, let me show you how to slice those," he said, moving to take hold of the sheath of leather. "You want to take care not to weaken the leather when cutting the slits," he said, his hands moving expertly in demonstration. "Jesses are only good if they're secure. What's the point of a steel swivel that can hold an elephant if the jesses are so weak it couldn't hold back a sparrow? There. How's that?" he said, holding up a perfectly slitted pair.

"Looks good."

"Yeah, well, I've been doing this for years. Now you try."

He watched as Lijah worked the leather. As with most things in bird care, attention had to be paid to the details. Once, he'd found a hawk hanging by one leg so high up in a tree Harris couldn't get to him, all because of bad jesses. But the old man's enormous hands worked as daintily as a seamstress's making French knots, he thought, looking on with admiration.

"You're good with your hands."

"Yes, I am. They been good to me over the years. I can build just about anything with some wood and nails. Done some ironwork, too. And I'm handy with a net, if you ever need help there." He held his hands up and looked at them with more respect than admiration. "Always wanted to try these fingers on a piano, but we never hooked up. I like to think we'd make pretty good music."

Harris took a breath, rubbing his palms together, knowing that the next conversation would determine if this particular versatile man would stay on at the center.

"A bit cold today, don't you think?"

"Cold? Nah, it's not that cold. 'Posed to warm up to the forties by midday."

"Really? That's good. Good. We can put the birds out to weather." He cleared his throat and tried again. "But the nights are cold, aren't they?"

Lijah chuckled softly as he worked the leather, nodding his head. "Oh, yes. The nights sure are cold."

Harris waited a moment or two before saying, "I imagine it's cold, even in that cabin."

Lijah's hand stilled and he lowered the hand tools. He sat for a moment, not moving, then he sighed heavily and turned to face Harris with an open expression.

"I don't mean no disrespect," he said somberly. "I keep it clean and I'm careful not to disturb nothing."

"I know," Harris replied. He paused. "Lijah, do you not have any place to stay?"

"No, no. I'm staying with friends—just down the road a piece. But getting back and forth to see Santee every day got to be troublesome. See, I need to be close. I need to sit with my bird a while to see her through this. I reckon like you did for your child back when she was in the hospital."

Harris felt a strong sympathy for the man's situation. Lijah loved that bird as any father loved a child. "I understand," he replied. "But damn, Lijah, there's no heat in there."

"I do all right." A sly smile slipped across his face. "It's a sight better than sleeping in the car."

"Lijah, it's not right, you sleeping out there in the cold. We'll have to figure something else out."

"You don't have to worry none. I'll just clear out of that cabin and find somewhere else. It ain't no problem for you."

"But where will you go?"

He shrugged. "Don't matter. Like I said, I have friends. And it's only temporary." His expression altered to worry.

"I hope this don't change your thinking on letting me keep coming here. Leastways, till Santee be well. I like working near these birds. And I daresay I'm doing a good enough job here?"

"You know you are. In fact, too good. You're coming near every day now and that's more than just volunteering. I don't want to take advantage of your generosity."

"You can't take advantage of what I'm giving freely," he replied with his serene smile.

"Well, I certainly don't want you to stop coming. There's no fear of that. But the conditions of your working here have suddenly changed. You're working as hard as any of the full-time staff, but the problem is, I can't afford to pay you a full-time salary."

He drew his shoulders back. "I never asked for money."

"I know you didn't. But you deserve it. So, I've been thinking. What would you say to a salary? We could negotiate a fee that you feel is fair."

Rather than brighten with enthusiasm, Lijah seemed a bit wary. "I thank you for the offer," he replied. "It's kind, to be sure. But all that strikes me as too permanent. I ain't looking for a job. I always pay my own way and earn my own keep. Done so all my life. And I don't want to *charge* you for working here because I'm only here on account of my bird friend. Here's the way it is. I like keeping to myself, like coming and going as I please. I just need to sit with Santee a while to see the bird through this. Then, when she well, we can make our way back home. Soon, hopefully." He met Harris's gaze. "You need to understand that when Santee leaves, I'll leave with her."

"I understand that." He sighed, reaching a decision. "I suppose we could open up the cabin early this year. Put a kerosene heater in, open the plumbing, fix up a bed, and you could join us for meals in the house. Though after you've tasted Miss Major's cooking, you might forgo that pleasure," he added with a smile. "What do you say? You can stay for as long or as short as you wish."

"In that case, I thank you for your offer and accept."

They shook hands and smiled in that companionable way that men often did when they were relieved and comfortable with the way a situation was resolved.

"I confess," Lijah said, that wry smile playing at his lips again. "A couple of those nights near froze my vitals off. But we're heading toward spring, so I'm hopeful."

"You won't freeze another night, not if Miss Majors has anything to say about it. She's the one saw you creeping out of the cabin at dawn and has been worrying about you ever since. Knowing her, she'll have that place in right order before nightfall."

Lijah's brows rose. "Miss Majors? That your new lady friend?"

"Good God, no! She's the nanny. She only just arrived yesterday and will be staying in the house with us, looking out for Marion, cleaning, and—heaven help us—cooking our meals. Speaking of which, what have you been eating these past few weeks?"

"I'm an old man and the appetite ain't what it used to be." Amusement sparkled in his dark eyes. "I been making good use of the microwave in the clinic to heat up a can of soup or stew. And from time to time I stay with a relative or a friend I know lives nearby. They can't stop feeding me. 'Course, there's biscuits, jerky, the kind of things I can pack up. Oh, and I come to like that Slim Fast in a can. Tastes pretty good. Only thing I miss, though, is a good hot cup of coffee in the morning."

Harris released a smile, amazed—as he often was in life—

at how things sometimes came around full circle. He put his
hand on Lijah's shoulder.

"Today's your lucky day. I happen to know just where you
can find one."

Brady Simmons traveled to the Coastal Carolina Center
for Birds of Prey vowing to make everyone at that rehab
joint as miserable as he was.

He sat in the passenger seat of the family's Ford pickup
that belched smoke and whined like a tortured animal every
time it shifted into high gear. If being seen in that sorry-
ass piece of tin wasn't embarrassing enough, his mother was
driving him.

Not being allowed to drive was all part of this mother
lode of punishments that had been dumped on him since the
police pinned the shooting of that eagle on him. That bird
wasn't even dead and his own life had been wiped out, as
far as he could tell. It was bad enough that he had to spend
every Wednesday afternoon and Saturday morning for six
long months doing so-called community service hours. He'd
a done that without complaint. He deserved it. He shouldn't
have pulled the trigger.

But why did they have to go and punish his whole family? Just on account of him doing something so stupid? The
authorities told them they was lucky to only have to pay
eighteen hundred in fines. *Lucky?* They weren't no wealthy
family that could just write a check for that amount. That
was about every cent the family had put away, and then
some. Mama had cried for days about that and wouldn't talk
to his father, blaming him for being so pigheaded as to tres-
pass on government property and to drag his son right along
with him. And if trespassing weren't bad enough, she'd hol-

lered, he had to go tell him to shoot the goddamn national emblem!

All of that was true. Brady wouldn't have fired if his father hadn't pushed him to do it. But he'd do it again if he could stop the nights of fighting between his parents.

Always the next morning, his mother would tell Brady that his father was a good man and only drank when he was worried. Problem was, he was worried all the damn time since the authorities banned both of them from hunting and fishing anywhere in the United States. Brady couldn't care less about himself. But *that* was a lethal blow for Roy Simmons. Let them do what they will to his son.

Though Brady doubted his father would obey it, anyway. And he had the nerve to tell Brady to act like a man? God, he hated him and all he stood for. There was a time Brady had looked up to his father. Roy Simmons always told his sons that a man had to live and die by his honor.

What a crock, Brady thought as he swallowed down the ball of hurt that bobbed in his throat. He turned and looked sullenly out the window at the blur of green pine along Highway 17. Good ol' Roy Simmons had caved at the first threat of trouble. And look what honor got me, he thought.

As far as Brady could tell, all that honor had brought him was having to stand in shame before a judge while he called him every kind of vile snake that crawled upon the earth before laying down a sentence that sounded like a living hell to Brady, but that everyone claimed was lenient on account of him being a minor. He'd been branded a delinquent and forced to serve time at some godforsaken outpost for birds.

"We're here," his mother announced as she turned off the highway onto a narrow gravel road in the middle of nowhere. When she stopped at the gate, she waited for him to climb out and open it, watching him like a hawk each step till he climbed back in the truck. When he settled in she reached out and slapped the back of his head.

"What?" he asked with a scowl.

"Sit straight and do something with your hair," she said, her mouth turned down at the corners. "You look like you just fell out of bed."

"I'm gonna be scrubbin' bird shit, Mama."

"Don't talk to me like that," she warned, her voice rising. "You just change that attitude, hear?"

Brady rolled his eyes and slouched farther into the seat. He'd heard that expression so many times it blew right over him like the wind.

"You want to do right in there so there's no more trouble. We're counting on you, son, to get this whole incident behind us."

Brady kept his lips tight, horror-struck that he felt a cry about to burst out and tears stinging his eyes. *They were counting on him....* Didn't she think he knew that? Didn't she know what this was all about, anyway?

He turned his head away from her, crossing his arms and leaning against the door. As his mother shifted into First and began pulling off, he caught sight of a big ol' white rooster sitting up on a pine bough. It seemed to look him straight in the eye as Brady passed.

__Flocks.__ Most birds of prey are considered solitary and breed in single pairs. Sometimes, however, raptors will come together to form large, cohesive flocks for migration or to form communal roosts in winter. Flocking is also a means of protection for smaller raptors as well as a means to gain information about food sources.

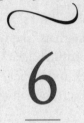

6

THE COASTAL CAROLINA CENTER FOR BIRDS of Prey was a small five-acre sanctuary surrounded by the 350,000 acres of wildlife refuge. All that protected land was seen by many folks to be too much to set aside. Others believed it wasn't near enough.

Harris was of the latter frame of mind. Not that many years ago, Harris could drive for miles without seeing much beyond salt marsh, pine woodlands and scattered homes burrowed along black-water creeks. It was a bird heaven. Raptors, shorebirds, songbirds—they all could migrate through the free coastal Carolina skies, find plenty of food sources in the maritime forests, perhaps even decide to take up residence, if only for a breeding season. Now, new subdivisions littered the highway, bringing with them high wires that crisscrossed the sky, speeding cars, noise, trash and the destruction of natural habitat.

His work could be pretty discouraging. Every day there

were calls for help. He'd gone to pick up hawks whose wings were broken from flying into electric wire while in fast pursuit of quarry; picked up countless owls and vultures with head trauma after being hit by a car while eating roadkill; treated ospreys whose chests and talons were ripped open by improperly disposed of fishhooks and line; put down a suffering raptor shot needlessly from the sky or poisoned by the misuse of sprays and insecticides. Over the years, he'd come to realize that most people weren't even aware that there was a lot society could do to prevent these senseless casualties.

Truth was, most people didn't know what the heck wildlife *was*. Folks—good folks—moved to big, new homes carved out of the wilderness, eager and excited to live among all that natural beauty. They lived day after day right smack next to a black-water creek or a vista of marsh, maybe even had a dock, and didn't have a clue what to do with it. They'd never learned how to cast a net or a line in the creek, or pull up a crabpot from the dock loaded with the most succulent meat God put on earth, or squished their toes in the pluff mud searching for hidden clams. Rather, they walked in clean-soled shoes along tended paths in a park, peeked at nature and breathlessly declared it wild.

But Harris figured if they learned to play with what lay in their own backyard, they'd learn right quick what wild *was* and what wild *did* and be eager to protect it. Education was the key.

Today, however, his commitment to education was being sorely tested. Harris placed his hands on his hips and waited at the edge of the parking area at the raptor center while an old Chevy truck rounded the bend and whined to a stop. He wasn't happy about this young hooligan coming to the center, but the court had argued that allowing Brady Simmons to do community service in support of the raptors he had defiled was an important form of education, perhaps even a message to the community.

Well, maybe, he thought as he watched the disheveled teen in baggy jeans, sweatshirt and torn jeans jacket slink from the truck and slam the passenger door with force. There was work that needed doing, but he'd sure as hell not let that kid anywhere near his birds.

The driver was a stout woman, pale and pasty, dressed in faded black slacks, a cable-knit green sweater and tennis shoes. Her blond hair was the same color as the boy's, only streaked with gray, so he figured she was the boy's mother. But that was where the comparison ended. Brady Simmons was tall for his age, with a boy's leanness and a man's broad shoulders. A troublemaker, he thought, tightening his jaw when he spied the spiked hair and pierced ear.

The woman led the boy along the dirt path with a rolling gait. "Mr. Henderson?" she asked in a rural drawl. When he nodded she said, "I'm Delia Simmons, Brady's mother. This here's my son." She turned to locate him.

The boy came up behind her, hands deep in his pockets, head ducked and eyes averted.

"Brady," she said sharply. "Say hello to Mr. Henderson."

Brady raised his eyes and shot out his hand so fast it barely touched Harris's before he retracted it back to his pocket, mumbling "hello."

Harris could see the frustration raw in the mother's eyes at her son's lack of manners. But he remained silent, doing nothing to make either of them feel more relaxed or welcome. His resentment against the boy and his father, and thus this woman by association, was like an unhealed sore on his hide.

"He's here to do whatever you tell him to do," Delia Simmons declared. "He knows what he done was wrong and he's here to make amends." She nodded her head several times, as if adding exclamation marks to her statement.

"We'll keep him busy enough."

"Uh-huh. That's good." Another nod. She must have sensed which way the wind was blowing for her son, because she looked Harris full in the face, her pale eyes appealing. "He's real sorry for what he's done. Brady's a good boy. Works hard around the place. Helps me with the kids, that's for sure. He's smart, too. The teachers tell me so all the time, and he's never caused us no trouble before. Fact is, I blame his father for the mess Brady's in, him bringing the boy into the government woods in the first place. We're hoping that he'll do his time here and that'll put this whole mess behind us."

The line sounded too rehearsed to suit Harris. The boy shuffled his feet and looked off at some point in the far distance, no doubt wishing he were there. Wishing he were anywhere but here. Harris gave Mrs. Simmons a stern glance that told her this was not some parent-teacher conference she could bluff her way through.

"The whole mess, as you put it, will only be behind us once that eagle is healed from the load of pellets that hit her. It'll be behind us once your boy learns that shooting federally protected birds is simply not tolerated. You see, Mrs. Simmons, the only reason I agreed to allow your son to do the community service here at my center is because I have the hope that your son will learn enough by being around raptors not to ever *want* to shoot them again. Nor any other bird—not an eagle, hawk, owl, not even a sparrow. And that he'll pass on what he's learned to his peers. *And* his family."

Then he shifted his gaze to the boy. "You got that?"

Brady swung his head around, eyes widened in surprise at

the direct question. Recouping his cool, he shrugged non-committally, then looked down at his feet.

"I didn't hear you," Harris said.

"I *get* it."

Harris studied the boy, but his passive expression revealed little besides contempt.

"Then that's settled," Harris said to Mrs. Simmons. "I expect him here every Saturday morning at nine sharp and every Wednesday afternoon by three. We won't be waiting on him to show up. Three late shows and he's out. You can pick him up today at two, unless he wants a lunch break, in which case you can pick him up at three. He brings his own meal, water and whatever else he wants. Any questions? No? Then we'll be seeing you later this afternoon, Mrs. Simmons."

"I'll be here at two, since I didn't make a lunch. Hear, Brady?"

"Yes'm. Two o'clock."

Harris turned to the boy. "Come on, then," he said, catching himself from calling him *boy*. "Let's get started." He fixed him with a stern look. "I hope you won't make me think this was a mistake."

Harris found Elijah in the rear of the clinic, cutting long strips of AstroTurf. Already he'd covered two six-foot perches. They were leaning against the wall looking tightly fitted and clean.

"Hey, Lijah! Mind if you slow down a bit? There's someone I'd like you to meet."

Lijah turned from the perch he was bent over to face him, a greeting on his lips. The smile of welcome slipped, however, and recognition sparked in his eyes when he saw the blond young man at his side. He straightened from his task and turned to face them with his shoulders erect.

Harris waved the boy closer. He followed with dragging feet. "This here's Brady Simmons. I suspect you know who he is."

Lijah nodded without comment. Even in his baggy jacket and faded pants, Harris thought a king could not be more regal. Turning to the boy Harris said, "This is Mr. Elijah Cooper. It was his eagle that you shot."

Surprise and confusion flickered across Brady's features. Harris was gratified to see the boy's cheeks flush before he ducked his head.

"Lijah, you recall we talked about this boy doing community service here?"

"I recall."

"And you're fine with that?"

"I don't have a problem, long as he don't give me a problem."

"Right. I thought it only fitting that I put him in your charge, if you're willing."

"I'm willing."

"Well, there's no shortage of chores to be done, we both know that." He looked around at the rows of stacked dog kennels lined up along the wall. Each one of them was filthy with streaks of black, green and white smears of bird mutes, spores of mildew, mold and mud. "Looks like we've got an overflow of kennels that need cleaning. We could maybe start him off with that."

Brady's head shot up. "I thought I was going to be working with the birds."

Harris's eyes flashed. He wanted to tell him hell would freeze over before he'd let him touch his birds. He took a moment to rein in his anger at the kid's arrogance before saying in a level voice, "Let's get this understood right from the start. No one gets to care for the birds without approval.

Not any volunteer. And you, Brady Simmons, are not a volunteer. You're going to have to work extra long and extra hard to earn that approval from me. We're all here to serve those birds. It's not the other way around."

"That be right," Lijah interjected with feeling.

Brady shot the old man a wary glance.

"You'll start working with a by-product of birds. See that bottled soap over there? And those scrub brushes? And that hose? Lijah here's going to show you how to use all that stuff along with some of that muscle power you've got to scrub clean every one of those kennels."

Brady's eyes smoldered in dismay at seeing the fourteen dog kennels ranging in size from small to extra large. "All of them?"

"Well, that's all there are for now. More come every day. They'll keep you busy."

"But…they're covered with caked-on bird shit!"

Harris was enjoying the boy's agony and had to hold back a smile. "We prefer to call it mutes. Makes it somehow easier. But the truth is, bird shit is just part of living with birds. You'll be scrubbing a lot of mutes in the next six months. Mutes from kennels, mutes from perches, mutes from pens, mutes from towels. We all do it. Pretty soon you won't think twice about it. Isn't that right, Lijah?"

"Don't bother me none."

Harris grinned, then turned to the boy. "See what I mean? So, I'll be leaving you in Lijah's excellent care."

Harris could readily see from the boy's mutinous expression that none of this was sitting well with him. But there wasn't a darn thing he could do about it. Brady Simmons would have a lot to reckon with in the next few months. Every act had consequences, and young Brady was about to find that simple truth out.

★ ★ ★

Ella sat at the oval wood table chewing a pencil nub and making up what was turning out to be a very long grocery list. The situation was dire. After she'd finished cleaning up that pitiful breakfast, she'd spent the better part of an hour prowling through a dank-and-dingy pantry and dusty, over-crowded cabinets. There were old, dented pots and pans, very few modern conveniences and a scarcity of food in the shelves other than tinned goods and condiments, most of which were unsuitable for a diabetic diet.

Marion would need a diet low in sugar, fats and salt with plenty of whole grains, fruits and vegetables. She'd need lots of good snack food, too, so Ella had added boxes of raisins, packages of cheese and crackers, small cans of juice and nuts to the list, all stuff that could be packed up if they went out somewhere. Looking over the list again, she thought they'd all be healthier in the long run, even if it meant there'd be no more late-night snacks of chocolate chip cookies for her. She sighed as she picked up her coffee cup. Late-night cook-ies were her one bow to decadence, but she couldn't very well eat cookies when little Marion could not.

She added a few more cleaning supplies, then smoothed out the list with her palms, satisfied. When she saw a child in the hospital, it was an emergency situation. She patched up a problem as best she could, then sent the child off. This time, with Marion, she'd be able to *prevent* the problems. She could make a difference in the quality of the child's life. Even the length of it.

The image of a small boy lying still on a hospital bed flashed through her mind. Ella removed her glasses and rubbed her eyes, the pain of the memory pricking fresh. She would not fail *this* child, she vowed.

Opening her eyes, she checked her wristwatch. It was high

time for sleepy little girls to wake up and have their blood tested.

The backstairs to the attic bedroom were very narrow and steep and they creaked under her feet. She pushed open the narrow door to a marvelous room bathed in winter's pale light pouring in from two gabled windows. It was a child's room, small, but airy because the ceiling rose to a point. Her lips spread in a smile. The walls and gingham curtains were both a lovely, little-girl pale pink. A Berber rug kept the floors toasty for bare feet. There were the usual toys and dolls tossed in baskets along the wall, a small white table-and-chairs set, and affixed to the wall with pushpins was an assortment of Marion's artwork.

Ella walked to the single bed nestled under an eave and gazed down at the child sleeping half in, half out of the blankets. What was it about the sight of a sleeping child that stirred a woman's heart so? she wondered. They held the innocence of angels in their faces. As she watched the child's rhythmic breathing, saw the soft blond hairs stir with each breath, she felt her commitment to the child surge with renewal.

"Marion?" Bending at the waist, she brought her palm to Marion's forehead and gently, almost shyly, stroked the downy hair from her face. She let her fingertips trace the curve of her jaw, then travel to her shoulders, which she gently shook.

"Marion? Time to wake up!"

The eyelids blinked heavily a few times before gradually dragging open. Ella watched as the round blue eyes slowly focused, then saw her sweet smile freeze and fall to a frown when recognition sank in.

"You're still here."

"Yes, sleepyhead, I'm still here. And I'll be here tomorrow, too."

Marion whined petulantly and turned her back on Ella. She was cranky and out of sorts. Ella immediately worried about her insulin levels.

"I remember promising you an outing today. I thought we'd go to town to the grocery store. Maybe we could find something to make the day special. Would you like to come?"

"Okay," she said with a condescending sigh.

"Why, thank you, Miss Marion, for allowing me the pleasure of your company. I think we might even have a nice time. If we try."

Marion looked over her shoulder, still showing a forced scowl. "I'm hungry."

"I'll bet you are and I've got breakfast all ready for you. But you know what we have to do first, don't you?"

Harris could hear the screaming from clear across the yard.

"What the hell," he muttered, stopping en route to look up at the gabled windows as though he half expected to see someone come flying out of them.

"Sounds to me like they're mighty busy in there at the moment," Lijah said at his side. "Maybe I'll come by later for that cup of coffee."

Harris nodded his agreement. "Might be a good idea."

While Lijah took off for the far side of the yard, Harris's heels dug into the soft earth on a direct path to his house. Didn't this thin-lipped, bossy nurse know how to deal with the child better than he could? Or was she just skilled at giving *him* orders? Well, he'd had about enough for one morning, he thought as he stormed into the house.

His words stuck in his throat as he stood in the doorway.

Ella Majors was at the table, calmly pouring cereal into a bowl, seemingly oblivious to the howling going on upstairs.

He shut the door behind him. "What, may I ask, is going on here?"

"I'm getting Marion's breakfast ready," she replied, looking up with a serene smile. Her brown hair was pulled back in a martinet's style and the white shirt under her sweater was buttoned to the throat. She was the very picture of control amid chaos. Somehow, the image only irritated him further.

"While she's screaming?"

"Oh, she's just mad, is all. I had to prick her a few times. First the test, then the shot."

"And you just left her crying up there all alone?" His voice was rough with anger.

Ella slowly put the cereal down, then gave him a cold, hard stare.

She wasn't a big woman—average height, slender and small of bone. When she pulled those bony shoulders back and glared at him with those dark brown eyes, however, she made herself appear formidable, like a hawk that fluffs its feathers when threatened.

"I'm sorry," he said at length. "I didn't mean to sound harsh. It's just—"

"She's fine," Ella interrupted, her shoulders lowering a bit. "Really. She just needs to get her anger out and there's no point in giving her an audience. That's what she wants, you see. To manipulate me." Her thin lips twitched in mirth. "Like she does you."

He was taken aback. "No, she doesn't."

"Oh, yes, she does. She plays you like a fiddle."

He shifted his weight as an embarrassed smile eased across

his face. "I guess she might, from time to time. What were her blood levels this morning?"

"High," she replied, her smile slipping as she grew serious. "Quite high, actually. It was clear when I woke her up that her insulin levels were way off. I tested her, then immediately gave her an insulin shot. No easy task, as you well know. Frankly, Mr. Henderson, I'm concerned. I need to get a handle on her blood levels. They're all over the place."

"I— Well…they've been hard to maintain."

"Granted. And the shift with my arrival adds stress, but we must make some immediate changes. We can start by getting her on a fixed routine. No more sleeping in late. That's never good for a diabetic child. And no more backing off from her temper tantrums. She'll get tested at regular intervals. And no more tempting sweets in the house. That's an accident waiting to happen."

"Look, I know I've screwed up. I missed the symptoms, and now I obviously can't manage her care. I've failed her, okay? What more do you want me to say?"

"Oh, no, Mr. Henderson! Please. I wasn't being critical of you! I don't think you failed her."

He didn't believe her.

"Quite the opposite. You've done marvelously well here on your own. Diabetes is a tough disease to handle. There's so much to learn and do, especially at the beginning of this crisis. You've brought her around again and, after all, you did hire me to come here and care for Marion. As for missing the symptoms… No one can single you out for blame. I can't tell you how many parents have told me the same thing when their child lands in the emergency room at the hospital. They think that, somehow, they are to blame. That they've fed their child the wrong foods. The truth is, nothing you or they did contributed to the onset of diabetes. You can't blame yourself or think you've failed."

He said nothing to this. He could not.

"Managing her blood levels is a daily—hourly—struggle. I'm a nurse. I've studied the disease, dealt with it many times. Honestly? I'm more worried that *I'll* fail you and Marion."

She tucked a tendril of hair behind her ear as she took a deep breath. "If I sound like a general sometimes, forgive me. You wouldn't be the first one who's thought that. It… it's just my way of approaching a problem. I like to attack it head-on. But the truth is, neither of us is alone in this struggle. We have to work together."

Harris felt the weight of his guilt slip from his shoulders like a glacier crashing to the sea. Suddenly, he saw Miss Ella Elizabeth Majors through different eyes. She wasn't being critical, she was being supportive. She wasn't blaming him as a failure. Rather, she was afraid of her own failure.

Hearing that helped to put his own worry into perspective. He wasn't alone on some precipitous branch, like poor ol' Pee Dee. He and Ella were partners in this effort. Looking at Ella again, the sharp angles of her face appeared to have softened as she looked at him with concern.

"Working together… I like that idea," he said.

"Me, too."

"You know," he said, sensing that they'd just crossed a line in their relationship. "A good start to all this might be if you stop calling me Mr. Henderson and just call me Harris like everyone else does."

"All right. Harris. And please, you'll have to call me just Ella."

"Okay, Just Ella."

He noticed that her color deepened at his weak attempt at

humor, making her brown eyes come alive. It felt oddly like flirting.

As though she sensed it, too, she pressed her hands together and spoke in a rush.

"Last night Marion may have had too much to eat for her bedtime snack, or she may be having low blood sugar during the night. It's hard to tell right off the bat. I gave her a peanut butter and jelly sandwich, just to stabilize things a bit. The little minx only ate it when she thought I wasn't looking," she added, smiling ruefully at the memory. "I'm afraid I'm at the bottom of her list of favorite people at the moment."

The screaming upstairs abated. Ella looked up for a minute, her ear cocked. In another moment, all was blissfully quiet. She looked at him as a knowing grin crossed both their faces.

"More coffee?" she asked brightly.

Ella Elizabeth Majors was in her element. She saw the household as just one charming but dusty carpet that needed a good shaking and to be laid out straight. In the past few days she'd literally rolled up her sleeves and cleaned the house with relish. She felt she was starting to gain control of this unruly house.

She wasn't so confident with Marion, however. She had a whole new sympathy for Harris's efforts as a lone parent. At the moment, the little girl was sitting at the table quietly eating a hot breakfast. Ella didn't want to do anything to distract her, even if it was only the calm between storms.

It wasn't really the child's fault that she was so temperamental. Marion had been living on a schedule that revolved around the lives of the adults in her life, going to bed late and sleeping late the next morning. The first thing Ella did was put Marion on a new schedule in order to better monitor her blood sugar levels. This meant literally dragging the complaining child from her bed every morning and proceeding to poke her with needles. Each day began with a tantrum instead of a smile.

But these were minor skirmishes compared to what she knew would be the major battle: the television. Marion spent hours in front of the television, watching one children's show after another with a glazed look on her face. Ella had yet to see her play with any of the dozens of toys she had lying around the house or go out of doors in the fresh air. She knew it would be easier to get the housework done with Marion sitting passively on the sofa. It was the obvious mode of baby-sitting she'd received thus far. But her first priority was to care for Marion, not the house.

So Ella's plan for today was to keep the television turned off.

It wasn't long before she heard the telltale clank of the spoon hitting the cereal bowl and the scrape of a chair. Ella wiped her hands on her apron and came around the corner from the kitchen to stand at the threshold of the living room. She watched, pensively, as Marion trotted over to the television with her doll, Lulu, tucked under her arm. With a yawn, she reached out to turn the television on.

Ella tucked her arms around herself and waited.

When the television didn't turn on, Marion pushed the button again, then again with frustration.

"It won't go on," Ella told her with a calm voice.

Marion swung her head around to face her. "Why not?"

Ella licked her lips and stepped into the room. "There won't be any television for a while."

"Is it broken?"

It would have been so much easier to lie and tell her yes. After all, she was only five years old. She didn't need a long explanation. The truth was Ella had simply unplugged it. But Ella didn't want to begin their relationship with a lie. Better that Marion understand the new routine, she thought to herself. Then she could come to accept it.

"No, it's not broken," she replied calmly. "I just made it so it wouldn't work for a while."

Marion looked at her disbelievingly, then she scrunched up her face and whined, "But I wanna watch TV!"

"Let's take a walk instead," Ella suggested, holding out her hand. When Marion angrily crossed her arms and turned away in a snub, Ella whispered a prayer for strength and tried another tactic. "Do you want to play one of your games? I'm pretty good at them. You pick."

"No! I wanna watch TV!" This time more loudly and persistent.

"Marion, I care too much about you to let you sit there all morning like a vegetable. There are lots of fun things we could do." She saw the anger sizzling in the child's eyes and knew that this was going to be a showdown. Ella racked her brain, trying to think of what might tempt a five-year-old. "How about we play dolls? Or color in some of your coloring books? I'll get some paints for later, if you like. I love to paint and could teach you. What do you think?"

Marion squared off and shouted with all the rage and anger pent up inside. "I *said* I wanna watch TV!"

Ella held her ground, clasping her hands tight before her. "Well, that's not going to happen. You might as well accept that and think of something else you'd like to do."

"No!" She marched like a mad general over to the television and tried again to turn it on. When, of course, it wouldn't work, she grew so furious she raised her hand and hit it. "Ow!" she cried out, cradling her hand against her chest and letting the first tears flow at this final indignity.

It was too pitiful to watch and Ella drew near to wrap a consoling arm around her.

"I hate you!" Marion screamed, backing away as though she loathed Ella's touch. "You're mean. You only make me do what you want me to do. You never let me do what I want to do!"

"Marion…"

"I wish you never came here. I want you to go away from here. And never come back!"

"I'm sorry you feel that way, but that doesn't change the fact that you are not going to watch television this morning."

It was all too much. Marion threw herself across the sofa and began writhing and screaming at a high pitch. Her face was turning as red as a stoked fire that was going to burn hot for hours.

Ella took a deep breath, trying to contain her own simmering frustration and maintain a nurse's calm in the face of crisis. "When you're finished, come join me in the kitchen," she said, trying to speak loud enough to be heard over the screaming. "I'm cleaning out the cabinets and you might want to help."

"I hate you! I wish you never came here!"

Ella felt slapped by the words and, chewing her lip, turned on her heel and headed for the kitchen. There, she grabbed the bucket of soapy water, dropped to her hands and knees and began scrubbing. She was a pediatric nurse, she told herself as she put her back to the task. She knew that Marion was simply overwhelmed with the changes going on in her life. All her fears of hospitals, illness and needles, coupled with the anxiety of a new caretaker and schedule, had proved too much for her. And who could blame her? She had to get pricked with a needle six times a day!

Ella reminded herself that she'd dealt with tantrums at the hospital many times over the years. Some children screamed until they were so upset they threw up. Others held their breath till they turned blue or passed out. Most people didn't realize that tantrums were hardest on the child. The uncontrollable nature of their own fury terrified them. In the hospital, Ella had been skilled at helping a child calm herself, and more often than not, the tantrums gradually subsided.

But Marion's tantrums were happening with increasing frequency, not less. Ella's hand stilled and she sat back on her haunches while the water dripped down her thighs. What was she doing wrong? she wondered as the screams pierced her skull. Was she coming on too strong? Was this new schedule too strict? She'd only been here a short while.... Maybe it was too soon to start restricting things Marion liked to do. Maybe she was setting up a power struggle that Marion could only lose.

Ella closed her eyes and listened to the heartrending screams of desperation pouring out from the next room. Her shoulders slumped as all her confidence popped and dissolved like the soap bubbles in the bucket beside her. Maybe she couldn't do this job, she thought with despair. She prided herself on running a tip-top unit, but this wasn't a hospital, she scolded herself. This wasn't an adult. She was being too tactless, too unyielding for the everyday tending of a small child.

"I hate you! I wish you never came here!"

She dropped the sponge and brought her hands to her face, feeling enveloped by the screams as well as her failure. She didn't hear the door open, or the footfall across the room, so she startled when she felt the strong hand on her shoulder. She sucked in her breath and looked up in alarm.

Harris crouched down at her side. She was assailed by the

scent of the leather from his jacket. He didn't bear a look of anger, as he had the first time his daughter screamed bloody murder. She was surprised to find compassion etched across his features.

She sniffed loudly and wiped the embarrassing tears from her eyes. "I didn't hear you come in."

"How are you holding up?"

Ella released a short, choppy laugh and looked at her hands. "Not too well, as you can see."

"It's been a rough morning, huh? Let me warn you. This can go on for hours."

"God help me…"

"I've got some earplugs in my desk drawer. Found they worked wonders for me."

She met his gaze and they shared a commiserating smile.

"How did you stand it for so long?"

"I didn't. I hired you."

Their chuckles broke the tension and the howling seemed to grow more distant.

"I'm wondering if it was a mistake to hire me." Her hands tightened on her thighs. She felt exposed and fearful that she'd revealed too much.

"What happened?"

"I turned off the television."

He grimaced.

"I'm not being mean, or at least I hope I'm not. I'm just trying to get Marion to *play*. She can't just sit around and watch television all day. But…maybe I was insensitive. She told me that all I do is tell her what to do and not do and it suddenly hit me that she's right. A lot of *do's* and *don'ts* is the recipe for a tantrum."

"No, it's not your fault. You know, she didn't always have these temper tantrums. They started when she came back from the hospital. I guess I'm to blame. I must've been doing something wrong."

"Listen to us. We're both so eager to accept the blame." She sighed and shook her head, feeling like she was regaining a bit of her equilibrium. She could think clearly again. "It's more likely that she tried so hard to be a good girl in the hospital that when she came home to safe turf, she felt comfortable enough to let all that frustration out. And to punish you, too, of course, for taking her there in the first place. Children aren't logical, you know. It's all trial and error. Once she saw how effective her tantrums were, she was smart enough to keep using them. Kids do this sort of thing all the time, the little darlings." She sighed, then exhaled, thinking. "And with me... She's upset and frightened by the new changes. But I'm doing the right thing," she said with conviction. "I know it."

She looked up. He was so near, listening intently. His hair was tousled and unkempt and she thought his eyes were the most brilliant blue she'd ever seen.

"Thank you," she said.

"What for?"

"For your support. I needed it just then. I think I'll be all right now."

He smiled and his eyes kindled. "Seems only fair to return the favor." Then he rose and took a step back. The moment was over. "I'll leave you to it, then. I just came by when I heard the helter-skelter. Wanted to make certain you were still alive." His grin widened as she joined him in a brief laugh. "Just remember—the earplugs are in the top drawer of my desk," he said, then turned and left through the back door.

All the dishes, pots, pans and cooking paraphernalia were lying on towels across the floor while Ella finished washing the cabinets. She paused, suddenly aware that the screaming had stopped. She pulled her head out from the depths of the wood cabinet, and breathing the cooler, unscented air, she reached up to pluck out the earplugs. The house was blissfully quiet. Too still, in fact, for comfort. She'd best check on Marion, she thought. Most likely she'd fallen asleep on the sofa, exhausted.

When she turned, she was startled to find Marion standing at the door of the kitchen with a sheepish expression. Her hair was smeared with tears and her eyes were red and swollen. There was an air of fearfulness and expectancy—and defeat—that touched Ella to the core. Ella knew that this was a critical moment. No words came to mind, so she responded with her heart. She opened her arms wide.

Marion's lower lip trembled with uncertainty, she sniffed loudly, then she impulsively dashed across the room to fall into Ella's arms. Ella scooped her into her lap, wrapped the child tightly to her chest and rocked and rocked, crooning that everything was going to be all right, reassuring her what a good girl she was and telling her for the first time how much she cared for her. Marion clung tight and whimpered, seeking a safe harbor.

Holding her, Ella swore to herself that she'd be that harbor for this motherless child. She'd care for Marion as if she were her own. As she crooned and rocked, she blocked out of her mind the warning niggling in the recesses of her brain to be careful. Marion wasn't her child and the gods had warned it was dangerous to steal fire.

The rest of the morning was relatively peaceful. Marion had inspected each and every kitchen utensil on the floor. Then she stood on a chair at the sink, which Ella had half filled with mild soapy water while a thin trickle of water dripped from the spigot. Ella figured she'd be long finished cleaning the cabinets before water could fill that enormous farm sink.

Afterward, she took a sopping wet Marion to her room to change into dry clothes and a thick sweater. Then together they gathered the wet clothes into bundles with the rest of the laundry. Ella hadn't done laundry yet and had to ask Marion where the washer and dryer were.

"Are you sure, honey?" she asked, following Marion out of the house to a woodshed yards away.

"Uh-huh. It's in there," she told Ella, pointing.

The chilly wind tossed their hair as they made their way across the yard. Ella set down the basket on the cold earth. The shed was tilting to the east and it looked like one good gust would finish the job. Lifting the makeshift wood latch, she cautiously tugged the door, stepping back as it creaked open. When she was satisfied nothing would jump out at her, she peeked inside.

Sunlight poured through the dusty motes, revealing an old washer and dryer set against one wall, a deep freezer on the other and countless rusted tins and dusty bottles stuffed into any other available space. Cobwebs hung like drapes across the small paned window and three black garbage bags took up most of the middle floor. Ella walked through the little remaining space to the closest bag. With two fingers, she gingerly picked it open and rummaged inside. A pungent odor escaped the bag, and inside, she found towels of all colors and shapes, all of them heavily soiled with bird dung. She closed it back up and twisted it tight.

"Is this where they wash the towels for the clinic?" she asked.

Marion nodded.

"And you do your laundry in here, too?"

Again, Marion nodded.

"Lord help me," she muttered, her worst fears realized. She opened the rusted washer. It creaked loudly, and looking in, sure enough, she found a load of wet towels waiting to be dried. In the dryer she found a load of scruffy towels.

She drew back and crossed her arms, deliberating. This was the laundry room. Feathers floated in the breeze and the floor was covered with a fine white powdery substance she could only guess was dander of some sort.

Ella shook her head and chuckled as she reached for a broom and dustpan. "I swore I wasn't going to get roped into the clinic work, but I suppose we could fold a few towels, don't you?"

Marion leaned against the door. "I don't know how."

"You don't know how to fold a towel? It's easy. Think of it as a new game. I'll teach you."

The singing drew him in. Harris was walking from the clinic, hoping for a little lunch, when he heard two feminine voices belting out choruses of "Old MacDonald" coming from the woodshed. Marion's high-pitched e-i-e-i-o mingled with giggles, was the sweetest music he'd heard in a long time. He detoured, stopping when he was close enough to see, yet not disturb them. The door to the laundry shed was wide open, revealing a tidy laundry room, freshly swept and with all the supplies lined up in a row on the dusted shelves. A pile of folded towels lay on the freezer. Beside it, Ella stood folding a large towel while watching Marion attempting to fold a smaller one. The child mostly just rolled it up with her chubby fingers and pressed it on to the tilting pile. Marion's towels would all have to be refolded, but she didn't know that. Anyone could tell the child was blissfully proud of her efforts. Her smile spread from ear to ear and her eyes sparkled.

Harris stood mute and still, but inside, his blood was roiling and tears blurred his vision. This was the Marion he knew before the onset of her illness. This was the Marion he missed.

Ella looked up and saw him standing there. Their eyes met. Her hands stilled, then lowered as she brought the towel to her chest. They stood for a moment, sharing a commiserating look across the yard—his filled with gratitude, hers with understanding. He didn't need to say a word. Nor did he approach and disturb the child singing loudly, happily, off-key, oblivious to the fact that a turning point had been reached in their world.

There might be mice in the fridge and feathers in the laundry. There would be mornings of burned toast and soggy bacon, and evenings of bitter tears and insulin shots.

But Marion was singing. And like the canary in the coal mine, this signaled all would be well.

Eagles: Majesty in Motion. Eagles are very large and powerful birds of prey. With broad, planklike wings and dark plumage, they soar with a stately steadiness that has inspired nations for centuries. While both the bald and golden eagles reside on the continent, the bald is the more widespread and, as the national symbol, the most recognized and revered.

7

DAYS WERE NEVER LONG ENOUGH IN THE WINTER, Ella thought to herself as she carried an armful of heavy wool blankets, flannel sheets and a pillow across the yard to the cabin. She found that when the sun lowered on the horizon and the sky turned dusky, especially on chilly nights like this one, lassitude settled deep in her bones.

When working in the hospital, each minute was so hectic she usually wasn't aware of the time or the weather outside the thick glass windows, or whether the sun was high or low in the sky. Here in the country, the sun regulated her days. She rose at daybreak with the birds, and like them, wanted to tuck her head into her feathers and roost when the light faded from the sky.

Today, however, she still had much to do before sleep. She'd already gathered wood into the basket for the fire and had finished stoking the flames, satisfied that the house would be warm through dinner. Her primary task now was to finish preparing the cabin for Elijah so he could move in. Harris had agreed that Lijah should sleep in the weighing room until the cabin was ready. They'd fashioned a small cot for him that could be readily disassembled for the workday. It wasn't much, but it was only temporary, and more important, it was warm. In the meantime, Ella had turned her attention to the cabin, sweeping out the cobwebs, polishing the panes of glass and washing inches of dirt from the floor. She'd purchased a kerosene heater that was up to the task of warming a small space, a rug, a few blankets and sheets. Now she was on her way to meet Harris's bird handler, Maggie Mims, who had volunteered a twin-size mattress and box spring as well as a spare table and two chairs from her home.

Maggie was already at the cabin when she arrived. She was a big-boned woman, tall, with broad shoulders and chest, pronounced cheekbones and brick-red hair cut short to frame her face. She wore a nylon rain jacket over baggy khaki pants and thick rubber-soled boots. Her cheeks were flushed with the effort of trying to single-handedly maneuver the floppy twin mattress from her minivan through the cabin door.

"Here, let me help you," Ella said, trotting closer. She set the bedding on the car's tailgate and hurried to grab an end of the mattress.

"You must be Ella," the woman said with a smile that showed a line of large white teeth.

"And you must be Maggie."

"Guilty as charged. Heck of a way to meet, but I'm glad you showed up. This mattress is not so heavy as it is darned clumsy. And you know the saying—two hands are better than one."

"Or, timing is everything, as my aunt Rhoda always told me," Ella said, getting a better grip on the corner. She was smaller in height and width than Maggie, but she was strong. "Speaking of which, I'm ready. On the count of three. One, two, lift!"

The two women readily lifted the mattress and carried it into the cabin. The matching twin box spring was already in the room and on the frame. It took up most of one wall. Together they moved the small table and two chairs in, then closed the door against a brisk, damp wind that stung their cheeks and threatened a sleety rain.

"Let's get that heater going," Maggie said, rubbing her palms together. "It's colder than a witch's titty in here."

Ella laughed, liking Maggie's blustery manner immediately. It reminded her of her aunts. While Maggie lit the heater, Ella laid down a cheery, brightly colored hooked rug and draped heavy, navy curtains across the two windows, more to cut the draft than for decoration. As the wind howled louder and louder outdoors, inside, the small space grew warmer and cozier.

"Lijah will be appreciative of all you're doing," Maggie said as they worked together to spread the bottom sheet across the bed. "It just isn't his style to ask for anything for himself. But he's always the first one to lend a helping hand to others. There are givers and takers in this world, and Lijah is one of the givers."

"What's he like? I've invited him to meals but he's yet to show up. He's accepted fruit and cheese, sandwiches, that sort of thing, but so far I've only been able to lure him to the house with my coffee. He fills his thermos, thanks me profusely, then leaves without eating a bite."

Maggie chuckled softly to herself. Everyone at the center had heard about Ella's cooking.

"He's kind of aloof, don't you think?" Ella asked, spreading out the top sheet.

"Aloof?" Maggie bent at the waist to tuck in her side of the sheets. "No, he's not that. He's just not much of a talker. Unless he's got something to say. Then he's freehanded with advice. Lijah calls himself a Watcher, and I'd say that pins him down pretty good."

"A Watcher? What does that mean?"

"Just what it sounds like. Walk around the area and you'll understand. Sometimes you'll turn around and see Lijah looking at you. Not in a weird way, nothing like that. He just has this peaceful gaze, like he was staring out at the sky and you just happened to cross his line of vision. But I get the sense he sees everything that goes on around here. Owls are like that, too, you know. They just sit quietly in the tree, turning their heads left and right, catching sounds and sights like radar. I wonder if that's what makes him so popular with the birds."

"Is he?"

"They just love him. I've never seen anything like it. Most of the time the birds are really jumpy when a person walks into their area, especially someone they don't know. Not Lijah. He can walk right into their enclosure and they don't seem to mind. He does move quietly, maybe that has something to do with it. But I think it's something more. When I asked him about it, he just smiled in that way he does and shrugged."

Ella made sharp tight hospital corners on the sheet, then spread out the two wool blankets. Maggie grabbed hold to help, making quick work of the job. It was nice working with another woman again, she thought. Ella had grown up with her aunts, and at the hospital, the nurses shared stories during the breaks or quiet moments on the floor. She'd not realized how much she missed the natural flow of feminine conversation.

At the dinner table, she tried to start conversations. Harris was polite and offered short responses to her questions, but he was quiet by nature and felt comfortable with long lapses of silence. It was the opposite with Marion. She was a typical chatty five-year-old who had a lot to say about everything. Ella did little else but nod and occasionally say, "Oh, really?" So, having a give-and-take chat with another woman—one she instinctively liked—was a pleasant treat.

"You were a nurse, right?" Maggie asked.

"A pediatric nurse. I worked in the emergency room, and before that, intensive care." She paused, remembering the pounding of feet, the orders called out in staccato, the way the adrenaline flowed during an emergency. "It got pretty intense sometimes."

"I'll bet. It can get like that at the clinic, too."

"I imagine it's not a whole lot different. Except, of course, the stakes are lower."

"True, but you don't think that when you're fighting for a raptor's life. I suppose the biggest difference is that, for us, when the injuries are so bad we can't fully rehabilitate, we put the bird down. It's kinder that way. It would be cruel to release the bird back to the wild to suffer."

"Can't very well do that in a hospital."

"Nope." Maggie chuckled. "Though sometimes I think it might be more humane. So why be a nanny? Seems an odd career change."

Ella sighed and rested her hands on her hips while she considered her answer. "Not really. You see, I love children," she said honestly. "I always have. That's what led me to pediatrics in the first place. I was your typical wide-eyed idealist when I first started out. I wanted to heal the world. I thought I could make a difference, not only with medical care but with kindness and patience when a child was scared, sick and alone."

"That doesn't sound idealistic. It's what compels so many of us to volunteer."

"Except I didn't realize how painful it would be when I failed. It's very hard to watch a child die."

Maggie's hands stilled. "I can't even imagine."

"They kept telling me I'd get used to it, that in time I'd develop a shell. But I never did. I persevered, day after day, for more than ten years. I'm not boasting when I say I was good at my job. I could communicate with the kids, and all their screaming didn't agitate me. I have a long streak of patience." Her lips twisted into a wry grin. "Some folks might call it stubbornness."

Her face grew somber again as she brought back to mind the hard times of nursing: the psychological punishment of seeing the "repeaters" return to the E.R. again and again, until the vicious spiral tragically ended. Or knowing that no matter how hard she tried, that sweet child was going to die and nothing she could do was going to make a difference.

"Looking back, I think I crammed all that pain down and held it boxed up inside me until, one day, it all just burst out and I couldn't take it anymore. I…I simply couldn't go back."

"I'm sorry. I didn't mean to pry."

"No," she replied quickly. "No, you didn't. It helps to be able to talk about it. Anyway," she said, grabbing the pillow and beginning to stuff it into the pillowcase, "that's why I quit nursing. At least for a while."

"You're going back to it?"

Ella nodded. "I told Harris I would stay for one year. At the very least, in that time I should be able to get Marion's levels stable and establish a routine for the two of them to follow. I hope I can last that long. It's strange, given what I just told you, but sometimes I miss that adrenaline rush. I miss all the excitement. The pace here is so slow. I'm used to go, go, go. Making quick decisions and giving orders. I can be a bit of a drill sergeant." She shook her head and pressed the pillow to her chest. "Poor Harris. I'm sure I'm not the easiest woman to live with."

Maggie muttered, "You wouldn't be the worst."

"What?" Ella asked, her head snapping up.

"Oh, nothing."

"Come on, now. I didn't hold back. What's that about a woman?"

"Curious, are you?"

"Not really."

When Maggie snorted with disbelief, Ella's cheeks flamed and she fluffed the pillow. "Well, okay, maybe a little."

"I see the way it is now."

"You can stop wriggling your brows, I don't mean it that way. It's perfectly normal to be curious about someone you live with. I mean, as a nanny. Oh, stop it," she said, joining Maggie's laughter. "You know what I mean."

Maggie laughed as she placed a down comforter atop the blankets. "I'm just having fun with you. Well, I don't know much, that's the truth. Harris is pretty tight-mouthed."

"Tell me about it."

Maggie laughed again and sat down on the bed. Ella sat on the chair and leaned back, surprised by the depth of her own curiosity.

"I only met her once," Maggie began. "I gather Fannie, his wife, is quite a bit younger than Harris. The only thing I've ever heard him say was that she wasn't ready to settle down. Of course, I doubt Harris would ever say a mean word about anyone—even a woman who up and left him and their child soon after she was born."

"How awful for them both. Poor Marion…"

"Boggles my mind. There's more to it, I'm sure, but the details are hazy. Anyway, Harris was left to raise his child single-handedly. And I think he's done a pretty fine job of it, considering. The center was just starting out when Marion was born. Fannie used to help him care for the birds, so you could say she walked out on the center, too. Harris had a brand-new baby and a brand-new birds of prey center commencing all at the same time. It was pretty overwhelming. He had to work round the clock," she said with a sigh.

"Still does. He's the heart and soul of the place. This whole thing was his vision. He saw the need, fought for a license and built this place from nothing. We have the clinic building now, the bird pens, and we're still growing. But back in the early days, Harris had the birds in his spare bedroom and a dog run out in the back!"

"Now I understand the mice in the kitchen fridge. And I found feathers in the closet corners when I cleaned them out."

"Lord, I'm not surprised. He used to have more rats and mice in his fridge than food for him and Marion. Used to do surgery in the kitchen, too. Right smack on the table."

"Really?" Ella said, making a mental note to scrub the table with bleach.

"We were all pleased as punch when the clinic building was donated to the center. Harris and Marion could finally have a life of their own, separate from the birds. He built the pens you see out there, the resident birdhouse and the weighing room. His next big dream is to construct a real flight pen. He has so many dreams. You've never met anyone so dedicated."

"A man can be too dedicated," Ella said softly. Catching the sharp look of criticism in Maggie's eyes, she hastened to explain. "Marion needs her father, too. She's only five years old and she adores him. We're making progress, but she's made it quite clear that I'm *not* her mother. It's like she's afraid I'm trying to encroach on that sacred bond. And I can tell she resents that I'm doing everything for her around the house, things her father used to do. I'm sure she views it as my butting in there, too. So, while I realize he's needed at the clinic, he's needed at home, too."

Maggie put up her hands. "I'm staying out of that one. I recommend you do, too. Do your best, but don't try to change things with him. You think you're stubborn? Just wait. He's the king of stubborn." Her lips held back a smile. "Though he likes to call it focused."

They both burst out laughing.

"Well, we'll just see," Ella said.

"Mmm-hmm," Maggie said, shaking her head. "I swanny, I don't know about you two. I've never seen two goats more likely to bop heads."

Maggie stood up, then smoothed the wrinkles from the comforter in long strokes. When she straightened again, she loomed tall over Ella, her face thoughtful.

"Seriously, Ella, be patient with him. Visionaries are a unique brand of people. They inspire us. They challenge us to live up to the possibilities. But sometimes, they don't see the forest for the trees. They work with a single-minded focus, forgetting mundane things like eating, putting on socks and kicking back to relax once in a while. They feel responsible and they give *everything.* You see, Harris doesn't mean *not* to be there for Marion. In his mind, I'm sure he thinks he's doing everything he can. I know he's riddled with guilt that she got so sick. I mean, here he takes care of all these birds, notices whenever the slightest thing isn't right, but he missed these big problems in his own child. You've got to know that digs deep. He may not tell you this, but he's so relieved that you're here. *I'm* glad you're here, too. I've worried about him and Marion both and do my best to keep an eye on them. Sherry does, too. But she's getting old and I've got my own husband and children to hustle home to at the end of the day."

Ella was slow to respond, not sure what to say. "I'll do the best I can."

Maggie smiled reassuringly. "I know you will." Then she turned serious again. "I guess what I'm trying in my own clumsy way to say is…Harris is a good man, Ella. He's spent his whole life taking care of others. First his mama. Then his wife. And now Marion. He doesn't know how to let someone take care of him for a change. He doesn't know how to slow down and enjoy life. He's never had the chance."

As though uncomfortable with the heightened emotion, Maggie waved her hand and said in a rush, "Oh, listen to me. I was his first recruit here and we've worked together from the start. I guess I've grown a little territorial about him."

"And you want me to go easy on him?"

"Yeah, something like that. And I don't want to see him get hurt."

"Hurt? By me? How could I ever do that?"

"Like I said, I'm just a worrier."

"You must really care about him to say all this to me."

"I do. We all do. And we care about little Marion, too. We've all taken turns baby-sitting for her ever since she was a baby. She runs around the place, getting underfoot, even though she's not supposed to be near the birds." She shrugged. "We've made do as best we could. But that's what life is all about, isn't it?"

Ella took a deep breath and nodded. She certainly knew better than most how to make do.

She was glad for this conversation with Maggie and for the insights gleaned. She learned that she was clearly the outsider, the new kid on this block of spirited, complex characters. She only hoped she'd fit in.

"It's late," she said, rising to a stand. "Time to fix dinner." She crossed her arms and surveyed their work. Even sparsely furnished, the cabin was filled. The bed was piled high with blankets and the bright colors of the hooked rug warmed the room as much as the heater. "It's not the Ritz, but I think Lijah will be comfortable here."

"I hope you'll be comfortable here, too," Maggie said. Then, impulsively, she stepped forward to wrap her arms around Ella in a bear hug.

"Welcome."

The cold snap in the Lowcountry finally ended. February winds blew the gray clouds out to sea and ushered in skies of blinding azure clarity. Brady wiped his brow, then hoisted the large kennel and stacked it on the row with all the others—nineteen in all. The past two Wednesdays after school and two whole Saturdays he'd scrubbed off bird shit so baked on it was like chiseling rock. It didn't matter what they called it—mutes, dung or guano—shit was shit, as far as he was concerned. He'd bent over these damn kennels and scrubbed till he'd worn through two wire brushes and chapped his hands raw.

But he was done now, and looking at all the kennels stacked up neatly against the wall, he couldn't deny a kind of satisfaction that surprised him. More fouled-out kennels would be coming soon enough, if the number of injured birds he'd seen brought in were any indication. Mostly owls, though he didn't know why. It was kind of sad, seeing them all banged up. Sometimes one of their eyes was badly smashed. And the folks that brought them in were real worried about them. That surprised him, too. He'd grown up thinking wildlife was just out there for the taking. He'd never wondered about how the animals or birds were faring or what to do if he saw one hurt. Nature took care of itself, didn't it?

Brady was getting used to the place. It was weird at first, being around all these wild birds. They glared at him when he went by their cages, almost as much as the people did.

Sure, he knew the staff would be mad at him when he first came here. Everyone knew *why* he was here, after all. But he didn't know it would rankle, even after a few weeks. Harris was the boss around here and everyone took his or her cue from him. Harris never said anything mean to him, but he wasn't cutting him any breaks, neither. Maggie only came by to stick her nose in and check up on what he was doing, more to let him know she was keeping an eye on him. Other volunteers came and went; there were different ones every day. Most of them were decent. At least they said hello. But some of them only gave him a glare, just like the birds. Not that Brady cared. *As if.*

The only one who treated him decent was the old man. He couldn't figure that one out, considering it was his eagle that got shot. When Brady had first heard that Lijah would be in charge of him, he figured the old man would make his life at the center a living hell. Not that scrubbing kennels was fun…but Lijah treated Brady with the same respect he treated everyone else.

"The kennels finished?"

Brady spun around, heart pounding. Swear to God, he could never hear that man approach. Did he walk on air or something? Lijah was carrying two cans of Coke and, coming near, handed one of them to Brady.

"Figured you'd worked up a thirst, eh?"

"Thanks." He gulped down some soda, wiping his mouth with his sleeve. "Didn't know I could work up such a sweat when it's cold outdoors. Some of those kennels were a bitch to clean."

"You done a fine job," Lijah said, approval ringing in his voice. "Ain't complain none, neither." They both stood and drank their Cokes in silence, looking out at the kennels as though they were the most interesting things in the world. When they finished their drinks, Lijah took the cans, rinsed them, and put them in the recycle bin while Brady put away the cleaning supplies and wound up the hose.

When his chores were done, Brady stood with his hands in his pockets, rocking on his heels and wondering what to do next. Lijah stood a few feet away, one foot in front of the other. He had this serene look on his face while he stared out over the compound with his hands held behind his back. Brady didn't interrupt him. His daddy had taught him never to interrupt an elder but to wait until he was spoken to.

After a short spell, Lijah faced him and said in an easy drawl, "It's time you see what all this work here is for."

Brady hustled to follow Lijah's long stride across the yard toward the medical pens. He felt excited, especially since he'd expected to be handed a shovel and pickax and told to start digging the ditch along the road. That's what Harris had said, anyway. Brady was real curious about the raptors, but he'd never told anyone this. He was careful to keep his face passive as he followed Lijah. He'd learned it didn't pay to let anyone know how he really felt.

The med pens were housed in one long unit separated from the clinic by a grouping of overgrown shrubs and shaded by leggy pines and an old live oak tree. Lijah undid the latches and swung open the wood-and-screen door. Stepping inside, Brady saw that there were nine pens in all, four on each side of a cement walkway and one far in the back. They were made of wood with inch-wide spaces between that allowed him to peek inside. Overhead, a green plastic dome and screening gave the area the feeling of a conservatory.

A teenage black girl was in there, carrying a pale green plastic tray loaded down with fat white rats and black mice, some of them gutted, and a few large fish. She carried these to the birds with grace, as though she were serving royalty.

Brady was struck by how beautiful she was. She was slender and nearly as tall as he was. Beneath her fleece jacket she wore the same white T-shirt with the Coastal Carolina Center for Birds of Prey logo on it that all the volunteers wore. Everyone except for him, of course.

"Morning, Clarice," Lijah said, holding up his hand in greeting.

"Morning, Lijah," she replied with a dazzling smile. Then she glanced toward Brady and her smile fell to a scowl. "What's *he* doing in here?" she asked. "Harris said he didn't want him near the birds."

"He's with me," Lijah replied evenly. "Go on about your business."

Clarice's finely arched brows furrowed with displeasure, but she did as she was told. Brady watched with rapt attention as she opened up a pen and quickly slipped inside. He heard a rustling of feathers against wood and her voice, soft and low, crooning, "It's okay. I'm just leaving you some breakfast."

Lijah cleared his throat and Brady swung his head toward him.

"Close each door soon as you pass through," Lijah told

him. He refastened the main door behind them. "Every pen really have to be closed fast fast. Watch how she bolts each door two times."

Brady watched Clarice close one pen, then move with her tray delicately balanced on a slim hip into the second one. Each time, she carefully unlatched and latched the door.

"Don't ever forget these the wild birds and they want to git out at ya! Sometimes they do, even when you're careful. Last week one of them screech owls sneak out quick. They're little and fast and can go right through a small opening. Took us forever to catch him. If we keep this outer door shut, they can't get out into the wild. If they do, they're gone for good. They ain't heal yet and most likely won't survive out yonder. You have to be real careful or one'll escape."

"I won't be allowed to work in here with the birds, anyway."

"Keep what I say in mind. You never know."

Brady moved over to the first pen and peeked inside. Two black vultures sat high on the upper perch. They were ugly cusses. With their bald heads, wrinkled skin and long black feathers held close, they looked like craggy old men in overcoats, hunched together on a park bench. When he drew nearer, they fluffed up a bit and hissed at him, sounding like acetylene torches at full blast. Then one of them threw up a vile-smelling substance.

"Whoa, take it easy, man," he said, stepping back.

"You shouldn't go so close," Clarice scolded. "That's their defense."

Brady ducked his head.

"Move slow slow," Lijah instructed him with his gentle tone. "Keep down the talk. They ain't like people around so close. It ain't natural."

Lijah walked to Pen 3, stopped and bent closer to look

inside. From the corner of his eye, Brady watched him and thought the old man's face fairly glowed with affection.

"That her?"

"That's her."

Brady was curious but held back, filled with dread.

"Hey, Santee," Lijah said in a low, soft voice. "How's my best gal? You better today? You sure look fine. Someone's here to meet you."

He looked over to Brady and gave a quick, encouraging wave of his hand. Brady stuck his hands in his pockets and drew near, peeking between the wooden slats.

Inside, a bald eagle stood on a perch close to the ground. She was a big bird, with shiny black feathers and a white crested head. Her low brow hung over her yellow beak, making her bright yellow eyes appear more ferocious.

"I don't think she likes me."

Clarice heard this and snorted.

"Probably not," Lijah replied, ignoring her. "Truth be told, she ain't like most of us. That's okay, though. Ain't supposed to like people."

"Well, she gives a whole new meaning to the word *glare*."

Lijah chuckled softly, still looking at the eagle like a father would his favorite child. He turned toward the sound of Clarice coming out of the last pen. "Yes, she sure can give a man a time."

"They're all fed," Clarice said to Lijah. "I'll be back later to check for leftovers. So how are you doing? I heard you're staying in the cabin by the pond now."

"Yes," Lijah replied.

"Do you like it?"

"I do. It's warm and clean. And most of all, it's close to Santee. I can't complain."

"Well, we miss you. Everyone does. Mama about had a hissy fit when she heard you were camping out in the woods this time of year. And at your age!"

"Your mama can fuss."

"She wants to know if you can come round for service tomorrow and then have dinner with us after. I'm to pick you up."

"That's fine. Tell your mama I'd like that. Do I need to bring something?"

"Just your stories." When he was about to object, she said in a rush, "Really, Lijah, it's our pleasure. I'll be by around ten, if that suits you?"

"Suits me fine."

Clarice bent to pick up her chart and tools, then headed for the door. "Bye now. See you Sunday." She gave Brady a cool once-over before offering Lijah a farewell smile filled with warmth and affection.

Brady turned his head and pretended not to notice. He looked into the pen and carefully checked out the eagle's bandaged wing. It was spotted with bright red blood.

"How's she doing?"

"Fair to middling. Her wing's healing pretty well, but she ain't eating like she supposed to."

Brady saw the large fish that Clarice had left lying on the stone at her feet, untouched. Santee didn't seem the least interested in it.

"Why not?"

Lijah shrugged. "I ain't know. It's a worry."

"Well, she looks pretty good. I mean, I wouldn't go in there and mess with her, that's for sure. Look at the size of those talons. She looks ready to rip me apart."

"Eagles are that way," Lijah replied, eyes on the bird. "Most birds of prey be that way. They can't let it show if they're feeling poorly or if they're injured. They cover up their hurts, so other birds or animals don't think they're weak. Otherwise, *they* become the prey."

"I hear that," Brady said. It wasn't so different from surviving at school, and sometimes, even in his own home. "I hope she'll be okay," he mumbled.

"Oh, I expect she'll be fine. Her attitude is all right. She got her nest to get back to."

"I heard that the eggs never hatched."

"No."

"How many were there?"

"Two, most likely. Maybe three."

"Will she lay more?"

"Not this year."

Brady felt the weight of his guilt triple. "I…I never meant to hurt her."

"I know you didn't, son."

Brady looked up sharply. Something in the way he said that, and the knowledge gleaming in the old man's eyes, sent Brady's heart pounding. No one was out in the field that morning. There was only him and his daddy.

"I heard you were the one that found the eagle lying on the ground," he said.

"That's right. I been behind her, going to her nest."

"Following her? You mean, you saw her get shot?"

"Saw it and heard it."

Brady's face suffused with color and he stammered, "Y-you saw who shot the bird?"

A long silence preceded his answer. "I seen a tall, broad man carrying a shotgun. And a boy carrying a rifle."

Brady's eyes widened.

"And I know it was buckshot they took out of my bird."

Brady ran a hand through his hair, mumbling a profanity. "You ain't gonna tell nobody this, are you?"

"If I was, I'd already done so."

"I don't get it."

"I expect this here's something you and your daddy have to work out."

Brady exhaled, relieved but still confused. He kicked the gravel, sending a few stones flying.

"I'm curious," Lijah said. "You might let Harris know. He'd ease up on you some."

"No!" Brady blurted. "I don't want him to know. Nobody's to know. You got to promise you won't tell no one."

Lijah rubbed his jaw awhile in thought. "Seems to me you're carrying a heavy load for a boy so young."

"That's the point, isn't it? My being young? If I took the heat, then the penalty would be lower, me being a minor and all. My daddy couldn't afford a higher fine. It was hard enough for the family to come up with the eighteen hundred. And he sure couldn't do the jail time. What would my mother do? There's five kids at home! Besides, I'm the eldest. I'm supposed to watch out for them."

Lijah's eyes gleamed in understanding. "There's a saying. A man's done the crime, he does the time."

Brady looked sharply up at Lijah and his eyes appeared haunted. "Don't matter," he said, his voice rough with emotion. "I'm just as guilty whether there was buckshot or a plug from a .22 pulled out of that eagle. I pulled the trigger. And I have to live with that."

He stepped back, putting his hands in his pockets and hunching his shoulders. There was a long silence that followed while Brady stared at the ground and Lijah turned to watch Santee.

At last he faced the boy and said, "You have to decide."

Brady exhaled a huge sigh of relief and nodded gratefully. He ran his hand through his hair again in a self-conscious manner and shifted his weight from foot to foot.

"I don't know that cleaning up a bunch of kennels or digging a ditch is going to help your Santee heal," he said. "I mean, I know it's not much. It's nothing compared to what Harris does."

Lijah turned to fix his gaze squarely on him. Brady could feel the force of it clear to his marrow.

"I respect that you come to work on time," Lijah replied. "I respect that you work without a mumble or whine. You do a good job, too. Ain't cut no corners. And I respect that you never talk back when certain folks treat you less than kind."

Brady raised his head and felt his chest expand. He'd been unaware that the old man had noticed any of this.

"I'm going to tell you a story." Lijah pointed one of his long, gnarled fingers toward the Med 1 pen. "Look over yonder at Buh Buzzard," he said, pointing to a black vulture. "He likes nothing more than to spread his silver-tipped wings up high in the elements. If you set back and watch him up yonder, it looks like he just floating along real lazy-like on the wind without a worry in this world. But truth be told, Buh Buzzard do work! His job is to clean up the fields. Buh Buzzard likes dead lamb, dead cow, dead horse, snake, alligator—all kind of critters, long as they dead. He do a fine job keeping the roads clean of roadkill, too.

"Now look at my Santee. Buh Eagle is a powerful bird. She don't just fly. No, sir. She *soars*. Way up with the high wind, her black wings stretched wide. You never see Buh Eagle wobble in the wind like Buh Buzzard do. Eagles fly straight like an arrow and go way up to the clouds. Looking upon Buh Eagle while she soars sets the soul to singing and makes people want somehow to act right. More strong and true. Guess that's why so many people want Buh Eagle as a symbol, like we do for this here country."

Lijah shook his head and put his hand on Brady's shoulder.

"Folks tend to think Buh Buzzard is a lazy scavenger, good for nothing but trash. They like to point to Buh Eagle as noble and better than other birds. Think a minute about how the world would be without Buh Buzzard. Likewise, Buh Eagle. They both do their own work. They both know their worth. And that's why they both can stretch their wings, catch the wind and rise high up yonder in the elements, flying and giving praise."

Brady turned to look at the vultures in Med 1 and the eagle in Med 3. Both were big black birds and he knew that both of them would confront him if he got too close. But he felt he understood them a little better.

"I guess I'd still rather be like an eagle than a buzzard," he said.

Lijah laughed then, spreading his lips and showing white teeth. "We all would, son. We all would."

Harriers: The Versatile Hunters. The northern harrier is the only member of this family in North America. This talented hunter is a medium-size bird with narrow wings that is often found cruising low and doggedly over open areas. When flying high, however, the harrier is often mistaken for a peregrine falcon or Cooper's hawk. Often called a marsh hawk, it is distinguished by a white rump patch.

8

IT WAS VALENTINE'S DAY. OSPREYS WERE RETURNING to the Lowcountry and red-shouldered hawks were courting. Harris could hear their high-pitched "kee-yer" in the sky. There would be a frenzy of nest building soon, he thought as he walked across the compound.

He saw his house framed by the majestic longleaf pines in the distance. Yellow light flowed from the paned windows and a ribbon of gray smoke curled from the chimney to dissipate into the winter sky. It was a handsome house, he thought with pride. Solid, well situated. A good nest.

He stopped to pick a sprig of pine to add to the two bouquets of flowers he carried in his hands. His step quickened. He was eager to be home.

Harris set the flowers on the chair outside the door, then stepped inside. The warm air was redolent with the scent of basil, oregano and bread baking in the oven. He sighed with satisfaction as he stood at the threshold and simply took the sight in. He could hardly believe it was his own home. Yes, there was the same couch, chairs and tables. The same pictures hung on the walls. Yet everything was different. What was it about stepping into one's home when everything was clean and tidy, when dinner was cooking and the table was set that made a man feel all was right with the world?

It had been a long while since he'd felt the tension in his chest ease when he came home. For so many years, going from the clinic to the house was merely a transition from one place of work to another. Now, for the first time, he understood what it meant when men he'd known talked about the sense of peace they had when they returned home at night and closed the door to the world behind them.

This was all Ella's doing, he knew. This prim, tidy woman had stepped into the chaos of their world and brought order. Closing the door, he followed the sound of voices in the kitchen. The small dining table was decorated with a red tablecloth, and paper cutout hearts were sprinkled over it.

"Daddy's home!"

Marion bolted from the kitchen into his arms. He bent to hug her tight against his legs and kiss the top of her head. He heard Ella's footfall and raised his eyes, smiling at her. She was wearing jeans and a bright red sweater. To her shoulder she'd pinned a paper heart trimmed with a doily on which her name was written in large, clumsy letters, obviously by Marion.

She returned the smile shyly, then brushed past them with a hot serving dish in her hands. "Your timing is perfect. The pizza just came from the oven."

"Look, Daddy. Ella made a heart pizza."

"It's beautiful," he said, looking at the homemade pizza

made into the shape of a heart, bubbling hot and covered with sausage and peppers. His eyes gleamed with admiration. He knew that she'd done this to make something for Marion that didn't involve candy, cookies, cakes and other sweets so popular for the holiday. "Very clever. Smells good, too." He looked at the pizza with puzzlement. "But why did she make a heart-shaped pizza? Is there something special about today?"

Marion's face fell. "It's Valentine's Day. Did you forget?"

"Valentine's Day? Today?" He scratched behind his ear. "Is that the day we get presents under the tree?"

Marion laughed and leaned against his legs. "That's Christmas, Daddy."

"Oh, yes. That's right. Then is this the holiday when that bunny comes and brings us baskets?"

"That's Easter," Marion said, with a pretend scold. "You know that."

"Then what's today?"

"This is the day we give something to the one we love."

"Well, I love you," he said, cupping her cheek in his palm. It amazed him that her little face could still be framed by his hand. "So I guess I'd better have something for you, right?"

She nodded, her eyes hopeful.

Harris turned to wink at Ella, who stood close by, eyes dancing, enjoying the exchange. Then he went to the front porch to retrieve his gifts. The sky had turned dark and somehow the scent of the pizza was more sharp and tantalizing in the cold outdoor air than in the house. Coming back inside, his heart expanded to see his daughter's face so animated.

"Will these do?"

"Flowers!" she exclaimed. "For me?"

"You did say I should give them to the one I love, didn't you?"

He handed a bouquet of pink daisies to Marion, who held them to her chest as though he'd given her the world. Seeing her face was as gratifying as it was humbling. Ella stood by, beaming with pleasure, her hands clasped to the kitchen towel in her hands. He stepped forward and held out a dozen red roses to her. He felt the awkwardness of the moment and said in a rush, "These are for you."

"For me?" Ella's eyes rounded as she lifted the slightly faded bouquet from his hands. She lowered her face to the red petals and her cheeks flushed with color as she inhaled deeply. In that moment he thought she looked quite feminine, even pretty—and out of character for the former head nurse who had taken this little house and marshaled it into order. It pleased him to see the transformation.

What a stroke of luck it had been when, earlier today, he'd overheard Maggie and Sherry talking, all amazement, about the fresh flowers they'd seen for sale at Snell's Market down the road. Snell's was a tiny corner market along the highway that carried a scarcity of sundries, a bottle of this and a package of that, candy, a large jar of pickled pigs' feet, tobacco, Coke and horrid sandwiches on white bread wrapped in plastic and kept in an ancient fridge. So to see fresh flowers there sent everyone agog.

Reminded that it was Valentine's Day, however, he'd hurried to his car and drove down in time to buy one of each of the two types of bouquets, the last in the bucket of water by the door. They weren't the most glorious selections, but looking at Marion's and Ella's faces, that didn't seem to matter. Their obvious pleasure at receiving the rather sorry-looking flowers from a market bucket was a lesson for him in how small acts of kindness could have meaningful consequences.

Ella fingered the bright green conifer branch with puzzlement. "This is an unusual bit of greens for a bouquet."

"That was my contribution," he replied. "It's kind of symbolic. During incubation, the eagle brings sprigs of conifer to the nest. I'm not sure why. Maybe for shade for the eaglets, or maybe for deodorizing. Or maybe just to say thank-you to the nesting female."

"What a lovely thought."

"Daddy must love you, too, Ella," Marion said innocently.

Ella's face colored almost as red as the roses as she plucked at a petal.

Harris gulped in dread. He'd meant the roses as a gesture of friendship and gratitude. He hadn't wanted Ella to feel left out. Seeing the blush deepen on Ella's cheeks, however, he realized the roses implied a romantic feeling that he'd never intended.

"I, uh, wanted to say thank you for all you've done. To let you know I've noticed. I—I thought you'd like them," he stammered. "For your table."

"Oh, yes. Of course," she replied, a tad too quickly. "For the table. They're perfect." She turned and headed toward the kitchen. "I'll just put them in water."

Ella couldn't escape Harris's sight any quicker. Her blush had betrayed her, and she knew by looking at the utter dread on his face that he was horrified she might interpret his gift in the wrong way.

And she had. What a silly fool she was to think, even for a moment, that his intentions were romantic! She was so embarrassed, yet, she couldn't help her imagination. She'd never received flowers from a man before. So today, on Valentine's Day, to receive red roses was the ultimate romantic gesture.

And the gesture meant more to her than he could possibly have imagined. Women—lonely women in particular—dreamed of such moments. The way her heart had soared when he'd given them to her, the way he'd smiled in that reluctant way of his...

"Stop!" she scolded herself, feeling her heart rush once again. She was behaving like a silly girl with a crush. It was humiliating. She was angry with herself for allowing such childish notions to creep into her heart and then cloud her mind. What was she thinking? She was here to care for the child, not the man. If she allowed this nonsensical thinking to continue, she'd jeopardize the positive relationship she was building with both Marion and Harris.

She filled the vase with water, added preserver, then snipped off the ends of the roses. As she placed each one into the vase it felt like a thorn prick in her heart. With each rose she told herself that Harris was only being kind, that he was bringing roses for her table, not for *her*.

"Hurry up, Ella!" Marion called from the table. "The pizza's getting cold."

"Coming!" She took a deep breath, fixed a smile on her face, then carried the flowers to the table. "Don't these roses make my table look pretty? Harris, why don't you start slicing the pizza while I put these daisies in water, too? I'll only be a minute."

He hesitated. "I hate to cut it. It looks so nice."

"It'll taste nice, too," she replied. "Maggie helped me with the dough and I used a jar sauce that's delicious. I think you're safe."

He smiled then, too, and she wasn't blind to the relief on his face that the tense moment had passed and all was well. Carrying the daisies to the kitchen sink, Ella told herself she would guard against such a show of emotion in the future.

They sat together at the table and Harris held out his hand
to her for grace, as was the custom for Marion and Harris
before the evening meal. Ella took a breath and reached out
to take hold—Harris with her left hand, Marion with her
right. Ella found the physical contact of this ritual both comforting and disturbing for so many reasons. Holding Harris's
hand—the simple, physical act of touching him—was so rare
and so personal that she felt it intensely. It was hard to con-
centrate on the words of prayer. Ella had grown up serving
dinner to guests at her aunts' Victorian Inn. So the act of
sitting down for an evening meal, much less the formality of
praying beforehand, was foreign. The whole scene was too
close to the dream of a family she'd harbored all her life, like
the one in the Norman Rockwell print that her aunts hung
up in the dining room at the inn every Thanksgiving. A father, mother, children, grandparents all gathered around the
table for a family dinner.

A family like this one.

She held tight to their hands, whispering a prayer of her
own.

"Do you want to say grace tonight?" Harris asked Ella.

"It's *my* turn, Daddy."

Ella tried to stop her smile. "Marion's learning about taking turns."

"Ah, I see. Well, then. Marion, would you lead the
prayer?"

Marion began dutifully. "Thank you, Lord, for the pizza.
Thank you for my flowers. And thank you for Ella's flowers,
too. Right, Ella?"

Ella felt a faint blush renew as she nodded and said a firm
"Amen."

"What did you do today?" Harris asked when they drew
their hands back to their laps.

He began each mealtime with the same question. She appreciated his effort at sparking conversation for her sake.

"Well, we spent most of the day cutting out paper hearts," she replied.

"I practiced my letters," Marion declared.

Ella pointed to the large paper heart with crooked lettering on her chest, eyes dancing.

"Very impressive."

"And I called my aunts," Ella added. "To wish them love. They were so excited to get the call. I forget they're getting older and worry about me."

"How old are they?" Marion wanted to know.

"Ancient. But they'll never tell and they hold on to the family documents with tight grips. They're the matriarchs of the Majors family. They call themselves The Maidens."

"Why?" asked Marion.

"Don't talk with your mouth full, honey. Because they've never married," she replied, thinking to herself that maidenhood seemed to be a genetic trait in the Majors family.

"Never?"

"Never. They've been asked. Rumor has it that Aunt Rhoda was left standing at the altar. It caused a great scandal. I'm not sure what the story with Aunt Eudora was. She'll never tell. It's all very hush-hush. They've lived in that house all their lives, were born in it. They took care of my grandfather, their daddy, after Grandma died. Then, after he died a few years later, they turned the big old house into an inn. It made sense. They'd spent their life caring for others. Dear Aunt Rhoda and Aunt Eudora... They're all arsenic and old lace. Their warmth and vitality is infectious and they bring such joy and laughter to the Victorian Inn and all the guests lucky enough to pass through it."

She chuckled with affection, thinking of her aunts' flamboyant natures, even though she'd often found them a bit ostentatious and downright silly while growing up. She was as grounded as her aunts were flighty. They lived for the moment, and if they had a fault, it was extravagance. They loved beauty in all its forms. Ella had always secretly felt that in this regard, she was a disappointment to them. When she'd first arrived at their home she wasn't much older than Marion was now. She'd overheard her aunt Eudora say, "Ella looks a little like a mouse, don't you think? It's a pity the dear girl inherited the worst features of both her parents."

Ella had cried herself to sleep that night, not because she'd thought the statement cruel, rather because she thought it true. She had her father's large brown eyes, but they were set too far apart and framed by her mother's lashes, so short and pale they appeared not to be there at all. Her nose was straight but sharp. Her mouth was wide, like her mother's, but the lips were thin like her father's. And though her hair wasn't blond like her mother's or auburn like her father's, but a brown referred to as mousy, it nonetheless was her one vanity. It was thick and shiny and grew almost to her waist like a glorious sheath of shimmering silk, a throwback from some ancestor that neither of the aunts could name.

But she did inherit her father's sharp intelligence and her mother's New England common sense, and for these gifts she was both proud and grateful.

"What about your mama and daddy?" asked Marion. "Are they old?"

"Oh, no. They died when I was young."

Marion looked stricken.

"It's all right," she hastened to assure the little girl. She knew the child was thinking of her own mother. "That was a long time ago and I'm reconciled."

"What happened to them?"

Although Marion was asking all the questions, Ella could see from Harris's expression that he was as keenly curious.

She placed her pizza on the plate and wiped her fingers. "My father was a family doctor. My mother was his nurse. Every day they traveled over Wallingford Mountain to Rutland and back where they had a clinic. Sometimes they'd hurry to the hospital at night if there was an emergency. Between their working hours, emergency and travel, they were gone a lot.

"One day they were coming around a sharp curve on the mountain road just as a hay wagon was coming around from the other side. It was dark and rainy. The roads were wooded. Neither one saw the other." She shrugged. "I was five when I went to live with my aunts. They're dear souls and I love them very much. Though they have never ventured outside the Northeast, they always encouraged me to dream big and travel the world."

"And you did!" Marion exclaimed. "You came here."

Ella picked up her pizza. "Yep. I came all the way to Awendaw," she said, her eyes sparkling in a tease.

"Lucky for us," said Harris.

Ella swallowed hard and looked at her plate.

"And how was *your* day?" she asked Harris, steering the conversation in another direction. "What were you up to while we were cutting out paper hearts?"

He frowned with worry. "Actually, I was hoping to discuss this with you later."

She looked up with concern.

"We've got a problem at the clinic. Sherry's mother had a stroke. She'll have to go there to check on her."

"Oh, that's a terrible shame. She must be so worried."

"She is. She's the only daughter. She's going up to Orangeburg tomorrow. She needs to be there to help make the decisions. Her brother doesn't know what to do and Sherry will understand all the medical terms." He sighed and looked at his hands. "She has to go, of course, but that leaves us short-staffed, right as we head into spring, the busiest time of the year."

"How long will she be gone?"

"She doesn't know. It's too soon to tell. Like I said, it's a problem."

"Don't you have other volunteers to fill in the gap?"

"Not with the medical experience needed. It's hard to find someone who can read X rays, give shots, draw blood, plus have the knowledge to treat trauma injuries. Even if I were to train a volunteer, it would take a long time. Time that I just don't have to give right now." He shook his head, looking at his hands. "No. For this job you just have to know the biology." Looking up again, his face was pensive. "The job's not much different from what you did in the emergency room at the hospital."

Ella could see where this was headed. She kept quiet, but inwardly steeled herself.

"I was wondering...I was *hoping* that you could lend a hand in the clinic? Just for a short while. Until I can find someone else."

"Harris, I don't know anything about birds."

"I know, but you're a nurse. You know the basics. I can give you a crash course on the rest."

Ella shook her head firmly. "I came here for Marion. I have no wish to play nurse to raptors."

"It won't be for long."

"No." When he opened his mouth to speak again, she rushed on, firmness in her voice. "Really, Harris, it's just not my thing. There are *animal* people and there are *people* people. I'm a people person. I always have been. No dogs, cats or birds for me."

Disappointment flooded his features, but he tightened his lips against further argument. He put his napkin on the table and pushed his plate away. "As I said, it was just a hope. Sherry will have to leave soon. I'll be taking on her load so that'll mean I'll be coming home later. I'll likely miss eating dinners with you, and I'll have to go back out at night."

"Can't you take a break to eat with Marion? I mean, you have to eat. I'll have dinner ready on the table."

"It doesn't work like that. A lot of birds will be coming through in the next few months. When they come in, I have to treat them. There's no one else. You've worked in an E.R. You can't just leave someone injured to go get a bite to eat. You eat when you can."

Ella knew this was true and said nothing.

"Speaking of which, I have some birds to check on now. Sherry had to leave early today, what with the news and all." The chair scraped the floor as he drew himself up and left the table.

Ella rose, too, and was clearing plates when the door closed. She paused to look across the room. The red drapes were drawn against the cold, the fire was crackling and soft yellow light flowed from a corner floor lamp. A homey scene that felt suddenly empty.

Marion slipped from her chair and went directly to the television.

"Marion? Where are you off to? There are dishes to do."

"Aw, do I have to?" Marion groaned and hung her shoulders, but she obediently went to the table and helped clear the silverware.

Ella hid her smile at the theatrics, pleased that Marion was slowly getting into a fixed routine. She wanted the child to appreciate she had a role in making the household hum. It had been difficult at first to get her to agree to anything. She'd had a lifetime of having everything done for her by Harris and a string of baby-sitters. To do more required an investment in time by the caretaker. Never one to cut corners, Ella had begun teaching Marion rudimentary chores. Now Marion made her bed in the morning—even if it was only smoothing out the blankets. She cleared the table after meals—if only the silverware. And she picked up her toys and clothes—some of the time. The biggest chore of all, of course, was cooperating with the system of checks and balances for the diabetes.

And Marion was flourishing with the routine. They'd come a long way to getting her blood sugar levels even. She rose early in the morning without grumbling and looked forward to her bath and bedtime story at night. Her attitude was pinking up just like her cheeks.

Marion came in to dump fistfuls of forks and spoons into the sink. They splashed noisily into the water.

"All done."

"Okay, then scoot!"

Ella leaned far back to watch Marion dash from the kitchen into the living room. Passing the sofa she grabbed hold of Gaudy Lulu, then surprised Ella by not going to the television after all. Instead, she went to the window, pushed back the curtains and stood on tiptoe to peer out for her father.

Ella's heart pinged and her brow furrowed as she returned to the dishes. No matter how good the routine and how well she and Marion were getting along, the child still pined for time with her father.

Ella began washing the plates, her thoughts spinning. She'd always found the ritualistic washing and rinsing good for reflection. Her mind traveled again to Harris's request that she help out in the clinic. She wished he hadn't asked. It put her in the annoying position of having to refuse. Yes, she had the medical skills, but she really didn't want to use them on birds. Especially not birds with talons, sharp beaks and an attitude. She had every right to say no, yet she still felt guilty doing so.

Her mind was at war with her heart. When did one put one's own interests ahead of another's? Already Harris hardly spent time with Marion. If he was forced to put in more hours at the clinic, the poor child would never see him. It was a heartbreaker to see the way Marion's eyes filled with longing whenever her daddy came into view.

Ella's hands stilled in the sink. She thought back to the time when she was a little girl waiting by the window for her own father and mother. That terrible waiting… She'd missed them even before they died.

Ella looked over again at Marion. The child held Gaudy Lulu close to her chest and leaned in a dejected pose against the window. Ella turned off the water and left the last pot in the sink. Drying her hands, she walked directly to Marion. She crouched low and gently drew the child away from the window and into her arms.

"Hey, little one," she said close to her ear. "How about a nice, warm bath? I'll even put in bubbles!"

An hour later, Ella tucked Marion into bed and sat beside her to read a bedtime story. This was the favorite time of the day for both of them, when their chores were done, the blood tests and shots were out of the way and they could just stretch out together and enjoy a moment's peace. Marion rested her head against Ella's chest as she read. Ella had never known how poignant such a simple gesture could be.

"Mmm…you smell sweet," Ella told her, bringing her nose to the gold downy hair.

Marion nodded her head, accepting the compliment as fact. Then she turned her head and leaned back against her shoulder to get a good look at Ella. She studied her face for a while and Ella felt she was somehow being measured, though against what standard she couldn't imagine. She already knew that Marion did not find her pretty.

"You smell good, too," Marion announced with authority.

A smile tugged at Ella's lips, but Marion was so serious that she put on a serious face and replied soberly, "Thank you."

Tonight they chose Marion's favorite, *Goodnight Moon*. Marion loved the simple but lyrical sentences that never failed to lower the lids and elicit sleepy yawns.

"That's me," Marion said when they'd reached the last page. She pointed to the picture of a small bunny tucked into a great big bed. Marion often liked to pick out a character in a story to be.

"Yes, that's you if you want it to be."

"Is that the mother?" Her small finger pointed to the female bunny in the rocking chair across the great green room.

"No," Ella replied. "That's the old lady who takes care of the little bunny. The one who whispers hush."

"Oh. Then, is that you?"

"Yes," Ella replied with a self-deprecating chuckle. "That's me."

Marion was silent for a moment, then she twirled a strand of hair and said softly, "She *could* be the mother. If I wanted her to be."

"Do you want the lady in the book to be the bunny's mother?"

Marion didn't say anything as she looked at the picture book spread open on her lap.

"Do you miss your mother?"

Marion nodded. Ella could feel the motion against her breast go straight through to her heart.

"Do you ever get to see her?"

"No. I want to, but Daddy says she can't come 'cause she's far away."

"Ah. Well, that's a problem, then. I'm sure she wants to see you."

"I know." Her tone was dejected, as if she'd been told this a million times before.

"Do you have a picture of her? We could put it here by your bed so you could say good-night to her every night. Just like the bunny does."

"Daddy won't let me have a picture of her."

Ella didn't know what to say to this, suspecting that was a long story only for grown-up ears associated with it.

"Do you remember what she looks like?"

"She's pretty. Like this." Ella held up the Gaudy Lulu doll that she slept with every night.

Ella looked at the statuesque doll with the enormous breasts and the pinched waist and wondered if Fannie was, in fact, beautiful, or if Marion just thought of her mother as such. Looking at Marion's pretty, doll-like features, however, Ella knew that it was likely her mother was beautiful.

"Oh, then she's very pretty."

Marion nodded, settling that point.

"When did you last see her?"

She sighed and rubbed an eye with a curled fist. "I dunno.

A long time ago," she said with a yawn. "I was this many." The fist uncurled three fingers.

"Maybe she'll come to see you again soon," Ella said. "Would you like that?"

Marion suddenly closed the book and shoved it from the bed. It hit the floor with a muffled thud. "I'm sleepy," she announced as she hunkered under the blankets.

Letting the subject drop, Ella rose and tucked the blanket under Marion's chin. Then she bent low to smooth the hair from her face and kiss her tender cheek.

"Good night," she said softly.

Marion slipped her hands under her pillow and closed her eyes. "Tell Daddy to come give me a kiss."

"I will."

Ella turned off the bedside light and followed the beam of light from the hall to the door, picking up a few items of clothing en route and tucking them under her arm.

"Ella?"

She turned and peeked into the dim room again. "Yes?" she replied in a hushed voice.

From the darkness, she heard the child's high-pitched voice, hoarse with sleepiness. "I want the lady in the book to be you."

Ella stood motionless at the door, too moved to say a word. She had cared for hundreds of children over the years, had saved lives by the score. But never had she felt the unspeakable sweetness of a child's head against her breast as she read a story, or experienced the delicate bond that existed between a woman and a child she loved.

For she was beginning to love Marion. And, thinking of Bobby, this frightened her deeply.

"Sleep tight," she said, and closed the door.

★ ★ ★

Much later, Ella stood leaning against a wood pillar on the porch, gazing at the stars. The air was crisp, reminding her of spring nights at her home in Vermont when there were no noises except for the calls of night birds and insects, and no lights except for the moon and the stars.

This sky, however, was strictly South Carolina. A wisp of a crescent moon, the likes of which was not seen in the north, sliced a sky filled with stars so bright they looked like diamonds of the highest color and clarity set against black velvet.

She was here under a Carolina moon, but her northern memories were tugging at her heart. All this talk of her aunts, the memories of her childhood and her affection for a child mingled together to form an unsettling concoction, bubbling up images in her mind.

If she closed her eyes, she could see Bobby's pale face the last time she spoke with him.

In retrospect, she'd known right away that he was in trouble. All her instincts warned her that this time his illness had gone too far. But duty pushed back all her inner alarms and she'd worked on automatic pilot to do a preliminary evaluation, then sent him upstairs to the pediatric ward. If only she'd taken the time to hold his hand and talk to him. If only she'd stopped asking questions and giving orders long enough to look at his sweet face one more time and tell him that she would stay by his side.

But, of course, she couldn't have done any of that. She was a nurse on duty. And it had been another busy night in the emergency room.

Diet. Birds of prey are opportunistic. They never know where or when they'll find their next meal. The crop is an enlarged space in their esophagus that can store large amounts of food, so a raptor with a full crop can survive five to seven days without eating. Raptors often swallow their prey whole. The fur and bones go through the system and are later coughed up as a pellet. Pellet analysis can provide a good look at a raptor's diet and habitat.

9

IT HAD SNOWED THAT NIGHT. INSIDE THE RUTLAND General Hospital, Ella Elizabeth Majors stood at the window watching the flakes fall.

"Look! It's snowing!" said an excited voice coming up beside her. "Can you believe it?"

"Can't say I can," Ella replied with a smile of greeting for Denise, a fellow pediatric nurse. "It's already snowed four times and it's only November."

"I still think it's magical each time," Denise said, coming to stand beside Ella. She crossed her arms against her white uniform and watched the falling flakes with a wistful expression.

"That's because you're from Florida and don't know any better. Snow can be beautiful when it's fluffy and white like this, but it gets dirty and difficult pretty quick."

"Nothing you say can change my mind," Denise replied. "I've never seen snow like this, or built snowmen. That all might seem boring to you because you've grown up with it, but for me, it's pretty wild."

Ella pulled a corner of her mouth into a wry smile. "Glad you like wild, 'cause with this icy snow, it's going to be a wild night."

As though on cue, the E.R. doors burst open, followed by the sound of pounding feet and calls for assistance as a team of medics raced through the hall pushing a gurney.

"Here we go," Ella said as her training clicked into high gear. She turned and raced toward the gurney, voicing clipped orders to the medics and other nurses standing by. But her voice caught in her throat when she caught sight of the small child on the gurney.

"Oh, no," slipped from her mouth. It was Bobby D'Angelo, a six-year-old boy with juvenile diabetes. She ran up to take hold of the gurney and ask the med assistant, "He's a diabetic. What's his status?"

"Low insulin levels—dangerously low. He went into convulsions."

Her eyes expertly searched Bobby's face for medical clues. She didn't like the pastiness of his skin or his labored breathing.

"Bobby? Bobby, can you hear me?" When the boy dragged open his eyes, she smiled with relief and squeezed his hand. "So you came to see me again, huh, Bobby?"

His eyes blinked sleepily and a shaky smile of recognition spread across his small face. "Ella?"

"How're you doing?" she asked him, stroking back a shaggy bit of black hair, then resting her palm on his forehead. His skin was clammy with sweat.

"Okay," he replied in a foggy voice. He licked his dry lips.

"Yeah? Maybe not feeling so good? And thirsty?"

"Uh-huh."

She walked alongside the gurney as they rolled him into the triage room. There, she quickly got to the business of checking his stats: listening to his heart, checking his eyes, his reflexes and blood pressure. Bobby was familiar with the routine and cooperated without complaining. He was what the nurses referred to as a "frequent flyer," one of the kids who bounced in and out of the E.R. She'd seen hundreds of kids like him over the past ten years as a pediatric nurse, but there was something about Bobby that tugged at Ella's heart-strings. He'd chipped away at her resistance until she began looking over her shoulder each time a little boy was brought into the E.R. He came in far too often, however, and after each episode it took him longer to recover.

"Do you remember when you last got your insulin?"

He shrugged noncommittally.

"A long time?"

"It's not Mama's fault. I just forgot."

She heard Denise mutter with disgust behind her, "Six years old and he thinks it's his fault."

"Let's double-check your levels, okay?" Ella said sooth-ingly, careful not to let her anger against the mother sound in her voice. She patted his hand, gauging the temperature and texture of his skin.

As she administered the insulin stick, she cast a quick glance over her shoulder to the admissions desk. She recog-nized the thin woman with flame colored hair in a short, tight black skirt, a white, puffy jacket, her hair piled high on her head with sparkly pins. Ella knew that on closer inspec-tion she'd find tracks on her arm.

The attending physician walked in and Ella quickly gave him the intake report. After the exam, Ella returned to Bobby's side.

"Okay, big guy, we're all done here," she said, smiling into his eyes again as she affixed a bandage. "Your room is waiting for you!"

His face scrunched up with worry—unusual for him. "Will you come with me?"

Ella wondered about his fear but forced a wide smile on her face. "I'll be up just as soon as I can."

He smiled weakly.

"Are you hungry?"

He nodded, embarrassed to be so.

"I'll get something yummy sent right up." She patted his hand and he gripped hers tightly. Her heart clutched as she looked into his eyes and squeezed back.

"Ella?"

She brought her face close to his. "Yes, sweetie?"

"Don't blame my mama. It's my fault. I just forgot."

She smoothed back the lock of damp hair from his forehead and swallowed back the emotion rising up her throat. She couldn't comprehend that kind of selfless devotion. It broke her heart. There was a special place in heaven for young children who had to take care of their parents. And a special place in hell for those parents.

"I won't blame anyone, sweetie. Especially not you. And do you know why?"

He shook his head.

"Because you're so very good."

His heavy lids drooped with relief and fatigue. In a rare impulsive gesture, she bent over to place a kiss on his clammy cheek. Her heart pumped with affection for the boy and she vowed then and there that she wouldn't let him go through this again. She swore that, even if she had to adopt him herself, she'd not let this child's life be threatened by negligence again.

As another nurse began rolling the gurney off to the pediatric ward, she felt his small hand tighten in panic on hers. "Don't worry, you know the routine," she told him with a reassuring squeeze. "I'll be up to see you later. I promise."

As she'd predicted, it had been an unusually busy night. Hours later, Ella made her way to the elevator and up to the pediatrics ward on the third floor, relieved no one stopped to ask her about the teddy bear she carried in her arms. She openly discouraged sentimental attachments between nurses and patients. Such bonds only proved difficult to handle when the patient was dismissed for home or, sadly, died. Again and again she'd seen nurses get overly attached, then crash and burn when the child didn't make it.

As the elevator rose, she plucked at the stuffed bear's ears and smiled, allowing herself to wonder what it would be like to care for one child instead of so many? To allow herself to love one child, without reserve. She had so much love to share.

The elevator door swooshed open to the pastel-colored walls of the pediatric ward. Ella knew this floor as well as she knew her own home; she actually spent more waking hours here.

"Hi there," she said cheerfully to the nurse sitting at the station "Which room is Bobby D'Angelo in?"

"Room 317. But Ella, wait! You'd better not go in there right now. There's a code."

The words jolted Ella and she took off at a run for his room. From the hall she could hear the terse, staccato orders of the medical team. Drawing near, she saw the crash cart with the defibrillator. She stood out of the way of the team as they frantically worked over the limp child. Her gaze sought out the slim, erratic line of the heart monitor.

"Don't die, don't die, don't die," she prayed with each beat.

Time became a blur of motion and shouts. The team wasn't giving up on this young child, calling again and again for shock. Ella clutched the stuffed teddy bear against her chest each time the child's frail body jerked with the force of the electricity. And after each convulsive jolt, Bobby's arm lay slack on the sheet. The skin was ghostly pale and so painfully thin she could see his blue veins travel from wrist to elbow like rivers.

Ella's gaze fixed on his slender hands. They lay flat on the white sheets, palms up. His small fingers curled ever so slightly. Ella recalled that he'd been afraid and she wanted to reach out and hold on to his hand. To hold on to his life.

A high humming sound pierced the silence of the room. Her own hands loosened and the teddy bear fell to the floor.

That had been the last night she'd worked as a nurse in a hospital. The next day she'd left, turning a deaf ear to all her friends, counselors and the administration. "It's tough, I know," they told Ella. "You're a veteran. You've been through this before. Children die. It's part of our job."

But that was just it. She'd been through it too many times. She'd seen one child too many die.

It didn't help that she mentally kicked herself for falling into the trap she'd helped others avoid, but she could keep it from happening again. She vowed she would not allow another child to creep into her heart the way Bobby had. When she'd taken this position as nanny, she told herself she would be a better caretaker if she were kind and loving, yet kept personal emotions out of the equation.

Now, standing on the porch under a late winter sky, Ella could only wrap her arms tighter around herself and laugh at her foolishness. Did she really believe such a ridiculous vow was even possible? No matter how far away she traveled from Vermont, she couldn't distance herself from the memories she carried with her like excess baggage in her mind. She had to gather her courage and move forward with her life. She had come to South Carolina for warmth. It was time to loosen the ice from around her heart and let the warmth in.

Across the yard, a faint light glowed from behind the heavy navy curtains on the cabin's windows. Ella smiled, imagining Lijah lying in his warm bed covered with all those blankets, maybe smoking his pipe. She could catch the slightest scent of cherry tobacco in the night air. Lijah had told her, as many times as she would listen, how much he appreciated her fixing up the cabin and letting him "put his feet to his own fire."

Her head was pounding from too many memories and the emotions they stirred. Often fresh air helped and she breathed in slowly, exhaling through pursed lips. She brought her hands to her head and undid the clasp that restrained her hair. Immediately, her head felt a little better, and she brought her fingers to her scalp to massage the tension away. Before long she heard a steady footfall approaching the house. Her stomach tightened and she quickly began winding her long hair into a braid.

The porch light illuminated Harris's face as he looked up from the bottom of the steps. "Are you all done for the night?" she asked him.

"For today, anyway," he replied, climbing the stairs with

a heavy tread. "Tomorrow it starts all over again, bright and early."

"When you've got sick patients, there's always something that needs doing."

He reached the top of the stairs and stood facing her. His face was pale with fatigue and his arms hung loose at his sides. She had to fight the urge to reach out and brush the wayward lock that fell onto his forehead.

"Sherry called," he said. "Her mother will be in the hospital for a few more days, then moved to a rehabilitation facility. She'll have to leave right away."

"That doesn't give you time to find a substitute."

"No, but I don't plan on finding one, anyway."

"How long does Sherry expect to be gone?"

"Who knows? Her mother had a massive stroke. Everything's up in the air right now. She'll know more once she talks to the doctors."

Ella sighed and leaned her back against the porch pillar. The silence dragged on between them.

"Did Marion get to bed okay?" he asked.

"Finally. She was wound up from the excitement of the holiday." She glanced over at him. "We talked about her mother."

His brows rose, then settled in a face rigid with expectation.

"Harris, tell me about Fannie. I'm not prying. I need to know in order to help Marion."

"There's nothing you need to know."

"Why won't you let her have a picture of her mother?"

"She does better when she doesn't think of her."

"But she misses her."

"No, she misses the idea of a mother. Not her mother."

"Are you sure?"

In the moonlight, his face appeared as smooth and inflexible as granite. "Look, Ella. You don't know anything about this. It's complicated."

"Nor do I need to. All I know is that Marion needs some contact with her mother. A picture, the ability to talk about her, *something*."

"I said no. It would be too painful."

"For her or for you?"

His eyes flashed and a muscle twitched in his cheek. "This is my house," he said in a voice grown harsh. "And Marion is my child. There'll be no discussion of her mother."

She opened her mouth to speak, but he raised his hand in a halting gesture.

"This is one decision I expect you to abide by. Without any argument."

She tightened her lips and jerked her head up to look at the stars, holding her tongue with great effort.

"Ella, it's not that I don't trust you," he said. Then, with more feeling, "I do."

She swung her head back to look at him. He had the uncanny ability to fluster her.

"In fact, I was thinking that earlier tonight, while I was working at the clinic. I didn't have to worry about Marion, about her medicine, about her getting to bed all right, about the million things that run through a parent's mind. For the first time since I can remember, I could relax and do my work, knowing that you were here."

"That's a great compliment and I thank you for it." She paused and clasped her hands before her. "Seems we were both doing a lot of thinking tonight." When he half smiled in response, she felt bold enough to continue. "Harris, I'm very fond of Marion. In fact…I've come to love her. But I don't want to replace you in her life. I don't think I *could*, really, at least not while she's young. But as she gets older, there is always the danger of you becoming less important in her life. Diminished, somehow, by disappointment or perhaps just the passing of time without you in it."

"I don't understand," he said, wariness creeping into his eyes.

"It's very simple, really. You need to spend time with her."

His face bore the look of defeat, like someone weary of this argument and powerless to change the status quo. "Ella, I don't know what to tell you. You know how things are right now. With Sherry gone, it'll only get worse."

Ella pressed her hand against the harsh grain of the wood pillar. This decision had been building in her mind all evening, despite her internal arguments against it. Now, however, she could see her course clearly, as though she'd been fussing at a puzzle and suddenly the pattern crystallized.

She'd come here to help Marion, but she couldn't help Marion without helping the father. Their fates were intertwined. She'd seen that readily enough but hadn't known quite how she could help. The last piece of the puzzle, however, was the part she hadn't seen—or hadn't wanted to see. She couldn't help either of them without helping herself, too.

She licked her lips and pushed out the words. "That's what I wanted to talk to you about."

His eyes filled with question.

"I've been thinking about what you asked me over dinner," she began. "To help at the clinic. I still don't think I'll be as much help as you seem to think I'll be, but I'm willing to give it a try."

His face froze for a moment while he took in her answer,

then he brightened with astonishment. "Ella, that's wonderful! Thank you. You don't know what a relief this is."

"I wouldn't thank me yet."

His smile slipped as he caught her reserved stance. He cocked his head and looked at her as though trying to figure things out. "Wait a minute. What about all that 'animal person-people person' stuff you talked about? You seemed so firm. What made you change your mind?"

"A person," she replied, her lips twitching. "A little person."

"Marion?"

"Who else?"

"What did she say to make you change your thinking?"

"Nothing."

He seemed perplexed.

"She didn't have to. Did you know she stood at the window, watching for your return tonight?"

His face went blank. Obviously he didn't.

"It's not the first time. She waits for you to come home for dinner every night. And the last thing she tells me after we read a bedtime story and I tuck her in is, Tell Daddy to come give me a kiss good-night. Every night she asks the same thing."

"I always do."

Ella lifted her shoulders in a light shrug.

He raised his brows with innocence. "I do," he repeated, insistent.

"Sometimes she is awake and knows you're there. Sometimes it's so late she's already asleep and she doesn't. Like tonight. Trust me, Harris. You don't want to promise to be there, then not show."

His face clouded and he looked off into the distance.

"I have personal reasons for changing my mind, too. Tonight, when I saw her standing at the window, I recalled how I used to do the same thing at her age. I stood for what seemed forever, wondering where my parents were, why they couldn't be home like other kids' parents. Wondering what was wrong with me that they could leave me behind." She walked along the porch, absently picking up sticks and bits of debris blown in from the wind and gathering it in her hands.

"When I was a grown woman, I was able to understand why my mother chose to leave me in my aunts' care. She wanted to work alongside my father. He was a workaholic. If she hadn't, she never would have seen him. My father was my mother's first priority. Not me," she said without a hint of self-pity. "I like to think they were very much in love.

"And yet…as a child I couldn't rationalize any of that. At Marion's age, I felt abandoned, hurt, even angry with my mother and father. Their careers, their dedication, even their love for each other—none of that mattered. At five, all I wanted was my mother and my father back. Life is fleeting, Harris. There will always be our work and deadlines and immediate problems to solve. But Marion will only be young for a short span of time. Blink and you'll miss it. Blink again and she'll be gone."

He stood motionless, his eyes haunted.

"So," she said, rubbing her palms together. She looked up, took a deep breath and gambled. "I have a proposition for you."

"A proposition?"

"Yes. What I have in mind is a cooperative effort. I'll come to the clinic to relieve you, and in exchange, you'll come to the house to take care of Marion."

"What?"

"The work will get done, but Marion will be spending time with you."

He shook his head. "That won't work. We'll still be one person short at the clinic. The work will pile up."

"Then we'll both have to work longer hours. I don't mind." Her face became resolved. "But the sacrifice won't come from Marion. We won't hire sitters for her. That's not what I came here for."

His eyes stared blankly at the distance and she could tell that he was working this out in his mind. She figured that was only fair. She'd gone over it a million times in her own mind while waiting for him on the porch, and each time the answer came out the same.

"I don't know if it will work," he said slowly.

"It will."

"But there is more work than one person can do."

"We'll manage."

"How? Be realistic, Ella. Where are we going to find the time for this trade?"

"We won't find the time, Harris. We'll make the time."

He pursed his lips in thought, but she saw fear in his eyes.

"What are you really worried about? Don't you think I can handle the birds?"

"No, it's not that at all. I'm sure you can. Frankly, it's me I'm worried about." He ran a hand through his hair. "I'm not sure I can handle my daughter."

She suddenly understood the source of his reticence and tried to think of a way to encourage him. "What about the male eagles who lose their mate while rearing their young? You told me that if someone provided enough food, he could be very resourceful and manage to raise an eaglet on his own. Remember? All you have to do is trust your instincts once again and know that you are not alone. You're surrounded by people who will help you raise this particular little eaglet." She wagged a finger at him. "But there *is* one thing you'll have to worry about," she added, releasing a grin. "*I'll* be the one leaving you food."

Harris lay on his bed, his fingers interlaced behind his head, and played back his conversation with Ella for the tenth time.

You're not alone.

He couldn't wrap his mind around those words. He'd always been alone. Maybe not physically. In his lifetime he'd always lived with someone: his mother, Fannie, Marion. But they were females who needed his care. Whether that was by fate or his own design, he didn't know. The fact was, there hadn't been anyone with whom he could share his thoughts, his hopes and aspirations, even his dreams. He'd had no one to help ease the burden of all his responsibilities. Ever since he was nine years of age and his father had abandoned him and his mother, he'd been the caretaker. He'd learned to be self-sufficient. He'd grown up not depending on anyone or anything other than himself. And over the years he'd become unwilling—or unable—to open up to another person. He'd thought he didn't need anyone else.

He was a fool, of course.

Closing his eyes, he could still readily bring forth the image of Fannie, only seven years earlier, when they'd married and he'd brought her to his bed. The sight of her beautiful body, so lithe and willowy, upon his sheets still stirred him and brought a yearning ache that was his only companion for too many nights. He was a man in his prime with all a man's insatiable hungers. Yes, he needed someone else.

He sighed and turned on his side, punching his pillow

under his head. When he closed his eyes, this time he saw Ella standing on the porch, as he'd seen her earlier when he'd walked from the clinic. He'd stopped in the shadows to watch her. She'd reached up to undo the clasp and her hair had cascaded down her shoulders like a waterfall. He'd never seen such hair! The rich brown strands caught the moonlight like phosphorescence on waves, and for a moment he was mesmerized by the sight of her slim, tidy figure leaning against the pillar while her luxurious hair swirled around her, stirred by the breeze. He'd felt a little like a voyeur, but he couldn't drag his eyes away. It was unusual to find Ella relaxed and caught off guard.

The moonlight had shone on her face and her expression was dreamy, like she was a million miles away. For the first time he'd realized that she had a whole life that he knew nothing about, memories that might include lovers, and it startled him to think of Ella in that way. He'd been careful to avoid that line of thinking. They were living together in the same house, after all.

Tonight, however, he saw Ella as a woman, with a woman's wants and desires. And once the image was planted in his mind, he couldn't shake it.

Harris gradually drifted to sleep, thinking of Ella, hearing Ella's words floating in his mind. *You are not alone.*

***Ospreys: The Dashing Fish Hawks.** Ospreys are large black-and-white raptors with crooked wings and sharply curved talons. With their banditlike eye markings, they cut a handsome pose as they fearlessly dive, talons first, under the water's surface for prey. They eat fish exclusively and are common to coastal areas and inland lakes.*

10

ELLA AWOKE THE FOLLOWING MORNING FEELING as though her world had subtly changed. It had been a sleepless night, full of unbidden memories and momentary panics and regrets. By the time the light of dawn seeped through the curtains, her eyes were puffy and she could feel the faint thrumming of a headache in her forehead.

The day, however, would not wait until she was ready to rise, so she dragged herself from the bed, then stretched and yawned noisily. The house was silent save for the rush of water from the shower informing her that Harris was already up. She peeked through her bedroom curtains. Outside, a fine mist settled over the pond, clouding the view of the pines beyond. She could barely make out the roofline of Lijah's cabin in the fog.

Slipping into her robe and slippers, she hurried to the wood-burning stove to add a few pieces of wood, then went directly to the kitchen to make coffee. She was pouring two cups out when Harris came into the room. He was clean-shaven and dressed in jeans and a blue flannel shirt. His hair was still damp from his shower and slicked back from his broad forehead, making him look sleeker, sexy.

She felt self-conscious at being caught undressed and tightened the robe closer around herself. Last night they'd moved one step closer, and this morning they'd awakened to a heightened awareness that made them dance around each other with all the awkwardness of blushing teenagers. Her hands needed to keep busy, she thought, and she grabbed the sponge and wiped up the few grains of spilled coffee from the counter.

"Chilly this morning," he said, stopping beside her.

She could feel his presence surround her, smell the faint scent of soap on his skin more powerful than the freshly brewed coffee. "Coffee's ready."

"Thanks." He leaned closer to grab his cup and took a few sips. "Mmm. Good."

"Ayah," she replied, slipping into Vermont vernacular.

He noticed and a small smile crept into his eyes.

"You're up early. Breakfast will be in just a minute."

"Don't trouble yourself. I've got to get to the clinic. Got a call late last night. Someone's bringing in an osprey from Mount Pleasant. They want to drop it off before they go to work."

"Okay." She poured milk in her cup, keeping her eyes averted.

They stood a few feet apart, he leaning against the counter, she standing erect by the sink. They each sipped their coffee, the silence between them as heavy and as concealing as the low-lying fog. When she cast a furtive sidelong glance his way, she blushed to find his gaze squarely on her.

"Well, I'd better get going," he said, pushing away from the counter.

"Will you be back for lunch?"

"Don't think so. Things are backed up."

"We'll miss you." She hadn't meant to put it quite that way. Looking abruptly up, she saw a faint smile tugging at his lips as though he were pleased.

He walked toward the door, gulping down the dregs of his coffee. She followed him, opening the door and pushing wide the screen door for him. He smiled a brief thank-you, acknowledging the courtesy, then passed through the door. As she stood flat against the cold metal screen she felt the scrape of his leather jacket against her breasts as he walked by. She had to close her eyes and hold her breath, so overpowering was this brief, inconsequential brushing of his garment against hers.

He hesitated on the back porch. "Ella?"

"Yes?"

"About last night..."

"Oh, it was nothing..."

"No. I mean, yes, it was. What you said. It meant a lot. Thank you."

She opened her mouth to reply, but as she looked into his blue eyes shining with such sincerity, her mind grasped for words that wouldn't come. So she merely nodded her head and ventured a shaky smile.

He returned a smile so swift she doubted she saw it, but it left her feeling like the morning sun was shining directly on her face.

Ella let the screen door close between them and set down her cup. My God, she thought with prickly shame, it was ridiculous to feel this way. The man simply said thank you and her heart was fluttering as if he'd made a flowery confession of love.

She hurried to the sink and leaned over the rim to catch sight of him as he walked across the field. She did this most mornings and each time she thought he cut a handsome figure in his jeans and leather jacket. His long legs strode with a determined gait, and she knew him well enough to know that his mind was already on the myriad duties he had before him that day.

"What're you looking at?"

Ella swung away from the window. "Marion! You're up. Are you hungry?"

"You were looking at Daddy again, weren't you?"

Ella saw the twinkling in Marion's eyes and the smirk on her lips and knew she'd been found out. She sighed. "Come along, snoopy," she said, grabbing hold of the child's hand and leading her back upstairs. "Let's get this day started."

"Morning, Ella."

Ella looked up from the skillet of bacon sizzling on the stove to see Lijah peeking his head through a small opening of the kitchen door with an empty plate in his hand. She smiled broadly and waved him in with her mitt-covered hand. "Just in time!"

"When I smell that coffee brewing in the morning, I know it's time to come on by and return the dinner plate."

Laughing, Ella grabbed a mug from the cabinet. For the past several weeks she and Lijah had struck up a quiet routine that began when she brought a plate full of dinner to the cabin. He'd seemed reluctant at first to become beholden in any way. As friendly as he was, he was a private sort. But she'd grown frustrated with his refusals to join them at the dinner table and wouldn't take no for an answer. She started knocking on his door, making it impossible for him to refuse the plate of a warm dinner. The following morning when he came to return the empty plate, Ella wasn't blind to the longing in his eyes when he spied the pot of freshly brewed coffee. And being a coffee lover herself, she was totally sympathetic. She'd poured him a cup then, and he'd come by for a refill every morning since.

"Here you go, sir. The cream's on the table."

"Appreciate it."

As she wiped the counter she watched as he bent over the table and poured a liberal amount of cream in the coffee, added two heaping teaspoons of sugar, then stirred with the same care and precision as any prim lady at a tea party. The spoon made a rhythmic clinking noise as it went round and round.

"Look there!" he said, pausing before drinking and pointing to the coffee. "See all the bubbles in the coffee? Means money's coming."

"Harris will be happy to hear that. He's hoping to get enough to start building a proper flight pen."

"That's a fine thing. I'd be happy to help him build it. Santee needs to exercise."

He brought the mug to his lips, sniffed, then closed his eyes and sipped noisily. After he swallowed, he slowly lowered the mug with a hearty, near reverential "Ah."

She smiled, enjoying the ritualistic performance. "Coffee okay today?"

"Ain't had a good coffee since my Martha crossed over. She could make a fine cup."

This was the first time she'd ever heard him mention his personal life. She'd wondered if he'd ever married, had children or family of any kind. She figured he was connected somehow to the local Gullah community that held him in such high esteem. Clarice had explained to her that Elijah was a walking encyclopedia of the Gullah culture. A living treasure.

And yet, looking at the old, slightly stooped man, she couldn't help but be mystified at how this man who had so much knowledge and was held in such esteem by so many came to be so unattached to personal possessions and people that he could simply take off and follow an eagle.

She leaned forward. "Martha was your wife?"

"She was."

"When did your wife pass on?"

"Long time. I done stop count."

"You must still miss her."

"My heart hurts and ever will. Though, she ain't never gone for true."

"Come again?"

"She's still here with me."

Ella stilled her hands at the sink. "How is she still here?"

His eyes softened as he took on a wistful expression. "I hear her voice in the wind," he said, speaking as much to himself as to her. "When I pass through the marsh on a soft, moist night, and I look up, this here mist floats by and I think whether it's my Martha. Other times, when I go way deep in the woods where the sun dapples through and the earth greens up, Martha comes close and walks with me. Yeah, then things still just like before."

He sighed and was quiet for a moment. Ella sensed a great loneliness in the old man. When he spoke again, he looked up at Ella with a benign expression, but his eyes betrayed him with a moist film.

"The spirit ain't go soon as the body do, that's for true. It lingers awhile. We just have to know how to talk to it."

She leaned across the back of the chair, lured in as much by the melodic quality of his voice as the images he created.

"And how do you communicate with spirits?"

He pursed his lips. "You have to be dear. They find their way in if the door is open. Singing is good, too. Opens the soul up."

"I hear you singing at night, when the owls hoot. Are you communicating with your Martha then?"

His face darkened as he frowned. "Ain't the same thing. When an owl hoots after hag holler time, that's a bad sign. The singing quiets the owl and cuts his power."

"Does it work?" she asked, surprised by this. She'd found the owl's music mysterious but enchanting.

His eyes sparkled with mischief. "I've got a nice cabin to sleep in and a hot cup of coffee every morning. That seems a good turn of luck."

She chuckled, understanding better why the local people often called Lijah to dinner on Sunday to hear his stories and get a dose of optimism.

"You sure I can't get you a little breakfast this morning? It's no trouble. Just a little bacon and some grits."

"Grits, you say?" He eyed the pot carefully.

"I haven't burned it yet."

He smiled wide, an admission as to why he'd dodged so many breakfasts in the past. "Well, guess I can be nice and try a little bit."

She laughed again and served a bowl for him as he took a seat at the table. Then she put a plate of bacon beside it. She was inordinately proud of her efforts this morning. The bacon slices were evenly cooked and crisp. She held her breath, waiting.

Lijah took a bite and nodded with appreciation. "That *do* be good."

Ella smiled, then walked with a lighter step to the back stairs and called up. "Marion! Come on down for breakfast!"

She heard a commotion on the floor above. "Coming!"

"Where Harris at?" Lijah asked.

"He left about half an hour ago. He wanted to check on an osprey that came in this morning."

Lijah shoveled in a few mouthfuls of grits, finished a slice of bacon, then wiped his mouth with a napkin and rose from the table. "Thank you, Ella. I best go help. There's plenty work to do. Clarice is the only volunteer today and young Brady ain't coming till three. Miss Sherry's going on, you know."

"I know. I'm planning on coming to the clinic to fill in for her. Or at least to try."

His brows rose at this.

"Why are you so surprised?"

"I just never figured you for having much interest in the birds."

"I don't. Harris roped me in. But I roped him in, too, so we're even." She twisted the kitchen towel in her hands. "I hope you won't tell anyone this, but I'm a little afraid of the birds."

"*You're* scared?" He shook his head in disbelief. "I didn't figure you to be afraid of much."

"I'm not. But these big birds look so ferocious. I don't know why, they just do. I hear from Maggie that you have a way with the birds. That you can go up close to them and they don't squawk or get all flustered. I can't seem to go near a pen without them rearing up and flapping their wings. I'm worried they'll hurt themselves more if I get too close. Is there something I could learn to make them not so afraid of me?"

He scratched his jaw in thought. "Seems to me, if you're afraid of them, then they're picking up on that. Not in your words, of course. They feel you. You have to feel them back. Signals and things."

"What kind of signals?" she asked, not having a clue as to what he was talking about.

"Birds of prey be powerful hunting birds. Remember that! They're wild. You have to be careful. And respectful. Especially when you going toward them because they're real fussy about their no-go area. You don't want to just march into they space, hanging over them or moving real quick. It makes them mean and nervous. Believe me, they'll let you know when they don't want you coming any closer. Some might raise they wings and puff they feathers, and commence screeching to appear bigger. Or some might crouch low and hunker close to the ground. If they do that, slow down and give them a chance to settle.

"And don't stare at them, either. It's tempting to look at them, but they'll mad up then." His eyes narrowed to make a point. "If they think you're nasty, they carry a grudge worse than a lover gone bad."

"Lord, I have a lot to learn."

"It's simple, really. Communicating with birds ain't much different than the way you communicate with all spirits. You just have to open your heart and let the warmth inside come spilling out."

He shuffled toward the door but turned before leaving. The smile across his face was full of reassurance. "Don't worry, Miss Ella. I see your heart. You'll do just fine."

Brady's heart was full of anger and resentment as he plowed the pickax in the gritty soil. He figured he must have hit the earth at least one hundred times that afternoon but it still didn't come close to easing the fury simmering in his chest. He paused to lean on the wood handle of the tool and mop his brow with his shirt. He couldn't believe it when he'd arrived at the birds of prey center this afternoon and Harris told him to start digging the culvert down by the gate.

He looked across the road to the pine tree where the white rooster sat on a low-lying branch, watching him. "What the hell?" he said to the rooster. "Doesn't that jerk know slavery ended in the South?"

The rooster only stared back impassively with his dark eyes.

"Shit." Brady picked up the ax, lifted it over his shoulder, then heaved it to the earth. "What does Harris know, huh? He thinks he's, like, the king of the place. Everyone jumps at his bidding. Do this." He landed a hit with the ax. "Do that." Another hit.

He looked up at the rooster, who hadn't moved a muscle.

"I'll bet you wouldn't jump for nobody, would you?" Brady laughed, thinking that extremely funny. "Nope," he said, getting a good grip on the wood handle. "Not you. And not me, neither. Not for Harris Henderson, that's for damn sure. I've got enough of that at home with my own father."

The pickax hit the earth again, this time clawing out a big chunk.

His father had been in a hellish mood since the judge took his hunting license away. No matter that his kid had to serve time twice a week every week for six months. No matter that they had to sell Mama's family piano in order to pay the fines. Brady knew that what really stuck in Roy Simmons's craw was the feds taking away his one passion in life—pointing the business end of a .22 at some critter and blowing it to kingdom come.

Not that he blamed his father for being angry. Brady knew he counted on hunting to bring home enough food to the table. Whether deer, fish, bird or just mangy squirrel, meat was meat. And Brady figured it took away his daddy's sense of worth not to be providing. Brady was man enough to see the problem with that.

But he did blame his daddy for dealing with his anger with liquor. He didn't even try to go out and find more work. It was like he was sliding down some slippery black hole he couldn't climb out of. The angrier he got the more he drank, and vice versa. Things at home were getting pretty mean. His mama couldn't hide the bruises no more. There were just too many of them. And his daddy was taking good shots at him, too. He had to do *something* to keep the anger targeted at him instead of his mama or the younger kids.

Not that it was hard to do. Hardly. His daddy blamed him for being the cause of all his troubles. Roy was blaming him for things that happened clear before he was even born. But when Roy was in the drink, it didn't matter what craziness sprang to mind—he believed it. And nothing or no one could stop him from his rants.

"One of these days…" he swore, picking up the ax again. One of these days he was out of there. As soon as he could, he was going to pack up and leave and never come back. He'd be like Lijah, hiking around the country with no cares and no worries.

"What you lookin' at?" he said in a snarl to the rooster. It was starting to get on his nerves the way that white bird kept ogling him for hours on end. "Go on, now. Quit staring at me." He paused to wipe his brow, muttering under his breath. "You think I should stick around? Like you? Just watching everything? You're a dumb shit for hanging around here. And for what? For Mama? Why doesn't she just pack up and leave herself? Why do I have to be the one to protect her? Let the other kids step up to the plate. I've done my turn."

Down came the pickax, and again and again until Brady paused, catching his breath. Even though the temperature was only in the forties, he was sweating so much he had to remove his jacket.

"Hey, there," someone called from up the road.

Brady turned his head to see Clarice walking toward him, carrying a brown bag in her arms. She had a free-and-easy, long-legged gait, swinging her hips to the left and right. Her shiny black hair was tied in countless thin braids today that were pulled back at the sides and made a knot at the back of her head. He stood a little straighter and reached up to smooth down his hair.

He couldn't figure Clarice out—or his feelings for her. She was one of the prettiest girls he'd ever seen, though not in the way he usually thought was pretty. Not like Jenny, his girlfriend. Jenny was like most of the girls he went for: blond, with big blue eyes and a willing disposition. Clarice was…well, he couldn't quite say what it was about her that intrigued him. It was more the way she acted than the way she looked. Real confident and smart, like she knew what she wanted and was going to get it. She was a pain, too, and liked to put on airs. Especially with him. But she'd gotten a lot nicer to him in the past few weeks, doing things like bringing him a Coke or a snack when she brought one to Lijah, saying hi, just things like that. It got so he kept an eye open for her whenever he came to the center.

"I thought you were working down here," she said as she came closer. "But here you are, lazin' around. You're like those guys I see on road crews, just leaning on their tools and catching some rays."

"I'm taking a breather," he said in defense. "It's hard work hauling this pickax."

"I wouldn't know," she said with a jaunty lift of her chin as she passed him. "Why's the gate open?" she wanted to know. "It's supposed to be closed at all times."

"Ask the Boss Man. He told me to keep it open while I dug the culvert."

She couldn't argue this and it pleased him to have the upper hand, for once.

"What are you doing down here?" he asked.

"I've come to bring the rooster some corn."

"Oh." He looked over at the bird.

He swung the ax a few more times, all the while watching Clarice from the corner of his eye. She walked over to the pine tree and tossed handfuls of dry corn to the ground beneath the rooster.

"What for you doing that?" he asked.

"I should think it's obvious."

"If you're so worried about the rooster, why don't you just bring him up to a pen or something instead of leaving him here?"

"He's not ours to bring anywhere. He came on his own and sits here, watching who goes in and who goes out. He must like being here or he'd leave." She tossed another handful of corn to the ground, then closed up the bag. "We leave corn once in a while just to make sure he has enough to eat."

"It's weird, his being here. Isn't it? I mean, why'd he come and what's keeping him here?"

She walked a little closer to him, her arched brows gathered. "I don't know. But Lijah says that every animal has a powerful spirit. Or a totem. They're sort of like messengers of the spirit world to humans."

Brady lifted his brows and rolled his eyes. "Right."

Clarice huffed at the snub and said sharply, "I'm obviously wasting my time. You wouldn't know what I was talking about, anyway."

"You're calling me stupid now?"

"Those are your words, not mine." She began walking away.

"Wait," he called after her. He wasn't really interested in this totem stuff. He just wanted to talk to her a little more.

She turned her head in a saucy manner and gave him a look that said, *what?*

"So, tell me about this totem thing."

She looked at him, narrowing her doelike eyes as she considered whether or not she'd answer him. Her eagerness to tell the story obviously got the better of her because she walked back toward him, stopping before she came closer than a few feet away.

"We don't know for sure, of course. But you have to admit it's strange that this rooster just showed up and started sitting in that tree. He's been there for a couple weeks already."

Brady only shrugged. He was watching the way Clarice's gull-wing brows lifted when she grew animated about a subject.

"Harris thinks it's an omen for the birds of prey center," she continued. "I heard him talking to Lijah about it."

"What'd they say?"

"If you knew your Bible, you'd know that the cock crowed after Peter denied Jesus three times."

"So? What's that mean? Someone's gonna deny the center or something? Okay, I'm *sorry*," he said when she bristled again.

"Are you always so smart-mouthed?"

"Just sometimes." He smiled with such boyish charm he lured a tentative smile from her. "I'm sorry. Go on."

"Lijah said that roosters are watchful and vigilant. They're always looking out for others."

Brady looked over to the rooster. *You too, huh?*

"Anyway, Harris thinks that the rooster must have chosen the center. Totems do that, you know. They choose."

"Uh-huh," he said, absently scratching a streak of dirt from his face. "Hey, you go to Lincoln High, don't you?"

She looked up at him, taken off guard by the quick change of subject. "Yeah. So?"

"So… So do I."

"I know. I've seen you there."

"You have?" He was surprised. "Lincoln's a big school. What year are you in?"

"I'm a senior."

"Oh, yeah. Lijah told me that."

"He told me you were a junior."

Great. Thanks, Lijah. "You must be all about looking at colleges now."

Her face brightened and he could tell by the way she straightened that she was proud. "I've been accepted at Stanford. Early decision."

"Stanford? In *California?*" He couldn't believe she'd want to go to a college anywhere out of the South, let alone clear across the country. "That's a long way from home."

"I love it there. I can hardly wait. I'm going into premed. It's a great school and thank God I got a scholarship."

He felt a flash of jealousy run through him. A scholarship? *Of course.* She was a black girl. Everyone knew all they had to do was check the box and they got money.

"You must be pretty smart." He meant that sarcastically.

She took him seriously. "I work hard and get good grades."

Something in his expression caused her to stiffen and he knew she'd clued into his thinking. Her voice took on that haughty sharpness she used when she was mad and going to put him down.

"You know, lots of people have a 4.0 average these days. So I guess it was my SAT scores that nailed the scholarship."

He kicked the dirt, feeling mulish. She was fishing for him to ask what her scores were but he wouldn't give her the satisfaction.

Clarice didn't wait. "I had a perfect score in math," she said, driving home her point. "Only a 750 in English." She lifted her shoulders with false modesty. "I also got accepted at Duke and Radcliff."

"Yeah?" he said, shot down and embarrassed.

"What about you?"

He rubbed his cheek and looked away, feeling the dagger dig deeper. "I haven't even taken the SATs yet." He lifted one shoulder slightly. "Not that it matters. I'm not going to college."

"Why not?"

"I can't afford it."

"That's no excuse. You can always apply for a scholarship or financial aid. The money's out there. You can't *not* go to college because of money."

"Yeah, well…" He shrugged self-consciously. "I guess you ain't seen my grades." He used the word *ain't* deliberately. "Like I said, it don't matter, anyway. I don't want to go to no college. Can't wait to get out of school as it is."

"Oh."

He dug his heel in the dirt and shifted his weight. "California, huh? I guess that's cool. Sometimes, far away can be good."

Now he was really embarrassed because her expression changed and he could tell she felt sorry for him and awkward that she'd rubbed her success in. He wished he could just fall into the ditch he was digging.

"Well, hey," she said, her voice high with enthusiasm. "I think you should go for it. It's not too late, you know."

For guys like me it is, he thought. If she only knew what his life was like, she'd skip the pep talk.

"Well, I'd better get to work."

"Yeah, me, too. See you."

She smiled before she turned away and he didn't read any of the malice or distrust in her eyes he'd been expecting.

He watched her walk away with her confident stride and gentle swing of the hips and wondered with a pang of anguish what it was that some people were born with that made them winners, while others, no matter how hard they tried, just seemed destined to be losers.

Before hoisting the ax, he took another look at the rooster. As always, it sat with its head cocked and its little dark eyes staring directly at him.

"What you lookin' at?" he said begrudgingly. "You think you're my totem or something? Well, you can just forget that."

The rooster suddenly shook its feathers, spread its wings and flew down to the ground. It walked straight for him in that head-bobbing, leg-kicking, challenging strut that shook its bright red wattle. Brady was so startled that he took a step back, nearly tripping over the pickax lying on the ground.

"Well, okay then," Brady said, holding his hands out and getting his balance. "Don't get steamed." The bird stopped a few feet away but Brady didn't take his eyes off it. "You go on and eat your bittle and let me dig my ditch, hear?"

He turned to hoist the ax and commence digging. The rooster strutted back to the pine and scratched for corn.

Brady shook his head, muttering, "Damn crazy bird." But the truth was, he was getting to like that stupid white rooster. They were two of a kind. They both knew what it was like to be living on the outside, looking in.

Kites: The Graceful Aerialists. These slim, finely proportioned, medium-size birds have long wings and tails and a distinctively graceful flight. Kites' aerial maneuvers are acrobatic as they catch insects in the air over open spaces. They have distinctive plumage, shape and flight style—especially the American swallow-tailed— yet at a distance they are difficult to distinguish from other birds. Kites include American swallow-tailed kites, Mississippi kites and black-shouldered kites.

11

THE FOLLOWING WEDNESDAY ELLA WALKED with Harris from the house to the clinic. Today was her first day as part of the medical staff. Lijah and Maggie had both volunteered to keep an eye on Marion for the time it would take Harris to guide her through the crash course. He'd been wonderful. Every night and every spare minute, he sat across the small dining table and played tutor while she crammed like a college student. She'd studied the anatomy of birds, the terminology and abbreviations used, and grasped an overview of the needs of an injured bird versus a resident one.

Yet she still felt as green as any new volunteer the moment she stepped into the quaint, low-ceilinged, white clapboard building that housed the medical clinic. Right off, she was hit with a pervasive, overpoweringly pungent odor that she couldn't identify. She wrinkled her nose and peeked around. "What's that smell?"

"What smell?"

"*What* smell?" she asked, looking at him incredulously.

"Oh, that. We skin and gut mice for the birds. That's probably it."

"Oh. That."

He grinned and shut the door, cutting off the rainy wind and the last breath of fresh air for her. "You'll get used to it."

She rubbed her arms and looked around.

"You seem nervous," he said.

"Nope. Just terrified."

"Whatever about?"

"Oh, everything. About being a nurse again," she admitted. Then, because of a sudden rush of self-consciousness about broaching this tender topic, she added, "For raptors. I've read all about them in the books you gave me. That's all well and good. And Maggie's been great to walk me around the past few days to get me acquainted. At least I'll know the difference between a red-tailed hawk and say, oh, a Mississippi kite. Did you know I didn't even know a kite was a bird? I thought it was some toy made out of paper and string. Until I came here, I looked up in the sky and called everything bigger than a sparrow a hawk."

He started to laugh and his slanted glance held no criticism. "That's what most people do," he reassured her.

"Still…pointing at a hawk in the sky and walking into a small pen and grabbing hold of one by the talons is another thing altogether. Harris, I've got butterflies and I don't know why. It's not like I've ever had a bad experience with a bird, at least not that I can remember. I mean, Alfred Hitchcock's film The Birds didn't traumatize me as a child or anything like that."

"*I* was pretty freaked by that movie," Harris replied. "If he'd used raptors, the film would've been a lot more violent."

She didn't laugh. He didn't seem to be taking her fears seriously.

"It's not your style to be nervous, Ella. Anyone who can go *mano a mano* with Marion when it's time to give a shot will have no problem dealing with the beaks and talons of even the largest raptor." He seemed pleased to see her rueful smile escape.

"Now, just relax," he told her, and this time his voice was gentle, reassuring. "We'll get you accustomed to the place slowly. Take off your jacket and let me show you around. Keep in mind I've been working with a skeleton crew, so it's a bit disorderly. Speaking of which," he said when the clinic door opened. "Meet Marie. She's one of our senior volunteers."

Marie came into the clinic shaking the rain off of her yellow slicker. She was an attractive woman in her fifties with an unassuming manner and lively eyes. The kind of woman you liked instantly.

"Morning, Marie. This is Ella Majors. She's going to be taking over for Sherry."

Marie's eyes sparked with acknowledgment as she put out her hand. "Thank goodness. We sure need you."

"I'm pretty green when it comes to birds, so I'll be counting on you and the other volunteers to help me out."

"That's what we're here for. Oh, speaking of green," she said, turning to Harris. "The water's dripping from the hose outside the clinic and there'll be a swamp there soon if it's not fixed. I think the washer's broken. Probably from overuse, the way you've been working that poor kid. Brady must've scrubbed every one of those kennels. And the perches! I can't believe it. They're all repaired and covered with new Astro-Turf. Between him and Lijah, the place is really shaping up. They're the Dynamic Duo."

"I'll fix it," he readily replied.

They chatted a few minutes in a friendly manner, but just as in any hospital, when duty called they cut the talk short. Marie moved on to begin the morning feeding while Harris guided Ella on the tour.

The clinic was an old house that had been remodeled to fit their needs. She found it a comfortable combination of charm and efficiency. Ella followed him down a long, narrow hall and through the five small rooms. Of these, the most important was the treatment room, and adjoining it, a small critical-care room where the kennels housed seriously ill and injured raptors. Across the hall was a second, smaller treatment room where drugs were stored in a locked glass cabinet. There was a book-lined office where a steady supply of hard candy and pretzels could be found, a closet-size X-ray room and, lastly, a food-preparation room and mini-laboratory. Lots of natural light flowed throughout the clinic, bringing out the contrast between the white walls and the honey-colored wood floors. It was, she decided, a cheery workplace.

They walked from room to room while Harris explained everything, from the location of the BID, SID and QID charts to the medications of choice. Yet all she heard was a buzz in her head as she looked at the clinic with a nurse's eyes. A *bit* disorderly, he'd said? Her worries and fears about the job were swept away by a familiar racing of her blood as years of nursing training kicked in—hard. Her fingers itched to work.

To her mind, there was limited space, and from the looks of things, every person was doing multiple tasks. In the food-preparatory area, the countertops, sinks and the surrounding areas came into contact with food, blood, tissue and mutes. The forceps for both feeding and medical use were soaking together in a sink of soapy water. Charts were set down on the counters during food prep, then carried from the food-prep area down the hall to the treatment area. All manner of wonderful, life-saving work was going on of which Harris could be deservedly proud. No doubt about it. But all Nurse Majors saw was a hotbed of cross-contamination.

"That's the general layout," Harris said when they'd finished the tour. He crossed his arms with the satisfaction and pride reserved for those who've built something wonderful from nothing. "I know there's a lot to take in all at once, but you'll get a better sense of the place once you actually start working here. Any questions?"

"Oh, a few," Ella replied, her eyes ablaze. She began rolling up her sleeves with the intensity of a woman on a mission. "Where's the bleach, some soap, paper towels, a clean sponge and the broom?"

A few days later when dusk was falling, Ella leaned against the gleaming counters of the food-prep area and thought to herself that she really should be heading back to the house to relieve Harris of his child-care duties and begin dinner. That thought floated lazily in her mind as she took a long, slow perusal of the cabinets, counters, equipment and tools of the clinic. Nary a tweezer nor a gauze pad was out of place.

She was proud that she'd made her own small contribution to this already well-managed clinic, even if she hadn't yet handled a bird. But Lord, she was tired. Her legs felt like lead from so many hours of standing and her hands were raw from scrubbing. Even the thought of having to make dinner seemed beyond her tonight. When she'd put in long hours at the hospital, she could come home and eat a bowl of cereal and be content. Here, however, she had Marion and Harris to cook for. Ella had a whole new appreciation for the plight of the working mother. She brought her hand to the back of her neck and began massaging away the knots, holding fast to the final few moments of quiet.

The door swung open, interrupting her peace. Surprised, Ella swung her head to see Harris step into the clinic along with a crisp gust of rainy wind.

"There you are. We were getting worried about you."

"I was just finishing up. Is it terribly late?" She darted her hand to her hair, tucking in the wayward tendrils. For the past several days they'd literally bumped into each other dozens of times in the confined space of the clinic. He never failed to fill the room with his presence and make the breathing air seem scarce. "I'm sorry. I took off my watch since I was scrubbing."

"It's not that late," he replied, closing the door behind him. His jacket dripped and he smelled of rain. As he pushed back his hood, a few drops of water clung to his long lashes while his eyes roamed the gleaming counters and cabinets. "Looks great," he said, admiration glowing in his eyes. "Really, I hardly can believe it. You've turned the place around."

"It's all part of my secret plan. Now, *I'm* the only one who knows where everything is so everyone has to come to *me* to find something. See? Instant indispensability!" She tapped her head. "Good ol' Yankee ingenuity."

"I'm impressed. No more cross-contamination, right?"

"You bet."

"I have to admit, when you first started this project I was a little skeptical—and even annoyed. You seemed to be only

making more work, not lessening the demands. But now…"
He nodded with affirmation. "I can see it was well worth the
effort."

She flushed at the compliment. "And it will save time in
the long run. Not to mention, save birds' lives, too. And
that's the point, right?"

"I knew it was the right thing to do to get you involved."

"Temporarily," she hedged. "I'm still not a bird nurse."

"Not yet."

He held her eye and Ella couldn't help the laugh that escaped with a shake of her head.

"Speaking of which, I've got to do a follow-up check on
the barred owl that was brought in. Want to try to handle
your first bird?"

"Now? Tonight?"

"There won't be a better time. It's peaceful and quiet."

She felt her heart rate accelerate. "I'm pretty tired," she
replied in way of an excuse.

"It won't take long. Come on, Ella. You're going to have
to learn some time or another. Might as well be now."

He cajoled her into the critical-care room where rows of
kennels lined the two shelves. The close space was pungent
with the odor of bird mutes. Ella tightened her arms around
herself to quell her shaking.

"This is the one. Number 2036," he said, pulling back the
towel that draped the kennel."

The brownish-tan-and-gray owl stared out from the grate
with its enormous, soulful black eyes. Its left wing was bandaged, as was one foot, and yet he stood straight and silent,
like a wounded soldier, anticipating her every move.

"He's beautiful," she said.

"Yeah, I'm partial to barred owls. The southern species
are tamer than their northern cousins. I like to think their

mamas taught them their manners. Makes him a good bird to learn on. Don't be fooled by its sweet face, though. All owls can give you what-for. Especially the great horned. Now, *that's* a tough old bird. Got to know what you're doing there." He handed her a pair of thick, black rawhide gloves that went nearly to the elbow. As he studied the bird, she could see concern etched into his features. "Remember, a raptor's feet and talons are their best line of defense. Always wear gloves."

Ella licked her lips and felt her breath quicken as she stared back at the seemingly docile owl. There was something about its stillness that unnerved her. "I don't know if I'm ready for this," she said, backing off a step. "What if I hurt him?"

"It's always a chance we take, but you have to start somewhere. This owl is in pretty weak shape so he won't fight you much. Someone found him ensnared in barbed wire, struggling like the dickens to escape. He's lucky the lady who found him cut the wire instead of trying to disentangle him. Still and all, there's lots of tissue damage on the wings and a deep wound on the foot. Okay, let me show you how it's done," he said, moving closer to her.

She felt her heart thudding in her chest so loudly she was sure he could hear it as he came to stand behind her and raise his hands to encircle her arms. She stiffened when his fingers made contact with her skin.

"Relax," he told her. "You're shaking like a leaf. There's nothing to be afraid of."

He couldn't know, she thought as she tried to still her trembling, what turmoil his touch could bring her. He couldn't know how long it had been since anyone had touched her, even innocently, like this. Her skin was like arid soil when the first drops of rain fall—absorbing, awakening, quickening, coming alive again and greening.

"Get in close so you can block his escape route," he was saying, his breath close to her ear as he guided her arms. "Always hold your hands in the ready...like this... That's right."

She nodded in the crook of his arm, feeling his soft chamois shirt against her cheek.

"The main thing is to go in real slow and calm, so as not to frighten him too much. You don't want him banging his wings around in there. That might cause feather damage. Once you've got him, gather the bird's wings and gently fold them close against the body," he explained, guiding her arms. He removed his hands but remained standing near. "Ready to try?"

When he stepped aside, she took a deep breath and nodded, feeling the cool air rush between them to clear her muddled thoughts. She had to focus, she told herself as she looked back at the dark eyes of the owl.

She brought to mind the day—oh, so many years ago—when she'd had to give an injection to a child for the first time. Her hands had trembled then like now and she was equally certain that she'd hurt the child, somehow send him into a death spiral thus failing miserably as a nurse. She hadn't, of course. The whole procedure had gone smoothly, yet afterward she was shaking more than the child. Remembering that incident, and how she'd survived it, helped steady her nerves. She'd get through this, she told herself. She just had to have confidence.

The owl stared wide and alert as Ella slowly opened the kennel gate. It creaked on the rusted hinges. The owl didn't move, but she sensed its nervous coiling of muscle as her gloved hands moved into his space. Gentle, gentle, she told herself as she inched her way closer. Suddenly, the bird lunged back against the far wall of the kennel, flapping its one unbandaged wing loudly against the confined plastic walls. She squinted her eyes against the fury of wing beats and moved in, panic welling up in her chest as the owl thrust its feet and talons at her and began viciously biting her glove. She moved quickly to grab hold of its legs, and once secured, she reached around with her free hand to fold in the flapping wing.

"Good! You've got him," Harris said from behind her. "Now, bring him out and keep a good grip on his talons. That's right," Harris said, watching her every move.

Reassured by his guidance, she followed his instructions.

He stood back and put his hands on his hips, grinning. "Congratulations, Ella. Nice job."

Ella flushed with pleasure and released a long breath of pent-up air. She held in her arms this wonderfully wild creature. It was, she knew, a rare privilege.

"I can't believe I'm holding an owl," she said, a bit breathless from the exertion. She looked down at the beautiful bird held secure in her gloves. "I've always loved owls. I used to try to find them in the woods in Vermont. I'd prowl around looking for whitewash on trees or pellets on the ground. I liked to pick the pellets apart like a treasure to discover the tiny bones of rodents. Sometimes I'd see one roosting in a tree but always at a distance. Never this close. I feel like I'm breathing rarefied air."

She looked up then and saw him gazing at her intently, as though he were trying to understand who she was and take her measure.

"Anyway," she said, feeling a sudden cockiness, "I guess this wasn't so hard after all."

As though it had heard, the owl turned its head on its amazing axis and nipped her chest.

Ella gasped in pain and lurched back. She kept a firm grip

on the bird but leaned away from the curved beak that was holding fast to her breast.

Harris lunged forward to pry open the owl's beak. The T-shirt was puckered but no blood seeped through.

"You okay?"

Ella peered down her shirt at her bruised skin. "He didn't break the skin, but ouch, that hurt!"

"A love bite," Harris said as he put a towel over the owl's head.

"Yeah, great," Ella murmured, her chest still stinging and her pride prickling. "Talk about a comeuppance."

"You did great, Ella. You stayed calm and kept hold of your bird. I didn't expect you to get bit right off the bat. We all get nipped sooner or later, but it's official now. You've gone through hazing with flying colors." He smiled at her so brightly the pain eased. "Welcome to the club."

A few weeks later, Harris sat on the floor of his living room across a playing board from Marion. It was only ten o'clock in the morning, but they'd already dressed and undressed Gaudy Lulu a dozen times, played several hands of Old Maid and long ago abandoned the dollhouse. This was the third round they'd played and Harris thought he was about to lose his mind.

Marion, however, seemed to be having a wonderful time. She was chattering away like a magpie. He could make little sense of her nonending, convoluted sentences and found his thoughts drifting off to other matters. Occasionally he'd mutter a mechanical "uh-huh" or "oh, yeah?" response to Marion's questions.

His mind wandered to what Ella was doing in the clinic that morning. Two owls—a barred and a screech—had been admitted the day before with serious eye trauma. The screech's left eye was so bad it was unlikely it'd regain sight. And some Good Samaritan had brought in an osprey all the way from Beaufort. The ospreys were only just arriving in the Lowcountry, setting up nests, and already this poor fellow was found with its chest impaled with multiple fishhooks. It was in pretty bad shape and would require very tricky treatment. Was Ella up to it? he wondered. If he could just slip into the clinic for a few minutes...

He pursed his lips knowing he couldn't. He'd already had several arguments with Ella on this point since they'd started this arrangement. His job was to stay a few hours with Marion and not turf her off to someone else. Ella had taken to her job like the proverbial duck to water. All her nursing skills came into play, as he'd suspected they would, and she proved to be adept at treatments. She was still a little gun shy at getting the raptors from the kennels, but the other, more experienced volunteers were able to cover that for her. Once at the treatment table, Ella had no difficulties dispensing medical care.

Hell, the truth was, she'd come on like gangbusters, sending the dust flying and turning the place around, just as she had in the house. The clinic had never been so clean and organized.

At first he'd been a tad disappointed that the first thing she'd see at the clinic were microorganisms on work surfaces. Sure, he knew that bacteria could be transferred into a bird's body with fatal results, but most people who worked here were awed by the fierce beauty and commanding presence of the raptors. Most developed strong feelings and a dedication to rehabilitate them. Ella seemed a little standoffish with the birds. Her emotions connected instead with preventing contamination, cleaning and disinfecting. Little typed signs were posted all over the clinic for infection and disease prevention, each with numbered instructions under headings such as: Wash your Hands! Keep Food Off the Treatment Table! Keep Medical and Food Instruments Separate!

The volunteers joked about the signs, but beneath the humor he saw respect.

He had to admit he was a little jealous. While Ella was making a difference in the clinic, all he was doing was sitting on the floor, rolling the dice and moving some blue peg around a brightly colored game board.

"Daddy!"

He blinked, realizing that Marion had been calling him. "What?"

"It's your turn," she said, clearly exasperated.

"Oh. Okay. Sure." He picked up the dice and rolled it. Six. He looked at the board with a blank expression. "Now, where am I?"

Marion frowned and pushed away the board. "I don't want to play anymore."

Harris couldn't disguise the relief on his face. "You don't have to. What do you want to do next?"

"Watch TV."

"Nope. Not an option. Want to pick out another game?"

She shrugged, keeping her eyes on the ground.

"What about this one?" he asked, pulling from the cupboard some silly game where they had to do surgery on a battery-operated game board.

Marion shook her head no.

"What's the matter, honey?"

"Nothing."

"No, tell me."

She just groaned and stretched out on the floor as if she was tired.

He felt a sudden panic. "Are you feeling sick? Is that it? Maybe I should check your blood."

She snapped her head up and her eyes were narrowed. "No! You don't have to check my blood."

His stomach dropped, thinking that they were headed for a temper tantrum. They hadn't had one in weeks and it just went to prove that he wasn't up to taking care of her. He stood up, reaching out for her hand.

"Come on, let's just do it."

"No, Daddy! I don't need to." She mulishly kicked the playing board, sending the pieces flying.

Convinced her blood sugar was dropping, his heart began pounding. "Stay there," he ordered as he hurried from the room to gather the test kit from the bathroom. How could he have not noticed, he berated himself? He'd missed the signals. Again. His hands shook as he took the test kit from the bathroom shelf.

When he returned to the living room, Marion was gone.

"Marion?" he called. Even as he looked for her in the kitchen and raced up to the bedroom, he knew in his bones that she'd run out. He pushed open the back door and ran outside, feeling panic rise in his chest. "Marion!"

The little girl was nowhere to be seen. He did a quick run around the house, then across the lawn straight for the clinic. He burst through the door, breaking all rules by raising his voice.

"Ella! Is Marion in here?"

Ella rushed out from the treatment room wearing an X-ray apron. Her face was tense and alert. "What? Is she missing?"

"She ran out of the house."

"How long ago?"

"Just minutes."

Ella took a breath. "She can't have gone far. Let me get this owl back in the kennel and I'll help you look. She's got to be right around here."

Harris turned on his heel and headed for the med units. Inside, he found Clarice and Brady scrubbing out Med Unit 8 while the two ospreys inhabiting the space were huddled in the corner as far away from them as they could get. But no Marion. Coming back outside, he saw Ella running toward him from the clinic.

"Where have you looked so far?" Ella asked.

"The house, the clinic, the med building."

"How about the resident birds? She likes the crows."

"The crows," he muttered, the connection clicking in his brain.

They ran together to the resident pens. He was very much aware of her support as she trotted at his side. As he rounded the curve of shrubs, Harris's throat constricted with relief when he spotted a small child's form standing beside Lijah inside the crow pen.

"Thank God," Ella said, breathless as she came to a stop beside him.

Looking at Marion, Harris thought she seemed calm and attentive, bending at the waist to get a closer view of the smaller of the two crows. Gone was her fury and any signals that she might be having a blood sugar attack. It was obvious that she was engrossed in whatever Lijah was telling her. Harris saw the gentle smile on Lijah's face, too, and it didn't escape him that the old man was enjoying this brief interlude with Marion.

"She doesn't look any worse for wear," Ella said. "In fact, she seems to be having a wonderful time with Lijah."

He pushed his hair from his face and waited for his breathing to catch up to his heart rate. "As long as she's not with me, she manages pretty well."

"Don't be so hard on yourself. Everyone loves Lijah. He just has this way about him."

"But I'm her father. Put me in there with her and she'll throw a tantrum."

Her mouth settled in a crooked smile. "What happened this morning?"

"Damned if I know. One minute we were playing Chutes and Ladders, and the next she was kicking the board and telling me she didn't want to play anymore. I thought she was having an insulin reaction."

"Was she?"

"I don't think so now. But how could I know with diabetes? It's like riding a damned roller coaster. I was getting the kit when she snuck out."

"So she knew you were going to test her?"

He pursed his lips and nodded curtly.

"Let's take a walk."

Spring had not officially arrived in the Lowcountry, but the soft promises of redbuds and cherry blossoms, greening marshes, creamy saucer magnolias and a palette of pastel colors floated in the balmy breezes.

They took off down the gravel road, traveling nowhere in particular. As she walked shoulder to shoulder with Harris, Ella was keenly aware that their relationship wasn't employer-employee any longer as much as colleagues, perhaps someday friends. They'd shared too much to maintain such formality between them. Their dinnertime was no longer the torturous effort at communication. The talk was lively, full of questions and reports about their days and banter about people and birds they both knew.

Neither one spoke right now, however. She sensed that

they were walking toward a new plateau in their relation-ship. The gravel crunched beneath their shoes and the song-birds called in the trees. Usually Harris kept his eyes to the sky, unconsciously scanning for birds. Today, however, she saw that his eyes were on his feet as he placed one foot before the other.

"I can't tend to Marion. It just isn't working," he said at length.

"It's only been a few weeks. Give it more time."

"Marion doesn't want to spend time with me."

"I don't know how you got that idea. She adores you. She loves spending time with you."

"This morning we were playing a game and the next thing I knew she was kicking the board away and quitting. Does that sound like she was having a good time?"

"Were *you* having a good time?"

"Me? That's not important. The idea is to make Marion happy."

"Then you didn't have a good time."

"No."

"I think we've just found the heart of the problem."

"What do you expect me to do?" he said, his voice rising with frustration. "Dolls and board games are not fun for me."

"Then why play those games with her?"

He seemed perplexed. "You told me she needed playtime, so we played."

"Who chose the board games?"

"She did. We pulled them out of the cabinet and she picked out the ones she wanted to play."

"But think, Harris. Who decided to play board games in the first place?"

He didn't answer.

"I'll wager you did."

"What's wrong with board games? I grew up playing them."

"There's nothing wrong with board games, except when that's all you play. How many days have you depended on that as the basis for interaction with your daughter?"

He didn't have to reply. She could read the answer in his troubled expression.

"In the end, Harris, you chose things to do that you *didn't* enjoy—for her sake. And she tried to play those games with you—for your sake. So with all the best intentions, you both ended up miserable."

She walked a bit farther beside him, letting the words sink in. They came to the fork in the road. If they turned to the right, they'd travel along a well-worn truck path to where the woods thinned and you came to a breathtakingly wide vista of marsh framed like a picture by the woods. Instead, they bore left, traveling farther down the dirt road that led to Highway 17. The highway, with its zooming trucks and cars, seemed a thousand miles away as they walked in a rural hush. Everywhere she looked, palmetto trees stood side by side with pine and she thought it was an amusing parallel between herself and Harris.

They came to the gate, but the white rooster was nowhere in sight. Harris went over to the culvert to stand with his hands on hips, head down, inspecting Brady's work. The wind did its job of tousling his longish strands of brown hair. He needed a haircut, she thought. It was the kind of thing she would notice and he wouldn't. Harris was oblivious to how attractive he was. It was one of the things she liked most about him.

She walked to his side and looked up into his face, fighting the urge to reach up and smooth back the hair. A simple enough act, but one that implied a level of intimacy they hadn't reached. He turned his head when she approached and she felt lost for a moment in the closeness of his blue eyes.

"Penny for your thoughts," she said.

"I don't even know who my own daughter is," he confessed.

Her face softened with sympathy. "Marion's a bright child who desperately wanted you to be having a good time playing with her. She probably figured out that you weren't, or that you'd lost interest, and she grew desperate. So when you mentioned testing her blood, she slipped right back into the behavior she knew always got your undivided attention."

"A temper tantrum."

"Like I said, she plays you like a fiddle."

He gave off a short, self-deprecating laugh as his mind recalled how he'd sat on the floor giving mechanical answers to Marion's questions, not really engaging. "The poor kid. She was probably exhausted from all that chatting."

She laughed, well acquainted with Marion's nervous chatter. They started walking back up the road toward the compound. Her short-legged stride worked double time to keep up with his long-legged one.

"How'd you get so smart about children?" he asked suddenly.

Ella flinched. He was offering a backhanded compliment, she knew, but it still pricked that beneath the surface was the question: How could a woman without children of her own know so much about them?

"You forget I've worked with children for years and studied child psychology," she replied, giving her pat answer. "And," she added, "I know Marion."

"What's the secret, then?" All pretense and humor fled from his face. "I love my child, but I can't seem to *connect* with her. How can I start to enjoy spending time with my own daughter instead of dreading it?"

"By sharing with her the things you love."

He stopped walking to turn toward her. "How?"

"Harris, you have so much to share. So much you can teach her. Why get stuck in a room indoors when what you love is outdoors? Go out with her! Take her on nature walks and share your world with her. Give her glimpses of who you are. And then, let her loose! Cut the line and just let her fly. Then follow to where she takes you. Marion's very good at structured games where there are rules to follow and she knows what to expect and what's expected of her. I was stunned when I first arrived to see that she really doesn't know how to free play. To let her imagination soar. And, no offense, but the apple doesn't fall far from the tree."

"Ouch."

"I'm not criticizing you! But when was the last time you actually had *fun* with your child?"

He walked awhile, pondering the question with a troubled expression.

"If you have to think that long about it," she said with a chuckle, "the answer is it's been way too long. Oh, Harris, you've been a wonderful provider for Marion. No one could dispute that. You've taken good care of her. But all that caretaking is a lot of responsibility. A lot of plain, old-fashioned hard work. Right?"

"Of course."

"Well, it shouldn't be. It should also be a pleasure. And it's not just you. Do you know I used to tell other nurses not to form attachments with their patients? I was so smug. I'd figured everything out, you see. By keeping myself emotionally at a safe distance, I could make all my relationships safe. I could get a lot done, not having to waste time talking to patients or thinking about what they might need to ease their mind, not just their body. Or, God forbid, that I should actually care about them." She paused while her mind traveled back to a time months earlier, to one child in particular.

"A little boy named Bobby D'Angelo taught me how wrong I was. How one person could make a difference in a child's life." She exhaled heavily, regaining the control she could feel slipping at the mention of his name.

"Who's Bobby?"

She stopped walking. He took another step before realizing she wasn't beside him. Turning, he looked at her with question in his eyes.

"You don't have to tell me, if you'd rather not."

In point of fact, she would rather not, especially since he had been so closemouthed when she'd asked him about Fannie. But this was a step toward honesty between them, and rather than take a step backward, she decided to move forward.

So she told him about Bobby, about his diabetes and death, and how it had driven her away from nursing. How it had driven her from the cold of Vermont all the way to the small town of Awendaw, South Carolina, and an outpost of healing called the Coastal Carolina Center for Birds of Prey. As she talked they resumed walking up the road toward the center. He listened quietly, but at some point in the telling he wrapped an arm around her shoulder, drawing her closer, safe, as she exposed her inner thoughts. This time, she wasn't nervous or flustered. His nearness felt natural.

When she finished they walked in a silence so deep they could hear the crunch of their footfall on the gravel and, overhead, the piercing *keyer-keyer* of a distant hawk.

At length he said, "When you're hurt like that, it's hard to let anyone close again."

"Yeah," she replied softly, wondering if he was referring to himself and Fannie. "I came here determined not to allow myself to be close to a child again. But what happened?" She cast him a sidelong glance and they shared a knowing smile. "Yep. Marion knocked down those walls and forced her way into my heart. And thank God. Because that's what a heart is meant for. For love, Harris. And caring. And sympathy and kindness and forgiveness and compassion. Those are the qualities that make us human. The mind is where the ego rules. The soul resides in the heart."

They stopped again and he let his arm fall from her shoulder as he faced her, his eyes searching. Ella followed her impulse and reached up to smooth back the long lock of hair from his forehead.

"Just do with Marion what a wise old man told me to do with the birds," she said. "Simply open up your heart and let all the warmth come spilling out. You don't always have to be productive, or fix things, or feel like you're taking care of her. Just *be* with her. All you have to do is set aside time and take your cues from her. Play her games. Then you'll truly be connecting with your daughter."

"You make it sound so easy."

"That's the secret. It *is* easy."

She smiled then, and he marveled at how it transformed her face into something of quite extraordinary beauty.

Vultures: The Cleanup Committee. Vultures are large black birds with unfeathered heads. Though they have much in common with raptors in their flight and hunting behavior, they have recently been classified as more closely related to storks. These carrion eaters are gregarious in feeding and roosting habits. Vultures have expansive wings that can catch greater lift than other raptors, allowing them to soar the wind with seeming effortlessness.

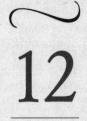

12

"WE HAVE TWO MORE ORPHANS COMING IN today."

Ella looked up from the chart and grimaced at Maggie's announcement. This was, she'd learned, the expected response at the Coastal Carolina Center for Birds of Prey.

As cute as raptor orphans were, the danger of imprinting nestlings to humans was very real. The nestlings identified with whatever moving, vocalizing object cared for them. Once imprinted, the effect was irreversible and the bird could not be released to the wild. Not to mention, feeding a fast-growing raptor was labor intensive. The volunteers had to wear Burkas when they went into the pens to leave food or pick up leftovers—which was several times a day for those hungry babies.

Secretly, however, Ella's heart pinged whenever an orphan

was brought in. She'd been working at the clinic for several weeks already, and whenever she saw one of those big-headed, big-footed, down-covered fuzz balls looking at her with their innocent eyes, her maternal instincts started kicking in, mulishly knocking down all the rational arguments. And when they started chirping for her when she came near their pen, she was putty. Not that she'd ever let Harris know. He was firm that it was best for the orphans to be returned to the nest whenever possible and groaned when an orphan was brought in. Intellectually, she agreed. But it was a classic case of her brain warring with her heart.

But later that morning, when she opened up the covered transport box and found two of the gawkiest, homeliest-looking birds she'd ever seen, Ella had second thoughts.

"Vultures?" she asked dubiously. "But they're not birds of prey."

"No, but we take them in, anyway." Maggie came closer, donning light gloves en route. She bent low to look inside the box. "Oh, my, bless their little hearts. They're so young! They can't be more than two or three weeks old."

"Poor babies," Ella said, crooning. She bent closer. "Where did your mama go, hmm?"

"It's a sad story," Maggie replied. "The parents were attacked by dogs."

"I don't understand. How did the dogs get them both? Did the wind blow the nest down?"

"Vultures nest on the ground, or sometimes in old buildings. But the wind does knock a lot of nests down. You know that osprey orphan we have in Med 8? Someone saw the nest floating down the Intracoastal with the nestling just sitting in it. Really. He was moseying down the waterway." She chuckled. "We call him Huck Finn—but don't tell Harris. He has a thing about not naming the birds."

"The nest just fell into the water?"

"Yep. Thank goodness someone spotted it before it went under. What's sad is we don't know what happened to the other nestling. But we can guess. It's tough coming up as a raptor."

Maggie hunched over the box to carefully grasp a vulture and lift it out. Like Harris, Maggie's movements were slow and deliberate. Nonetheless, the vulture nestlings immediately began huddling low and hissing.

Ella stepped aside, giving Maggie space to move the nestling to the treatment table. The nestling's soft bones and blood feathers could bend and break easily if the bird flapped or was mishandled, and Maggie was the more experienced handler. She put the nestling into a towel-lined bowl for a weight check, but before covering it with the towel, she called Ella over.

"Look here," she said, lifting up the nestling's wing. "The flight feathers are already in blood, which is good. When they're this young, they pretty much just eat, sleep and burrow under mama. This gives them a better chance at survival. Okay, little one, let's check you out."

Together they weighed each of the orphans, checked their eyes, feathers and blood, and to their relief, found them in good health for ones so young. Then while Maggie held each one, Ella slipped into a Burka and fed it small chunks of cut-up and skinned mice. Using forceps, she gently tapped the beak with the meat, one side then the other, just like the mama vulture would do. The nestling opened its mouth again and again, greedily eating its fill. At last, both nestlings were fed and settled together in one large kennel with a heating pad.

"Look at them," Ella said, shaking her head as she took a final view of the baby vultures in the kennel. The two stared back at them, curious and pensive. "What a pair. With those long legs, big beaks and all that tan fuzzy down, they look like two homely chorus girls in feathered boas."

"Or drag queens."

They both chuckled again as Ella lowered the flap. She knew that these two would get names.

While Ella was tending to the orphans, Harris was tending to his own little girl. Today was the first day of spring, his favorite season in the Lowcountry. All around them, the earth was ripening. The days were growing longer and warmer, and Carolina jasmine was bursting with its heavenly scented yellow flowers. He knew in a few more weeks the sunlight would lure out the dogwoods, azaleas, wisteria and scores more wildflowers, making their father-daughter walks seem like visits to the fairy world.

Taking Ella's advice, he wanted to share something he loved with his daughter. Hand in hand they walked through the thick pinewoods that surrounded their home. Harris hadn't known that Marion loved to climb trees. She was like a little monkey, scuttling up the gnarled, perfect-for-climbing limbs of live oaks.

It amazed him to realize that Marion was her own little person, with her own ideas and talents, not some miniature of himself or Fannie, nor even a combination of them. She was curious about things that he didn't find remotely interesting. And then, when he least expected it, she'd ask a question about something he could share, like when she asked him about the lichen on a tree bark. It was like watching a flower unfold.

The warm sun on his back made him feel as slow and lazy as an old alligator on a bank. Marion, on the other hand, heard the drumming of a woodpecker and took off with a squeal in the direction of the tree. She scrambled up the bottom limbs, but the bird, quite naturally, flew off. Harris watched with amusement when she stomped back, her face flushed with frustration.

A short while later, he caught sight of a rabbit several yards off, munching away at the tall grass that nearly camouflaged him. Harris squatted down and waved Marion over. When she drew near, almost trembling with anticipation, he first put one finger to his lips to indicate silence, then pointed to the rabbit. It stilled its chomping and was eyeing them warily.

"That marsh rabbit is in a freeze," he said, still holding the rabbit's dark gaze.

"He's trying to hide. Shh…be very still."

"Where Daddy?"

"Just over there, beyond the dogwood."

Marion gasped at spotting it, then took off after the rabbit, her arms held straight out, crying, "Stop! Stop, I won't hurt you!"

"Marion!" he called after her.

Predictably, the rabbit disappeared in two leaps with Marion in hot pursuit.

"Come on back!" he called to her.

"Daddy, make it stay," she whined, breathless when she returned. Her cheeks were pink from the run and a fine bead of perspiration lined her forehead.

"It's long gone, honey," he replied, trying hard not to chuckle. "And it's been a long time since I could catch a rabbit."

"He won't play with me," she cried, leaning into him. "None of them will play with me." Tears moistened the tips of her lashes.

"Well, of course they won't play with you. You keep chasing them. Animals don't like that. They think you're going to eat them or something."

"But they won't stand still so I can catch them."

"You shouldn't chase them. And you shouldn't catch them. They're wild."

"*No,* Daddy," she said, angry that he didn't understand. "Then I won't have anyone to play with."

"You have me."

She pouted and looked at her feet. He obviously wasn't what she had in mind.

Or what she needed, he realized. She'd had a long line of baby-sitters. Occasionally, one of them would bring their child along. But usually Marion played alone. Ella's words came back to mind. *She doesn't know how to free play.*

He reached out to brush a damp tangle of hair from her forehead.

"Ella does that," she said with a sigh.

He remembered in a flash the feel of Ella's fingers on his brow. "Do you like it when she does?"

Marion nodded.

So did he, though he didn't mention it. "Do you like Ella?"

Marion nodded again, then craned her neck to look up at his face. "Do *you* like her, Daddy?"

"Why, sure I like her."

"I mean, do you really like her?"

"I just said I did."

"I mean, do you love her?" Her eyes sparkled with curiosity.

"Marion, where's this coming from?"

"I dunno. I think she loves you."

He could have been knocked over by a feather. "What makes you say that?"

"Well, you two are together an awful lot."

"That's because we're working together now. You know that."

"Yeah, but sometimes she looks at you in a funny way. All googly-eyed."

"She does?"

Marion nodded and began bulging her eyes out and fluttering her eyelashes.

He laughed and playfully shoved her away. "She does not. She doesn't like me in that way."

"Oh, yes, she does," she replied in a singsong manner.

He thought about that for a moment, surprised at how pleased he was to think it might be true. Thankfully, Marion didn't pick up on how he was looking at Ella a lot lately, too, *in that way.* "Would it bother you if she liked me? Or, say, if I liked her?"

"It'd be okay, I guess." She thought about that for a minute. "You'd have to take her out on a date."

He barked out a laugh. "What do you know about that? You're only five years old."

"I'm five and a half, Daddy."

"Oh. Well, then…" he said with a roll of the eyes.

"Besides, I see it on TV. When a boy likes a girl they go out on a date. She gets dressed all pretty and he does, too, and they go someplace nice."

He could only stare at this little tin-tyke. He couldn't believe she was giving him dating advice. "Ella was right," he told her. "You've been watching way too much television."

Now it was Marion's turn to roll her eyes. "Oh, Daddy, it's not just on TV. Everybody knows that. When Linda was baby-sitting me, she told me how much she liked David and how much he liked her and they went out on dates all the time. So, that's what you have to do."

"I do, huh?" He put his hands on his hips. "I'll have to think about that. Come on, now. Let's head back."

They made their way through the woods to the small pond near the house. Lijah's cabin was perched on a small rise on the other side, and beyond, almost hidden by the long, soft fronds of the giant longleaf pines, was their house. Ella had hung ferns from the porch ceiling and placed big clay pots full of geraniums and trailing ivy by the front door. The beds around the trees were neatly raked, the shrubs trimmed, and in front of the house the rich black earth had been tilled for what would soon be her flower garden. It was a welcoming sight, made more so by the fact that, inside the house, he knew Ella was waiting for them.

"Daddy, look!" Marion exclaimed as they neared the pond.

"Now, look at that," he replied. Among the tall stalks and cigar-shaped spikes of the cattails, a turtle was basking in the sun. "That's as fine a specimen of a yellowbelly slider as you'll ever see."

He was just about to tell her that the yellowbelly sliders on the South Carolina barrier islands were larger than others, how they nested in May and June and laid about ten eggs. He was about to share this and all sorts of tidbits, but in a flash Marion was tearing off toward the pond, her little legs pumping and a look of fierce determination on her face.

"Marion, don't run at it!" he called out after her.

She ignored his call and reached the pond just as the turtle slid quickly away into the water. The gentle *plop* echoed loudly and the turtle was gone.

"Daddy!" she cried in frustration.

Harris put his hands on his hips and rolled his eyes.

Neither one of them saw Lijah standing by his cabin, watching and smoking a pipe while a small smile tugged at his lips.

Later that week, Marion stood inside the crows' pen with Lijah. She looked up at him and scrunched up her face in doubt.

"You're sure that crow can talk?"

"Not just now, missy, but he can. If you teach it to."

Lijah was down on one knee and Marion was leaning against his shoulder, listening to him with rapt attention. Most mornings, Lijah found Marion hanging around the crow pen, peering in and jabbering to them. She especially liked Little Crow, having watched him grow from a nestling. Lijah figured that she thought of Little Crow as just another child to play with.

She tilted her head from left to right. "I never heard of a bird that could talk."

"Missy, there be lots of birds that can talk. Parrots, mynahs, even budgies." He pointed a long finger to Big Crow and Little Crow sitting on a perch a few feet away inside their pen. "Buh Crow, though, he the cleverest of birds. Did you know that when lots of crows are all flocked together, they send lookouts high up to a branch? The scouts sit quiet and keep their eyes peeled. If they see something bad, they let loose that screechy *caw-caw* they do to warn all the mama crows and their children. You know the one I'm talking about." He cupped his hands around his mouth, took a breath and released a perfect imitation of a crow's cackle.

The two crows roused their feathers and hopped with animation from one perch to the other, their shiny black eyes alert with curiosity. Marion giggled and covered her mouth.

"Sounds just like an alarm, don't it?" he said, grinning

slyly. "Sometimes when they migrating south, the winter roosts number a thousand, maybe more. When they take high, high to the sky…" He shook his head, grinning wide. "It's something to see."

"But how can I teach it to talk?" she asked with persistence.

"It's not hard, but it takes a heap of patience. You got patience, child?"

She nodded her head with the positive confidence of a five-year-old.

"Okay, then," he said, eyeing her seriously. "Let's do like this. Come every day to visit Little Crow. He be young and has the temperament for it. Don't be in a hurry. Bide your time till things are peaceful between you and Little Crow. Then, when you sure you got his eye, go on and tell him hello."

Marion burst from his side and ran up to the small crow and called out, "Hi, Crow!"

Little Crow cawed and flustered, flung open its wings and joined Big Crow on the opposite perch. Both crows glared back at her while nervously hopping from the perch to the wall and back.

"They never like me," she cried.

Lijah waved her back to his side. She returned, shoulders drooping and mouth downturned.

"They don't like the way you scared them, is all."

"I didn't mean to."

"I know, missy, but that don't change things. First, you have to tie your mouth and listen, 'cause here's the way you got to do. You ever see Buh Rabbit out in the field?"

"My daddy showed him to me."

"Then you know how it is. Buh Rabbit's daddy tells him he mustn't jabber or hop all the time if he wants company.

He tells little Buh Rabbit to come up real quiet on soft feet when he come visiting so he don't scare off his friends. Then he just sits real peaceable, his whiskers as still as the grass."

"But how can he play if he just sits there?"

"That's the way they like it. It's a heap of fun, if you play right. You like to try?"

"I guess," she replied, not at all convinced.

"Come on, then."

They sat on the pea gravel of the pen. Lijah leaned against the wall with a heavy sigh. Marion sat close to him, Indian style. After only a few minutes, Marion got antsy.

"Say, how long do we have to sit like this?"

Lijah turned his head and looked into her eyes, then slowly shook his head.

She squirmed a bit but got the message. After that, they sat quietly for what seemed to her a long spell while the two crows cocked their heads and eyed them with curiosity. Her bottom was getting cold and she wanted to scratch her nose, but next to her Lijah didn't move a muscle. Thinking of Buh Rabbit, she tried to keep very, very still. Eventually, the crows hopped to a closer perch for a better look. Marion looked at Lijah expectantly, but the old man didn't move.

Then, to her utter delight, Little Crow hopped to the gravel and began pacing in a circuitous route, closer and closer, eyeing her with his shiny black eyes. Marion felt bubbles of excitement race under her skin. It was so odd because her heart was pumping and it felt like she was running through the field, hopping and laughing, even though she wasn't moving a single muscle. When Little Crow stopped smack before her and stared right at her, she knew it was time.

"Hi, Crow," she said in a very soft voice.

Little Crow cocked its head but he didn't scamper away.

Then Big Crow hopped closer and landed smack on Lijah's shoulder.

When she looked up at Lijah this time, she saw his dark eyes gazing at her with a sparkle in them, and a wide, knowing grin stretched across his face. She grinned, too, from ear to ear. She suddenly understood why she was having so much fun just sitting still and quiet like Buh Rabbit.

The crows were playing with her.

That evening after dinner, Harris stepped out into the darkness to do his evening rounds of the pens. Clouds were moving in, carrying sweet-smelling rain and moist breezes, the kind that makes a lonely soul long to search out another. And for him, the other soul he wanted to walk with that starry night was Ella.

The sound of high-pitched laughter drew his gaze back through the window into the house. Ella and Marion were at the sink, laughing. A smile formed at his lips.

He smiled a lot lately. In the mornings, when he awoke to the smell of fresh coffee. In the afternoons, when he came home for lunch to find Ella and Marion working together in the flower beds or painting pictures on the back deck. And in the evenings, when they did simple everyday things like cleaning up the dishes or folding laundry or washing hair. He felt a nostalgia that was absurd because such simple family joys had never been part of his life's experiences. They were only memories of dreams he'd had as a boy.

Ella and Marion were always together, and whether they were laughing or Ella was firmly dealing with one of Marion's outbursts, the bond between them was tangible. The kind of connection he'd always envisioned between a mother and child. The way it never was for Marion and Fannie.

Why couldn't Fannie have felt this way for her own child?

he wondered. What aberrance of nature could cause a mother to leave? Did *he* drive her away?

He turned sharply from the window and began walking from the house—away from the guilt that always stabbed whenever he thought of his wife.

Instead he put Ella back to mind and the image of her was as soothing as the touch of her fingertips on his brow. He smiled with chagrin. Before she'd come, he had worried that she'd be an intrusion into his life. Little did he know how true that would turn out to be—and for reasons he'd never imagined. He looked over his shoulder as he passed the rear of the house. In the soft glow of interior light he could see her face in the window, animated and full of life as she played with Marion. He'd never known anyone so vital and with so much eagerness to share. He paused to take the sight in and it occurred to him that he'd never seen anyone more beautiful.

Ella. He chuckled and shook his head in wonder. She was like a terrier. Small, determined—and stubborn. Lord, had he ever known a more stubborn woman? She'd turned his whole life around. All he'd wanted was help and support with Marion. He'd hoped for a simple routine in his home life, a little less mania and a lot more peace. Ella had brought all this into this life, it was true. But she'd brought so much more.

She'd brought joy. Despite him. Marion hadn't been her biggest obstacle—he was.

Ella. What was he going to do with his feelings for her, he wondered as he began walking again? He couldn't deny them any longer. Even a five-year-old child could tell which way the wind was blowing. Most nights he lay in his bed tossing and turning, or with his hands behind his head just staring at the ceiling, listening to the spring love songs outside his window and wondering if she heard them, too, in her bed just down the hall. Hell, he was no better than one of the thousands of courting, testosterone-filled songbirds claiming out a bit of Lowcountry turf. He sighed and pounded his heels into the soft soil as he walked over the grounds. This was a complication he hadn't planned on. He hadn't been looking for love.

But love had sure found him.

Harris was completing his rounds when he heard a low bass singing, barely audible, coming from inside the med pens. He recognized it as a Gullah spiritual he'd heard in his youth. He followed the sound to Med 3 and was not surprised to find Lijah sitting on the pea gravel inside Santee's pen. What did surprise him was seeing the eagle resting mere inches away in a roost position, feathers fluffed.

As he drew near, however, Santee's proud beak rose and her breast feathers filled out as she stared at him with her yellow eyes shining fierce. When Harris looked away, Santee lowered her chest and settled, but her eyes remained wary. Lijah only looked up and smiled that wide, open grin of his.

"I swear, Lijah, there's no way I could tell someone what I'm seeing right now without folks saying you're doing the voodoo on these birds."

He chortled, amused at the notion. "I ain't hold to that no more. Used to. Back when my wife was doing poorly. Chewed the root and all." His gentle shrug told the rest of the story. "Even in my heart I know everything happened like it should." He slowly turned his head to look at the eagle. "No, ain't no fix between me an' Santee," he said, affection ringing in his voice. "We're just friends. I'm worried about her though. Something ain't right."

"Not right? How do you mean?"

"I can't specify. I'd appreciate it if you'd check her out to-morrow."

Lijah's eyes flickered with worry, like a father with a child. In a flash, Harris recalled the horror of sitting in the emergency room, waiting to hear news about Marion. He'd never known that kind of fear before.

"Can you bring her in first thing?"

"We'll be there."

Harris looked at the eagle. To him, Santee looked well enough. But come to think of it, Maggie had reported that Santee had more than the usual leftovers the past few days. Besides, if Lijah said something was wrong with that eagle, then it was a fact.

"That bird does dote on you," he said, drawing closer to the pen. "Makes me wonder. I've not been blind to the way *all* the birds act with you, not just Santee."

"They know me same as I know them. See," Lijah tried to explain, "every bird has its own self, same as people. Spend enough time with them, you can see it, clear as day. Take Chance," he said, referring to the golden eagle. "He the bully. You never can turn your back upon him. Cinnamon... now, that hawk can sulk and whine if you let her. But give her the chance and she's sweet as syrup. Oyster the sport. All you have to do is watch him soar to know that it be pure fun for him. And Risk?" he said, with a shake of his head. "That falcon be the teacher's pet. And don't she know it. Loves to show off."

Listening to the descriptions of the birds, Harris realized Lijah was right on the mark.

"They show who they is and how they feel all the time," Lijah continued, "if we watch close. And you know with their sharp eyes, a hawk can figure what mood we be in before we even reach the pen, just by the way we walking or the way we move our hands. It the same with people as birds. Problem is, we don't pay enough mind. Most folks look, but they don't see."

Harris grew agitated. They were getting close to what he really wanted to learn about. Whether this something extra—this gift—he coveted so desperately really existed. He'd heard tell of it, wondered about it, but had never really witnessed it—until he'd seen Lijah with the birds.

"When we exercise the birds, if there's no tidbit on my glove, sometimes they won't come. But with you, they do come. Every time. Even without the food." He leaned forward against the wood frame. "I've thought about it, and I've come to the conclusion that it's habituation. The birds got used to you tending them. So they didn't bate and come to you expecting a reward. It's a simple form of bird learning."

"Is that a fact?"

Harris saw the humor shining in his eyes and chuckled in a self-deprecating manner. "Well, old man, how do you explain their coming to you when you call?"

"I never claimed I could explain anything. I just ask the bird to come and it comes."

"You mean, you *will* it?"

Lijah opened up his palms in a gesture of frustration. "I mean *I* just do and *they* just do. I can't put words to it. Son, why you have to work things till you agonize the brain so? You have to learn to let things *be*. You have to be natural, not control nature." He shook his head as a smile played at his lips. "Your little missy, she's a lot like you. If you just settle and listen and watch, you'll get what I'm talking about by and by."

Harris shifted his weight, then cleared his throat. "Will you teach me?"

"Son," he asked, troubled. "What can *I* teach *you?*"

Harris's mouth felt dry. He licked his lips. He had to ask. "Teach me how to communicate."

"With who?"

"The birds, of course."

The old man's eyes seemed to grow cloudy in rumination. When he spoke, he appeared weary. "See, that's the thing right there. Ain't nothing you can do just with the birds. Or just with people, or pets, like some folks think they can. It be about *you* and how you do with everything around you. Even the elements. Like this," he said, holding up his hand and showing two long, brown fingers entwined. "It don't work like this." He separated the fingers in two. "Don't work like this, neither." He brought the fingers in to form a tight, angry fist. "Just like this." Again he relaxed his hand and raised the laced fingers.

Harris stepped closer to the wood bars that separated them. "I'd like to learn how."

Lijah nodded his snowy head and sighed heavily. He rose in a stiff manner to a stand, putting his hand to his back. Beside him, the eagle shook open its wings, startled, and honked its guttural cry.

"Hush now, Santee, and mind your manners before you wake the others. Good night," Lijah said to the eagle on leaving the pen. "Good night, Harris," he said as Harris fastened the door behind. "I'm weary, my bottom done gone cold and I'm heading for my bed. Santee and I will see you in the morning. And after, maybe we can go to the birds together, if you want."

"I would. Thank you."

"I ain't done nothing yet." He turned to leave, then quickly turned back. "Oh, one more thing I been meaning to ask. That boy, Brady?"

Harris tilted his head. "What about him?"

"He got the gift for true. He needs to do more."

"Are you forgetting what he did to that bird in there?"

Lijah's face grew solemn. "I know exactly what happened that morning. And I'm telling you, I been watching that boy real close. He be healing same as my Santee." His face set in resolution. "And if the birds trust him, that's good enough for me."

Still, Harris was resistant. "Ella's already after me to have him help Clarice with the feeding and leftovers, which is more than I'd ever intended. Just what else do you have in mind?"

"I won't tell you your job," Lijah said archly. "I'm just saying that boy can be more help to you than you might know."

"I'll think about it."

"And another thing," he said, lifting his finger into the air.

"You've got a lot to say tonight," Harris said with a wry grin.

"I do," he agreed, returning a slanted smile. "You been working that young woman awful hard. She tending to everyone's needs, except maybe her own."

"Which lady?"

Lijah gave him a look that said, Now, just who do you think you're fooling?

"You mean Ella."

"The weather's fine. Show that woman a good time, hear?"

With a final wave, Lijah left. Harris stayed back to lock up the med enclosure, then stood for a while staring after Lijah as he walked across the grounds under the shifting moonlight in his stiff-legged gait. He continued staring after him, lost in thought, long after the old man disappeared from his sight.

Hearing. Although most raptors rely on their remarkable eyesight for hunting, they also have an excellent sense of hearing. Northern harriers fly close to the ground with their heads cocked to use both sight and sound. Cooper's hawks hunt quail by following their calls. Owls have highly developed ears that can hear sounds ten times fainter than the human ear can detect. Owls depend on hearing to locate their prey, even in total darkness.

13

BRADY SAT BY THE GATE OF THE CENTER EATING a sandwich and waiting for his ride. He preferred to wait here rather than up at the center where everyone would know his mom still had to drive him. Mostly Clarice. That would be really embarrassing. He only had to hold out a little while longer. His parents had told him they'd suspend his license until he finished his community service, but his mother was getting fed up with having to drive him back and forth twice a week so Brady figured it was just a matter of time before he got the keys back.

Not too far away from where he sat, the white rooster was pecking at the corn he'd tossed. Every Saturday and Wednesday the two of them had been hanging out together and sharing lunch. Neither of them spoke much and that suited Brady just fine. Working with the birds was exhausting, and he didn't know why, exactly. It wasn't just that he was doing physical labor. It was more that when he was in the pens with the raptors, feeding them or just picking up the leftovers, all his senses were on high alert. He tried hard to keep his voice low and his movements slow. He was always aware of where they were in the pen and he never stared directly at them. He did this to make them feel comfortable around him.

And he did it for Clarice, too. He couldn't believe his luck when Ella had asked if he'd like to team with Clarice for the feeding shifts. He'd agreed on the spot. Later on, he figured both Lijah and Clarice had put a good word in for him or else that tight ass, Harris, would never have let him near those birds. But ever since Ella had started working there, things had been different. The place was a lot cleaner and more organized, even a know-nothing like himself could see that. Just her being around made folks seem to smile more, like they knew things were on the upswing. And they were being nicer to him, too. Even Harris. Anyway, it didn't matter which of them moved that mountain. In the end, he and Clarice formed a volunteer team. Brady grinned as he bit into his ham sandwich. Sometimes, the Fates were kind, he thought.

He didn't know what to make of Clarice Gaillard. She wasn't just pretty. She was smart. The kind of real smart where she didn't have to talk down to him or boss him around, like some kids did when they had something to prove. Anyone could tell she really loved being with the raptors, especially those teeny screech owls, and she passed that enthusiasm on to him. That's what he admired most about her. She was real good at stepping back and giving him a chance to try new things instead of hogging the birds to herself.

Like when he'd been learning to grab hold of the birds.

He was nervous at first, damn nervous. The little ones, like those screech owls, were so fast and they tried to escape right under your arm. And those big ones, man! Those talons could make mincemeat out of his face if he screwed up. Seeing tiny Clarice move in and grab those talons with precision and speed was, well, it was a challenge to his manhood. He couldn't wuss out when a girl could do it. He did pretty good the first time, too. He liked the way she'd smiled then, warm and with approval shining in her eyes. He hadn't seen that look too many times in his life and it made him want to try all the harder the next time.

After a while, he got so he could collect a raptor as good as her. It was all about reading the birds and thinking about how nervous *they* were instead of himself.

He heard the sound of a car's wheels crunching the gravel and got up out of the way of the gate. The rooster scuttled farther back into the woods to stand just at the perimeter of the trees. Soon he saw a white Ford sedan round the bend. It slowly came to a stop at the gate, the window rolled down, and Clarice stuck her head out.

"Hey, Brady. What are you still doing here?"

"Waiting on my ride," he mumbled, about ready to die. Goddamn, he thought. Why couldn't his mother have come on time for once?

"Still? Are you sure she's coming?"

He looked down the road as if checking to see if she wasn't coming at just that second. "Yeah, she'll get here." He looked back and shrugged his shoulders, averting his gaze. "I don't mind waiting, if it doesn't start to rain again." He looked up with speculation at the gray clouds in the sky. "Anyway, I'm just sitting here, eating my lunch."

"Oh, yeah? I haven't eaten mine yet. Want some company?"

The question caught him by surprise. He got a little heady. "I already have company," he said with a wide grin, stepping back and gesturing toward the rooster. "But you're welcome to join us."

The western sun shone in her eyes so she had to squint and raise her hand as a shield. But he could tell she was smiling. "If you're sure I'm not interrupting your conversation…"

"Nah," he replied with a short laugh. "We've already solved the problems of the world today."

She laughed and he thought it sounded like bells trilling.

"In that case, I'll just move the car out of the way, if you don't mind opening the gate for me."

He couldn't believe the way his heart was pounding as he opened the gate and then closed it after she passed through and parked the car on the side of the dirt road. Where would they sit, he wondered? Did he have anything he could offer her? He looked in his brown paper bag. All that was in there was a half-eaten ham sandwich, an empty bag of chips and two broken Oreos.

He looked up and there she was, standing beside him, smiling and looking around, her beautiful dark eyes alighting anywhere but on him. Brady wondered with a quick stab of surprise if maybe she was a bit nervous, too.

"Where do you sit?" she asked.

"Over there. There's a big rock by the tree. You go ahead and take it," he offered with clumsy chivalry. "I'll sit on the ground."

"Thank you."

He sat down on the earth, sorry for the rain they'd had the past few days. While he dug into his brown bag for the remainder of his shredding white-bread sandwich, Clarice pulled out a bunch of green grapes from a Ziploc bag and began eating them, popping them between her full lips one by one.

"So, you and that rooster are getting to be pretty good friends, huh?" she asked.

"Yeah. I kinda like sitting down here with ol' Buh Rooster. That's what Lijah likes to call him. Sometimes he calls him Chanticleer, too, after some rooster in a story. Lijah's always telling me stories while we're working. That man's a bottomless pit of stories, as far as I can tell."

"Of course he is," she said, matter-of-factly. "He's a *griot*."

"A what?"

"In Africa, our people called our culture keepers 'griot.' Gullah/Geechees continue that. It's what you call a historian. Except, what he knows isn't written in books. Our history is passed on through word of mouth. He knows things that happened in our community from way back to the slave days. It's part of the oral tradition of our culture."

"You're Gullah, but you don't talk like him."

"I've been educated by mainland teachers. I was taught that the Gullah language was not a good thing. It's sad. The language isn't spoken much anymore, except by the elders. As the old people pass away, much of the language passes with them." Again, her brow furrowed and she dropped her hands to her lap.

"Sometimes I worry that everything's sort of dying away," she said. "The Gullah cooking, arts, medicine—even the stories—are disappearing just like the farms and the fishing holes on the Sea Islands. Disappearing to bulldozers for fancy new houses and resorts and roads that will change the face of the Sea Islands forever. But we're fighting to keep the culture alive. We've come together as the Gullah/Geechee Nation. We have a queen mother and a council of elders to keep the language and traditions of our people. That's why a griot like Lijah is, well, honored by the Gullah/Geechees. You see? There is more to understanding our people, just like there is a lot more to Lijah."

"Then what's he doing sleeping in a cabin like he's got nowhere else to go?"

Her lips pursed as she shook her head. "My mama's real upset about that, I can tell you. It's not like he doesn't have anywhere to go. He's got his own house in St. Helena waiting on him and there isn't a family that wouldn't take him in as an honored guest, if he asked. But you know Lijah. He likes to be free to do what he wants, when he wants."

"Don't we all?"

"What's so strange about that, anyway?" she said, her voice rising in defense. "It's not like the roaming storyteller hasn't been around since the time of the knights. Only then they called him a bard."

"Hey, don't get all fussy with me. I wasn't saying anything against Lijah. I wouldn't do that."

She took a breath and exhaled slowly. "Oh, I know." She plucked at her grapes. "It's just that I worry about him, too. He wasn't always this way. I think it all started after his wife and children died."

Brady swayed back and put out his hand. "Whoa, slow down. What's that about his wife and children?"

"Now don't go telling him I told you this," she fussed at him.

"Who am I going to tell? Come on, Clarice," he cajoled.

She popped a grape in her mouth, considering. "It's not like it's a secret," she said. "Most everyone knows so I guess I can tell you. It happened a long time ago. In the sixties, I think. His two boys were out fishing one day when a nasty squall came up all of a sudden and overturned their boat. They were far out and both of them drowned."

"Damn…"

"Lijah just stopped telling the stories after that. And I guess his wife never got over it. I don't know the particulars, but she wasn't quite right in the head after. Lijah took care of her for years until she passed on—oh, about ten, fifteen years ago. She was all he had in the world that mattered and when she was gone, too, he just put away his tools and gave up boat-making.

"That's what he was. A boat-maker," she explained. "He never used plans, but people used to come from all over for one of Elijah's boats. My daddy has one and says he's never seen the like. Anyway, sometime after his wife died, he began telling the stories again."

"Huh. Why do you think?"

"Who's to say? Maybe telling the stories brings him closer to her? To his children? Or maybe he can lose himself in the telling for a little while." She sighed and popped another grape. "I hope so."

"And now he just follows this eagle around?"

"I guess. To hear him tell it, the eagle chose him."

"Maybe it's his totem," he said with faint sarcasm.

Clarice tilted her head and gave him a slanted smile. "Maybe. Or maybe he just needs something to cling to. Whatever, he seems to have found peace and God knows he deserves it."

She stopped talking and he didn't know if he was supposed to say something. He couldn't think of anything to add except, "Well, he's a good friend to me. I'll do anything I can for him."

Clarice ate the final grape on her branch and gathered her things. "I better get going. I've a lot of homework tonight."

She looked down the road, then at her watch. When she looked back at him, her brow was furrowed with concern.

"Listen, are you sure you don't want me to drive you home? It's looking like it might start raining."

He was torn between wanting to go with her and talk some more and having to deal with her seeing his crappy house. Pride won out. "No. Thanks, but she'll get here soon."

"It's no trouble."

"There'll be hell to pay if she comes and I'm not here. But thanks."

"Okay, then."

He walked Clarice to her car. With each step he agonized how he could work it so they could talk again like this. Not a date, he told himself. He was already dating Jenny and he liked her fine. Clarice was more like a friend. He just wanted to spend some time talking with her. She made him think of different things than he was used to, things that made him feel better about himself.

Clarice climbed into the car. He wanted to ask her to meet again but his tongue felt frozen in his mouth.

"See ya on Saturday," she said.

"Uh, yeah. Sure."

She started the engine. It revved and purred and still he couldn't say anything. He stepped back, telling himself that working with her on Saturday would be fine. They could share lunch again.

"Oh, wait," she said, poking her head through the window. "I won't be here on Saturday. I'm taking advanced placement tests. See you next Wednesday, I guess."

"Clarice," he blurted out. Suddenly a whole week seemed too far away. "I was wondering. I mean, if you're not too busy studying, maybe we could get together. Have lunch or something," he added feebly.

Her brows came together and he could see she was troubled by the suggestion. "I don't know…"

"No big deal. I just thought, you know, we could do something. Like friends."

Clarice put the car in Neutral and looked at him through narrowed eyes. "Friends," she repeated.

He shrugged, trying to seem nonchalant. "Yeah."

"I guess we could," she said, without much enthusiasm. She was clearly hesitant. "Maybe after the test."

"Yeah? Good. We can meet at school and go someplace."

"Don't you have to be at the clinic on Saturday?"

"Oh, yeah. I forgot," he said, putting his hand to his forehead. What an idiot he was. "I meant after. What time are you done?"

"Actually, I'm done around two. About the same time you are." Her fingers drummed on the steering wheel. "Okay, how about we just go for some ice cream at *Ye Ole Fashioned Ice Cream*? I can meet you there. Say about two-thirty?" She put the car into gear and looked up at him, a smile in her eyes. "As friends."

Ella found Harris inside the mews repairing the wire fencing. It had been a stormy several days but the rain had ceased at last and the birds were allowed out to weather, even if the wind still blustered. He stood at the far end of the wire enclosure with his broad back to her, but Cinnamon spotted her approach and began her shrill food-begging call. Harris's hands were engaged on the wire wall but he turned his head and spotted her over his shoulder.

"Hey," he said in a lackluster manner before returning his attention to his work.

Ella didn't reply. She walked along the outside of the mews where the golden eagle, three falcons and two Harris hawks stood on their perches, hunkered against the wind. With each step she tried to walk soft-footed, as she'd seen Lijah do, but her tread pounded and sloshed in the mud as if her boots were made of lead. One of the falcons jumped from its perch as she passed, jangling its bell and fluttering as though she'd just scared the bejesus out of it. The others watched her warily as she passed.

"Is it my smell?" she asked as she drew near to Harris.

He shook his head but did not turn to face her. "They just don't know you well. Give them time."

"I don't know," she said, putting her hand on the honey-combed wire screening. "Lijah doesn't get so much as a peep, and even Brady can walk right up to them and they don't seem to get all flustered like they do with me."

She thought she heard a harrumph and looked sharply up at Harris. White petals from the flowering shrub on the opposite side of the screening lay scattered on his shoulders. The rain had created marshy conditions and they were all joking that they'd have to drag out the canoes to get from one pen to another. Not that Harris had been laughing. He'd been brooding and his face was as cloudy as the skies. He'd barely said a word to her at last night's dinner or at breakfast, and his cool greeting was the last straw.

"Look," she said, stopping before him on the other side of the wire fence. "I know you're put out that I assigned Brady to a team with Clarice. But you're making much too big a deal out of it. He's a good volunteer, he knows the territory, and you know better than I that there are certain jobs that require two people to get them done safely."

Harris turned his head then and she saw his jaw was set. "Brady is *not* a volunteer."

She tsked with frustration. "You're splitting hairs. He's here to work, no matter what got him here."

"No matter what got him here?" he asked, his eyes wide with incredulousness as he took a step closer. "He shot an eagle, for Christ's sake!"

"I know, I know," she said, leaning forward and grabbing hold of the wire fence. "And if you'd take a minute to look past your prejudice, you'd see the boy is sorry! Lijah has forgiven him. Seems to me you should, too."

She met his stare even while her fingers tightened on the wire. She'd learned that his smoldering anger could be a formidable thing, as could her own. She'd also learned that he was fair. Sure enough, after a minute the fire in his eyes banked and his shoulders lowered.

"Maybe. Lijah told me he'd let that business pass long ago," he said. "Told me the wise man held no grudge."

"I respect his opinion," she said softly. "He spends more time with Brady than anyone else. In fact, he's the one who came to me with the suggestion."

Harris's mouth slid into a crooked grin. "He came to you, too, huh? The sly fox. He tells me he thinks the boy has potential."

"So does Clarice. She's changed her opinion of Brady, too. She asked for him to be her teammate. Harris, you told me to do what I thought best at the clinic, and I did. You can't be second-guessing every decision I make. That will drive us—and everyone else—crazy. Clarice needed help and Brady was the best one for the job. That's all." She paused, then added with a hint of pleading in her voice, "Aw, Harris, you should have seen him when I told him he could work with the birds. His whole face lit up, as if I was giving him a gift!"

He listened, but he seemed unwilling to change his stand

on the issue. "So," he said with a shrug. "You've already given the okay. It's done. What do you want me to do now?"

She tilted her head and studied his face, wondering if he was really so obtuse about his influence around the center. Come off your high horse and give the kid a break, she thought to herself.

"Nothing," she tersely replied, turning to move away.

"Ella—" He took a step toward her, placing his hand against hers on the fence.

She slowly turned back, acutely aware of their hands touching, separated only by a thin pattern of twisted wire. She raised her eyes to his.

"I'm sorry," he said quickly.

"It's okay," she replied in the next breath.

Her stomach muscles quivered as she stared into his eyes and read a message of longing and need every bit as wild and real as her own.

"I *have* been giving you a hard time about this. Way out of proportion. I shouldn't be."

"I should have talked to you about it first. I knew how you felt."

"No, it was your call."

Such polite words, she thought with pained amusement. Why couldn't they speak the same dialogue that their eyes were communicating? She felt the warmth of his skin against hers and wasn't imagining the press of his weight.

Cinnamon began her high, shrill calling. Ella dragged her hand away as Harris took a step back. It was one of the volunteers carrying a tray of mice and fish to the med pens. She was dressed in a rain slicker and rubber boots and paused to call out a cheery hello as she passed.

The moment was gone, and Ella was glad for the interruption. She'd struggled to reach a place of comfort where they could live and work together as colleagues without her imagination getting in the way.

But he'd lured those emotions out from her again like a magician pulling brilliantly colored silken scarves from a hat, one after the other in a glorious, mesmerizing, seemingly endless string. Was she imagining the second glances, the palpable tension between them when they stood side by side, the countless moments of awareness? She thrilled at the magic of it all, even as she scolded herself for falling victim once again to what she told herself had to be the mere dreaming of a lonely woman.

He had the profile of a hawk, Ella thought as she looked at his long forehead and strong, pointed nose. Even in the twilight she could see the early tan Harris had from working longer hours in the spring sun. A farmer's tan, he jokingly called it, because it cut a line on his arm and neck where the T-shirt ended. He was standing outside the med pen that housed a pair of eagle orphans that had arrived by special courier from Florida earlier that day. Everyone had been very excited to receive them, no one more than Harris.

"I thought I'd find you in here with those babies."

He acknowledged her with a smile, then returned his attention to the eaglets. "They're pretty amazing."

"Those little guys sure caused a lot of excitement today," she said as she walked to his side. The shadows in the pens deepened, but she could still make out two distinct, dark brown shapes housed in the kennel.

"It's rare to have a pair sent to us so young."

She didn't reply. From the way he looked at those eaglets, Ella knew that the eaglets' age had nothing to do with his awe.

"Their parents were shot when they were only chicks, so the rehab center in Florida removed the nestlings and raised them till they could stand and tear their own food. Both parents care for their young, did you know that? They're amazingly good parents and move about the nest with their talons balled into fists so they don't accidentally skewer their young."

"What will you do with them?"

"We'll put these eaglets into the hack box in a few weeks, when they're old enough to fledge."

"A hack box?"

"Haven't you seen it? That's that box high on the tower over on the other side of the pond, back in all those trees. It has iron bars on the front of it so they can see the outdoors but they can't get out and they're protected from predators. It'll be like living in a nest up there. Gives them a bird's-eye view of what's to come, you might say. Then, after they start to call it home, we'll remove the bars and they'll be free to try their wings and get the hang of hunting. It's a sweet moment to watch an eagle take its first flight."

"I hope I'll be able to see it."

He turned and smiled with such brilliance that she felt singled out for the gift. It was no wonder so many people were devoted to him.

"I'll make certain you do," he said.

She backed away toward the next med enclosure. "All the courtship songs I've been listening to outside my window must have been fruitful," she said, looking between the slats. "The orphans have been coming into the clinic in droves. The med pens are like a nursery!"

"It gets like this in the spring. It'll keep us busy."

He'd said *us* and she liked the feeling that she was included.

Ella strolled from pen to pen, checking on her patients. It brought her back to the nights she would check on all her patients at the end or the beginning of a nursing shift at the hospital. Her patients were *birds* now, she thought with both humor and amazement that fate would bring her down this road of destiny. This was, she knew, a step in her healing.

She walked first to Med 1 to check on those two silly vulture orphans. There was something about them that made her smile every time she saw them. They were getting bigger by the minute and were loaded with personality. Though they were inseparable, lately they'd commenced squabbling between them, just like two-year-old kids. If one had a bit of food, then the other one wanted it. In the past few weeks their soft gray down had given way to sleek black flight and contour feathers and they'd grown to almost their full height. But they were still kids. The two adult vultures were perched on the highest ledge, probably as far away from the young ones as they could get. The orphans were housed in the kennel on the ground. Peeking inside, she saw them sleeping, one's head resting upon the other's flank.

As the sun lowered, the diurnal birds were settling down and the nocturnal birds were just getting frisky. There was a commotion and vocalizing coming from Med 2. She peeked in. There was a gang of owls lined up on the back perch, as far from the humans as possible, with their throats bobbing and their large yellow eyes staring back.

Ella looked over her shoulder and said, "Do you realize we're up to eight great horned owl orphans in here? Look at them. They're wide awake and ready to party."

"And they keep coming," he said, walking to her side. "People have been bringing them in from everywhere. They find them on the ground where the nestlings probably fell from their nest and, meaning well, they drop them off at their local veterinarian. Problem is, they don't leave a name, address or phone number. So we don't know where the orphans came from and we don't have anyone to call to ask. It's frustrating because nine times out of ten the orphan is still in good shape. Young owls hop around their nest and from branch to branch to test their wings when they get a bit older. Naturally, some of them fall. I'd have preferred to put these owls right back in their nests where they belong."

"What about this guy?" she asked, moving over to Med 4. Inside, with two adult barn owls, was an orphan that had arrived in early March looking like a big dandelion puff with a heart-shaped face and enormous eyes.

"I don't know about him. The X-ray I did this afternoon showed a huge callused area around the fracture. And that wing droop hints at some possible nerve damage. It doesn't look good."

The owl really was adorable with the final puffs of down on the head and neck, the last vestiges that revealed he was as yet a hatch-year owl. Otherwise she would've mistaken him for an adult. It was hard to accept that this beautiful bird would have to be put down if he couldn't be completely healed.

"I hope he makes it," she said, looking into its fathomless eyes. "Speaking of which…how is Santee?"

Harris frowned and walked over to Med 3. Ella followed close behind to visit their star patient. Everyone loved this eagle. She was a regal bird, large and powerful yet well mannered. She deigned to tolerate their presence—as long as they kept a distance. Except for Lijah, of course. Harris had agreed that only Lijah would feed her, clean her pen and bring her in for treatment. Ella looked at the eagle with a nurse's eye and saw the drooping of the wings and the way she preferred to stand directly under the heat lamp. She clearly wasn't well.

"She's having a hard time. Unfortunately she contracted aspergillosis, a respiratory disease common in raptors. I put her on an antifungal, gave her some fluids and put her in the nebulizer box for some vapor to help those lungs. The heat lamp will help, too, especially with all the rain we're getting this week." He slipped inside the pen and turned off the heat lamp for the night to avoid the risk of fire. Santee watched every move he made but did not stir from her perch. When he came back out to the hall again, he studied the eagle for a few moments longer with concern etched on his face.

"We'll keep her dry and her bedding clean," he said. "There's not much more we can do."

"How is Lijah taking this? I haven't seen him today."

"He took it pretty hard. You should have seen his face. His chin was dragging on the ground all morning. You know, usually we hear wheezing before we catch this thing, but he just knew something was wrong."

He wiped his face with his palm, pausing to squeeze the bridge of his nose.

"You look exhausted," she said, her voice rich with sympathy.

"I *am* pretty tired," he replied, dropping his hand. He looked at her then, his eyes traveling across her face. "No more than you. You're working as many hours as I am. Maybe more." His expression changed and his eyes lit up.

"What?" she asked him suspiciously, sensing something more coming.

"I was thinking… Actually, someone pointed out to me recently that we could use some time off. What do you think?"

She leaned a shoulder against the wood frame of the pen and smiled skeptically. "Yes, I suppose a day off would be nice. We never really discussed days off or vacation time in my job description, you know."

"No, and clearly I've been taking advantage."

"Yes," she replied with a straight face. "Yes, you have. I've been meaning to report a complaint. I'm sure there's a nanny union out there somewhere."

He tucked his fingertips in his pockets. Suddenly, she felt the air charge between them.

"I was looking at the schedule and tomorrow is going to be very light. And Maggie will be here all day. It's a good idea to grab the good days when they come."

"Makes sense."

"Supposed to be a nice day, too. The rain's stopped."

"Thank heavens."

He cleared his throat. She held her breath.

"Do you want to go fishing?"

She released her breath in a puff. Fishing? She'd expected him to ask her to a movie or out to dinner. Was fishing a date, or just an act of kindness, like the roses? She didn't want to fall into that trap again. The light was fading fast, and against his tan, the blue of his eyes seemed backlit by the bright white. She looked at her sleeve to pick off some dander, telling herself for the hundredth time that they were just friends. Friends could go fishing. That's what friends did.

"Sounds like fun," she replied with hesitation.

"Great. I have a favorite fishing hole." He grinned self-consciously. "I reckon every fisherman has his favorite spot, but this one's mine. It's out in the creek along the sand flats and there are holes there for mullet and holes for shrimp. We're going for mullet. You'll love the spot. You'll feel like you're a million miles from the rest of the world. There's nothing more relaxing than sitting on a dock with your toes dangling in the water just waiting for the fish to jump." He looked at her and his eyes glowed. "I'd like to take you there, Ella."

Their eyes met and she felt a sudden shyness. She tucked a tendril behind her ear. "I'd better get back to Marion," she said, moving her hand to indicate departure with her thumb. "She'll be looking for me. Just let me know when you want to go…"

She hurried out like a convict making good an escape. Each step toward the house she scolded herself for letting her imagination get the best of her and kept repeating, friends… friends…friends…

And yet, something in the spark in his eyes when she'd agreed to go made her suspect—and, God help her, hope— that this might lead to something more.

Vision. *"Eagle vision" or "eyes like a hawk" are human expressions, but they refer to the highly developed visual capacities of raptors. They have binocular vision: the ability to focus both eyes on an object at the same time. Birds of prey can scan the ground or water from hundreds and sometimes thousands of feet in the air, pinpointing their target with the precision of a bombsight.*

14

HARRIS AND ELLA BEGAN WALKING DOWN THE gravel road with fishing poles and gear in their hands. Ella was keenly aware of several pairs of eyes watching them as they left.

Earlier that morning, Marion had asked a litany of questions about where she and her daddy were going, why she couldn't come along, and whether this was a real date. Maggie, who had agreed to baby-sit Marion for the few hours they'd be gone, was curiously silent. Her lack of enthusiasm spoke volumes and Ella vowed to talk to her about it later. When they'd left the house, Lijah stood by his cabin, smoking his pipe and watching them walk off with a faint smile on his face. Even the volunteers hawked them as they went about their chores.

"What in heaven's name did you tell them we were doing

today?" she asked Harris as they passed by the compound. She reached up to self-consciously smooth back her hair.

"Oh, nothing much. Just that we were eloping."

She laughed and playfully socked his arm. "You'd think we *were*. For heaven's sake, we're just going fishing."

"I guess they need to get out more. I don't know," he said, dismissing them. He turned his head and his smile was playful. "Let's not worry about them or what they're thinking, Ella. Let's just let today be for us."

That silenced her. Her heart was beating a rhythm of its own as she matched his long-legged strides down the gravel road.

The nesting season was well underway in the Carolinas. The wintering raptors—eagles, owls, ospreys—were already in residence and rearing their young. Now the stage was set to welcome the songbirds and other summertime residents. Early migrants were out claiming territories while grasses and twigs were being piled in nests and boxes. The trees were alive with their chattering.

When they reached the fork in the road, Harris led her to the right along a grassy truck path that led toward the creek. The farther they marched toward the water, the scrubbier and denser the terrain became. Her booted feet caught in the thick thatches of smilax and jasmine that nearly obscured the path, but he was quick to reach out and steady her.

The landscape wasn't as cragged and mountainous as her home state, Vermont. Nor as vivid a green. But the longer she lived here, the more she realized she couldn't keep comparing the two. It was apples and oranges. The beauty of the Lowcountry was seductive, more sultry than majestic. There were mysteries teeming in the winding creeks and rivers. They snaked through vast greening marshes that breathed in and out with the tidal current like a living creature. It was a land of myths and tall tales told by old men and young boys on docks, aboard boats and around dinner tables throughout the region.

They made their way through the dense woods and clinging vegetation to where the sky suddenly opened up and a breeze whisked her hair, pungent and cool. She lifted her chin and breathed deeply of moist air that spread through her veins like an elixir. Harris stopped to raise his arm and point.

"That's my creek," he said, pointing to a quick-flowing creek that wound its way through the green cord grass and around ancient, gnarled live oaks, some more than a dozen feet around. His gaze shone with pride of possession. "Not that I own the creek, of course," he said. "More like it owns me."

"It's a beautiful view. How long ago did you buy this land?"

"Oh, about twelve or thirteen years ago, back when I was still working for the state. I worked in the Francis Marion forest next door, so when this place came on the market, I came right over to check it out. Hurricane Hugo had just come ripping through here, tearing up houses and trees and sending all the Spanish moss north. Land was cheap then, so I jumped. It's a good thing, too. Couldn't afford to buy a parcel of land here these days. Hugo hit the Awendaw and Georgetown areas real hard. Including the birds. That's what was real eerie. After the hurricane passed, we'd come into the forest and it'd be real quiet. Unnatural. Some birds left before the hurricane came. Thank God for instincts. But a lot got caught and died, too."

"Is that what got you interested in rehabilitating birds of prey?"

"I was interested in them long before. Since I was a kid,

actually. My grandfather loved hawks. Taught me how to spot them in the sky. He passed that love on to my mother and she passed it on to me. It's in the genes, I reckon. Though Mama loved all kinds of birds, not just raptors. We had this list she posted in the kitchen. Every time we spotted a new bird, we had to add it to the list. I guess she was the first one to teach me about categorizing. She tried to help birds that were sick or wounded around the farm, too. Nothing elaborate. She just did what she could. That's when I began the dream to start a rehab center. I knew we could do better." He shrugged. "Years later, I did what I could on a bird-by-bird basis. Gradually got a license, some backers…it was pretty rough. It just took a while for the pieces to come together. Life is like that sometimes."

He grasped her hand and flashed a smile. "Come on, Ella. The fish are jumping."

As his large hand wrapped around her smaller one, she felt as though the pieces of her life were coming together, too.

He brought her along the sand-and-mud path to the old dock that was here when he'd bought the place and had somehow survived Hurricane Hugo—though just barely. It stretched out a long way into the creek.

Ella balked at the edge. "It looks pretty rickety. Are you sure it will hold us?"

"Well it *is* old and worm-eaten, and it *has* seen better days, to be sure. But I think it's sound enough to carry the weight of a man and a little thing like you. Leastwise, I hope it is."

"Harris…"

"Come on, scaredy-cat."

They took off their shoes and started to laugh spontaneously, as though they were kids again with toes wiggling, free of constraints. Their spirits shot skyward as they walked to the end of the dock, feeling the scratchy wood on their soles.

Standing at the end of the dock, he set his hands on his hips and took deep breaths. The sharp and pungent air filled his lungs and nose.

"Mmm…smell that? Nothin' else like it in the world. That there's pure, unadulterated pluff mud. My spring tonic. A good whiff of that does wonders for the soul," he said in a grand manner. He cast a sidelong glance over at Ella.

She sniffed, then crinkled her nose in response. "I guess it takes a little getting used to."

She seemed a little lost standing at the edge of the dock with her hands behind her back, staring past her toes at the murky waters below. He had to admit it was a heady thing to see the always efficient and competent Ella Elizabeth Majors out of her element. Did she think this place was as special as he did? he wondered. Then wondered why it mattered so much that she did.

"You ever catch mullet?" he asked her.

"Catch it? The only mullet I've ever heard of is a particular hairstyle some men wear—God love them."

"Mullet is a fine fish, the true taste of the Lowcountry," he said, bending to move the bag of supplies closer to the edge of the dock. "Though some folks might just call it low class. They catch it only for bait. Ask any country boy, though, and he'll tell you that when you take a bite of the mullet's moist flesh, you can taste a little bit of the muddy creek it came from. You won't find it in a store, though. Nope. You have to catch it yourself and eat it fresh. Folks around here have been doing just that for a long, long time. I learned how to catch mullet from my father when I was a boy."

He opened the canvas bag, then said in a lower mutter, "About the only thing he ever taught me."

Ella looked back at him, perplexed, and he was relieved when she only asked, "Can I do something to help?"

"As a matter of fact, you can." He bent over the canvas bag of supplies and pulled out some corks, a spool of line, a bag of hooks and a Ziploc bag filled with what looked like soggy bread. This he handed to her. "Your job is to chum the waters. It'll attract the mullet to the bait."

Ella opened the bag, then gagged and held the bag at arm's length. "Oh, whew! This smells awful! What is this stuff?"

"Mash for bait. It's mostly bread, with a few other secret ingredients tossed in that fish find irresistible. It might stink to you, but mullet think it smells like French perfume. Now, the trick is not to put a lot in all at once. You want to spread out just enough to lure them in close, but not too much that they eat their fill and skip the bait."

"Right. Thanks for clearing that up."

"Just use your best guess. I'm going to set up the poles."

If he'd known how much fun it was going to be to watch Ella wrinkle up her nose, pick up small bits of the smelly bait mash with two fingers, then hold her arm out over the creek to drop chunks into the water, he'd have brought her here a lot earlier. Still, he thought, his eyes kindling as the bait fell into the water with graceless plops, she was a good sport about it. She went ahead and did it without complaint. He didn't know a lot of women who'd do that.

"Is that enough?" she asked, eyes pleading.

"Looks good. Here's your pole," he said, handing her a stiff cane pole with a light line attached.

She looked at it blankly. "Thanks. So... I just put the hook into the water and wait for them to bite?"

"Ella, this is a time-honored sport! Most people use a cast net. Catching mullet with a hook and line is as much luck as anything else, as far as I can tell. A good mullet fisherman makes it looks easy. Ha! Don't you believe it. These ol' fish have a real soft bite. When you see the cork wiggle, you'll want to hook it and haul it, real quick."

"I haven't the faintest idea what you're talking about," she said with a giggle.

He shook his head ruefully. "Didn't they teach you anything useful in all those schools you went to?" He sat down on the edge of the pier, patting the wood at his side. Ella took the cue and settled in beside him. "It's easy. Just drop your line in," he said with a drawl. "Then let me know if you see your cork bob."

"See the cork bob," she repeated. "Got it."

She was laughing and he chuckled, too, feeling the spring sun begin to soften his bones.

They sat on the edge of the pier, legs dangling in the cool water, and held on to their fishing poles. As the sun rose higher in the sky, they shed their jackets and rolled up their sleeves, leaning far back on their elbows. Soon, they forgot about their poles dangling in the water.

"This sure is a beauty spot, as we'd say in Vermont," she said, showing her face to the sun.

"Yep. Shore is, as we say in South Carolina." He grinned at her in a teasing manner. "I grew up on a creek not too different from this one, down in the ACE basin. Maybe that's why the minute I saw this creek, I knew it would suit."

"Look at those egrets clustered in that gnarly old oak across the water. There are one…two…four…six of them. Amazing. They're so beautiful."

"You'll see a lot of birds out here. Egrets, ibis, herons, and there are osprey nests, too. I've put a few orphans in that one right over there."

"Where's the nest?" she asked, squinting.

"Right over there, along that hammock. Look up in the branches of the dead tree."

She sat up and followed the projection of his outstretched hand. "Oh, yes. I see it now. It's sure a scrappy-looking thing, isn't it? And big."

"Ospreys are pretty creative when it comes to nest building. It's a big pile of sticks, grass and about anything they can scrounge up. I've seen nests with foam cups, plastic food containers, twine, pretty ribbon, even a bicycle tire, though I'd liked to have seen the osprey get that up there. Even saw a Barbie doll in one." His eyes sparked with humor. "I guess I'll have to tell Marion to be careful where she leaves Gaudy Lulu, else we'll be seeing it up in that nest over there."

"I'm not sure that'd be such a terrible thing," Ella said with a laugh.

"Nope," he conceded. "They like things that are shiny. I'm sure they'd love that sparkly dress."

They laughed again.

"Once they build their nest, ospreys are site loyal. Like eagles. They'll keep coming back to the same nest year after year. They're monogamous, too. I respect that."

"Which? That they're site loyal or monogamous?"

"Both. It's not like they've taken vows to stay together forever and ever." He looked off at the nest and his eyes narrowed. "Not that vows keep couples together, anyway."

Ella turned her gaze from the nest to peer into his face at that comment, and he immediately regretted the slip.

"What they have is a strong instinct for where they're from and where they'll stay. A commitment to the nest is a commitment to each other."

"That's quite romantic, when you think about it."

He chortled. "Don't let a biologist hear you say that."

"So, this land is your nest, so to speak?"

"You could say that. Though it won't be for long if I can't make a go of the center." He lifted his shoulders as if to say, Who knows what the future will bring?

"That's true for all of us," she said.

"Even the ospreys. Sometimes they return to their nest in the spring to find an owl has already taken up residence in it. No matter how they fuss, they'll never oust the owl."

"What do they do then?"

"They move on. Build another. The ol' biological imperative."

"Fannie lived here with you, didn't she?"

His face grew shuttered at the sudden change of subject and he answered warily, "For a while."

"Maggie tells me that she used to help you with the birds."

He sighed, knowing he couldn't avoid talking to her about his wife. He'd have to sooner or later, anyway, if he was to be honest and fair with Ella.

"I've known Fannie since she was a young girl. Between my mother and me, she grew up around birds and raptors. So helping me with them came easily."

"Does Marion look like her?"

His eyes glazed as he searched back through the years for the image. "She has her looks, but Fannie's beauty was... stunning."

Ella felt a sting of jealousy for the woman she'd never met but whose memory was her rival. She knew that she was not a beautiful woman. Not even pretty. The most people could say about her own looks was that she was pleasant-looking— a far cry from stunning.

Harris ran his hand through his hair and blew out a long stream of air. "Fannie," he said again, and she couldn't tell whether his tone was resigned or troubled.

Ella waited, unaware that she was leaning forward, holding her breath.

"She was about ten years younger than me. I thought of her as a little sister at first. She lived down the road with her mama and her so-called family. They were pretty messed up. Her mother had a lot of men Fannie called uncle come through. They'd stay for a while, then rob her or beat her—sometimes both—before they'd leave. It was a pretty sad situation. Anyway, Fannie just showed up at our house one day. She couldn't have been more than eleven." He paused and his gaze turned inward, back to those days along the Edisto.

"I'll never forget the way she looked the first time I saw her. All long, thin legs and big eyes that held way too much sadness and experience for a kid so young. She came looking for odd jobs, and she ended up staying at our house more than her own. So when I started working full-time, I hired her to keep an eye on Mama. She cooked her food, brushed her hair, that kind of thing. She wasn't that great a cook and never cleaned the house, but she was great with my mother. Sometimes she'd read to her, sometimes they'd just talk. I'd come home and hear them giggling away. My mother adored Fannie. They were a lot alike. Both beautiful and funny. But needy. I didn't know that about Fannie at the time, of course."

He pursed his lips in thought and she urged him in her heart to go on.

"We spent a lot of time together growing up," he continued at length. "When my mother died…it just seemed right that we get married."

Ella had to struggle to keep the surprise from her face. Did he love Fannie or just feel sorry for her? she wondered. The question lingered on her lips, but she didn't dare voice it.

"What was wrong with your mother?" she asked instead.

He shook his head, then glanced off at the fishing pole. "She was a diabetic."

Ella sucked in her breath. "You didn't tell me that. Harris, you know the genetic link to Marion."

He nodded his head. "She was also an alcoholic."

"Good Lord, that's a bad combination. So, that's what killed her."

"No. That was only the means. My father killed her when he left her, years before she ever touched a drop. In fact, she used to say she didn't like the taste of alcohol. But after my father just up and left, well…" His expression turned cold. "She must have taken a sudden liking to it."

"Why did he leave?"

"Because he was an asshole," he said bitterly. "Why does any man up and leave his family?"

"There's usually a reason," she said softly.

"If there was a reason, I'd guess it was money. Nothing original there. He was a tomato farmer, like his father before him. For a while the business was really good and he made a lot of money. But when the bottom fell out of the market and the farm went belly-up, I guess he couldn't stand the pressure. So when the going got tough, rather than see it through, he just went out one night and never came back. No letter, no phone call, no nothing."

"I'm sorry."

"Don't be sorry for me. She's the one to feel sorry for. She used to sit by the window and wait for him, night after night. Left the porch light on for that worthless son of a bitch." He shook his head. "It was pitiful. Once she finally accepted the fact that he wasn't going to walk through that door, only Johnny Walker could comfort her. Not that I didn't try."

"How did you get along? You were just a boy."

"Mama had to sell off the land, bit by bit, to make ends

meet. We didn't need much and we knew how to make a dollar go a long way. And her drinking wasn't constant. At the beginning, she could go through long periods without touching a drink. Those were the good days. I can remember being so happy coming home to the scent of a meal cooking and seeing the house all picked up instead of a mess. Each time I used to pray it would last. Every damn time. Then, just when I was getting hopeful, all of a sudden something would send her spiraling and she'd go on another binge. I did the best I could to take care of her during those periods. I'd fix her something to eat before I left for school and make us dinner when I came home."

"She was negligent. They should have taken you away."

"She was my mother, Ella. I loved her. I was all she had."

Ella tightened her lips against the familiar raging in her heart. She'd dealt with so many negligent mothers in her career, face-to-face in the hospital as she struggled to patch up the bruises or illnesses of their children in the emergency room. In her mind she saw Bobby's mother again, the tracks on her arm, the way she sauntered out of the emergency room after dumping her son there. She looked at Harris and felt for the boy who had endured so much.

"Sometimes love isn't enough. The child's needs are more important than the mother's."

"I did fine," he said, rejecting her pity. "*She* was the one that needed help. She was the diabetic."

"Then she was slowly killing herself. She had to have known that."

"I don't know that she cared."

"Didn't she care about *you?*"

"Of course she did," he said, his tone defensive. "You're only hearing the bad about her. She was a lovely woman.

Gentle and smart. It's not her fault she was born with two horrible diseases that took control of her life."

"But, Harris, she allowed the diseases to take control. She could have tried to stop the drinking and get her life back. To be a better mother to her child."

"You don't know, Ella!" he fired back. "You weren't there when he walked out. You didn't see her face. It killed her. He took the best part of her with him."

"You're right," she said calmly. "I didn't know her. But I knew a lot of women like her. Though their stories may be different, the ending is always the same. The children suffer. You suffered, Harris." She reached out to place her hand on his shoulder. He flinched beneath her palm so she quickly took it away.

"We got along okay," Harris replied.

Ella heard Bobby's voice in her mind. *Don't be mad at her, Ella.* She backed off, not because she agreed with Harris, but because she didn't want to alienate him the first time he opened up to her. Her heart bled for the childhood he must have endured with parents like that. But she couldn't feel a lot of pity for his mother. What never failed to amaze her was how the child always forgave the mother, no matter how severe and how obvious the neglect.

From across the water came the high, shrill cry of an osprey. They both looked over toward the nest. The male was perched on a branch higher than the nest, a sleek, gleaming fish in its talons. He looked like a bandit with the black eye band as he tore at the fish with savage pokes of his beak. The female stayed at the nest, watching him eat until she could stand it no longer and cried out again her complaining whistle. At last the male finished his meal and brought the remainder of the fish to the nest for her to eat.

"He's a good provider," Harris said of the osprey, approval ringing in his voice.

Ella looked at him as he watched the male fly off to hunt again and thought to herself that to understand the osprey was to understand Harris. Site loyal. A good provider. But what about monogamous? He'd divorced Fannie, which didn't fit the pattern.

"What happened to Fannie?" she asked, knowing she should let the subject drop, but unable to. "I heard she had an addiction of her own. Is that why she left?"

He laughed shortly and it was filled with bitterness. "I seem to have a history of addicted women, don't I?"

"No," she said, gently. "More a history of taking care of dependent women. It's no wonder your mother and Fannie got along. They were birds of a feather. I'll bet Fannie let your mother drink while she took care of her."

Harris blanched. "There was no stopping her when she wanted to drink."

"If she didn't leave the house, how did she get the alcohol?"

"Alcoholics are very resourceful. If you don't know that, then you don't know the first thing about what it's like living with one. Deliveries, friends, a few dollars greasing palms… Yeah, Fannie too, I'm sure. I used to pour the stuff down the sink, but it got to the point it didn't matter where she got it from. She always got it."

"You let her get it."

"What?" He was stunned by the comment. And angry.

Ella didn't back down this time. "You were the one in charge, Harris. At some level, you allowed the drinking to continue. That's called enabling."

"I know what that is," he fired back. "I'm not an idiot. And you don't know what the hell you're talking about."

"I think I do," she persisted. She was seeing the painful pattern of denial unfold, and though it was clear to her, she doubted Harris could see any of it. Without resolution it would remain embedded in the family and move on to afflict Marion as surely as the diabetes had.

"You can fire me for this, Harris, but I've got to say it. Marion might have your mother's disease, but she's not your mother. She's not Fannie, either. Don't hold back your affection from her. She's not going to hurt you. Marion has so much love to give you, if you'll just give her the chance."

"I'm not afraid that she's like my mother, or even Fannie!" His face was distorted with pain. He pinched his lips and looked off across the creek. When he spoke again, his voice lowered. "I'm afraid she's going to die. That I'm going to lose her, too. And it will be my fault."

Ella held her breath as, suddenly, she understood it all. He'd told her this, many times, but she didn't hear him. He was afraid that he'd somehow slip again and she'd die—because of him.

She put her hand on his, and this time, he didn't flinch or pull it away. "I understand that kind of fear. Really I do. Do you remember I told you about Bobby? I was afraid to take this job. Terrified to handle another case of diabetes. But I knew if I didn't, I'd never reconcile his death and I'd spend my life crippled with wondering what I might have done. How I might have changed things that night, if only... You don't know how I was tortured by those two words. *If only*." She paused. "I probably always will be.

"But I have another chance with Marion. So do you. I can't tell you that Marion won't get into trouble again, no matter how hard both of us try. With juvenile diabetes, serious complications are a reality. We have treatments, but not a cure. But we can take care of her, every day. The better care she has, the better her chance of avoiding the problems. She's a wonderful, vibrant, healthy child."

Harris closed his eyes. He didn't want to see the light shining in Ella's eyes. It was like too much sun on already tender skin. She'd been so damned determined to get the truth out, digging deeper and deeper. He'd be mad except he must've wanted to get to the truth himself, because he didn't stop her. He hadn't always distanced himself from Marion. They'd been close before the illness. After all, it had been just the two of them. If he looked at himself honestly he could see that Ella was right. His attitude had changed since the diabetes. His fear kept pushing her away.

When he opened his eyes he saw a gleam of silver flash at the surface, like dozens of torpedoes.

"Mullet!" he exclaimed, sitting bolt upright.

"What?" She jerked her head around.

He leapt to his feet, going for the net. "Quick! They're coming for the bait."

"But my cork isn't bobbing!"

The water rippled with the motion of countless mullet, a few jumping clear from the water. Ella climbed to her feet, holding tight to her pole. The fish ignored her hook and swarmed instead for the mash that was fast disappearing.

"Stand back," Harris called out, and with one fluid motion he tossed the net upon the bubbling water. Its edges flirted with the air, hung in the sky, then dropped into the teeming water. "Okay, we've got some!" he called, and tugged the net, dragging it in close to the pier. The captured fish struggled, his muscles strained and the net heaved as it broke the water. Ella grabbed hold of the net and together they hauled up the fish.

"How many are in there?" she asked, breathless.

He dragged the pulsing net farther down the pier, calling out, "Lots. Grab the bucket, Ella!"

Inside the net were at least ten mullet, each a foot to a foot and a half long. Each flipping hard on the pier. He scooped them up one by one and plopped them in the bucket.

"Harris!" Ella called, running back to the end of the pier. "My pole! It's moving!"

"Hook the fish, Ella," he called back at her, bent over the net, laughing. "Go on, you can do it! Just give it a yank, not too hard. Then pull that baby out of the water."

He paused to watch Ella holding tight to her pole, her cheeks red from the sun and wisps of hair flying. Her face was the very picture of determination. He knew he'd keep this image tucked away in his memory.

The pole bent near to the water before she tugged, firm and sure, bringing the pole far back. Out from the water came a glistening silver mullet, sailing through the air in one smooth motion. It landed on the pier with a thump.

"I got one!" she exclaimed disbelievingly, running with her arms outstretched to catch the mullet before it leapt back into the water. "And it's the biggest one!"

Harris chuckled as he brought over the bucket. "That's what they all say. It's a funny thing about fish. They seem to grow with each telling."

She laughed loudly then, happy. Happier than she'd been in a long time. The tension between them was over, and like a storm that rages then passes, the air in the aftermath seemed clearer and fresher than before.

Harris brought the fish to the shore and bled them by cutting the gills. Then he taught her how to scale them, giving Ella her first lesson in the law of the creek: You catch 'em, you clean 'em.

When they finished, they put the mullet on ice in the

cooler, rinsed their hands in the creek and then, reeking of fish and pluff mud, began their trek back to the house. Before leaving, Ella took a final backward glance at the creek.

Waiting for the truth to surface was a lot like waiting for the mullet, she thought. You have to chum the waters a bit, bait the hook, then sit back and wait for what comes up from the muddy bottom. And when it comes, it comes fast and unexpected, splashing to the surface.

Falcons: The Ultimate Flying Machines. Falcons have long, pointed wings and long tails for great maneuverability and are distinguished by a "mustache" under the eye. Falcons are the world's fastest animals. Every detail of their anatomy is built for speed. Large falcons dive at intense speed to deliver lethal midair blows to prey. Falcons include peregrine falcons, merlins and American kestrels.

15

THE SUN DID ITS WORK AND DRIED THE FIELDS, and the cooperative spring winds sent the clouds out to sea. It was a brilliantly lush afternoon when Lijah came up to Brady as he was trimming the hedge along the mews and tapped him on the shoulder.

"Come along, son," he said.

Brady set down the clippers eagerly because he'd learned that whenever Lijah had something he wanted him to see, it was worth taking notice. He followed Lijah to the large open field adjacent to the birds of prey center. Maggie and Harris were standing in the center beside some A-frame perches. Immediately, Brady spotted the sleek gray falcon, PEFA 14, that sat rooted to Harris's glove. Harris coiled a thin leather leash around his fingers and hand.

Lijah led Brady to the shade of a greening oak to watch.

He looked at Brady and nodded his head, as if to say, Now you're going to see something! Brady took a breath to tamp down his excitement and leaned against the tree. He was curious, sure, but at the same time resentful of anything Harris Henderson did. Harris had been riding him hard lately, giving him more and more different stuff to do, then checking up on him right after. It seemed every time he turned around, that guy was breathing down his neck.

He snorted with teenage insolence when he saw Harris walk across the field with the falcon. It was obvious to anyone watching that Harris cut a strong figure. Tall and erect, he held the bird with competence and confidence. Despite himself, Brady felt a stirring of admiration for that kind of mastery. It seemed to him that the falcon was an extension of the man's arm.

Harris walked toward the tall A-framed perch in the center of the field, oblivious to his audience. He attached the line to PEFA 14, then extended his arm to the perch. The falcon promptly stepped up onto the perch. Immediately, it turned to face Harris and the wind. Man and bird studied each other for a moment, as though reaching some kind of an understanding. Then Harris turned and walked several yards away to where a canvas bag lay on the ground. He stood with his back to the bird.

In the meantime, Maggie moved forward to face PEFA 14, effectively blocking the bird's view of Harris. She checked the slack between the spool of line and the jesses. The falcon shifted its weight, then stretched its pointy wings, eager to be off.

Harris would not be rushed. He took his time removing the dummy rubber lure out of the bag and affixing chunks of meat securely to it. Next he held out his arms to measure the length of line he needed, then tested it to make certain it ran through his hand as if on a pulley. When all was ready, he stretched out his arm and took a few practice swings of the lure, twirling it around, getting the feel of it.

All this time, Maggie stood in front of the young, eager falcon, obscuring its view. After a few swings, Harris pulled the lure line back in, then called out to Maggie that it was okay to step back.

"Here we go," Lijah said under his breath.

Brady tightened his arms around himself, surprised at how eager he was to see what would happen next.

For a moment Harris stood facing the falcon, lure in hand. The bird was poised and alert. Brady could feel the excitement in the air from fifty feet away. A slight wind gusted, ruffling the feathers around the head of the falcon.

Harris straightened and called out a hearty "Ho!" in two notes.

Simultaneously, he shot out the lure and began swinging it in wide, smooth circles in the air.

Instantly, the falcon took to the air with Maggie running right beneath it. Brady dropped his arms and straightened in anticipation as he watched the falcon fly with amazing speed straight for the lure. He's going to get it, he thought, holding his breath.

He did. Both of the falcon's feet came forward and the talons snatched the lure smack over Harris's head with a savage swiftness. Once caught, the falcon brought the lure to the ground where it wasted no time devouring the bites of meat. Harris allowed the bird to finish the reward, then stepped forward to place his hand over the lure. Immediately, the falcon stepped up onto the fist.

Brady watched the training with growing awe. It was sort of like hunting, only different. He didn't move as Harris repeated the process, each time allowing the falcon to catch the lure in the air and bring it down. After several successful catches, the bird was allowed to sit relaxed on Harris's fist with a full crop.

"What you think?" Lijah asked him.

Brady's eyes betrayed his excitement before he automatically shuttered his enthusiasm and hunched like a halfback. "It was okay," he said with a noncommittal shrug. "Don't seem so hard."

"Huh," Lijah grunted. "I thought maybe you'd like it."

"I do. But, shoot, I bet I could do that."

Lijah eyed him speculatively. "Think so, eh?"

"Sure. You swing around a toy with food in it. The bird goes for the food. That's just Pavlov's dog. Harris keeps doing it over and over. How hard can it be?"

"You think it's like a game, do you?" He drew his shoulders back. "Well, if that's how you think, then you ain't know the first thing about birds of prey." Lijah harrumphed and turned away.

Brady bristled and rammed his hands into his pockets. He'd been working with Lijah for months now, learning a lot about the birds from the old man. Things like the names of raptors, their habits, diet, personalities, stuff like that. But he was also learning how to approach them with respect and not make them jumpy. He and Clarice had teamed up, which was a big deal since Harris hadn't wanted him near the birds. It was Lijah who went to Ella and Harris about that, putting himself on the line. That meant a lot to Brady. There weren't many who'd do that for him. So to have Lijah dismiss him like that really hurt deep under his skin.

After Harris returned the falcon to the mews, Maggie brought out a larger falcon. This bird wasn't wearing a hood and looked around the surrounding area as if it owned the place. Brady sensed the moment the falcon spotted him and Lijah standing across the field.

"That ol' bird don't miss a thing," he said to Lijah, his voice conciliatory.

"They never do."

"How come he's not putting the creance line on this bird?"

"That's Risk. She's been here a long time and knows what to do. That other falcon is just learning what's what. If he didn't have that line, he might fly off." He chortled softly. "They all might fly off, that's for true."

"Oh, yeah? What keeps them from doing it? I mean, freedom is right there to take. Shoot, I would if I were them."

"They *choose* to stay."

When Brady looked back, puzzled, Lijah shook his head. "That's what I mean exactly. Birds of prey ain't the same as the rest of the birds. You can't just train raptors. They ain't like dogs neither. Those animals want to please. Not raptors. They be proud and independent. That being their nature, you can't go demanding obedience from them. Can't do that with a child, neither. All you can do is ask."

Brady listened, feeling the words take root in his heart. At sixteen years old, he'd had enough of people making him jump when they said jump.

"That's why," Lijah concluded, "to work with raptors, you first have to be humble."

"Humble?" he asked, confused.

"That's the truth," Lijah confirmed with a solemn nod. "And that be a hard, hard lesson for a man to learn. With a raptor, you're never the master. You're the student. You have to learn the ways of the hawk. To learn the spirit of the hawk." He raised his hand to indicate Harris and the falcon out on the field. "This time, son, open your eyes and watch what's really going on out yonder. Harris ain't just training that falcon. He working with her. Watching her, so she don't get tired. Watching the sky, so he don't put her in danger. Always watching, 'cause he cares. Now watch out there. They learning to be *partners*."

Lijah looked at Brady for a long moment, as though to make sure the message got through.

"Yeah, okay. I get it," Brady said, meaning it.

Lijah's eyes glowed with satisfaction. He turned his snowy white head again to watch Harris and the falcon. Brady had questions bursting at his lips that he wanted to ask, but he'd been around Lijah long enough to know when it was time to be quiet. So he bided his time and joined Lijah in watching the next exercise, hoping that this time he'd get a better understanding of what it was that stirred his blood so.

In the field, Harris set the gorgeous, sleek feathered falcon on the perch. Risk shook her tail feathers, ringing the affixed bell, then quickly settled into place. Maggie stood close by.

Harris moved into position farther away. This time, however, he didn't begin swirling the lure. Instead, he whistled, high and clear. The falcon spread her wide wings and with a burst of speed, climbed effortlessly to a good pitch in the sky.

Brady raised his face and watched with amazement as the falcon circled two times, a beautiful silhouette against a cerulean sky. Once again, Brady felt his blood race and his heart quicken. It seemed the falcon was waiting on a cue.

Then it came.

"Ho!" called Harris, and simultaneously he shot out the lure.

The falcon circled back and, in a dramatic plunge, shot from the air straight for the lure. The feet came forward, ready for the grab.

But with split-second timing, Harris pulled back the lure

just before the falcon could grab it. He swung it around again, keeping it close to the ground. Risk passed, then caught a lift of air and shot back up into the sky. Harris turned smoothly around, eyes on the falcon, and shot the lure out again. He moved seamlessly, slowly extending the distance of the line, each time allowing Risk to get within inches of the lure before pulling it back again, sometimes bringing the lure close to the ground, sometimes circling it backward over his head. Each time the falcon circled, then stooped, streaking across the sky for the lure. The two shared a dance of incredible skill, daring and speed.

Brady watched, transfixed.

After a few more passes, Harris slowed the swing and Risk caught the lure in her feet, bringing it to the ground.

"Good girl," Harris murmured approvingly as the falcon stepped up to the fist. Harris's exhilaration was evident on his face.

With the session over, Lijah walked directly over to them. Brady lagged behind, watching the two men talk for a while. Lijah must have said something about him because Harris turned his head to search him out, then turned back to Lijah, nodding.

Brady sauntered over to join the men with his heart in his throat. Harris always made him nervous. Probably because he was the boss. But in his heart, he knew it was more than that. There was something unspoken between them, a challenge, that they both felt. Brady didn't know why, but it was there, and they were both trying to deal with it.

Harris looked up as he approached, and Brady caught something different in his gaze this time. Less antagonism. He drew near with apprehension.

"Lijah tells me you were pretty taken with what you saw," Harris said to him.

"Yeah, I liked it okay."

"Interested in learning more about it?"

Brady's face lost its customary passiveness as his eyes brightened. "Sure."

"As you know, we're short on volunteers. Maggie could use some help with the resident birds. They need feeding and their pens need cleaning. But they also need exercise." He paused, considering. "You'd have a lot to learn."

Brady couldn't believe what he was hearing. "Are you asking me if I'd like to work with these birds?"

Harris seemed hesitant. "First off, you'd have to do it on your own time. As a regular volunteer. You'd still be working with Lijah for your community service. Cleaning and maintaining the grounds. That would have to remain the same."

"Sure. Okay, I don't mind."

"You'd have to come in another day. That'd be three times a week."

"Yeah, fine," he said, his enthusiasm ringing in his voice. "I don't care. I would've volunteered already but I didn't think you'd let me."

Harris held back his smile until he swung his head around to look at Lijah. Then he let it blossom across his face. "Well, I guess you were right about this guy."

"Yessir. I'm always right."

Harris laughed and looked again at Brady. "Lijah here seems to think you've got the making of a first-class falconer. Now, *that* is a real compliment. I've been around raptors all my life and I'm of the mind that it's not something that just anyone can learn. Either you're born with the gift, plain and simple—like Lijah here—or you come by it through hours of work and dedication." He looked at Lijah. "And understanding. But in either case, a falconer has to care about other people and animals more than himself."

Brady cast Lijah a questioning glance.

"Second, you've been brought up in the country. You understand the lay of the land. That's important, too."

"I just know that I like being with the birds. I feel comfortable with them. Like I belong."

Harris nodded. "That's a good start."

Brady released a quick grin of relief. "So, can I do it?"

Harris studied him and Brady felt as if his eyes were burning straight through him.

"Yes, I believe you can."

"What's that you're always doing with your hands?" asked Clarice.

Brady looked up from the piece of rope attached to the D ring of his book bag. Even without looking, the fingers of his right hand were still rapidly moving on the rope, tying an elaborate knot. He knew he was showing off, but if it impressed Clarice, that was fine with him.

"I'm practicing my falconer's knot," he said, proud that he could even say that. He'd been working under Harris and Maggie for three weeks and he'd already learned so much. "Harris says I have to be able to do it with one hand. That's because the bird's always sitting on the left fist. Like this," he said, holding up a Coke bottle in his left fist. "Now watch."

He dug into the book bag and pulled out the falconer's glove that was his prized possession. He thought it was a beautiful thing, all cream-colored leather that went halfway to his elbow. He never could have afforded to buy one of his own, but Harris had surprised him by giving him this one and it fit like the proverbial glove should. Just putting it on, he felt like a falconer. Brady moved his right fingers with the smoothness of a magician as he slipped the slim rope through the metal ring, then swiftly formed the classic knot.

"I've got it down pretty good. See?" He showed her a perfect falconer's knot.

"Mmm…mmm, just look at you," she said. "You're as cocky as that rooster over there, aren't you?"

He ducked his head but laughed. "Maybe I am. Me and Buh Rooster are feeling pretty good, aren't we, old friend?"

He turned to look over at the white rooster perched right over the Road Closed sign affixed to the gate of the Coastal Carolina Center for Birds of Prey. The rooster stared back at them, impassive as always.

"See? He agrees with me. He always does, you know."

Brady stretched his legs out and leaned back on his elbows on the old blanket. He sat beside Clarice beneath the old loblolly where they'd spent so many afternoons during the past months. The sun had warmed the Lowcountry to eighty degrees and spring fever was peaking. High school kids all along the southern coast could smell the magnolias blooming and knew summer break was just around the corner.

Lincoln High had closed early that afternoon, so Brady and Clarice thought they'd have lunch together before they headed up the road for their afternoon shift. It was a better idea than it was a reality. The gnats were swarming and the damp ground was beginning to seep through the cotton blanket. Still, it was a balmy day and Brady thought it felt good just to be sitting with the sun shining on his face and Clarice chatting away at his side.

"So, Maggie and Harris are reeling you in to the resident bird section, huh? I thought we'd try and keep you in the clinic."

"Not a chance. I'm really into the flying. It's in my blood. I'm not just saying that, Clarice. I know some ancestor somewhere in my history was a falconer. Had to be. It comes so natural." He looked at her across the blanket. She didn't laugh at him when he said things like that. His mother did, calling him some kind of fool.

"I feel like things are really starting to change for me, you know?"

Clarice smiled at him as she daintily scooped out her strawberry yogurt. "You're changing things for yourself, Brady. I've seen the way you've been hustling at the center. Seems like you're doing everything and you're always there."

"Nah. Only three times a week. Not that I wouldn't go more if I could."

"But you *can't*," she said, more as a scold. "Don't you even be thinking of going more. You've got to study. I've been busting my butt tutoring you and if you don't shine in those SATs tomorrow, you'll have me to answer to, boy."

"You're dreaming if you think I'm gonna do good." When he saw her narrow her eyes, he laughed. He just loved to rile Clarice. It was so easy. "All right, all right," he said. "I'm gonna do fine. Okay? Happy now?"

"I'll be happy when you score over 1100 on those SATs. Anything higher is fine, too. How was your history test yesterday?"

"Pretty good. Got an eighty-two."

"Hey, that's real good! Way to shine."

Her approval sounded sweet in his ears. He'd studied real hard for that test. Had to. If he didn't bring up his average he wouldn't pass the course. Only Clarice knew that he'd changed his mind about going to college. She'd gone with him to the school counselor and he'd found out that there was money there for him if he got his grades up. Even if he didn't get a full scholarship, they figured how he could start at the local community college until he earned enough for room and board.

"Are you ready for the SATs?"

"As ready as I can be."

"You've got to eat a good breakfast, you know. Have some meat for protein, maybe a steak or a hamburger. That'll give you endurance. Then you have a Coke for the caffeine to get you jump-started. The protein will keep your blood sugar levels from falling later in the morning. Works like a charm. It's my secret recipe for success."

"Oh, yeah? I'll tell my mama."

"And you've been doing those flash cards I gave you?"

"Yes," he said with a groan.

"Don't you go groaning at me, Brady Simmons. If you'd been reading a few books the past few years your vocabulary would be better. Like I told you, vocabulary is real important for the English score. You have to—"

He put out his hand and wagged it to make her stop. "Don't worry. I'm handling it."

She closed her mouth and her eyes kindled as she leaned forward. "I know you are, Brady Simmons," she said with sincerity. "You go in there tomorrow and show 'em."

His chest expanded. When she said things like that, he believed he actually could. He swallowed hard and sat up to lean forward, closer to her face. "I wouldn't be trying, if it weren't for you, Clarice."

Her eyes widened slightly, then her brow furrowed in worry as she backed away. "Brady—" she said, a warning in her voice.

She was interrupted by the sound of tires on gravel. Looking up, they saw a rusted pickup truck turning off the highway onto the dirt road.

"Shit," Brady drawled, his stomach dropping to his shoes.

"Who is it?" Clarice's voice was high with tension.

The truck pulled to a stop. A boy Brady's age stuck his head out from the driver's window. His left arm reached up to take off his sunglasses. The good-looking boy had a buzz cut and a chiseled jaw. Manigault Preston. His best friend.

"Well, well, well. What we got here?"

Nate stuck his curly haired red head out the passenger window, his eyes widened with mock exaggeration over raised brows and a smug smile.

Brady slanted a glance at Clarice. She was sitting straight-backed, her hands clasped so tight her knuckles paled.

"Hey, Manny. Nate," he said in a cool tone. "What you doing here?"

"We're about to ask you the same thing," Manny said. "You were 'posed to meet us at SeeWee's. Seems you forgot. *Again.*"

The doors swung open and the two tall, broad-shouldered boys in jeans and T-shirts stepped out, their boots kicking gravel as they landed.

"Yeah, you never have time for us no more," Nate said. He snickered. "Maybe now we see why."

Brady shot to his feet and walked forward to stand in front of them before they reached the gate.

"What's the matter? You ain't gonna introduce us to your gal?" Manny asked.

"Yeah, you got a new girl? Jenny's gonna be interested to learn that."

"Cut it out, you guys. She's just a friend."

"Oh, yeah," they drawled. "Sure she is. Now we see how it is."

"And all this time we thought you was workin' with birds."

They slapped his back and laughed.

"What're you guys talking about?"

"You gettin' some cream in your coffee, huh?" they said, giving him play punches.

"I said cut it out," Brady lashed out as he brushed off their arms.

Manny was bigger than Brady and looked over his shoulder to let his eyes slide over Clarice. "I'm Manny. This here's Nate. What's your name, honey?"

"I'm not your honey," she replied with a voice like ice.

"Oh, a live one."

"Brady, I'm going," she said, gathering her purse.

"Wait," he said, holding his hand out in an arresting gesture. Then to his friends, "Look. We work together at the birds of prey center. We're friends. Got it? Now, go on. Get out of here. You don't belong here."

Manny's smile hardened. "Hear that, Nate? We don't belong here. Now, what I want to know," he said, his anger tingeing the polite words, "is who says we don't belong here. You? Brady, you telling us, your friends, that we don't belong here?"

"Come on, Manny. Cut me some slack."

Clarice rose in a huff. Manny took a step toward her but Brady moved squarely in front of him. Manny's brows rose but Brady stood with his fists balled at his thighs, chin up, staring hard.

"You go on," Brady called to Clarice. "I'll meet you later." He cast a quick glance at Nate, who stood over by the truck, watching him warily. The tension rose between them while Manny and Brady stood toe-to-toe like snorting bulls, glaring at each other.

Clarice clutched her purse tight to her side, pulled up the blanket, then grabbed both their jackets. Tucking them under her arm, she walked quickly over to her car parked on the opposite side of the road. She had to walk close to the boys to reach it, but she kept her chin up, ignoring the stares that bore holes into her back.

When the car door closed and the ignition fired, Brady relaxed his fists and took a few steps back, his eyes still on Manny with a warning. Then he turned on his heel to walk to the gate.

"Look at that dumb-ass rooster, would you?" Manny said with a hoot. "It don't even move when he opens the gate."

"It's too dumb to live," Nate called out.

"Don't you pay them no mind," Brady said under his breath to the rooster as he stood with his hand on the gate, waiting for Clarice's car to pass. She cast him a worried glance as she went by, then drove on up the road. Once she was out of sight, he rolled his shoulders to release the tension cording like a falconer's knot in his neck.

Manny shifted his weight and shook his head in a show of bewilderment. "Now, you tell me what the hell that show was all about?"

Brady took his time closing the gate, aware of the rooster's eyes on him. "What show was that?"

"Shit. That macho act. I don't mind you trying to impress that sweet li'l piece of brown sugar. But you ain't got no call to dis your friends like that."

Brady walked straight to Manny's face and jabbed an index finger in the air. "That's a good and decent girl," Brady ground out. "I won't have you bad-mouthin' her."

Manny's jaw dropped open in feigned shock and he put out his palms. "What?" he said incredulously. He turned to Nate and repeated the gesture.

Nate laughed and shrugged with the timing of a good backup straight man. "What?" he repeated.

Manny's smile dropped. He stuck his hands in his pockets and said in a wounded tone, "What's all this trouble about?"

"You tell me what it's about."

"Some girl? She's nothin'. You and me, we go way back, Brady."

"I know it," Brady said. "You're a Manigault and I'm a Simmons and our families have been here since before the war, and we both been raised to treat a nice girl better than that. She's going to college. To Stanford. In California."

"Really?" Manny replied, impressed. Then with a smirk, "Well, you know why she—"

"Don't say it, 'cause you'll be wrong," Brady interrupted him.

Nate was getting bored over by the truck. "You coming or what?"

"Coming where?" Brady wanted to know.

"We drove all the way here lookin' for our good *friend*," Manny began with a sorry shake of his head. "Thinking for sure you had a good reason for ditching us like you did. Did you forget we was supposed to go hunting tonight?"

"Hunting? Tonight? Man, you know I can't go. I got to work here this afternoon and the SATs are tomorrow."

"Who the hell cares about the damn SATs?"

Brady pursed his lips.

"Come on," Manny whined, dipping his knees. "We got us some beer and some of Nate's mama's homemade jerky and a bunch of us are meetin' up at the Willard place. It'll be great."

"We have to show up at school tomorrow for the test. It's required."

"We'll be there."

The thing was, Brady wanted to go with them. It'd been a long time since he'd hung out with his friends, going fishing or hunting. Or just talking and goofing around, knocking back a few.

"I can't. Not tonight. Next time."

"God*damn,* Brady. What's going on with you? You're not the same no more."

"I got things to do."

That ended it. Brady saw in Manny's face the bitter realization that the things he had to do no longer included them.

Later, when his friends got back in the truck and drove off in a huff, Brady felt an odd loneliness inside, like they were driving off for good this time.

You're not the same no more.

He walked to the gate under the watchful gaze of Buh Rooster and came to a stop before it. The rooster cocked its head, shaking the bright red wattle, studying him with his shiny black eyes.

"You *are* one strange rooster, you know that, don't you?" he said with affection. "You just sit there and watch everything. A regular bump on a log." His smile wavered and he tightened his lips, pained by the confusion swirling inside his chest. "But I wish to God you could talk. Maybe you could tell me just what you're seeing when you look at *me.*"

Courtship. *Birds of prey have elaborate courtship behaviors. Most common are remarkable aerial displays of sky dancing, flutter-gliding and power flying. The male will also deliver food to the female, a symbol of his ability to provide through the long, arduous nesting cycle. Courtship behavior creates a bond between the male and female that concludes in mating. Some raptors, such as eagles and ospreys, form an exclusive bond and mate for life.*

16

THE EARLY MORNING COLORS WERE HAZY IN the soft mist. Harris stepped outdoors and immediately the heat and moisture enveloped him. The scent of spring blossoms was so cloyingly sweet he could almost taste them. The screen door swooshed behind him as he made his way down the wooden steps, still damp from the dawn's dew. As he did his habitual morning walk through the mews, he felt the lassitude of what would be a hot and humid May day seep into his bones.

The smattering of gray clouds in the dawning sky disturbed him. The forecasts had called for a mostly clear day, so he and Ella had planned to release a pair of great horned owls up along the Santee River. Rain could pose a problem.

The grass dampened his boots as he walked. Most of the resident birds were huddled on their perches waiting for the warmth of the sun to dry their wings. He was walking along the bird pens, pondering the road trip, when he heard Marion's voice call out in a seductive tone, "Hi, Crow!"

His step faltered. He turned toward the crow's pen where Little Crow sat perched close to the screening.

"Marion?" he called. No response.

But this was crazy. Marion had gone to Maggie's house to spend the night with Annie. He ran his hand through his hair, wondering if he'd imagined the voice. Unnerved, he began walking away.

He heard her voice again. "Hi, Crow!"

He spun on his heel and stared at Little Crow. This time he was sure he'd heard it. Damn, if that bird wasn't talking—and in Marion's voice!

"Well I'll be—" he muttered as understanding dawned. He hadn't thought it possible when Marion had gone on about how she was teaching Little Crow to talk. He'd tried to gently tell her not to get her hopes up. And she'd told him, with a scold that sounded remarkably like Ella's, that if Lijah said she could, then she would. And damn if she didn't do it, he thought, bursting with pride.

He walked back to the house, still grinning ear to ear. Ella was waiting for him on the front porch. It was a welcoming sight and his spirits rose even higher. Her long hair was pulled back in a braid that trailed down her back and her face was scrubbed and glowing. Climbing the stairs and stepping near, he caught the lingering scent of sweet soap from her morning shower. There was a natural quality about her that he found uniquely pretty. When she looked up at him and smiled, however, her whole face lit up and he was struck breathless with the same awe and wonder he'd felt when he'd watched the sun rise that morning.

"Morning," she said, her voice still husky with sleep. "Brought you coffee."

She handed him a thermos and he took it gratefully.

"Feels like rain," she said, worrying at the sky.

"I know. I feel it, too. Might pass over, though. Forecasts are iffy."

"Do you still want to go?"

He took a sip of the coffee and thought about it. They'd carefully picked a day with a good forecast and a light workload so they could take a canoe trip down the Santee River after they'd released the owls. For the past several nights, after Marion was tucked into bed, they'd had great fun checking maps and working out the details of the day trip. The canoe had been scrubbed, the supplies were ready, and Maggie had come by the night before to take Marion to her home for a few nights. She was the only woman with whom they felt comfortable leaving the diabetic child. Their ducks were in a row and who knew when they'd get everything to come together again.

"Let's do it," he decided.

Her smile broadened with pleasure. "I was hoping you'd say that. Shall we load up? The day's not getting any younger and I know two owls that are eager to find a new home."

They loaded Harris's pickup truck with the canoe and stuffed their gear in the shining silver toolbox. The owls they placed securely in transport boxes inside the truck's cab. They worked in a companionable silence, each feeling the excitement of a day's outing singing in their veins.

It was one of those days that couldn't make up its mind if it would be sunny or rainy. Clouds came and went across the pale blue sky as they drove north toward the Santee River. They didn't talk much. It was too early for conversation and they were satisfied just being together, sipping their coffees and listening to the radio.

The day was theirs. Ella had packed a lunch, plenty of cool drinks and a supply of bug spray and suntan lotion. She looked at Harris across the cab. He was wearing a baseball cap and tapped his fingers on the wheel to the beat of the music. She smiled at seeing him so relaxed. It was going to be a great day.

An hour later they turned off the highway and traveled along a road lined by cragged, dark-barked trees with halos of spring green arched over the pavement like the ribs of a whale. They slowly made their way along the winding road, keeping their eyes peeled for open fields that might be a suitable release spot for the owls. At last they reached the river's landing and the truck rolled to a stop. Ella swung open the door and jumped from the close air of the truck. The vista called her closer, drawing her to the water's edge. There she stood, arms dropped to her sides, in a quiet awe of the incredible beauty of black water against blue sky. Some of the trees were partially submerged by water the color of tea.

Harris came to stand by her side.

"It's so beautiful," she told him. There were no better words to describe how she felt.

"The water levels are high from all the rain we've had. We won't have to worry about scraping the bottom on the rocks." He winked. "But it'll be lively."

Ella turned her head. "Lively?"

"You do know how to paddle, right?"

"Well, yes, sure. I've done some canoeing in Vermont, but that was years back."

"It's like riding a bicycle. You'll be fine."

"Are you sure? This is different."

"How so?"

"This water's black, not white, for starters. And there aren't any alligators in Vermont waters."

"Aw, don't worry about them. They're very people shy. It's the water moccasins I'd be worried about."

"Oh, great. Thanks for telling me."

He chuckled, enjoying the banter, and surprised her by wrapping an arm around her in what she told herself was a friendly, jostling kind of hug.

"Don't worry, Ella. We're going to have a great time. Just you, me and the river."

He dropped his hand and she stepped back, flustered by his spontaneity. It was an affectionate gesture, like several he'd offered since their day at the creek. It was as though they'd crossed some barrier that day that allowed him to feel more at ease with her. She couldn't deny that they'd been closer in so many ways. In fact, if she didn't know better, she'd say serious flirtation was going on between them. Things like glances across a room, shoulders brushing, hands held during walks.

She watched him march up to the truck with a heady gait. He was positively boyish with excitement to get unloaded and hit the water. He even looked like a little boy with wisps of hair curling at the edges of the cap. He was dressed for the river in tan army-style shorts, a long-sleeved T-shirt and a rain jacket. She wore the same with the exception of a cotton scarf instead of a baseball cap.

"Ella! Let's get these birds out while the morning is still cool. They'll need time to settle before the sun gets high."

"I'm on my way."

They brought the two transport boxes out from the rear cab of the truck and gently carried them deeper into the woods to a clearing they'd selected. Harris had explained earlier that they were returning the nestlings to this forest because it was where they'd been found. The hope was that they'd settle into a habitat that could support two more hungry owls.

They set the boxes on the soft layer of mulched leaves and moss that covered the ground. Then, after putting on gloves, Ella slowly opened the folded top halves of the cardboard box. Immediately the young owl began clacking its beak in warning. Peeking in, she saw the two enormous yellow eyes staring back at her with glassy disdain.

"It's okay," she crooned softly as she carefully reached into the box and secured the owl in her hands. It jerked its body and pecked viciously at her glove. She was always surprised at the incredible power of the great horned.

"Ow!" she yelped as the beak pinched through the thick padding of the glove. "This one's got the right attitude."

"Good. He'll need it," he replied, opening up the second transport box.

Immediately more beak clacking began as Harris smoothly lifted the great horned owl from the box. They stood for a while, each with an owl in hand, as the owls turned their heads. This was Ella's first release and she felt a soul-stirring anticipation. It was probably her imagination, but she couldn't help but think the owls felt the same in these precious few seconds before freedom. They were alert yet quiet as their incredible lamp-lit eyes oriented them to the new surroundings. The woods slipped into an expectant hush as local birds checked out the unwelcome visitors.

Harris nodded his head and stretched out his arms. "Godspeed," he said, and then with a lift, he opened his hands. The great horned owl spread its broad wings, fluttering in an uncharacteristic manner as he took a rough start into the sky. But the owl quickly got its bearings and flew straight off toward the river with whispered wing beats. Soon, the brown speck disappeared from view.

This was a little disappointing, as Harris's owl was the older of the two and they'd hoped the two owls would stay close at first. She looked down at the hatch-year owl and felt a momentary pang of worry.

"I guess you're on your own now. Good luck," Ella said to her owl, and followed Harris's example, lifting her arms and opening her hands. She felt the separation as wing beats of air against her face as the young owl spread its wings. Hers was younger and clumsier than the first but took off, eager to escape the human hands that held him captive. No long flights for this novice, however. He flew straight up into the nearest oak tree to land on a thick branch. The owl just sat there, its eyes wide and its throat feathers bobbing like a nervous teenager on his first night out.

"Is he going to be all right?" she asked, feeling a sudden maternal instinct for the young owl she'd helped care for since it was first brought into the clinic as a nestling. She'd helped him through his cute, downy feather phase to see his handsome flight feathers come in and his natural aggressive attitude develop. She'd helped him past the phase of hand-feeding cut-up meat with a puppet and forceps all the way through "mouse school," where he learned to hunt live mice in flight cages. He'd graduated with the rest of his class of orphans and now it was time for him to make his own way in the world.

From nearby branches, two jays began chattering loudly in warning. Soon after, she could hear responses from deeper in the woods. The owl didn't move. This made the jays even madder because they began dive-bombing the young owl, one after the other. The owl ducked its head with each assault as it clung to the branch.

"Harris! He looks so confused and afraid," she said.

"That's to be expected. The jays see the owl as a predator. After all, he eats rats, mice, rabbits *and* birds. He's not welcome and they're trying to scare him off. But don't worry, he'll get the idea soon enough and defend himself. He'll probably sit tight for the day and start looking around for food come nightfall. He is nocturnal, after all."

"If you're sure," she said, still watching the owl.

"I'm not," he answered honestly. "Be careful not to give him human emotions. Nature is indifferent to us all, Ella. To pretend that it cares one way or the other is just being romantic."

It sounded a bit like a scold and she felt deflated. "I can't help but become attached to the orphans I've helped raise, even if it isn't scientific," she said in a huff. "In fact, I've had enough unemotional observation in my lifetime and I've come to the decision that I prefer romanticism—if that's what you must call it, thank you very much."

He turned and looked down at her, then took her hand and squeezed it, telling her with the gesture that he understood what she was feeling. They'd all done what they could for the owls. Release to the wild was the goal for all the birds they rehabilitated.

"Our work here is done. But we'll check on him before we leave, okay? Let's get on down to the river. The day's a-wastin'."

They walked hand in hand to the truck and together they lifted the canoe, then carried it to the shore and slipped it into the black water. While she held the canoe steady, he made trips to load it with paddles and gear, making sure the load was balanced and tied securely in. Finally he carried out the elaborate picnic that she'd prepared.

"What all have you got packed in here?" he asked, grunting as he hoisted the cooler in the canoe. "We're only going to be gone for a few hours."

"Just the things you need for a proper picnic," she said a bit defensively. "That's a thermos of hot soup," she said when he held it up with a questioning look.

"Hot soup? The weathermen said it's supposed to be near eighty today."

"They're never right. It's been pretty cool the past few days with all this rain. Besides, I just know that whenever we went on an expedition in Vermont in the spring or the fall, we never knew if the weather would turn and it would get chilly and damp. Call it insurance." She gazed up at the smattering of gray clouds with speculation.

"We shall see what we shall see," she said with a sigh, neatly putting the worry of rain aside. "Other than soup there are a few thick ham-and-cheddar sandwiches on crusty bread, a green bean salad and some Granny Smith apples. And for dessert, I made chocolate walnut brownies." She looked up mischievously. "I thought we could cheat today since Marion isn't here. That's not too much food, is it? It's the bottled water that feels so heavy. I brought plenty. Oh, and a bottle of wine."

"Wine?" he asked incredulously.

"Why are you looking at me like that? It wouldn't be a picnic without some reinforcements. We may have to work against the current to get back, but at least we'll be smiling."

"Hasn't anyone ever told you boating and alcohol don't mix?" he asked, reaching in and pulling out the bottle of wine.

"Oh, Harris. Don't be such a stuffed shirt."

"A what?"

"You heard me. Sometimes I think you need to loosen up a bit."

"*Me* loosen up? Isn't that the pot calling the kettle black?"

"What? You think I'm a stuffed shirt?"

"You stuff your shirt quite nicely, Miss Majors, but those buttons can be a little tight."

She sputtered with indignation, then seeing the tease sparkling in his eyes, erupted into a laugh. He joined her and, with a shrug, put the bottle of wine back into the picnic.

"Only for medicinal purposes," she declared.

"How about a bite of that ham sandwich now?"

"Oh, no, you don't. We have to earn it."

"You New Englanders with your work ethic. Well, fasten up that life preserver and hop in. It's time to start earning your lunch."

She fastened the preserver and, gripping the sides, climbed into the front of the tippy canoe. Once she was settled, Harris nudged the canoe from the shore onto the water. Her heart quickened along with the current, and, before long, they fell into the rhythm of the river. At first the canoe was wobbly, but between laughs and grunts they managed to get their paddling in sync. Harris steered in the rear of the canoe with long, strong strokes. Over and over her paddle broke the dark surface at a steady pace with Harris's and she found that this repetitive, rhythmic motion bonded them in a subtle yet powerful way.

They meandered along the winding waterway at the river's pace, slowing from time to time for conversation. She'd purposefully left her wristwatch at home, deciding that for at least today, she would not be its slave. They were on river time. The air was that soft and sultry kind that melted your bones. Birdsong filled the air. Occasionally she'd hear the plop of some amphibian—lizard, frog, alligator—as it broke the water's surface. She'd swing her head over to look, but every time she only caught the telltale rippling of the water.

Everywhere she looked was new and mysterious. Flowering dogwood peeked between majestic bald cypress trees more than one thousand years old and gnarled, twisting live oaks that lined the riverbanks. The long, drooping branches dripped lacy fronds of Spanish moss that skimmed the water's surface like a woman's sleeve when her long fingers dipped into the cool water.

Life slows down on the river, she thought. All that mattered was what was around the next bend. While she paddled, Ella enjoyed the sound of Harris's voice behind her, rich and melodious, as he pointed out the history of the area. It was as rich and complex as the landscape they slowly journeyed through.

He told her how the Spanish had come in their mighty ships in 1526, and how over the next hundred years, the English and French joined them to establish outposts in the New World. By 1729 Charleston was already a busy, wealthy seaport, which made some men wealthy and others eager to steal that wealth away. Famous pirates like Blackbeard and Caesar came to stake a claim. Harris regaled her with their stories, and those of the legendary "Swamp Fox," Francis Marion, and Christopher Gasden, a local planter who designed a flag that would inspire the colonists to battle with the slogan, Don't Tread on Me.

From time to time, Harris would interrupt his stories to call out, "Look there!" She'd turn her head to see what had caught his attention, smiling to herself at how much like his daughter he really was. Once it was a trio of fishing lines hanging from a tree, each marked with a different colored tape. Harris told her someone was going to have spot tail or catfish or maybe some wide-mouth bass for dinner. He pointed out rickety deer blinds nestled way up in the trees. What pleased her most, however, was when he tapped her shoulder and pointed up. Then she looked skyward to see a cluster of rare wood storks, white and majestic in the stark gray branches of a dead oak. She turned her head and smiled, pleased that she could identify these birds now.

As the sun reached its highest point, they pushed back their long sleeves, feeling the rays kissing their skin despite the increasing gray clouds. Suntan lotion changed hands, as well as repellant. The river had a brisk current and they were moving along at a good pace, yet as time passed, the sky darkened ominously. They should stop for lunch soon, she thought. Maybe even turn back. She debated whether or not to ask, but refrained, hoping against hope that the weather would hold and not cut even a moment of this time alone with Harris.

Her hopes were dashed when the first fat drops of rain splattered onto her forehead and landed in the water with rude, heartbreaking, plopping noises.

"Uh-oh," she said, stilling her paddle to look over her shoulder with a worried expression.

He grimaced and turned his face up to gauge the rain. "I was hoping we'd stop for lunch and be headed back before we got the first drops," he replied. "That's a pretty big cloud mass. We'd better head back. We don't want to get caught."

As though the heavens were waiting for him to finish his sentence, the sky opened up in a true Southern downpour, dumping rain in bucketfuls. They paddled hard but, even squinting, she couldn't see more than a few feet ahead of her.

"We have to get off the water and out of the boat," he

shouted over the roar of the rain. "Let's head for that small bluff to the left!"

The rain came down in torrents, a punishing, stinging rain that streamed down her face, blinding her. Still, she put her back to it, struggling against the current as he guided the canoe into the waves, zigzagging them toward the bluff.

"Harris!" she shouted in alarm. "The water is filling the boat!"

"Keep going, Ella. We'll make it. Paddle hard!"

Her arms felt like rubber and she was panting with each desperate stroke. Unable to see where they were heading through the downpour, she knew that they'd reached the shore only when the bottom of the canoe scraped sand. They scrambled like river rats from the canoe and dragged it up the muddy shore. Ella slipped, skinning her knee, then picked herself up and tugged some more. At last the canoe, heavy with all the gear, was safe on high ground.

Ella's arms drooped at her sides as she scanned the area. "There's nowhere to go!"

"You pull out the gear and I'll rig something up," he shouted. "Thank God for the tarp."

She wanted to weep, she was so exhausted, but she did as she was told, knowing it was critical to keep dry. They worked in double time, slipping in the muddy terrain. Harris pitched the large plastic tarp over the branch of a pine, then anchored the edges with large rocks. It was little bigger than a pup tent. He moved the gear to safety and was spreading a film of plastic on the ground when they heard the first rumblings of thunder.

"Come out of the rain!" he called, waving Ella under cover, away from the metal canoe that she was just finishing flipping upside down. She stumbled under the low tarp just as the first sheet of lightning scarred the dark sky.

In the dim light she saw Harris crouched and leaning against the pile of supplies. He'd wrapped a thin blanket she'd brought for the picnic around his shoulders and opened up his arm to her. She was on her knees in the low tent, shivering and dripping with cold water. She managed to slip off her life preserver with clumsy shakes, then crawled over to him, seeking shelter from the rain that pelted their little makeshift tent with relentless fury. Murmuring reassurances, he gathered her close and wiped the rain from her face with gentle strokes. Ella gathered her knees close and cuddled against him, relishing the feel of his arm around her shoulders as a sanctuary from the storm.

"You're soaked," he said.

"And freezing," she said, shivering. "That rain is icy."

"These sudden storms usually pass over just as quickly. We'll be safe waiting it out here."

Suddenly a fierce bolt of lightning lit up the sky, followed by a tremendous clap of thunder overhead. Ella jumped with a yelp and clutched his shirt with a tight grip.

"It sounds like it's right on top of us!"

"It's okay, Ella," he murmured by her ear. "We'll be fine."

"Are you sure? What if lightning hits a tree? I've treated people with serious injuries from trees exploding or falling down right on top of them."

He frowned and looked out of the tarp. He couldn't see anything except bent-over grass and driving rain. "We're out of range of most of the trees."

"But what if *we* get hit? I knew a man who wasn't even hit directly. He was just close enough to get a jolt. It fried his liver and screwed up his electrolytes. He still doesn't act quite right—and he's lucky to be alive. If it's a direct hit, you're toast."

"The odds of getting hit by lightning are astronomically slim. But if it will make you feel better, we can take off any belts or metal, just till the storm passes."

They fumbled in the close space and the metal felt like ice against her fingers as she undid her belt and slid it out from the loops. They set them far away on the pile of life preservers.

Afterward he wrapped his arms around her again, tightening the blanket. "Feel better now? Good," he said when she nodded against his chest. "There's nothing to worry about. We'll just ride it out."

She nestled in the stingy warmth of the blanket. "I hate thunderstorms. I always have."

"Really? I've always loved thunderstorms. When I was a kid I used to lie on my back and count from the moment I saw lightning in the sky till I heard the first rumbling of thunder to find out how far away the storm was."

"Everybody did that. Except I did it more out of self-protection than fun."

A low rumbling sounded, growing in crescendo.

Their eyes met and in unspoken agreement they began to count. "One, one thousand, two, one thousand." A searing bolt of lightning lit up the sky.

"That was close," she whispered.

He made a face of mock horror.

"My mother and father died in a thunderstorm."

His smile fell instantly. "I'm sorry, Ella."

"That's what caused the accident. The rain was really thick, like this, and the roads were so slick they couldn't see. I was only five years old but I remember it like it was yesterday. I was standing at the window of my aunts' house, looking out at the storm and waiting. Waiting for them to come home. I was so scared for them." Thunder roared again and she clutched him tight. "I *hate* this," she said in a hoarse voice. "I still have nightmares."

"Shh…Ella…I won't let anything happen to you. I promise."

She tucked her small hands under his jacket, close to his chest. The storm made the day like night as they huddled close under the tarp. "No one's ever said that to me before," she said in a soft voice.

"That he won't let anything happen to you?"

She shook her head against his chest. "I used to dream that my father said things like that to me, back when I was very little. When I got older, I dreamed that some man would. Someday. A childish dream. Like wanting to be a princess." She laughed ruefully. "Neither one of those dreams came true."

There was a long silence and she squeezed her eyes tight, feeling so exposed.

"You strike me as someone who doesn't need taking care of," he said.

He spoke in a soft voice, but in the small confines of the tent, the words seemed shouted. Or maybe it was because, though his words were true in one sense, they were so untrue in another that Ella cringed to hear them.

"I've always taken care of myself because I've had to. And, frankly, no one's ever stepped up to ask for the position. A person can be resourceful and competent and still need to feel cared for. Protected." She took a breath. "Not alone."

She felt his chest rise and fall beneath her palm.

"Do you feel alone, Ella Majors?"

Something in the way he said it, his voice hushed and husky, his breath coming fast, let her know that his question came from a source much deeper than mere curiosity. And she knew her answer would have consequences.

Words formed in her mind. *Yes, I've felt very much alone for a very long time, but never have I felt the pain of it so keenly as I have in the past few months as I lie in my bed, night after night, knowing you were lying alone, too, just down the hall. Knowing that I loved you and that you thought of me only as Marion's nanny. A colleague. A friend.*

She clutched his shirt, mouthing the words that she couldn't give breath to and suddenly she was crying. Her! Ella never cried and was embarrassed for the tears but couldn't stop them.

He brought his hand to lift her chin, saying, "It's all right, Ella. It's all right." His hand wiped the tears from her face, smoothed her dampened hair back as she took hiccupping breaths. He stroked her hair slowly, murmuring her name in a low voice while her crying ceased and her breathing slowed. She could feel his breath on her face—warm and so close—in rhythm with her own.

Her lids fluttered open and she saw his eyes staring into hers, so near that she felt she might drown in their blue depths. He moved toward her in degrees, and when at last he pressed his lips to hers, Ella closed her eyes again, breathing in his air. This time, she knew she was lost.

The kiss deepened and it was as if lightning struck, violently and unexpected. It sparked a fire so fierce and scorching that it blazed out of control, heating their skin, leaving them panting and tearing off damp clothing with shaking hands.

The storm outside raged. The wind whipped at the tarp, causing it to billow and shudder. Thunder rolled overhead, deafening in its fury, heralding the crackling lightning that lit up the sky, illuminating the two smooth, rocking silhouettes in the darkened tent.

Yet inside, Ella was unafraid. Closing her eyes she was

back on the river with the sun shining overhead, brilliant and clear, deliciously scorching their skin. She was in Harris's arms and his movements were smooth and soothing. They were blissfully in sync, their strokes repetitive, rhythmic, gradually gaining speed. She was caught in the current, flowing with the river, toward the warmth she'd been seeking and—at last—found.

"I'm sorry," Harris said to her after their bodies had cooled. "That shouldn't have happened."

He slid from her arms and moved to sit, stirring the close air of the tent. The storm had continued for what seemed like hours, but at last the rain had stopped. The humidity in its wake was as thick and heavy as a wool blanket. Outside the tent, a chorus of crickets and frogs swelled. It was a lonely sound.

Ella felt the emptiness of his leaving and shivered. She moved to sit as well, tugging the thin blanket higher up over her bare shoulder to drape her nakedness. She felt suddenly exposed.

"What shouldn't have happened?"

"I didn't bring you here for this."

"I know you didn't," she replied with a nervous laugh. "Don't be silly."

He sat motionless, looking at the ground.

She licked her lips, swollen and tender from his kisses, and voiced her deepest fear. "Are you sorry it happened?"

"Me? No!"

Ella could have wept for the relief that surged through her.

"But I had no right."

"Because I'm your child's nanny?" she asked, amused that he could be so concerned about such a minor technicality.

"No." He looked up at her. "Because I'm married."

Ella sucked in her breath. She felt blindsided. "You're married?"

"I thought you knew. We'd talked about Fannie."

There it was. Her name. His wife's name. It floated in the air between them.

"No! We didn't. Not really. I mean, I knew who she was, of course. But I'd just assumed you were divorced."

He shook his head.

Ella rested her forehead in her palm while she fought off a chill that was spreading throughout her body, causing her to tremble with despair as her happiness imploded within her.

"Do you still love her?"

Harris hesitated and suddenly he looked older. "I don't know. I suppose on some level, of course."

"But she doesn't live with you, right? Hasn't for years."

"No. Or, yes. Whatever," he said, exasperated. "She left when Marion was born and comes back periodically. Usually unannounced, when she needs money or a place to crash. She stays for a little while, long enough to get Marion's hopes up, then splits again."

Ella heard the bitterness in his voice. She also heard that he did not say Fannie had gotten his hopes up, too, as his mother had. She nearly reached to touch him then, to comfort him, to wipe the sadness from his face—but she could not bear to touch him again.

"Why haven't you divorced her?"

"I asked myself that question every time I found a note on the kitchen table saying she was sorry in some new way." He sighed then said plainly, "She's my wife."

"What kind of wife leaves her husband and child?"

"Ella." He said her name in the manner of wanting her to be patient, wanting her to understand. "Fannie's a drug addict. She had a problem with drugs before we were married. Her childhood was pretty messed up—I told you about that. Of course I knew about it and got her some help. She stopped using for a long time, and when we got married she really tried to make a good life for us. When she got pregnant she was so happy. I've never seen anyone more beautiful than Fannie when she was carrying Marion."

"Did she—"

"No," he said, shaking his head. "She didn't do drugs when she was pregnant. That's one of the things I'll always be grateful to her for. But after Marion was born… Maybe it was postpartum depression, I don't know. She'd sneak it and we'd have terrible rows when I found out. But when she started stealing drugs from the clinic, I went ballistic. I knew I couldn't handle it anymore and arranged to put her into the hospital, to help her. What else could I do? But she ran off before I could take her."

"Harris, I still don't understand. Why do you stay married to her?"

"I've known her since she was a kid, Ella. I've always looked out for her and she's done a lot for me. And for my mother. It's been hard but I'm no saint. I've asked myself, what if she was injured in some accident? Left paralyzed or in a coma. Would I divorce her then? Or what if she was schizophrenic and in a mental institution. Would I leave her then? The answer is always no. The vow says for better or for worse."

"What are you telling me?" she asked.

He took a deep breath. "That I'm sorry. I didn't mean to hurt you. I didn't mean for this to happen."

Ella brought her knees to her chest and wrapped the blanket around herself. Putting her chin to her kneecaps, she thought long and hard about all that Harris had just told her.

The most wonderful thing in the world had just happened to her and he didn't mean for it to happen. She had to squeeze her eyes shut against the pain.

"Oh, Harris," she replied, feeling defeated. "Where does this leave us?"

"That's totally up to you, Ella. I don't want you to leave, but I can't ask you to make love to me again. I want to. God, I want to. But I won't ask you—I swear it."

His eyes held hers for a long while, but she could not reply. His shoulders slumped slightly and he bent at the waist to retrieve his clothes and crawl out of the tarp.

Fresh air stirred and eddied the stale dampness inside the tarp. Ella grabbed her clothes and drew them near. They felt cold and wet and smelled of the river. She had no choice but to put them back on, half bent over, struggling with the drenched, clinging fabric.

He stuck his head back in as she was zipping her shorts. "I wish we had time to start a fire and dry them."

"No matter."

"You'll need to drink this," he said, handing her a cup of hot soup. "I guess you were right, after all."

The tomato soup was warm and soothing. She held the cup with both hands, relishing the warmth.

"We should eat, too, and drink water. We need to get our strength back so we can head home as soon as possible. We don't want to get stuck here if it rains again. Is that okay with you?"

"Whatever you think is best." Her voice was indifferent.

"That storm was pretty intense and the river's fuller than I've ever seen it. But it's really beautiful. There's a good current and we should make it to the next bridge in good time."

"Okay."

"Ella…"

"Don't say anything more," she said, lifting her face. "Please."

He tightened his mouth, nodded curtly, then left the tent.

They ate the meal she had so cheerfully prepared. Was it only yesterday? It felt to her that they'd been on this journey for days. They only spoke to discuss the plans for their river trip home. Then they took down the wet tarp that had been their salvation, packed the gear and dragged the canoe through the thick, slushy mud back to the water. Before they shoved off, as she bent to step into the canoe, Harris's arm shot out and he grabbed her hand. She turned her head, her gaze sharpening, surprised by his sudden action. He seemed earnest, even desperate.

"Ella, you have to know. Today meant a great deal to me."

He kept his eyes on her face, as though searching for some answer.

She had none to give him. She could only nod as if she understood, though she did not. She thought of the young owl, sitting alone in the tree on the dawn of his freedom, his throat bobbing, eyes wide, afraid of what was to come.

She looked at his hand on hers, holding tight, then tugged free and climbed into the canoe, settling herself in the front.

"I'll just be a minute," he said, and went to pick up any litter, any sign at all that they had ever been there.

The sun had begun its descent on the South Santee River and an anticipatory hush settled in the Lowcountry. Waiting in the front of the canoe, Ella floated soundlessly in the water. The colors of the sky darkened around her, deepening from rose to a brilliant ochre that was mirrored in the glassy waters of the river. In that moment, she could not tell where earth ended and heaven began.

She dipped the tip of her paddle in the water. Just one touch. It created a ripple that moved out in concentric circles, farther and farther, changing the reflection, breaking the stillness. She thought of her life with Marion, and with Harris, and how everything she did, and would do, had consequences that stretched out beyond what she might expect.

She prayed for guidance. She prayed for forgiveness.

She prayed for the strength to make the right decision.

Hovering. *This is the most energy intensive form of flying because there is no lift and flight must be generated by pure muscle power. Falcons, kites and osprey hover efficiently, and the American kestrel is so proficient it is nicknamed "Windhover." Kiting is similar to hovering. Used primarily when hunting, red-tailed and ferruginous hawks essentially face into the wind and fly in place by constantly flicking wings and tail to maintain position.*

17

POOLS OF LIGHT POURED FROM THE HOUSE AS they drove up. Ella's hand had been resting on the door handle for the tense, silent trip home. She climbed quickly from the truck, eager to escape the dark silence they'd suffered since the river. She was cold, damp, smelled of mud and river, and her heart was breaking. Yet she felt comforted by the sight of a place she'd come to call home and walked eagerly toward the light.

The screen door slammed open and Marion came flying from the house. Ella stepped aside to get out of the straight path to Harris. She was stunned when Marion ran to her, clasped her little arms tight around her legs and cried a heartfelt "I was so worried! I thought you weren't coming back."

A million emotions spiraled through Ella and the tears

she'd held at bay for hours began to leak. She lowered to her knees and wrapped her arms around the sobbing child.

"We just got caught in the rain," she said in a husky voice. "Nothing to fret about."

"Don't ever leave me again," the child scolded. "Stay with me. Forever."

Ella kissed her forehead and held her close, rocking her. She glanced up to see Harris with his arms crossed and his chin low upon his chest. She couldn't read his expression.

"Look! I've brought you a present," she said to Marion. She sniffed and swiped her eyes, then reached into the bag at her side and pulled out a book she'd found at a small shop near where they'd stopped for gas. The moment she saw it, she knew Marion had to have it.

"It's full of Gullah stories," she explained, delivering it to the child's eager hands. "Buh Crow, Buh Rabbit, the whole gang's in there. I thought we might have fun reading them. Who knows? Maybe we can tell Lijah a story for a change."

She looked toward Lijah, who had walked up from the cabin to greet them. He stood beside Maggie and her two children.

"I don't think you'll be finding a story in that book I don't know," he said.

"Can we read one tonight?" Marion asked.

Ella nodded, despite her exhaustion. "Of course. I've been looking forward to it."

"So what am I? Chopped liver?" Harris asked with his arms out.

Marion ran to his arms and was swirled around, squealing. Ella rose, grabbed her bags and went from the darkness into the house. Maggie hurried to her side.

"I was worried, too," Maggie told her, linking arms.

"I'm sorry. What idiots we were to leave the cell phone in the car."

"Marion didn't really catch on to how late it was getting until the sun set, so don't be too concerned. She actually had a great time while you were away. She and my Annie have become fast friends. I'm all amazement! Whenever I tried to get them together in the past, Marion never wanted to play with Annie. She just wanted to be left alone. Now she's all for playing games and loves to tell stories."

Ella managed a weak smile. Even this good news was unable to chip through the depression that cloaked her like lead. "So, she's learning how to play."

"You're doing a great job with her."

Ella's smile fell and she looked away.

"What's the matter?" Maggie asked, quick to catch the nuance.

"Nothing."

Their eyes met and they shared a glance that revealed that her pat response was a lie.

What might have led to a heartfelt conversation was cut off when Harris and Marion followed them into the house, chatting about the travails of the river. Immediately, Ella brought her bag close to her chest.

Maggie's glance shifted from her to Harris, knowing something of significance had occurred. However, she proved herself a friend by letting the subject drop. Instead, she looked over her shoulder to say something to Harris that made everyone laugh. Marion started running from person to person, pink-cheeked and bursting with happiness. She made silly statements and demands that were quickly met, clearly ruling the roost. Soon her new friend, Annie, joined in the silliness.

A buzz of chatter filled the house, punctuated with bursts

of childish laughter. Ella felt herself withdrawing. All the voices seemed muffled, like white noise. Lijah stood quietly, his shoulders slightly stooped, watching all with a vague smile. He turned toward Ella and their eyes met, his gaze searching. Ella looked down, stepping back from the group.

"I'm so tired, and I ache all over and smell so bad," she said, hand on the hall door. "Forgive me, everyone, but I need to get clean."

The hour was late. Ella lay on her back, stretched out on her mattress, her hands across her chest, like a body in state. The bedroom window was open and soft breezes fluttered the curtains and flirted with the hem of her pristine white cotton nightgown. She lay with her eyes open because every time she closed them, the image of Harris came up as if on a movie screen. Then she'd recall in exquisitely painful detail every moment spent under the tarp. They had lain, wrapped in each other's arms, for a long while after the explosive passion was spent. That tender closeness had been sweeter, and brought her a more profound pleasure, than the physical bonding they'd shared. It was unlike anything she'd ever experienced before. Was this what it was like to be addicted? she wondered. Once given a taste of something so mind-blowing and freeing, you simply cannot garner the strength to give it up?

For the first time in her life, she began to understand why some women could have an affair with a married man. Ella looked at the ceiling and reasoned why it wouldn't be wrong to love Harris. After all, Fannie had deserted him. She didn't even live with them and she certainly didn't care for them. Harris and Fannie weren't *really* married.

Yet, Harris stayed married to her. That bond was the unalterable fact. The lump in the crop that couldn't be swallowed. He'd said he felt committed to her, for better or worse. He loved her. Ella groaned with frustration and rubbed her forehead with her fist. She would think him a fool if she didn't find his decision so damned noble.

She'd been right about him that day at the pier. He *was* like the osprey and the eagle, birds he professed to have an affinity for. They were site loyal and monogamous. He'd told her that day! It was one more truth that had surfaced, glaringly evident. Only she'd been too blinded by her love for him to see it.

It was all too infuriating to think about. But if she allowed herself to carry that bird analogy to its conclusion, the other truth was that the eagle's mate was gone. The nest had been empty and now *she* was in the nest and caring for the young. If that was the way of nature, then let it be! Why should she feel so guilty?

The image filled her with hope. She told herself she was in the right. There was nothing immoral about a relationship with Harris. She'd not give Harris up without a fight.

Besides, what would happen if she *did* have an affair with Harris? she asked herself. Would anything change other than his coming down the hall to share her bed? She would still take care of their home and Marion, still assist in the clinic. No, she told herself, nothing would change.

Ella squeezed her eyes shut and wished she could convince herself of this, but a traitorous voice kept whispering in her mind that *everything* would change.

The night was quiet, void of birdcalls. She turned to her left side, then, restless, turned to the other. It didn't matter; her mind refused to settle. She opened her eyes, exhausted yet giving up the struggle for sleep. What was Harris doing now? she wondered. Was he lying awake, worrying about her decision like she was? Or was he lying in his narrow bed down the hall, sleeping soundly, oblivious to her suffering? She shifted her weight to lie once more on her back and stare through the pewter-colored night at the ceiling.

Men didn't have to worry about the reputations of the women they slept with. She'd be the *other woman*. The *home-wrecker*. And those were the kindest words that would be spoken about her. What would Maggie say, she wondered, then sucked in her breath, realizing with a burst of clarity why Maggie had been uneasy the day she and Harris had gone to the dock. Maggie *knew* that Harris was married.

Did everyone know but her? She moved her hands to cover her face, heated with shame at her stupidity and blindness. Why had she simply assumed?

Her fingers tapped her chest as her mind worked on and on. Hours passed. The moon rose high in the sky, casting its pale light in patterns across her room. Ella knew it had to be past midnight. The hour of the hants. Hag holler time.

The quiet was broken by the eerie, resounding call of the barred owl. There came no reply. Lijah had said that the call of the owl during hag holler time was a bad omen. She shivered and thought it wasn't the dead she feared. Traveling spirits held no worries for her. It was the ghost of the living that haunted her and prevented her sleep.

She sat up in her bed, frustrated and exhausted by her running thoughts and the restlessness that would not let her sleep. Only the weak believed in such tales, she told herself as she rose to her feet to close the window against the owl's lonely, repetitive call. She was not weak. She was strong and always had been. What was it that Harris had said? Something about how she didn't need taking care of? "Well then, so be it," she said with decision.

She opened her bedroom door and walked barefoot down the narrow hall toward Harris's room. The hall door was open to the living room. She reached out to close it tight, careful not to let it slam. Marion had been difficult to settle that night. She didn't want the talking she knew would begin soon to awaken her.

For she had a purpose this night. She would go to his room. Demand that he explain why he hadn't made his relationship with Fannie clear. Ask him why he'd wooed her these past weeks by holding her hand and exchanging hooded glances. Why he'd made her fall in love with him if he knew that this love would destroy her? She'd listen to his answers, no matter how hard they'd be to hear, because she needed closure.

Then she'd tell him she couldn't stay. No matter how she played it out in her mind, the one paramount truth was that he was married. She wasn't going to have a relationship with a married man.

All this she had in her mind to tell him. With each step her heart pounded so hard she opened her mouth to breathe in soft pants. She raised her fist to the door and knocked twice, in rapid succession, expecting him to call out a sleepy "Who's there?" from his bed. She sucked in her breath when the door immediately swung open.

Suddenly he was standing before her in long plaid pajama bottoms with his chest bare, stubble on his cheeks and his hair disheveled. He obviously hadn't been sleeping either; his red-rimmed eyes looked vulnerable. As they stared at each other in the dim light of a half moon, she heard her heart howling in her head, drowning out her well-rehearsed intentions, and she felt the trail of tears flowing down her cheeks.

"Do you love me?" she demanded.

It wasn't the question she'd come to ask him, but it was the only one she needed to know the answer to.

"Yes," he replied.

Ella released a long sigh as the inner howling subsided.

Sometimes decisions are made easily. Sometimes they are arrived at after stewing long and hard. And sometimes, she realized, they aren't really made at all. Sometimes you coast along like a leaf floating down the river and get caught in an eddy. Then you're spinning endlessly, helplessly, until some act of chance cuts you loose.

Love cut Ella loose. She took a breath, stepped into the current and said, "I love you, too."

The following morning at dawn, Ella rose from Harris's bed and slipped into jeans and a T-shirt. She'd slept a miserly few hours yet felt refreshed and eager to accompany Harris on his habitual morning walk. They walked closely together with arms entwined as lovers did, bumping hips. They couldn't bear to be apart, not even for a moment. First they took a swing around the pens, then he fetched Cinnamon from the mews. The sleek mahogany hawk was alert and ready for her morning outing, but she eyed Ella with scrutiny.

"I think she's jealous," Ella said with a light laugh.

"She's just not accustomed to anyone coming along on these morning strolls."

She exchanged glances with the wary-eyed hawk. "No, I think she's jealous."

"Interesting," he said, eyeing the hawk on his fist with haughty amusement. "She could be picking up on vibes. Hawks are territorial, you know."

So am I, she thought, but didn't say it.

The three of them took off on their walk. While Cinnamon sat on Harris's fist, Ella carried a mug of steaming coffee in hers. Eventually, Cinnamon seemed to accept her presence and stopped glaring. When they reached the point where the road widened, Harris lifted his arm and let Cinnamon fly free. She took off with purpose for a high branch of a pine. Ella could see the hawk was feeling quite pleased with herself as she shook her feathers in the early morning sun, jingling the small bell on her tail. Harris and Ella grasped hands and walked down the road as the hawk followed them—just like any dog on a walk—flying from tree to tree.

"Cinnamon is your favorite," she said, leaning into him. "You can't deny it."

"I have to admit, she's a charmer. And I've always had a soft spot for Harris hawks. My mother named me after them. She loved hawks, too, and I think she knew even at my birth that I was the cooperative sort." He smiled ruefully. "That I'd take care of her."

"Count your blessings. She could have called you Merlin. Or Cooper. Or Red."

He barked out a laugh. "Shouldered or Tailed?"

Ella wiggled her brow. "I'll have to look again." She tilted her head and searched for the hawk in the foliage. "I don't see her. Aren't you afraid she'll fly off?"

"No. She knows the routine, and every once in a while I give her a little treat, just to remind her." Saying that, he released her hand and reached into his canvas bag to pull out a small chunk of meat. He whistled, sharp and clear, and, extending his arm, tapped the meat against his fist. Ella saw Cinnamon check out the food on the glove, then spread her tail feathers with a jingling of the bell and emerge from the cloak of trees, straight to his fist.

"See?" he asked her as they watched the hawk tear at the beef with her sharp beak. "She knows on which side her bread is buttered."

He lifted his arm again and the hawk flew off. He then

hooked his arm in hers and they walked together, talking not of the past, but of things they wanted to do that day, tomorrow and in the days to come. Ella couldn't stop smiling. She had never known such happiness.

When they neared the gate, Harris stopped short and peered at the sky.

"Vultures," he said. "Something is dead." Immediately he whistled for his hawk.

Cinnamon did not return to his fist and Ella could see his face grow taut with worry.

Harris took a breath to calm himself, waited another moment, then whistled again with authority. The plaintive sound pierced the early morning quiet. From several trees back they heard the faint jingling sound of her bell, then Cinnamon burst from the foliage to come to his fist. Harris gave her a large piece of meat and ample time to eat it undisturbed. When the hawk was finished, he laced her jesses and kept her to his fist until they could find out what had caught the interest of the vultures.

They approached the gate, and the first thing both of them noticed was that the rooster wasn't around.

"Sometimes he goes off," Harris said, looking from left to right. "But I don't like this. Last night on my walk I came across a couple of young boys hunting. I chased them off but I didn't like their attitude."

"They had no business hunting here. This is private property."

"That doesn't stop them. It's worse in the fall. You take your life in your hands just walking in the woods."

"Harris, you don't think…"

His face was tight. "Nothing would surprise me."

She looked up in the sky to see a third vulture join the

others circling overhead. "You stay here with Cinnamon," she said. "I'll look around."

The ground crunched beneath her feet as she opened the gate and explored the area under the loblolly pine where the rooster usually could be found. The foliage was dense and a green anole was warming itself on the leaf of a neighboring magnolia. She pushed back a pine branch and carefully trod a short ways from the road, scanning the area. A white feather in the mud caught her eye. With a sense of dread she moved several steps farther into the woods.

"Oh, no," she uttered when she found him.

The rooster lay lifeless in a tangle of weeds. Blood as bright a red as its wattle stained its snowy breast.

The following day Brady turned off the highway onto the road of the center with a roar of his engine. The music was blaring and his elbow was hanging out the window. His parents had been so pleased with the upswing of his midterm grades that they'd relented and let him drive again. Brady was flying high these days. He'd passed all his courses and he thought he did a decent job on the SATs. Best of all, he was a member of the resident bird team. Today he was wearing his official Coastal Carolina Center for Birds of Prey T-shirt, given to him by the team at the last meeting. It was kind of a minigraduation ceremony and it had meant as much or more than any graduation he'd had before.

He pulled up to the gate and hopped out of the car to open it. Looking from left to right, he noticed that the rooster was gone. Where was that goofy bird? he wondered. It was the first time he'd not seen it watching him as he drove by. He kept his eyes peeled as he drove through and closed the gate after himself, but still no rooster.

"Hey, Harris," he said with gusto as he walked into the weighing room. "Lijah."

He clasped his hands on his hips and smelled the air. He loved this room best of all. Loved the smell of leather and the sight of all the falconry equipment neatly lined up on the walls. One glance at the large dry-mount chart gave him an instant overview of the weight and status of each resident bird. He felt at home in here and smiled openly, excited to begin his first day as a team member.

"Anybody see that crazy rooster this morning?" he asked, dropping his book bag to the floor. "He wasn't down by the gate."

Harris's brows gathered in concern and he cast a loaded glance across the room at Lijah.

Damn, Brady thought, catching the glance. Instantly, he felt deflated. What did he do wrong now? He shifted his weight, uncomfortable with the awkward silence. "What's wrong?"

"We had some bad news over the weekend," Harris began slowly. He paused. "We found the rooster lying in the woods near the gate. Somebody shot it."

Brady went still. "What? When?"

"We found him yesterday. My guess is he was shot sometime Saturday night."

"I don't believe it! Who'd shoot that rooster? He didn't hurt nobody."

"I don't know."

"But...why?" he blurted with pain and frustration.

Harris's lips were white with fury. "Because they can. I saw a couple of kids hunting around here on Saturday, but I can't be sure it was them."

Brady's gaze darted up. "How old?"

Harris shrugged. "I'd say about your age."

Brady felt anger surge through him like hot lava. He had to close his mouth tight before he spoke out the names hovering at his lips. He brought his fingers up to pinch the bridge of his nose, surprised to find tears pooling.

"I'm sorry," Harris said, putting his hand on the boy's shoulder. "We all know how much that bird meant to you. He meant a lot to all of us. We'll never know what brought him here or why he stayed. It's just not normal for a rooster to live in a loblolly pine like that."

"Where's the rooster now?" Brady asked, dropping his hand. His voice was thick, but he'd brought himself under control.

"I buried him," Lijah said in his deep voice. "Put him down by the loblolly. Thought he might like it there."

Brady met Lijah's eyes and saw the sympathy there. He nodded his head. "Yeah. That's good."

Clarice walked into the room, a worried look on her face and a large green potted plant with white bloom spikes in her arms. "Hey," she greeted them in a tentative manner, looking from one to the other.

Brady turned toward her. One look in her eyes and he knew that she'd come for him.

"I brought this," she said, indicating the pot in her arms. "It's a yucca plant. It blooms this proud, fine-looking white flower that sits high on a tall stem." She ran a finger along the pot's rim. "I thought, you know, it might be nice to plant near the gate where we laid Buh Rooster. To remember him by."

No one said anything.

"It was only an idea," she hedged, embarrassed.

"It's a fine idea," Harris replied. "I think we were all just moved by the suggestion."

"I'll plant it," Lijah said obligingly.

"If you don't mind," said Brady, "I'd like to do it."

Brady and Clarice drove down to the gate in Brady's car with shovels and the plant. It was a beautiful day, clear and breezy. Brady looked up and saw a long line of white puffy clouds in the sky.

They'd decided to plant the yucca directly over Buh Rooster. Brady worked real slow, careful not to dig any deeper than he had to. He didn't want to see no white feathers down in the earth. They got the yucca plant in, poured some water on it and stepped back. Brady leaned against the shovel pole and looked at the yucca plant. It looked so much smaller in the ground next to the tall loblolly than it had in the container. He hoped it would grow fast in the sandy, sunny soil and not die. Brady liked to think that the white flower would someday grow right from that ol' rooster, and in that way, he'd still be here. Next to the gate.

"You okay, Brady?" Clarice asked.

He shook his head. "Crazy bird. I didn't know how much he meant to me." He exhaled hard, clenching his fists at his thighs. "And now all I want to do is beat the crap out of Manny and Nate."

Clarice sucked in her breath. "You think it was them? How do you know that?"

"I don't. But I'm aiming to find out." He looked sharply at her. "Don't you be tellin' nobody about this, hear? This is *my* business."

"*Okay,* I won't."

He tightened his lips. The anger was so hot he couldn't reply.

"Don't get into any trouble about it, though," she cautioned.

"Don't matter. Trouble's never had a hard time finding me."

"Brady, you've been doing so great. You don't want to mess with that. Please. Don't make me worry about you now."

He turned his head to look at her, his feelings for her raw and exposed in his eyes. He let go of the shovel handle. It fell to the earth with a muffled thump. Slowly, cautiously, he took a few steps toward her.

Her eyes were soft, limpid with concern and a kind of surrender. When he drew near, however, she raised her beautiful, long-fingered hands and spread them out against his chest.

"Brady—" she said, stopping his advance.

"Clarice." He wanted to hear her name aloud. "If I did good, I did it all for you."

"Oh, no. Don't say that."

"It's true! I did it all for you," he repeated.

"Well, you shouldn't have!" she retorted, backing up in pique. "That's not right. Don't you get it? You can't make it out there working to please me, or your parents, or Harris or anybody. You've got to do it for yourself. Want it for yourself."

"But you got to know how I feel about you."

She shook her head and said fervently, "Don't go there. Please."

"You can't deny there's something."

Clarice took a long, pained breath and dropped her hand. "No, I can't."

Then, just when his heart jumped in hope, she dashed it quickly.

"But be real, Brady. There'd be so many problems and hassles that I can't even begin to list them. And why even bother? I'm graduating next week and then I'm going straight to California. I've got my own life. My own plans. Plans that don't include you."

"Oh." He stepped back, his face flaming, and stuck his hands in his pockets. "Forget it."

"Brady, it's not like I don't care."

He twisted his mouth.

"Don't do this. Not now. Let's just leave it the way it is."

"Yeah? And how's that?"

Her brows furrowed in her customary manner as she offered a tremulous smile, asking him with that smile to please try to understand. She took a step toward him and rested her hand on his arm. "Two people who worked together at something they loved. Who had some good times. Friends. I like to think good friends."

Brady exhaled hard, trying to get his feelings straight in his mind. Deep down, he'd always known nothing would come of his feelings for Clarice. He'd tried so hard to make a difference in his life these past months and she was always there to encourage him. Her smile, her tutoring, her belief in him. He'd actually started believing he could turn things around for himself.

Buh Rooster was there, too. Watching him. And even if it was weird, he thought the rooster *was* his totem. He'd never dare say it to anyone, but whenever someone wondered why the rooster just showed up at the gate, he wanted to say, "It was because of me. The rooster came for *me!*"

Now he knew he was just stupid and wrong about that, just like he was wrong about so many things. He was a dumb loser and he might as well accept that and stop thinking things would be different. Because no matter how hard he tried, things always seemed to end up the same. Dead and buried in the dirt.

"Brady? Tell me we'll still be friends?"

He looked at Clarice, shuttering his face, and shrugged. "Sure," he said. He bent to pick up the shovel and hoist it over his shoulder. "Whatever."

***Soaring.** When the sun warms the ground unevenly, bubbles of warm air rise in columns known as thermals. Raptors seek out thermals for lift, allowing them to fly upward with minimum effort. Raptors stretch out their wings and tails, catch a thermal and literally ride the wind.*

18

MAY WAS IN FULL FLOWER. THE SUN SHONE warm and both the earth and Ella Elizabeth Majors bloomed—sweet smelling, slow moving, swaying, glistening, opening to the pink light that shone across the Lowcountry. Seemingly overnight, the grounds of the Coastal Carolina Center for Birds of Prey crept from pastoral hazes of soft green and pastel blossoms to a sultry, lush jungle. Ella marveled at her first Lowcountry spring. She could no longer peek through leggy branches at the mews or the pens. She had to meander around thickets of tangled crepe myrtles and oleander, towering magnolias dramatic with eight-inch white flowers, twisting vines of flowering jasmine and, most exotic of all, stubby bushes bursting with delicate, waxy gardenias.

The women at the center were intoxicated by the sweet-scented breezes. They smiled more frequently and collected blossoms by the armfuls into vases, glass jars and bowls. They placed them on counters, tables, beside their beds, on any empty surface they found in an age-old attempt to bring a bit of springtime indoors.

On this morning, Ella opened the clinic's refrigerator to find gardenia blossoms lying beside plastic bins filled with fish, mice and rats. She chuckled at the delicious irony as she pulled out breakfast for the black vulture orphans. This was a big day for the pair. She and Maggie were moving them to an outdoor pen a distance away from the clinic. It was the last step toward their reunification with the wild.

Most of the orphans that had filled the pens were already freed. Harris had climbed up the tower to place the pair of bold young eagles in the hack box. Volunteers had released the great horned, barred and screech hatch-year owls in woodlands all around South Carolina. All that were left were the two vultures, dubbed by Maggie Tweedledum and Tweedledee.

"They certainly are tranquil about the whole thing," Ella commented when they finished weighing each vulture for the last time and affixing ID bands on their legs.

"I'm worried about that," Maggie admitted. "They should be picking and hissing. They're entirely too comfortable with us. You know, every darn time I fed them I stomped my feet and clapped my hands to make them afraid." She shook her head in worry. "Didn't make a dent."

"Well, there's nothing left but to keep our fingers crossed and give them a chance to go home. Tweedledum and Tweedledee are good to go."

"Tweedledumb and Tweedledumber, is more like it," Maggie muttered in feigned disgust as she lowered them into transport boxes. The pair looked up at her without fear as she closed the top over them. "Let's go."

Ella laughed again. Maggie wasn't fooling anyone. Everyone knew she doted on those two vultures. "Where are we taking them, anyway?"

"Down the road a ways, to The Restaurant."

"The Restaurant? What's that?"

Maggie smirked and bent to pick up the towels and a transport box. There was a skittering inside when she lifted it. "You'll see. Come on."

Ella carefully lifted her transport box with its traveler and followed Maggie out. It was another sunny day, clear and without humidity. They walked down the road at a companionable pace, turning at the fork that led to the creek. The bramble was thicker on this narrow path, and now that spring was in full flower it was slow-going. They wore jeans despite the heat to prevent scratches from the prickly stems of coral bean plants, briars, swamp roses and thistle.

"Mind your step!" Maggie warned.

Ella zigzagged around a large, bustling anthill.

"I swanny, you can always tell if a person's a Northerner by the way they walk through a field," Maggie told her. "They're looking at the trees and the flowers. A Southerner knows to keep eyes on the ground for fire ants. You only have to step on a hill once to never do it again."

"Harris is always telling me to keep my eyes on the sky."

"Yeah, well, he would. He wears thick boots, too, if you notice." They walked a bit farther before Maggie tilted her head and asked, "So, how're things between you two?"

"Things?"

"You know, are you getting along?"

"Why wouldn't we be?"

"You seemed a little put out when you came back from the river. I figured you had a fight of some sort."

That seemed like years ago to Ella now. "We did. But we worked it out."

"I'm glad to hear it. What with everything being off-kilter with the rooster getting shot and Clarice leaving, I couldn't really tell." They walked a little farther in silence. "So, everything is fine between you, then, right?"

Ella sighed and watched the ground. She knew Maggie sensed something was going on—was just dying to ask—and had held off as long as she could. Ella and Harris had done their best not to be obvious in the week since that fateful river trip, for Marion's sake, especially. Everything was too new, too sensitive, and she still felt too vulnerable. Her love filled her, suffused her with happiness, and she felt sure anyone who looked at her could see the glow. She didn't want to share it lest, like a wish, once spoken the spell was broken.

"We're very happy," she replied, hinting at the truth.

Maggie turned her head and studied her. "I hope you don't take this the wrong way—"

That phrase never heralded good news. Ella tensed as she walked.

"Be careful, Ella."

"What about? Ants?"

"I'm not joking."

Ella bristled. "Are you still worried about Harris? Do you think he's going to get hurt? By me?"

"No!" she said, stopping. "I think you are."

Ella's step faltered and she stopped walking.

"He's married," Maggie blurted out. "It's not a normal marriage, but he's still got a wife."

Ella hesitated before saying, "I know."

"Oh," she replied with a blank look. Then, focusing intently, "You do?"

"Harris told me that day at the river."

Maggie readjusted the transport box in her arms, but her

face was drawn in private thought. They began walking again along the path.

Ella struggled to find a way to ask the question that was preying on her mind. Finally, she asked hesitatingly, "Do you think he won't leave her?"

Maggie swung her head around and said boldly, "I wish to God he would."

Ella faced her and the two women shared a smile filled with commiseration. Ella saw a woman who could give to her family, to the birds at the center, to a friend and still have compassion left to share. And despite her generosity—or because of it—she wasn't afraid to speak her mind.

"What's she like?" Ella asked, needing to know.

Maggie clamped her lips in thought. "Beautiful is the first thing that pops to mind," she replied after a moment. "Manipulative is the next. Why he can't see that she's using him, and that he's wasting his time hanging on to that disaster he calls a marriage, I'll never know. He should cut her out of his life like a tumor instead of always being there for her when she's broke or needs a place to stay or whatever. I see the way he is with you. How happy he's been. Ella, this is a guy who hasn't been happy in a very long time. I'm sure he loves you." She paused again. "But mark my words. Fannie will return. And when she does, I just don't know what he'll do. Some patterns are hard to break."

Hearing it, Ella knew it to be true. "It's a chance I'll have to take."

"So, you love him that much?"

"I do."

Maggie shook her head with foreboding. "Then I hope it all works out for both of you. Just know that I'm here if it doesn't. For Marion, too."

"Thank you, Maggie. That means a lot to me."

A few steps on Maggie added, "My house isn't too far from here, you know. We live just minutes away. You should bring Marion by more often so she can play with Annie. We'll drink coffee or have lunch. It'd be good for both of them."

Ella understood the unspoken offer implied in this invitation. It occurred to Ella that Maggie was very good at listening and was good at keeping secrets, too. Both good qualities in a friend. She hadn't had a friend in a long time and confidences did not come easily for her. Harris she could talk to, of course, more and more each day. But should a problem rise between them, she might need someone who would understand and have her interests at heart.

"I will. I promise," she replied.

There was nothing more to say on the topic so they walked in silence until they came upon a large clearing in the woods surrounded by trees, some of them gray and scarred with death. In the center was a ten-by-ten chain-link dog pen, and in the center of this was a blue dog kennel. Clustered around the fence, peeking inside, were five vultures, both turkey and black.

"Well, here we are," Maggie said.

"What are the vultures doing around there?"

"They smell the food. Did you know that vultures have an acute sense of smell? At least turkey vultures do. The black vultures kind of come along for the treat. It evolved to help them find food. Those hungry guys over there are sniffing the leftovers I brought down earlier. We dump them here every week. The vultures, being smart, know this and are waiting to be served. Take a look," she said, pointing to the surrounding trees.

Sitting in the tops of trees, hunched with their black wings partially spread to the sun like kites, were another six to eight vultures. Waiting.

"Now I see why you call it The Restaurant."

"Yep. Vultures are communal. That's what makes this setup so perfect for these babies to learn about their own kind. We'll put the Tweedles in the kennel for a while where they can look out and identify with the other vultures. Then we'll wean these babies from the kennel to the wild. They'll have to learn, or else." She grinned. "It'll be a heck of a thing to get that kennel in the trees!"

"It's kind of unnerving seeing them all up there," Ella said, looking at the vultures gathered high in the surrounding trees.

"Nah. Think of them as just lining up, waiting for The Restaurant to open. It's a shame that vultures have a bad rap. My grandmama used to tell me to beware of being touched by a vulture's shadow on account you'd be touched by sickness or death."

"I was told that if I was bad, a vulture would catch me and peck my eyes out."

"See? That's exactly what I'm talking about! Most people think of vultures as these disgusting birds that only eat dead things. But what they don't know is that they aren't killers at all. They clean up those dead things that otherwise would make this a pretty dirty planet."

"A lot of dying happens in the wild."

Maggie nodded in agreement. "Did you know that vultures still gather at Gettysburg?"

"As in the Battle of Gettysburg in Pennsylvania?"

Maggie nodded again. "Fifty thousand men died in that battle," she began. "And countless horses. They say the fields were flowing in rivers of blood and the carnage of men and boys littered the field. After it was all over, they did their best. Eventually, the army buried the men, but the corpses of the horses were left lying where they fell. So the vultures did their job and cleaned the fields. They began appearing the day after the battle ended. More came every day, from all over. That winter they didn't migrate but stayed on, probably because there was a steady food source. Since then, more than nine hundred black and turkey vultures have returned year after year to the Gettysburg National Park."

While Ella listened, she watched as several more vultures gathered overhead, their black, broad wings gracefully circling, checking out the action below. When Ella and Maggie reached the dog pen in the middle of the field the vultures dispersed to a safer distance but watched carefully in their hunched-shouldered stance.

"Okay," Maggie said, opening up the chain-link gate. "Let's see how the Tweedles like their new digs. Welcome to your new home, guys."

It didn't take them long to prepare the kennel and lay a meal for the orphans, then to lock them inside the fence. Before they left, Maggie and Ella emptied the bucket of leftovers on the ground a few feet from the kennel.

Ella wrinkled her nose. "If those vultures have any sense of smell at all, they'll catch a whiff of that."

"Oh, they know," Maggie said, looking at the rustling of feathers in the trees.

They had not even left the clearing before the vultures flew to the carrion and began feeding. Sure enough, a few minutes later, the two orphans inched their way closer to the fence, closer to the adults, curious as to what the furor was all about.

Maggie and Ella smiled with satisfaction.

"Nature will out," Maggie said.

★ ★ ★

Harris received the phone call from a counselor at Lincoln High first thing the following morning.

"Hello, Mr. Henderson? This is Madeline Dreskin. I'm a counselor at Lincoln High School. I'm calling about a student who has been referred to me because of a fight that broke out on the school grounds. I was hoping you might find the time to come to my office and talk? The student's name is Brady Simmons."

Harris arrived at Lincoln High before noon. Ella had convinced him to wear a tie and it felt like a noose around his neck as he sat in a hard-backed plastic chair waiting for Miss Dreskin to finish with her appointment. Harris hadn't been in a high school in more years than he could remember. Were the boys always so big and muscular? he wondered. And the girls… Some of them looked like fully grown women and dressed like it, too. He felt like an old man in his tie and pressed shirt among all these kids in jeans, T-shirts, tattoos and body piercings.

The office door opened at last and a slight, fair-skinned young boy with acne slunk from the room with his eyes averted, as though embarrassed to be seen coming from the counselor's office.

"Mr. Henderson?"

He stood to meet her. Miss Dreskin didn't look much older than the students. She was small-boned and had an athletic prettiness. However, her suit and oxford shirt marked her as "the other" as clearly as his tie did, and coming close to shake her outstretched hand, he saw fine lines in her deeply tanned skin. Still, he bet she had her share of lovesick boys in the high school to fend off.

After they sat down on the standard, government-issue

chairs, she folded her hands on a manila file on her desk and looked at him earnestly.

"I have to be honest, this is a complex case," she began. "At first glance, I thought Brady Simmons was just another poor, toughened kid with no respect for authority, no care for his future, just biding his time until he can get out. I see a lot of those boys and there's not much I can do to help them. Then I saw the police report about that incident with the eagle. After I got past my flush of fury, I read on that he's been doing community service at your place. Seemed to me a just sentence." She opened the file and riffled through the pages. "The Coastal Carolina Center for Birds of Prey, right?"

Harris crossed his legs and nodded. "That's right."

"How long has he been working there?"

"Since mid-January. He came twice a week. Now he comes three times a week."

"And why is that?"

"That third day is on his own time. He's a volunteer."

She closed the file and pursed her lips. "I see. Is that customary?"

"Brady's the first case of his kind we've ever had. Other than a few staff members, most everyone who works at the center is a volunteer."

"How would you describe Brady's work at the center?"

"Good. More than good. He's reliable and hardworking. And let me tell you, he's had some of the worst jobs. Jobs most kids his age wouldn't do. He had a chip on his shoulder when he first started. I'll admit that. But he's come a long way. I'd go so far as to say he's part of our core team. I'm proud of the boy." He dropped his foot and leaned forward. "What's this all about, anyway?"

"That's what I'm trying to figure out. Brady's been in

a scuffle with a couple of boys. Boys that up till then had been his close friends. The school's put him on probation. But honestly? Early reports were that he started the fight. Brady would have been expelled from school except that the other boys involved refused to implicate him. And—" She smoothed her hand over the manila file in thought.

"Brady has been making remarkable progress in the past few months. He's brought his grades up to passing and better. He took the SAT prep course, and he's even been in to talk to the college counselor about applications and scholarships. Did you know about that?"

Harris shook his head. "No, but it doesn't surprise me."

"But now, a week before exams, he seems to have crash-landed. He's been skipping classes, not handing in homework and now this. I'd like to find out why before it's too late. You've obviously been a good influence on the boy and I'm wondering if you can help."

Harris looked at his hands, quickly reaching conclusions of his own. At least now he knew why Brady had shown up with a black eye and split lip. And he had a pretty good idea why Brady had started the fight. If his suspicions were true, he couldn't blame him one whit for knocking some sense into those boys. There'd been too many cases of his birds being shot. And he could not prosecute due to the uneasy peace between the resentful locals and the conservationists, who were seen as taking away land and hunting rights. In any case, he couldn't discuss his suspicions. That was Brady's private business.

He told Miss Dreskin instead about the influence of Lijah and Clarice Gaillard on Brady, giving them full credit for any growth the boy might have experienced. He concluded with the departure of Clarice from the center and the shooting of the rooster.

"I don't think it was the loss of any one of these alone that set him off," he said. "But maybe both of them hitting at the same time shook his resolve. I don't gather he gets much support at home."

"His mother tries, but she has four other children to worry about plus a job. That's a lot to juggle. His father never returns my calls."

Harris knew about absentee fathers and felt a sudden sympathy for the boy. "I'm not family and I only see him three times a week. What do you think I can do?"

She sighed, clearly uncomfortable with her lack of answers. "Brady has exams next week. Then he's out for the year. This is a critical moment in his life. I'd hate for him to fail now, when he's so close to turning things around for himself. If there's anything you can think of..."

He stood then and reached over the cluttered desk to shake her hand. "I'll do what I can."

When Brady arrived at the center the next morning, Harris handed him his falconer's glove and told him to fetch PEFA 14, the young peregrine falcon. Brady's eyes widened with surprise, but he did as he was instructed without comment. Harris hoped a flying lesson would instruct more than the bird on the art of flying.

He chose PEFA 14 not only because the falcon needed the exercise but also because, in an odd way, he seemed the most like Brady. Young, full of promise, but a bit "batey"—too quick to jump from the perch or fist. And Harris hadn't been blind to Brady's preference for the talented, cocky falcon.

They walked across the wide, flat flying field with Brady to Harris's right and the falcon, hooded, on his left fist. A breeze rolled across the field, swaying the grass and ruffling the feathers of the hooded falcon. It shook its tail, ringing the bell.

"This is far enough," he said to Brady when they reached midfield.

The boy dropped the canvas bag on the ground, then stood with one foot before the other, waiting. Harris reached up and deftly removed the hood from the bird. The young falcon's eyes were instantly alert and the ridge of his brow made him look all the more intense as he scanned his surroundings. PEFA 14 was a handsome bird, not yet grown into the blue-gray color of an adult, but with the bold, distinctive mustache markings. Watching nearby, Brady's eyes were as hooded as the falcon's had been, but Harris could read the signs of his excitement as readily as he could the young falcon's.

Brady stood with his broad shoulder muscles taut beneath the birds of prey center T-shirt that he'd been so proud to receive. His hair, longer now, tousled in the wind like the falcon's head feathers. Both Brady and PEFA 14 were on the verge of soaring, Harris thought to himself. Both of them were still tethered.

He thought back to his own jumbled-up feelings at that age. Sixteen was a tough age to be, full of wildly swinging emotions and merciless self-examination. It was an age of longing to be free to make your own decisions. To branch out on your own but without the legal support or the wherewithal to act. Harris knew what he had to do to train the falcon, yet he was on shaky ground with a boy but a breath away from manhood.

He asked, "Do you want to put the bird on your fist?"

Brady straightened with surprise. "Yeah! I mean, yes, sir."

Harris acknowledged the respect that spoke well of Brady's

intentions. "Then come on over here. Have you been practicing your falconer's knot?"

"Yes, sir. I've got it down."

"Well, let's see it," he said, handing him the long end of
the leash.

Brady knotted one end of the leather leash to his glove
with impressive dexterity, then moved his gloved fist close
to the falcon. "Step up," he said, and PEFA 14 stepped up to
Brady's fist without hesitation.

"He's yours now," Harris told him.

Brady held the bird at a good distance and angle. The
falcon sat comfortably on his fist and roused his feathers, a
compliment to the boy.

Harris nodded his approval and stepped aside, giving the
falconer his rightful space.

"Flying's a funny thing," he said to Brady, sure now of
the boy's attention. "Almost all birds can do it. But a raptor
doesn't just fly. It glides, hovers and soars. And raptors are
fast. Falcons, like the one on your fist, are the fastest of all.
They've been clocked in at dive speeds of up to one hundred
and fifty miles per hour. He'll target his prey from an aston-
ishing height, then ball up his feet, tuck in his feathers and
dive, knocking out his prey when he hits it. Hard."

He looked pointedly at Brady's black eye, letting him
know in that glance that he knew about Brady's fight at the
school.

Brady colored, catching the inference.

Nothing more needed to be said on the matter. "I reckon
they fly around forty to fifty miles per hour in level flight.
Not that that's anything to sniff at." He looked at the falcon
with admiration that could be heard in his voice. "Few creatures can compare to the perfection of a peregrine falcon in
the wind."

Harris pointed to Brady's wrist. "Watch your fist."

Brady had been so caught up in what Harris was saying that he'd let his wrist turn in, causing the bird to foot awkwardly.

"You've got to always be aware when a bird's in your care," he said sharply.

"Yes, sir." He quickly corrected it.

Harris looked at the boy and, in his earnest expression, read his heart. He'd worried that Brady would be insolent or churlish in training. Many young boys didn't like being corrected or told what to do, especially not boys who'd been raised with a hard hand and harsher words, as Brady had been. This young man had heart, just as that young falcon on his wrist did. Harris could see that now. They'd both do whatever was asked of them, as long as it was asked with respect.

"There was a time when only lords and kings could fly peregrine falcons," he told Brady. "Having one was a sign of status. A privilege. And a great responsibility, not only to the bird, but also to oneself. When you fly your bird, Brady, you fly with him. All the time and effort you work together forges a bond that is as profound as any you will ever know. When your bird succeeds, you'll be bursting with pride. And when he fails, as he sometimes will, you must accept it and bear it privately. No moping or outward displays of emotion. The falcon will come to depend on your consistent strength and wisdom. If you cannot commit to this, cannot commit to endure the ups and downs with the bearing of a king, then you should hand me back the falcon now and not attempt to fly the birds." He paused, then said with conviction, "But if you can, then this falcon is your responsibility to train."

He saw Brady's shoulders straighten as his chest expanded.

Harris's eyes gleamed and he nodded. "Very well," he said, and turned to face the wind. "Let's start flying."

Later that week, Ella heard Harris calling from outside. "Ella! Marion, come quick!"

Ella dropped what she was doing and came running from the house with Marion in hand. Her braid slapped against her back as they sprinted across the lawn toward Harris and Lijah standing at the edge of the pond. Breathless, they arrived to find the two men with wide grins on their faces.

"Look!" Harris exclaimed, pointing toward the hack tower at the opposite side of the pond. "I promised you that you'd see this."

"What is it, Daddy?" Marion asked when he bent to swoop her in his arms.

"Look up there, honey," he said, pointing to the tower. "See the eagle sitting up there on the ledge?"

"I see it!" Marion exclaimed, clutching him tight with excitement. "What's he doing?"

"Getting ready to fly," Lijah answered her. "His sister's already been flying for a couple of days now. She swoops by just to needle him, she does. He cries after her. Gets right up to the edge, tottering." He chuckled softly. "Thought the wind was going to take him a few times."

Ella drew near to Harris and Marion and felt bonded to them as they watched the young eagle about to spread its wings.

The fledgling threw back his head and cried its thin, reedy call. He would not acquire the white head and tail or the yellow beak and feet for another four or five years. Yet already he was full-size and bore the proud stance and threatening glare of the adult.

The eagle inched to the very edge of the platform, lured

by the siren call of the wind. He beat his wings again, as though to gather his courage. Harris had told Ella that an eagle's first flight was fraught with life-and-death peril. Yet his instincts urged him onward. This primal call demanded him to leap forward and take his place in the cycle of nature: to fly, to hunt, to pounce, to conquer, to breed, to nest. If he survived, his reward was to soar with the gods.

The young eagle flapped his wings in earnest, leaning forward. Ella clutched Harris's arm when the eagle teetered, almost losing his balance. But the wind caught him in an updraft and he was swept up, airborne at last! Ella felt her chest expand as she watched him sail over the pond, his knife-straight ebony wings slicing the blue sky. He soared right over their heads toward the open field, then began to angle downward. His first flight ended as he lowered to the earth in a graceless landing, tumbling clumsily to a careening stop. He stood still for a moment, comically looking about, unsure of what he was supposed to do next.

"He'll get the hang of it," Harris said, beaming with exhilaration.

"My heart done dropped to my shoes," Lijah said, shaking his head.

"I have to tell you, he had me worried there for a minute," Ella said, exhaling heavily. "I thought he was going to crash."

"He could have," Harris replied. "Only half of the eagle fledglings survive their first year. There's a lot to learn that first year besides how to fly. Now he has to learn how to hunt and he only has this summer to do it. Then he's on his own."

"You mean he won't go back to the hack box?"

"Oh, he'll keep hanging around for a few more weeks, as long as we keep bringing food deliveries. Sort of like what

344 Mary Alice Monroe

the parents would do so they don't starve while they're learning. This pair will keep showing up at the box until one day—" He shrugged. "They just won't come back."

"We should all be like Buh Eagle," Lijah said in his storytelling tone of voice. "When Buh Eagle's babies get big and the nest gets crowded, the mother eagle, she flies out and gets herself a nice fish or a varmint. Then she swoops by the nest with it dangling in her feet. Real close, so they can get a good look at it. Those hungry babies cry and beg for it. But she don't feed it to them. No, she don't. She calls for them to come and get it. She makes those grown children work for their bittle. 'Cause if she didn't, they'd be lazy and fat and never leave the nest. They'd never learn how to fly. All grown children got to learn how to fly and hunt and make their own nest. Yessir," he said, nodding his head. "We should all be like Buh Eagle."

Ella reached up to hold Marion's chubby hand, still sticky from the snack she'd been eating. Ella was thankful that Marion was as yet a nestling. It was, she knew, only a summer away until Marion went off on her own to school for the first time. That would be her first nudge off the platform, that brief airlift before returning for food and comfort. Someday, however, she would go off and not return home, and it was Ella's duty to urge her to go, to teach Marion how to fly.

Ella squeezed the hand and smiled up at the child in Harris's arms. He looked down at her, smiled and wrapped his free arm around her.

This was, she knew in her heart, one of those life moments she'd remember forever. It felt to her as though the sun was shining on the three of them, spotlighting them. Her family! She'd never felt such a bond. Her dream of a family of her own had come true. She'd grabbed the brass ring. Not the gold ring, not the one worn on the left ring finger of her hand. But as she stood beside this man and child she loved so completely, her heart trembled and she told herself that brass was good enough. After all, it was more happiness than she'd ever believed would be hers.

***Gliding.** Raptors tuck in their wings to glide downward at a controlled angle called gliding. By combining soaring and gliding from one column of rising air to the next, raptors can efficiently fly for many miles. Soaring carries the raptor upward on a thermal. Gliding is the downhill ride.*

19

IT WAS THE MOST ORDINARY OF MORNINGS. ELLA awoke at 6:00 a.m., dressed quickly, wound her skein of hair and prepared a simple breakfast of biscuits, ham and grapefruit. Harris was leaving for a flight demonstration and would be gone for the day, so Ella and Marion were busy packing a cooler of snacks and drinks for him. They were having fun writing notes to Harris on napkins so he'd be surprised when he opened them and he'd know how much he was loved. Marion prattled happily, campaigning again for a puppy. She longed for one and was close to convincing Ella to be her ally against her father. They were chatting about this when Ella heard the sound of gravel crunching beneath tires. She smiled, thinking Maggie was arriving at the center. Maggie had been busy lately and she hoped her friend could spare a minute for a cup of coffee and a quick visit. So she was pleased when she heard footfalls on the front porch.

"Come on in," she called from the kitchen. "It's open."

She heard the door creak and leaned back from the sink to look through the kitchen to the living room.

It wasn't Maggie. This woman was as tall as her but slender as a reed. Instead of red, this woman's hair was blond and worn shaggy to her shoulders, and she had legs that went on forever under her short skirt. She had the looks of someone who might once have been beautiful back when her skin was dewy and her eyes clear and full of youthful confidence. Though still striking, this woman looked tired. Worn-out by bad choices and hard living. She wasn't old, but time had not been kind.

Ella slowly dragged her hands from the sink and dried them on the towel hanging from her waist. She felt as if everything was in slow motion, the way she'd heard people describe what it was like the seconds before a car accident. They saw it coming, knew disaster was going to strike, but they could do nothing to avert it.

Ella knew who this woman standing in the living room was. Knew before Marion peeked around the corner, gasped and sprinted across the room, leaping into the woman's arms.

"Mama!"

"Marion? Are you my Marion?" the woman cried, her accent a heavy Southern rural. "No! I can't believe my baby has gotten so big! Let me get a good look at you." She leaned away from Marion's tight grasp to hold her at arm's length. "Why, you are the prettiest thing I ever did see!"

Marion's face was flushed with pleasure as she lunged forward again to hold her mother tight.

Ella watched in a desolate silence and felt as though Marion's arms were crushing her heart instead. She tugged at the towel and laid it on the counter, leaving her hand there to steady herself.

The woman detached herself from Marion's grip and rose to stand. She smoothed out her T-shirt, her fingers tipped with scarlet, while her gaze slowly circled the room with a proprietary air. Ella lowered her arms and waited until the gaze landed on her.

"Who are *you?*" the woman asked with a combative tone.

Ella drew back her shoulders and stepped into the room.

"It's my mama!" Marion exclaimed, reaching out to grab hold of her mother's hand again, eyeing her with adoration.

"That's right," she said, placing her free hand on her hip. "I'm Fannie Henderson and this is my house. And you are?" she asked again.

Ella gathered her hands together. "I'm Ella Majors, Marion's nanny."

Understanding dawned on Fannie and a kind of relief fluttered across her face. "You mean the baby-sitter?" She laughed shortly and her gaze insolently traveled over Ella. "Yeah, I should've known. You must be new. You're not the same one I met before." She turned back to Marion, dismissing Ella with her shoulder. "I swear, you sure go through them, honey pie," she said to the child. "I can't keep track."

"I should imagine there are a number of baby-sitters you haven't met. It's been what?—one year, two, since you've come by?"

Fannie straightened slowly, and when she turned her head, Ella could see the battle lines had been clearly drawn.

"I don't see where that's any business of yours."

"Anything that concerns Marion is my business."

"Is that so?"

Ella tightened her lips and glanced over at Marion who stood near her mother listening intently. Ella felt the force of a hundred words sizzling on her tongue, but Marion's rounded eyes silenced them. She returned a pointed gaze to Fannie, forced a tight smile on her face, then replied, "Quite."

Fannie smirked and looked down at her daughter. "Honey pie, where's Daddy? I want to say hello."

"He's at the clinic."

"Want to go with me to find him?" she asked, and when Marion nodded eagerly, the two of them began walking hand in hand toward the door.

"Marion!" Ella called after her. The child stopped short and twisted to look back at her, the picture of innocence.

Ella racked her brain, trying to think of a good-enough excuse to keep the child from going out the door with Fannie. There wasn't one, and it was silly, anyway. Of course Marion wanted to be with her mother.

"Never mind."

"Let's go, precious," Fannie said with a smug grin. The last thing Ella heard from the porch was Fannie's high-pitched laugh and, "Won't he be surprised?"

Ella didn't know how long she stood at the sink, mechanically washing dishes, pots, anything she could get her hands on. She had to keep working or she'd walk out the door straight to the clinic to find out what was happening. It wasn't long, however, before Harris came rushing into the house. He paused at the kitchen, a hand on the door frame, his gaze searching.

"Are you all right?" he asked, his words breathy from his run.

Ella nodded but kept her eyes on the sink. "Yes. Of course."

"I didn't expect her to turn up."

"I know. But she's here."

Harris stepped forward to put his arms around her. She leaned into him, resting her face against his shirt and inhaling his familiar scent.

"Let's get away. We can go fishing tomorrow," he said close to her ear. "We can spend some time to talk this through."

"Tomorrow?" she asked, stepping back and looking at him through disbelieving eyes.

"Sure. Why not?"

"You don't think I'd go on an outing with *her?*"

"She wouldn't have to come—"

"Oh, Harris," Ella said, tossing her sponge and splashing water. "Fannie is here. You have to see what her being here means to us. To Marion. That poor child is beside herself. She won't leave her mother's side for a second. Besides, even if she didn't come along, what kind of a day would it be, knowing we'd come back to her here? In our house."

She choked on the final phrase. "What am I saying? It's not my house."

"Yes, it is."

When she shook her head a few tears spilled down her cheek. "When Fannie had said 'my house,' it hurt because there was validity to it. When I say it, it sounds false in my ears, no matter how much I wish it were true." She grabbed for a towel and wiped the tears from her cheeks. "I knew this day would come, but I'd hoped it would delay a while. Oh, Harris, we've had so precious little time together."

"What are you saying?"

She looked up into his eyes. "Maybe I should leave."

"No."

"How can I stay with things the way they are?"

He opened his mouth to reply, but they heard the front

door swing open and Fannie's voice, high with forced cheer.

"Hello? Where is everyone?"

Ella and Harris exchanged a glance.

"We'll talk tonight," he told her, grabbing her hand. "We'll find a place to be alone. Promise you won't leave before I get back."

"Okay."

"I wish I didn't have to leave now," he muttered, almost a curse. "I'd send Maggie on this one but it's important and…"

"Harris?" Fannie called again from the front room.

"Go," Ella said. "You have to." She looked up with desperation in her eyes. "Just come back as quickly as you can."

Harris left for his flight demonstration. Ella found she couldn't bear to stay in the house while Fannie and Marion had a giggle fest and painted their nails while watching television. Leaving Marion in Fannie's care, she hurried to the clinic.

She found Maggie standing outside the clinic's narrow front steps beside the two black vulture orphans. The Tweedles were begging for food, standing in a low squat with their wings drooping.

"They're back!" Maggie shouted to her as she approached. She stood pink faced with her arms crossed as they waddled back and forth aimlessly. "They walked all the way back from their pen. *Walked!*"

"What went wrong?" Ella asked when she drew near.

"I don't know," Maggie groaned. "When I went to check on them the other day, they were plastered against the fence, just dying to join the other vultures. So we let them out.

They seemed okay the first couple of days, but..." She raised her arms in a futile gesture. "Here they are again."

"They're not the only thing that's back," Ella said ominously. When Maggie looked at her with curiosity she said, "Fannie's here."

Maggie's mouth dropped open. "No! When?"

"Just this morning."

"Does Harris know? Did he see her before he left for the demonstration?"

Ella nodded and put her hands to her face.

"Oh, sugar, how are you?" she asked, coming close and placing a comforting hand on Ella's shoulder.

"Oh, Maggie, it's been torturous. It was instant dislike. And the woman can't stop talking. She's watching television with Marion and there's nothing I can do to stop her. I'm just the *baby-sitter.* What can I say to the child's mother?"

"You can tell her to stop," she said with righteous indignation.

"No," she said, dropping her hands. "That's not my place. It's Harris's place."

Maggie made a face. "What are you going to do?"

"What can I do? I thought about leaving, of course. Right away. At least until she left again. But when I thought it through, I realized that I can't leave Marion. Who'd take care of her? She has to have her blood tested and her shots several times a day. Harris is busy and Fannie doesn't know the first thing about taking care of a diabetic child. The risks for Marion are too high for me to get emotional. No," she said with decision. "I won't leave Marion."

"Well, Fannie won't stay long. Not if her track record holds. How long can you hang in there for?"

"I don't know," Ella said wearily. "Not long. I'm not a

nice person. I'll crack and murder her in her sleep. A little shot of what we give the birds ought to do it."

"Don't worry about me. I'll never report it."

Ella laughed, short and pained. Then her smile fell and she grew serious again. "Oh, Maggie, this is so hard. I *hate* women like Fannie. She's my worst nightmare. I've had to deal with women like her for so many years. They expect everyone to take care of them, to pick up their mess—and that's exactly what I ended up doing, over and over again at the hospital. And it's so tragic because their messes are their children who've either gotten sick or hurt or beaten or die…" She put her palms to her eyes. "You don't want to know what I've seen. I just can't forgive women like her for neglecting their children."

She dropped her hands and her face hardened with resolve. "Least of all Fannie. She has Harris. She has Marion. They adore her, and she throws it all away. She doesn't deserve them." Her voice hitched. "Maggie, she'll hurt them again. I just know it."

Maggie reached out for Ella's hand. "No, she won't. You'll be there to stop her."

"I don't know if I can." Ella took a deep breath, collecting herself. "I'll have to talk to Harris alone. First chance I get. I'll tell him what I'm thinking. He'll have to make a decision."

"It's a long time coming."

"I'm afraid, Maggie," she said with whispered urgency.

"Don't be. Hey. What's to choose?" She tried to sound confident. "He loves you, anyone can see that. Hang in there. He'll send Fannie packing."

Ella sighed heavily and looked over at the vultures. They'd flown up to the roof of the clinic and were picking at the shingles with their hooked beaks. It wouldn't take long for them to start doing some serious damage.

Ella stayed in the clinic or the kitchen as much as she could for the rest of the day and into the evening. No pot, tub or appliance was safe from her desperate need to keep busy. She knew what she was doing. She was hiding out, too chicken to step out and deal with the bigger mess that was her life. So she scrubbed.

Harris returned home in the early afternoon, then he and Fannie had gone on a long walk together. Marion sat on the porch waiting for them like a left-behind puppy. When they returned, Marion ran out to meet them. Ella stood at the window and watched as the child bounded into her mother's arms and they embraced while Harris stood close, watching his wife and child. They made a charming family tableau against the backdrop of green trees and spring blooms, and Ella knew a desperate sense of foreboding.

She drew away from the window and busied herself setting the dinner table when they walked into the house. Harris carried Fannie's black zipped duffel bag and tote. His face looked beleaguered as he dropped the luggage to the floor. Fannie's eyes were red-rimmed but she was smiling. Marion, of course, was ecstatic.

Harris looked at Ella and said evenly, "Fannie will be staying here for a few days. Until she gets back on her feet."

There was a stunned silence during which Ella swallowed her defeat. "I see," she replied without a show of emotion. She tried to marshal her spinning thoughts. "Well then… We should see to sleeping arrangements."

Fannie laughed with disbelief. "Sleeping arrangements? I'll sleep where I always sleep. In my own room."

Harris shook his head. "Ella is sleeping in our…the front bedroom."

"Oh," she said, rubbing her hands. "Okay. Well, where are you sleeping then?"

"I'm sleeping in my office."

"In the office?" She rallied, shrugging one shoulder. "Okay. I guess I'll just bunk with you."

"No. It's a single, and anyway, that's not an option." His voice was resolute.

Fannie appeared momentarily frightened by the implication. Then, after mulling it over, she glanced at Ella, her brow raised in speculation. "Oh. I see how it is."

Ella didn't flinch or rise to the bait. She held her hands together and met Fannie's stare, waiting to see how this scene would unfold.

"Well," Fannie said, swinging her arms open in a self-consciously magnanimous gesture. "Hey, no problem. I'll just go on to the cabin. We can fix it up and I'll be fine in there. Kind of like my own little house, you know?"

"That won't work, either," said Harris. "There's someone staying there."

"Who?" she snapped, her voice rising with frustration.

"Lijah Cooper. My bird keeper."

"This is ridiculous! Tell him to leave! I need the place."

"I won't kick him out because you've suddenly dropped in for a visit."

"A visit?" she said plaintively. "A visit? I've come home, Harris."

His face hardened. "Now who's being ridiculous?"

A new voice entered the fray. "You can sleep in my room, Mama," Marion said as she lurched forward to wrap her arms around her mother in a protective gesture.

"Aw, thank you, precious," she replied, bending low to

hug her and kiss Marion's forehead. "I'm glad to know some-one wants me around here."

"I want you," Marion cried, burying her face against Fannie's legs.

An uneasy silence fell. Harris shifted his weight, then said, "All right. You can stay in Marion's room."

The sky was beginning to darken and the diurnal birds in the med pens were roosting. Lijah liked to sweep the hall at this time of the day, as much to spend quiet time with Santee as anything else. Volunteers didn't usually come into the pens at this hour so he was surprised when a strange woman poked her head through the doorway. She stepped inside, letting the door slam behind her.

"Is Harris here?"

She didn't look like a new volunteer so he figured she was that wife of Harris's that he'd been hearing about all day. She didn't seem his type. Her hair was piled high on her head with some sparkly clasp and she put lots of makeup on her eyes. His Martha used to call that type of woman a vamp.

"Well, now, he was here a while, but he left."

"Do you know where to?"

He'd seen Harris walk off in the direction of the hack box tower not ten minutes earlier. "Can't say."

She sighed with frustration, then narrowed her kohl-lined eyes in thought. When she raised them his way, he thought she had the look of a fox.

"How about Ella? Seen her?"

Lijah rested his palms atop the broom and leaned against it. He'd seen Ella race across the yard to meet Harris midway. He didn't look at Fannie, but answered truthfully. "I seen Miss Ella in the clinic this afternoon, about three o'clock."

She began walking down the hall, peeking between the

slats at the birds like some predator picking up a scent. "You know who I am, don't you? I'm Fannie Henderson. Harris's wife," she replied without waiting for an answer.

"Yes'm."

She slanted him a glance, then came to a stop at Med 3. "Is that the eagle Harris has been talking so much about? The one that's been shot?"

"She the one," he replied slowly.

"Really? She don't look so sick. In fact, she looks pretty good."

"She feeling much better now. Harris and Ella got her in tiptop shape. You won't see a prettier eagle than Santee."

"So how come she's still here? Shouldn't she have been set free by now?"

"I can't rightly say. Harris wants to give her time to test her wings. He'll know when the time is right."

"I heard that you're fixin' to leave when the eagle does."

"Yes'm."

"You're the one staying in the cabin, right?"

"That's right."

"Since this eagle came. That was about the same time Ella came, too."

"I reckon that's true."

"You've probably got to be pretty good friends with her by now."

"Miss Ella is a fine lady."

Fannie twisted her lips and stared back into Santee's pen, ignoring the restless footing of the eagle that indicated nervous discomfort.

"That's my cabin, you know. Harris built it for me." She spoke calmly but there was an edgy tone to her voice.

Lijah hadn't heard that fact before and wondered if it were

true. Feeling uneasy, he thought it best not to reply and see where this was heading.

Fannie turned from the pen to face Lijah squarely for the first time. "That's my house, too. And I'm home to stay." She said it as an announcement, as though to dispel any doubt in his or anyone's mind about her position. She took a final look at Santee before stepping away from the pen and heading toward the door. She paused before leaving, turned and let her gaze wander the nine pens. "You know, it's getting crowded around here. I think it's high time we let some of these birds go."

Harris leaned against the wall of the hack box and pulled Ella close beside him. It was a quiet and balmy evening with a breeze that cooled the skin and kept the bugs at bay. Ella nestled against his chest, holding tight. He rested his chin on her head, relishing the scent of her hair. It was second nature to him now to feel Ella's body close to his, to smell her scent, to feel the softness of her skin. They had spent every spare minute together, around the house and at work. Now they had to climb to the hack-box tower to hide away for a few stolen moments.

They sat high up in the eagle's aerie during those brief moments between light and dark when the vibrant colors of the coastline rose toward the heavens, leaving the earth in shadows. This introspective time always made him feel caught in a limbo between regret and hope, joy and despair.

He and Ella had talked for a long time about Fannie, exhausted themselves trying to explain their feelings to each other. Each had tried to be understanding, yet each clung to a position that felt unyielding to the other. To his mind, he'd made his decision to marry Fannie and had, duty-bound, stuck with it. He was not an impulsive man and would not abandon his family, would not leave like his father had—no matter how cruel the consequences. Yet, because of that decision, he faced losing the only woman he'd ever truly loved.

Ella broke the silence when the sun slipped below the horizon. Her voice was hoarse from the tension of holding back tears. "Harris, it's getting late. We should get down and back to the house."

He held her back. "Fannie won't be here for long. A couple of days. A week, maybe two."

"Then what?"

"Ella…" he said wearily. "We've gone over this."

"And it still isn't resolved! You're asking too much from me."

"I want this to work between us," he said with urgency.

"But it can't, not as long as you stay married."

"You knew I was married."

"I know," she admitted.

She sounded so defeated that he wanted to say something to reassure her, but there was nothing more he had the right to say.

"Fannie's coming here has changed everything. I *can't* stay with Fannie here, you know that! And I can't stay after she's left again, because now I've met her and she's real to me. Not some faceless villain out there somewhere. I can't pretend that she doesn't exist any longer. She's your wife. And that fact makes what we share illicit. Immoral. Wrong."

"Ella…"

She looked at him with more tenderness than he felt he deserved, and when she reached up with her small hands to cup his face, he lowered his lips to kiss her fingers.

"I love you," she told him. "And I'll stay for a little while. Not for your sake. For Marion's sake. She needs me and I won't desert her. But this is your mess, Harris. I'm not going to clean it up for you."

"You want me to divorce her."

She took a ragged breath and he saw the answer—*Yes!*—shining in her eyes. He sat up, running his hand through his hair in frustration. The eagles stirred behind him inside the hack box, startled by his sudden movement.

"There's another reason that I've held back on divorcing her that's not so noble."

He could hear Ella move behind him, then come to sit beside him, patient and attentive.

"If I divorce Fannie, as my wife she's entitled to half of what I own. I'd have to sell the property. I couldn't afford to buy her out, not with what the property is worth today. I'd lose the center."

"Harris, let it go," she said, and he heard all her desperation and love in those few syllables. "We'll get more money. You can always build another."

He shook his head no. If only it could be so easy. This question cut deep to the very core of him. How could he explain it to her? He looked back at the two eagles sitting beside each other, brother and sister. Bonded by birth but about to fledge. They'd likely never see each other again. But when they chose a mate, that bond would endure for their lifetime. They would nest and remain site loyal.

"It's not just about money. I've never yearned for material things. As long as I could make enough to provide for my child, my family, I've been content. But I've always had a deep instinct for home. My mother sold off the family land, parcel by parcel, then died and left me alone, with nothing. Ella, everything I am is *here*. I've made a commitment to this place and with it a commitment to my wife. The two are inexorably entwined."

Ella moved in front of him. Her hair hung loose around her shoulders like a luxurious cape and he could barely see her face in the dark shadows.

"Hold me, Harris. I'm afraid."

"I love you," he said vehemently, holding her close. "I know I have no right to say that to you. That I don't deserve to."

She put her finger to his lips, silencing him.

He lowered his head, meeting her lips with a kiss that he hoped would convince her of his love. Their kiss deepened with the night around them, and from somewhere near in the surrounding woods they heard an owl hoot. Harris buried his face in her neck and they held each other with a fervency that bordered on desperation.

Siblicide. *This phenomenon occurs in several species of birds. In a wild nest where two or more chicks hatch, the strongest nestlings may attack and kill the weakest. Siblicide allows the surviving chicks to obtain more food from the parents, thus increasing its chances for survival.*

20

A RECORD-BREAKING HOT SPELL STRUCK THE southeast coast. The only air conditioners in the house were in Ella's and Marion's bedrooms, so Fannie and Marion spent their days locked upstairs thicker than thieves. Ella heard the thumping of feet overhead and an occasional burst of laughter. In the evenings, while Ella sweltered in the kitchen cooking dinner, Fannie took Marion swimming in the pond. From the porch Ella could hear Marion squealing with delight and Fannie calling out "whoopla!" before every splash. When the pair returned to the house to change, the stifling air quickly dried the pond's moisture from their skin, then drew back out beads of perspiration around their foreheads.

The steamy humidity didn't break as the sun lowered. Fannie and Marion liked to stretch out on the sofa to watch television as a fan whirred and stirred the thick air around them. Ella moved from kitchen to living room setting the table, pausing with a stack of plates in her hands to gaze at the pair lying side by side. She couldn't help but notice the strong resemblance between mother and daughter. Their blond hair was exactly the same hue and Marion had Fannie's delicate bone structure. They looked like fairies with their hair frizzled around their heads and their cheeks pink and glowing.

They were bound together by blood and bone, Ella thought, and she felt the distance between herself and Marion widen. The child didn't even notice whether or not Ella was in the room. Ella tugged the towel from her waist to wipe the sweat from her brow and dab at her eyes as she returned to the kitchen.

Dinners were the worst. The rest of the day they could move about like planets in a solar system, each in their own, separate orbit. But at dinner they were forced to sit together and be civil. For the first few days since Fannie's arrival, Ella had escaped the ritual of mealtime grace by pleading kitchen duties. She played the role of nurse, nanny, cook and housemaid. Tonight, however, the ruse had worn thin and Harris pulled her aside in the kitchen and compelled her to sit with the family at the table.

"Who says grace tonight?" Harris asked when they assembled.

"Let Mama!" Marion volunteered.

"Why, okay, precious." Fannie wiggled her brows. "It's been a long time, though."

When they reached out to hold hands, Ella cringed at the thought of having to hold Fannie's hand. Fannie, however, thought the prospect very amusing and her eyes glittered. Ella looked over to Marion and instantly zeroed in on the streak of what looked like chocolate on her palms.

"Marion, what's that on your hand?"

Marion jerked her hand back under the table. "Nothing."

"It's chocolate, isn't it?"

"No, it isn't."

Ella's gaze met Harris's over the table.

"Let me see your hand," Harris said.

Marion swiped her hand against her pants, then held out her palm. Harris grabbed it, brought it to his nose and sniffed. "Where'd you get the candy?"

Ella looked directly at Fannie. "I told you Marion couldn't have sugar. It's not good for her."

"The kid was starving! Besides, what's one little piece going to do?" Fannie replied. "Lighten up, you guys."

Ella was too furious to reply. She turned to Marion and said in a firm voice, "You'll have to give me the candy. You know you can't have it. You'll get sick."

"No!" she shouted, pink-faced with fury.

Ella caught sight of the silver wrapping of a Hershey's Kiss slipping out of Marion's pocket. She reached for it, but Marion, seeing what was happening, was faster and grabbed it first.

"It's mine! My mama gave it to me."

"Marion, give me the candy."

"I don't have to. You're not my mama!"

"Marion…" Harris said, his voice stern.

"You take everything from me," Marion cried, targeting her anger at Ella. "You never let me have any fun. You're mean and ugly and I hate you. Here!" She threw the chocolate piece at Ella and clambered from her chair. "I wish you never came here!" she screamed.

"Marion, honey, don't," Ella said, reaching out to stop her. Marion skirted away and ran from the room, sobbing.

Her footsteps pounded on the rear stairs and her crying, hysterical with exhaustion from the day's excitement, was at a fever pitch. Ella ducked her head to hide her pained expression and picked the melting chocolate candy from her lap with two fingers. A blotch of chocolate stained her white blouse where she'd been hit.

"Don't you ever give that child candy again," Harris ground out, jabbing an index finger in Fannie's face.

"I won't!" she said, backing against her chair with a short laugh, her palms up in surrender, making light of the situation. "Jeez…"

"I'm serious, Fannie," he said, his voice rough with fury. "This is life or death for Marion and I won't have you screw up her blood levels. Whatever Ella says goes, have you got that?"

Fannie's smirk dropped and she appeared very contrite. "I'm sorry, Harris. I didn't realize. Honest, I didn't. It won't happen again. I promise."

He seemed appeased and dropped his hand on the table. "I'll go to her."

"No, let me," Fannie said, rising from her chair. "I'm the one who screwed up. I'll explain to her that I was wrong. And that Ella was right. Okay?" She looked at Harris, then at Ella, smiling sweetly.

After she left for Marion's room, Harris looked at Ella, exhausted.

Ella, ashamed for the tears building in her eyes, looked down at the plate of dinner that had gone cold.

That night, Marion pitched her first temper tantrum in months. Ella knew that emotions were running high and all of the child's pent-up frustrations were exploding. She'd mentally prepared for it, but though she was strong, it took every ounce of her strength to bring Marion, kicking and screaming, downstairs to the bathroom for her insulin shot. Her arms and legs were bruised from where Marion's fists and heels met muscle and she wondered, as she sat the child down on the toilet lid, if this wasn't her punishment for being too proud to ask Harris to help her. She'd wanted to prove her competence to Fannie, but instead the woman was hanging on the bathroom door watching the fiasco and making the matter worse.

"Marion, honey, stop kicking me," she said, breathless. "You know we have to do this."

"No!" she screamed, still kicking. "I don't have to do what you say. I want my mama!"

"What are you doing to her?" Fannie cried from the hall. She clutched the door frame, leaning in. "Stop it, you're hurting her."

Ella held firm to Marion's shoulders and swung around to face Fannie.

"Get out," she said through tight lips. "You're not making this easier for me or her."

Hearing that, Marion went ballistic and held out her arms. "Don't go. Don't go! I want my mama to do it!"

"Marion, she can't. She doesn't know how. Now stop it, this instant. We've done this hundreds of times. There's nothing to be afraid of. Come on, honey, be good."

"I don't want to be good. I don't want you to do anything. I want my mama," she cried piteously, arms reaching out for Fannie.

Ella took a deep breath and swiped a lock of hair from her perspiring face. She hated to ask but she had to get Marion under control. "Fannie, will you help?"

"Me?" she asked, straightening, her eyes wide. "Oh, God. What can *I* do?"

"You can hold her. Calm her down." She took a breath. "She wants *you*."

Fannie released the door frame with reluctance. "Well,

sure. I guess," she said, and entered the bathroom half smiling, half grimacing, with her arms held out to her daughter. She clumsily gathered Marion into her lap on the toilet seat. Marion clung to her like a drowning child, gasping for breath while Fannie stroked her head, crooning and rocking.

Ella had to turn away. When it seemed Marion was calmer, Ella took a deep breath, straightened her back and gathered her resolve. She brought the test kit to Marion with a nurse's cool efficiency. Though the child stiffened and whined, she had calmed down considerably in her mother's arms. Fannie followed instructions and Ella was able to get a quick reading. Marion's insulin levels were high, as expected. Still, Ella sighed with relief that they weren't worse, and after adjusting the insulin dose, she gave Marion the injection without any further hysteria.

Her medical treatments done, Ella put away her equipment and left the cramped bathroom. Neither Fannie nor Marion seemed to notice. Outside the door she leaned against the wall, squeezing her eyes shut and listening to the mother-child banter in the next room. She felt as pitiful as some dog under the table, waiting for fallen crumbs.

"It's too bad you have diabetes," she heard Fannie tell Marion. "I wish it were me, honey pie. I'd take those mean ol' nasty shots for you. It's just too horrible."

"I hate the shots."

"So do I."

Marion sniffed. "Mama, did you go away because I have 'betes?"

"Oh, no, precious!" she replied quickly. "Don't you ever think that, my darling girl. Mama didn't even know you had diabetes!"

"Then why, Mama? Why did you go?"

Fannie rocked Marion, holding her tight. "Oh, I don't

know, honey. It's complicated grown-up stuff. But it has nothing at all to do with you. I'm so sorry I left you. Really I am."

"Don't go away again, Mama. Please..."

"Hush now, baby."

Ella put her hand to her mouth and hurried from the confined house. She couldn't bear to listen any longer. Marion was like a baby bird, chirping with an insatiable hunger for love. And Ella had an endless supply of love to give her. What was breaking her heart—what Ella had to face, no matter how hard—was that the love Marion craved was not hers, but her mother's.

She hurried down the porch stairs into the yard. She didn't know where she was headed, and it didn't matter. Ella just had to get away from the house that was suddenly too small. She paused at the edge of the parking lot to lean against the sedan that had carried her from north to south. She'd carried such hope with her from the mountains to the shore.

She wiped a tangle of hair and sweat from her brow as she gathered her breath. The humidity had to break. The air was so thick she could hardly breathe. Beyond, in the darkness, she could hear the vocalizing of the restless birds as a storm approached.

She looked back at the Cape Cod house nestled between the pines. Only days earlier the three of them had seemed to fit so cozily in those cheery walls. Now one more person had entered the space and suddenly it was like an overcrowded nest at the end of a breeding season. Harris had taught her how, in nature, the strongest nestlings pecked at the weakest one, the misfit who couldn't compete. They viciously, mercilessly, drove the runt from the nest to teeter at the edge until it fell to its death. It seemed so heartless, even murderous, and for a flash she'd hated the birds and the cruelty that always clung to things wild.

She'd learned since those early first days here—they seemed like years ago to her now—to stop looking at things wild through human eyes. Those tame eyes filtered everything with conscience and ego. Humans always had to balance good with evil; right had to triumph over wrong. But there was no right or wrong in nature. No good or evil. What was, simply was. Harris had gone on to explain how, when food was scarce, the likelihood of survival for two nestlings was far greater than three. The nestlings were merely acting out an instinct developed over eons of time. In biology, it was all about the survival of the species. She couldn't pretend to understand it all but she did try to open her mind, as well as her senses, to all that surrounded her. To heed nature's lessons.

Ella walked back toward the house. Even in the dim light she could see her flowers that she'd planted with Marion encircling the porch. Climbing the stairs, she saw her mud boots lined up by the door beside Harris's and Marion's. Sitting down on the bent twig rocking chair, she recalled the many nights she'd sat here with Marion in her lap while they'd told stories or looked at the stars.

This had been her home. Her nest! Everywhere she looked she could see her mark, some proof that she lived here. She couldn't deny that she longed to always sleep in her down-covered bed with her smooth skin nestled against Harris's hard bone, to listen to the melancholy music of the owls outside her window, to wash dishes and Marion's gold-spun hair in the large porcelain kitchen sink.

Yet tonight she wondered if these had all been stolen moments. If she was the extra body in the nest. The runt in sparse times.

Ella curled in the twig chair, tucking one leg beneath her. She propelled the chair's rocking motion with steady, rhythmic pushes from her arched foot. A storm was rolling toward them from the northwest, a long line of black, menacing thunderclouds that had wreaked tornadoes and dumped rain on the prairie states then plowed southward. Oh, it was coming, all right. She could already feel the gusts of cooler wind cut through the thick, humid air. She tightened her arms as a rumble of thunder rolled across the wetlands. It sounded to her like the rattling of sabers.

She closed her eyes and thought of her mother and how she used to gather Ella up in her arms in a rocking chair and rock her back and forth like this. It comforted her to remember the way she could hear her mother's heartbeat if she laid her head against the pillowy softness of her breasts. Wrapped in her mother's arms she was safe, her lids would droop and she could fall into a sweet sleep, no matter what storm or bogeyman had frightened her.

Ella ceased her rocking and stared bleakly out at the night. Of course Marion wanted her mother. It was only natural that she should. This was not something Ella could debate or argue. The bond Fannie and Marion shared was marrow deep. They clung to each other now, safely ensconced high up in that cozy gabled room filled with yellow light.

And she sat shivering alone in the darkness, afraid of the thunder and wishing for the comfort of her own mother's arms. The wind gusted again, bringing with it the first drops of rain. She sniffed the air and could almost taste its cool sweetness as she swallowed hard, her heart fluttering madly, feeling as though she were teetering at the edge, waiting for the fall.

★ ★ ★

A bolt of lightning seared the sky, crackling, heralding the thunder that followed.

"Storm's coming," Fannie said, stepping out onto the porch.

Ella ceased her rocking.

"Marion's asleep. Hope that thunder don't wake her up. I had a devil of a time getting her settled."

Ella pushed against her foot, setting the rocker moving. "I know what you're doing," she said in a flat tone of voice.

"And what's that?"

"You've made me the bad guy."

"Oh, please…"

"The mean person who takes her candy away and gives her shots and doesn't let her watch television."

Fannie rolled her eyes. "I just told her she couldn't have any more candy. Like you wanted me to."

"No matter what you say to Marion now, we both know that you've set it up so that in her eyes you're the victim. Just like her. That I won't *let you* give her candy. That I'm *making you* help give her shots. And I've seen you sneak to turn the TV on when I leave for the clinic, like it's some kind of game. You're acting like her playmate, not her mother."

Fannie put her hands on her hips and moved to stand in front of Ella, towering over her. The two women stared at each other as thunder rolled in.

"We both know that's not what you're really mad about," Fannie said, her eyes sparking like the lightning overhead. "You're pissed that I left Marion in the first place. And now you're mad that I came back. That I'm moving in on this little love nest you've got going for yourself."

Ella's foot blocked the pendulous rocking and she abruptly turned away.

"But what really rocks your boat is that Marion wants me, not you. She wants *me*."

"Of course I'm upset!" Ella cried, unable to stop the burst of feeling. "I'm hurt and angry. God, I'm so hurt! I love that child. I want what's best for her. You've put me in the position of destroying all that I've built with her. I want to have fun with Marion, too. We used to do everything together and now I'm completely cut out of the picture, except to be the wicked witch. You've forced me into that role and I resent it."

"So what? You're not her mother."

Ella felt slapped and sucked in her breath. When she could speak she said with a pained defeat, "I know."

Fannie took a step closer and leaned forward, tilting her shoulder and saying in a lowered voice, "And Harris is my husband."

Ella raised her eyes to meet Fannie's. "I know."

Lightning cracked so close now it lit the sky, illuminating the treetops that waved and trembled in the increasing wind. Drops of rain splattered against them as the first rumblings of another clap of thunder began.

Fannie took a few steps back and angrily swiped at her hair. She seemed electrified and began pacing in the corner of the porch.

"You know something?" Fannie asked, stopping once more in front of Ella. "I'm mad, too. Not at you, but at me. Because I screwed up. Screwed up good. I hurt the two people I love most in this world. And I hurt myself, too. I've done some pretty horrible things. Things I'm not proud of. But I want to change."

"I've heard that before."

"I do," she repeated. "That's why I came back, see? I haven't used in months. I'm clean. Really I am. And I want a chance to make it up to Marion. I don't know about Harris. He may never forgive me. But Marion... She has so much room for me."

The sky opened up and the rain began coming down in earnest. It hammered the porch roof with a deafening roar and flowed from the roof in sheets. Ella rose from the rocker and headed for the door. Fannie reached out to grasp her arm and hold her back. Ella turned on her heel to glare at her, but Fannie's eyes were burning with intent and her grip was iron hard.

"I want to be a good mother," Fannie said to her, shouting to be heard over the storm.

"Then be one."

"The fact is, I can't do it alone." She released Ella's arm, crossing her own. "I...I need to learn to take care of her. I need to learn about this diabetes stuff, her diet and her shots. There's so much I don't know. I've seen you with her. You're good at it. So sure of yourself. Look, I know I'm the last person you want to help, but I have to ask. If not for me, for Marion. Please, Ella, teach me how to take care of my child."

Ella lay limp in the hot, soapy water of the claw-footed bathtub. From time to time she'd run a cloth over skin that held the memory of being thoroughly caressed. This was not the same body of the woman who had arrived at this strange sanctuary months earlier. The seasons had changed. The weather had gone from cold to warm, the trees from bare to lush with foliage. She had changed.

Her eyes slowly closed and she let the water settle around the curves of her breasts and kneecaps, white islands above the water. Her dilemma floated in her mind, repeating over and over again the decision she could not refute.

How many times over the years had she bitterly complained to anyone who would listen about all the mothers who had refused to participate in their child's illness? Or about those who didn't even bother to show up for the training classes, or simply turned a deaf ear to the instructions Ella had tried to offer? She used to pray that just one mother would come to her and say, "Please, teach me to take care of my child."

Ironically, the only woman who had asked was the only one Ella wished had not.

Ella was a nurse. That's who she was. And as a nurse she was committed to helping children thrive.

And so, she would help Fannie.

Ella closed her eyes, seeing the argument to its logical conclusion even as the last of her hopes and dreams drained from her. She would teach Fannie how to care for Marion and her diabetes. It was what she was trained to do. It was the right thing to do. And thus, by doing this, she knew she was opening the door for her own departure.

*__The Cleanup Committee.__ The common name "buzzard"
is the incorrect, slang term for vultures today. "Buzzard" is
derived from the French word busard, or hawk, and correctly
refers to buteos. Early settlers in North America, however,
incorrectly used the name for vultures. Vultures provide a
natural cleaning service for the world.*

21

THE TWO YOUNG VULTURES WERE WREAKING
havoc. They'd picked a hole through the roof and were
plucking out bits of insulation. They followed the volunteers
around whenever they carried trays of food to the pens until
someone relented and fed them. And now that they knew
where their next meal was coming from, they were perma-
nently roosting in the shade of a large oak by the weighing
room. They sat there now, shoulder to shoulder, watching
Harris labor with the heavy chain-link fencing.

Harris didn't know what he was going to do with them.
They were imprinted on humans and clearly had chosen to
live among them rather than with the other vultures. Yet he
didn't want to give up hope of reunification. He was moving
the dog pen from The Restaurant to the shaded area near the
clinic so that he could keep an eye on them until they got a
little older. Then they'd try once more to release them.

Inside the clinic he could see Ella's profile as she worked in the treatment room. For the past week, Ella had been teaching Fannie how to take care of Marion and her diabetes. She was a good teacher, slow, careful and patient with Fannie's endless questions and fears. Ella had used Marion's teddy bear to show the best spots for the shots and to let Fannie practice giving injections. Ella had naturally been hesitant to give Fannie any syringes at all, given her drug history, but Fannie swore on a stack of Bibles that she was clean. In the end, Ella moved forward with the instructions. Each day got a little better, at least as far as the training went.

Harris looked over at the house in the distance and no longer experienced that swell of comfort he had in the past several months. Once more, his house was a place of stress.

Their routine was their lifeline. Each morning they awoke to breakfast. He grabbed a bite and went to the clinic. Then he came back and they endured the clink and clatter of the silverware as they wordlessly cut and chewed their meals. Afterward, they escaped again to their chores. One day became two, then a week, then two weeks, and still they maintained this absurd civility. When Ella decided to spend more hours at the clinic, they altered the routine a bit and kept on going.

But the joy was gone. Ella was withdrawing. They barely spoke anymore, and when they did, it was only about business of one sort or another. She was loath to touch him. Even a brush of shoulders caused her to skitter away. The situation was like it had been at the beginning, only much worse because now they were going backward in their relationship. The strain showed in the brittleness of her voice and the pale color of her skin. When their eyes met she always dropped her gaze, but not before he caught a look of pain.

In contrast, Fannie was blooming. The healthy routine

and diet, as well as long hours in the sun with Marion, put the pink back in her cheeks. She'd stopped wearing makeup and she resembled more the beauty she had been when he first fell in love with her. She made frequent invitations for time alone or to share his bed, and several times she'd moved to embrace him, but he always turned her away. He felt little for her now.

Looking up, he saw Fannie was coming toward him, her stroll across the field easy and confident, as though she belonged here and had never left. She still wore those tight shorts and skimpy tops that exposed her flat midriff, styles better suited for a girl in her teens. He sometimes wondered if that was the age when her maturity ended. She'd likely end up one of those pitiful adults who never accepted adulthood. Peter Pans who clung to their youth by refusing to accept grown-up responsibilities.

"Where's Marion?" he asked when she drew near.

She pointed to the resident bird pens. "She wanted to say hello to the crows. Lijah is with her." She bent forward in a teasing manner while her eyes glittered. "Don't you worry none. I'm taking good care of our little girl."

He frowned and bent to renew his struggle with the unwieldy chain-link sections.

"What are you doing?" she asked, coming closer.

"Putting up the dog pen for those two vultures over there."

"Oh," she replied, casting a cursory glance at the birds. "Harris, can you stop a minute? So we can talk?"

He looked up hesitatingly. "What about?"

"You know what about. About us."

He sighed and straightened, looking at her steadily. "There is no us."

"I know. That's what I want to talk to you about."

He looked over his shoulder toward the clinic window. Ella had moved somewhere and was no longer visible. "Come on over here," he said, guiding Fannie to the shade of the oak.

She followed him, brusquely shooing away the Tweedles as they neared the picnic table. "Go on, get out of here," she said, clapping her hands.

"Leave them be, Fannie. They're not doing any harm."

"I can't stand those things. They give me the creeps. My mama used to tell me they'd eat my eyes out if I was bad."

Harris held his tongue against the words he'd like to have said about Fannie's mother. The vultures moved to the opposite side of the patio, watching them warily.

Fannie stepped up on the seat to sit on the top of the picnic table. Once settled she coyly patted the wood beside her.

He remained standing, putting his hands on his hips. Fannie shook her hair, then ran her hands through it, pulling it back from her face. It was meant as a nonchalant gesture but it struck him as too practiced.

"What do you want to talk about, Fannie?" he asked without enthusiasm. "Are you getting ready to leave?"

She let her hair drop and moved her hands to her knee-caps.

"You can be pretty cruel when you want to be."

"I don't mean to be cruel. Just realistic." He wiped his hands on his pants. "You told me you needed a place to crash till you got back on your feet. I figure you must be getting kind of bored about now."

She recoiled, hunching her shoulders. Her hair fell forward, cloaking her face. "I guess I deserve that," she said. Then she jerked her head up and faced him, eyes pleading. "Harris, I'm so very sorry for walking out on you and

Marion. I was sick, okay? Maybe not with a disease like your mama, but mentally. I was pretty messed up. I had a lot to overcome, you know that better than anyone. You know the way my mama was. All those so-called daddies that came through our place…" She shook her head, as though to scatter the memories away.

"That was a long time ago, Fannie. You're not a child anymore. You're not even a young woman. You're nearing thirty years old and you have a child of your own. You can't use that as an excuse forever."

"It's just…some things are hard to forget, Harris."

"I can't argue that," he said in a low voice.

"I wish to God I never got caught up in drugs. I guess I just needed to escape in any way I could. If only I was able to go back in time and change things." She dropped her hands and shrugged in defeat. "But of course, I can't."

He looked at her, squinting in the sunlight to see her eyes and mine the truth. "Did you need to escape from me? Really, I need to know. Is that why you started using again after we were married?"

"No! God, no. It wasn't you and it wasn't Marion. You were always good to me. I don't know what I'd do if I didn't have you to come home to. I need to know that you're here for me, Harris."

"Then why?"

"There's something inside of me that makes me feel so restless sometimes. Like my skin's crawling, and I have to go off and—" She was getting worked up, rubbing her arms and rushing her words. "I can't explain it! I've made a lot of mistakes, done things I'm not proud of. More than I can ever tell you. Just believe me, Harris, I've paid for my mistakes. I've learned my lesson. And I'm tired, so tired. All I want to do now is stay home and be with my little girl. And my husband, if you'll let me be a wife to you again."

"Fannie…"

"All I'm asking for is another chance," she pleaded. "I'm trying so hard, you can see that, can't you?"

"But for how long? Another week? Another month before your skin starts crawling again and you leave?" He could feel his pent-up anger and resentment building again.

"I won't go again. I promised Marion I wouldn't."

"Marion might believe your promises. I can't," he said, looking away.

"What do you want me to do?" she cried. "I'm her mother. She needs me, Harris, not Ella!"

Harris swung his head around again, glaring at the mention of Ella's name.

"Oh, I'm grateful to her, that's the God's honest truth. She's taught me how to take care of my daughter. But that's her job. We don't need her anymore. I know you have feelings for her, but her being here is confusing to Marion. We'll never have a chance to be a family as long as Ella's around. I can take care of the house now, too. And someday, when things settle down, I'd like to help you with the birds, the way I used to. We used to be a good team, you always said so."

She leaned forward to take his hand and hold it tight while her eyes pleaded. "Harris, honey, I'm still your wife. I still love you. And I want to make it up to you. I may not deserve much, but I deserve a chance. It's my place to be here. To care for our child. This is my home," she blurted out before succumbing to tears.

Harris wanted to put his arm around her, to console her, but he couldn't bring himself to do more than let her hold his hand as she wept. She cried copious amounts of tears that flowed down her cheeks till he couldn't bear it any longer. He moved closer to her as she sat on the picnic tabletop and wept, pulling out a kerchief from his pocket and handing it to her. She took it to swipe her face, then reached up to grasp him around his waist and press her face against the front of his jeans. It was a gesture of intimacy that made him uncomfortable but she held tight, still sobbing. Looking around, he saw only the Tweedles standing nearby, watching them with seemingly little interest.

"Sorry," she said when she brought herself back under control. "I've been holding that in for so long I guess it was like the dam just broke." She sniffed and wiped her nose and eyes with the kerchief. "I'll give this back after I launder it," she said with an attempt at a laugh.

"Mama!"

It was Marion, looking for Fannie.

Fannie laughed, more brightly than before. "That child does flash about. She's going to wear me down. And I love it," she added quickly. She looked up at Harris expectantly, waiting for some answer. "She's our child."

"Marion comes first," he said to her, moving toward an inescapable decision.

"Of course," she replied, her eyes opening wide with anticipation.

"I'll give you this one last chance, Fannie. For Marion's sake." His words caught in his throat. Hearing them, he realized he'd just repeated Ella's words.

Fannie lunged up to wrap her arms around him, delighted. She clung to him, pressing her body against him.

So, this was his decision, he thought dispassionately. After all the angst and sleepless nights, at the end of the day, it came down to duty.

"If you goof up on her medication, even once…"

"I won't!" she exclaimed, giddy with pleasure.

Marion rounded the corner, stopping short when she saw her parents in each other's arms. Her ponytail was askew and her knee was skinned, but she looked like any other healthy five-year-old running amok on a summer's day. She stared at them for a second, as though trying to figure it out. Then her face broke into a heartrending grin and she bolted for them with arms outstretched, throwing herself into her father's arms with complete faith and abandonment.

Harris bent to grab her and swing her up to his chest. Marion reached out her free arm and linked it around her mother's neck, then tugged, bringing both of them close to her so that they were all bound together in a family hug.

None of them saw Maggie standing near the door of the weighing room. Nor did they see Ella standing beside her before she turned and ran in the opposite direction, disappearing behind the cluster of oleanders.

Maggie found Ella leaning against a chinaberry tree, clutching her hands in fists at her sides and staring with a fixed expression out across the water. She was like a stone statue, holding herself hard and unyielding. It didn't seem natural.

"A good cry will do you good," Maggie said as she came near. "My mama always told me to let it all out and I'd feel better. She was right, too."

"No," Ella said. She was holding herself together by a thin rope and had to keep herself very still and breathe hard or she'd lose control. "I won't cry. For I have no one to blame but myself. I never should have let myself love him. Love Marion. They weren't mine to love. He was married. I knew that. He had a wife but I wanted him. I wanted Marion for my own. I stole the fire, like Prometheus. I knew it was wrong but I did it, anyway, and now I'm being punished."

She looked up at her friend and seeing the compassion in Maggie's eyes, she almost lost it. "Do you know how the gods punished Prometheus? He was chained to a rock while an eagle or a vulture ate his liver. Then it grew back and got eaten again. So the pain never stops, you see. Kind of like love. It's fitting, don't you think?"

"Cut it out, Ella. I don't believe that for a minute."

"It's true."

"He's not really married. He's only tethered and he's too dumb to undo the knots."

"What difference does it make? He's bound to his wife. I can't pretend any longer." She pushed herself from the tree, plucking a fallen leaf from her braid as she walked through the tall grass toward Maggie. She stopped short and looked at her tall, strong friend and was filled with gratitude that she had this anchor in her life.

"I thought this all through with that cool logic I'm so proud of. When I arrived, I saw myself as a helper to everyone. The efficient, competent Ella Majors back in form. I neglected to anticipate that I'd fall in love and want this happiness to last forever. I let myself believe Harris and I had something real. But I can see now that I've just been playing house. Living out some childhood dream. And I'm so angry at myself for falling into the trap."

"You're going to leave, aren't you?"

Ella tossed the leaf, then looked at her empty hands and nodded. "I have to. I'm not needed here anymore. Fannie has been giving Marion her injections and managing her diet. I've no reason to stay."

"But Harris…"

"Please, don't talk to Harris about this. Don't make this any harder for him than it already will be."

"Oh, honey, are you sure?"

"No," she said with a short, self-deprecating laugh. She laid her hand on Maggie's arm. "But it's what I've got to do. Promise me you'll keep an eye on things?"

"I always do."

They hugged and Ella felt the warmth of friendship swirl through her blood to bolster her resolve. Then she slipped from Maggie's arms and stepped back. There was never an easy way to say goodbye. She'd always found it best to simply wave, smile and walk away as quickly as she could.

Brady sat with his father in a johnboat on the Wando River. It had been a fair-to-middling morning of fishing and the sun was getting too high and hot in the sky. Roy was pulling in what he'd claimed would be his last fish of the day.

"Well, shoot, look at that. Ain't no more than an appetizer," he said in his gravelly voice, pulling the hook out of the spot tail's mouth.

"That one's undersized, Daddy. You ought to toss him back."

"Aw, no one gives a damn about that, anyway," said Roy, opening the fish bucket on the bottom of the boat.

Brady shifted his weight on the narrow slat and took a breath. "I do," he said.

Roy paused, the wiggling fish dangling from his hand. He eyed his son narrowly and considered. "You telling me you care about this puny fish?"

"Yes, sir."

His father shook his head and chuckled low in his chest. "If that don't beat all. Those tree huggers really got to you, didn't they?" He held up the fish to look at it up close. "Explain it to me how this one little fish is gonna make one scrap of difference in that big river out there?"

It would have been so easy to shut down his defenses as he usually did, to just shrug and let him toss that nothing of a fish into the bucket and leave it be. But something in his gut told him it was time to make a stand. Even if the issue was this puny fish, on this morning, in this boat, the consequences loomed large.

Once, months ago, his father had asked him if he was with him or against him, and Brady had fallen in line against his better judgment. Even against his own nature. He'd never felt right about that, never felt the same about his father—or himself—since that day.

Brady looked up at the man sitting only a few feet away. The years of hard living, hard drinking and smoking had coursed deep lines in his weathered face. His youth was long gone. That fact was clearly evident in the increasing amount of gray scattered in the coarse stubble on his cheeks and at the temples of his hair. Brady tried to see Roy Simmons as a man, not just as his father. Doing that made him feel more a man himself.

"You're right. I can't make a difference with every fish out there in the river. Or even one measly creek. That's too big. I can only do what I can do."

As he began trying to explain his newfound beliefs to his father, he was amazed when the belligerence on Roy's face slackened and he actually began listening to what his son had to say.

"See, if everyone went and kept the undersize fish they'd caught, that would be thousands of fish each summer that wouldn't grow to breed. Wouldn't be long before they'd die out and there'd be no fish left for anybody. But if I tossed my undersize fish back in the water, and the next guy did, and so on and so on, then we can all come back here and go fishing another day. So the way I figure it, it does make a difference if I put that puny fish back in this river. Leastwise, I'd know I did the right thing. A man can live with that."

His father shook his head and half smiled. But he didn't laugh at him. To Brady's surprise, he leaned over the edge of the boat and tossed that puny fish back into the river.

Roy looked at him sideways. "Happy now?"

Brady's chest expanded and he looked his father square in the eye. "Yes, sir, I am. Thank you."

Roy looked at his son, really studied him in the way he might if he were some stranger he came across and had the feeling he might have met him sometime before.

"You really like it at that bird place, don't you?"

"Yes, sir," Brady replied with a sinking feeling, wondering where this was headed.

"Your mama tells me you're going to keep volunteering there this summer. Even though your court time is served."

"I'm going to work there," he said with pride. "Harris gave me a job as a bird handler. He even gave me my own falcon to train. I got to name it, too. I call him Totem."

Roy screwed up his face. "What the hell kind of a name is that?"

"A good name. I like it. And I really like flying the birds. Daddy, I've finally found something I'm good at."

"Is that a fact?" Roy rubbed his jaw, his eyes sparkling with wonder. "Did I ever tell you your great-granddaddy used to hunt with falcons? Raised them, too."

Brady's brows rose in wonder. "You're kidding?"

Roy's face broke into a wide grin. "Yep. I'll tell you about him on the way back. You remind me of him. He was stubborn, too." He turned to the bucket, checking the day's catch before he sealed the lid. His movements were stiff, not as swift or agile as Brady remembered. "Well, we ain't got much, but we have something to give your mother for dinner. Ready to go home, son?"

Brady met his gaze and nodded. Then he turned and began pulling up the anchor out from the muddy bottom.

It was very early when Ella walked down the hall to Harris's bedroom for the last time. The dawn had not yet risen and the hall was black as night. Another rainstorm had pushed through the day before, clearing away the oppressive humidity and leaving the night air refreshingly cool. They'd left the windows open to cool the house. She could hear the pulls on the wooden blinds gently tapping as they fluttered in the wind.

She didn't knock on his door, afraid she might awaken Fannie and Marion sleeping directly upstairs. So she eased it open, grimacing when the hinges squeaked.

The moonlight from the open windows filled the room with soft gray light. The room was a shambles of tossed clothing and tilting piles of papers and books that appeared as shadowed lumps on the floor and desktop. She tiptoed around them to the twin bed in the corner.

Her stomach clutched as she looked at him lying on his stomach, deep in sleep and snoring lightly. She didn't want to wake him, didn't know if she had the strength to tell him goodbye. In the past several hours before dawn she'd written dozens of letters, yet she'd ripped them all up. In the end, she couldn't leave him another note on the kitchen table.

She reached out and touched the bare skin of his shoulder. It flinched under her touch. Gathering her courage, she shook him, gently at first, more firmly the second time.

He awoke with a start, jerking his head up from the pillow. She stepped back anxiously. He blinked, then looked at her with groggy, uncomprehending eyes.

"Harris, it's me," she whispered. "Ella."

He mopped his face with his hand, waking up more, and when he dropped his hand he looked at her again. His blue eyes shone in the shadows as he focused. He seemed surprised to see her at first, then pleased. His face softened to a lazy smile of welcome.

"Ella…" He moved to the far side of the bed and lifted the thin sheet to welcome her. His arm paused midair as he noticed that she was completely dressed in khaki pants and a T-shirt and that her hair was neatly wound and pulled back on her head.

"What time is it?" he asked, suddenly alert.

"Five o'clock."

He tensed and sat up on the mattress, pushing his hair back from his face. "Where are you going?"

"I don't know."

His arm shot forward to grab hold of hers. "Don't do this, Ella."

She pulled back, but he would not release her. "I have to go, Harris."

"No," he said urgently, drawing her closer.

"Please, let me go." Ella resisted, but he was stronger. He pulled her nearer, down to the warm, scented cocoon of his bed and into his arms. He moved his body to cradle hers and she felt the heat of his skin and the hardness of bone against her.

"You can't go," he said against her cheek.

Tears were pooling now and she put her small hands against his bare shoulder, afraid to let down her guard even for one moment. She strained against the force of him, pushing him away. "I must. I will."

"You'd really go?" he demanded in a strained whisper, looking into her eyes. "You'd leave me like this? Leave Marion?"

"Don't be unfair," she rasped, trying to keep her voice hushed. "We both know that you've made your decision. It's not the one I'd hoped for, but it's the one I must live with. You must promise me one thing, though," she said, her voice resolute. "You must promise to watch Marion closely. Make certain that she gets her medicine and follows her diet. You have to trust your instincts, and if you suspect anything, act quickly. Promise me!"

She felt his muscles relax as he gave up the fight. They looked at each other, their faces so close their breath intermingled in the space between them. In each other's eyes they saw the unspeakable sadness of defeat, knowing that it was over.

"I promise," he replied in a raspy voice.

She smiled a sweet, sad smile, then reached up to smooth his hair from his forehead. He closed his eyes tight.

"I tried to write you a note," she said, her voice gentler now as she loosened herself from his grip. "But I couldn't. I felt that what we'd shared deserved a proper ending."

"Ella…"

"No!" she uttered with a muffled cry, putting her hands over his mouth. "We've said all there is to say. Except goodbye."

She let her fingers lovingly trace his lips. "So, goodbye,

Harris. Each day with you and Marion was like a gift. I thank you for them. And I wish you much happiness."

"If you leave, you curse me with unhappiness."

"Goodbye," she whispered again, and kissed him, keeping her eyes open, memorizing every detail. Then, extricating herself from his arms, she slipped from the bed.

This time he didn't resist.

Habitat. *The area where an animal finds nesting sites, hunting territory and water is known as its habitat. Loss of habitat due to construction, draining and filling of wetlands, cutting of forests and the use of agricultural chemicals have taken their toll on raptor populations and is the greatest threat to wildlife populations worldwide.*

22

JUNE BEGAN WITH A HEAT WAVE THAT WOULD burn till the equinox. Local tongues were wagging about global warming and the upper-state folks were shaking their heads at ponds and rivers drying up. Everyone was praying for much-needed rain. Fires sparked in the tinder-dry grass, causing forest rangers to prohibit campfires. Only the tourists on the beaches were delighted with the weather.

Harris grunted under the weight of the lumber he was carting across the withered grass. The heat streamed down his face and chest but he kept on hauling like a beast of burden. At last he'd secured enough funding to begin his dream of building the large flight pens. He'd talked with Ella about the plans for months, couldn't wait to start building. Since she'd left, however, the joy had fizzled out of the project, as with most other things. He dropped the final load of wood on the ground. It landed with a loud clutter.

"Sit down and take a load off," Lijah told him, handing him a cold drink. "You work hard enough to cause the dirt to rise."

Harris slumped down on the pile of wood and took the drink. It was true. He was working round the clock, either at the clinic or training the birds or building the flight pens. Working was the only time he felt any peace these days, but it was exacting a toll. His back was sore, his arms felt like rubber and his stomach was growling. On top of all that, he was bleary-eyed. He hadn't had a decent night's sleep in the weeks since Ella left. And his appetite was off. He couldn't believe he missed Ella's cooking, too.

He almost chuckled just thinking back on those soggy pieces of bacon and lumpy grits of Ella's first few days. As with everything else, she'd kept trying. She studied cookbooks and practiced recipes from all over the world. She used to laugh and say the most exotic food she ever tried was good ol' Southern cooking. Okra was an enigma to her.

Fannie made fried okra better than anyone he knew and her grits were creamy smooth. But he had to admit, coming home to one of her meals wasn't nearly as much fun.

"That wouldn't be a smile I see on your face?" Lijah asked. "Ain't seen one of those since Miss Ella left."

Harris looked up, startled from his reverie. "I was just wool-gathering."

"Been doing that a lot, far as I can tell. Yessir, I miss her myself."

Harris took a long swallow from his soda. That old coot didn't miss a trick.

"That Fannie gal, she cut from a different piece of cloth, that for sure." Lijah sniffed in his haughty manner, making his opinion clear. "Can't trust a woman who don't make a decent cup of coffee."

"Give her some time," Harris replied wearily.

"Humph. That woman just flutters around doing no good. She won't cut her teeth to talk to me, but I seen her slinking 'round young Brady, offering him a cool drink, sweet-mouthing him."

"She gave a drink to all of us," Harris countered. He wanted to steer clear of the battle between Lijah and Fannie. He got an earful from Fannie about Lijah every night. The two were like baking soda and vinegar. Nonetheless, the image of Fannie smiling coquettishly at Brady took root in his mind and festered. She did seem to turn on the charm whenever the young man came near.

Hell, the heat was frying his brain, he told himself, putting the cold can to his forehead. A haze hovered over the ground and the sound of insects swelled and bellowed.

"Clouds coming," Lijah said, looking up. "Change in the weather."

"Hope so. We need the rain. You can cut this humidity with a knife. I'd like to finish the pen before the sky opens up, though. It's taking shape, don't you think?"

"This here's going to be a fine flight pen once we're done. And my Santee will be the first one to test it out."

"Yep. She'll be more than ready for it, too. Her lungs sound great and with a little exercise, I'd say she's set to go. She's a beautiful specimen of eagle and I'm glad she'll be back in the breeding pool. Though…" He slanted a glance at Lijah. "I'd be sorely tempted to find an excuse to keep her longer if it would mean you'd stay on, too."

"Can't do that," Lijah said, regret tingeing his voice. "Though I thank you for the sentiment. No, it's time for my Santee to go off and find Pee Dee. Then she can go on back home." He reached up to tug at his ear. "Same holds true for me. My Martha is waiting and I expect I'll be crossing over to meet her before too long."

Harris swung his head around to look closely at the old man. "Are you ill?"

"My spirit's fine. It's this old body that's feeling weary now."

"Let's get you in to see a doctor," he said, alarmed. "I know of a good one in Mount Pleasant."

"And what would he do if he find something? I ain't going to no hospital." He shook his head and waved his hand in a calming gesture. "Don't worry, son. Ain't something I can specify. Just aches and pains. It's the way it is when you get old. When you been in a body as long as I been in this one, you just seem to know when your boat's getting close to shore."

Harris rose and put his hand on Lijah's shoulder, guiding him toward the shade of the spreading oak tree. "You just sit down in that shade over there and relax. You're the craftsman. I'm the grunt labor. I'll finish this with Brady later."

"Maybe just for a spell. Mind you, I want these hands here to build this flight pen. It'll be something I can leave behind when I gone. Something with my mark upon it that I'm proud of."

"You've left your mark on every one of us, old man. We'll none of us forget you."

Lijah held his gaze for a moment, deeply moved, then nodded slowly. "That the finest mark a man can leave behind. That for sure."

"Mama, I'm not feeling so good."

"Aw, you're fine," Fannie replied, her eyes glued to the television. "Come on over and watch this movie with me."

Fannie was spread out on the sofa in the living room. Two

fans were whirling, but even oscillating at full blast they couldn't move enough of the thick, humid air to bring much relief.

"I don't wanna watch no more TV," Marion whined, stomping her foot petulantly. "We've been lying here all day."

"And we're gonna lie here all night."

"Ella used to take me for walks. Can we go for a walk? We can see the crows."

"In this heat? Are you crazy?"

She tsked loudly and pouted. "Can we play a game?"

"Precious," Fannie replied with an impatient drawl. She began tapping her fingers along the back of the sofa. "Can't you see I'm trying to watch a movie?"

Marion scowled. "I miss Ella."

Fannie swung her head around, scowling and sweaty. "I'm sick and tired of you whining about Saint Ella. *Ella did this… Ella did that,"* she said in a singsong manner. "Well, Ella's gone, hear? And I don't want to hear her name one more time. *I'm* your mama and *I'm* here."

Marion sighed lustily, wiped her sweaty brow and shuffled over to the sofa. She stood there for a while, watching the movie with a listless expression. Then she leaned against her mother, wrapping her arm around her and putting her head on Fannie's shoulder with a sigh.

"Oh, baby, don't do that," Fannie said, pushing her away. "You're all sweaty and it's too hot."

"My head hurts and I feel icky. Maybe I need to check my 'betes."

Fannie turned to look at her face carefully. "Your blood was okay a little while ago. Oh, it's this damn heat. You're just hot." She reached out to put her hand on her forehead. "You really don't feel so good?"

Marion shook her head.

Fannie chewed her lip, then her glance flicked over to the television set. "Tell you what. Go on in the fridge and get one of those orange juice packs. That'll make you feel better."

Marion's shoulders fell but she did as she was told.

Fannie heard the fridge open, then the footfalls up the backstairs as Marion went to her room.

Thank heavens, she thought with a sigh of relief. That kid was driving me nuts.

Harris returned home that night feeling gritty and sweaty after an afternoon of labor in the sun. Lijah was a remarkable craftsman. His large, gnarled hands could work a piece of wood till it was as smooth as silk, and Brady's strong back had been a boon to the project. At this rate, they'd be finished with the pen by the week's end.

He stepped into the house, and though the air was moving, it wasn't much cooler than the outdoors. The whir of fans and the blare of the television seemed deafening to his ears. Fannie was lying on her back in front of the television, her dirt-caked feet hanging off the armrest. The fans were aimed to whirl air over her slender body, clothed only in skimpy shorts and a bra.

Harris's face hardened and his gaze searched the room, landing on Fannie with reproach. The living room was cluttered with toys, a basket of unfolded laundry spilled over in the corner and dirty dishes lay on the table. When he saw the two empty beer bottles on the coffee table, however, an old trigger from way back clicked and he felt a bubbling fury well up. He slammed the door behind him.

Fannie heard the noise and swung her head around. Seeing him, she sat up on her elbows and said, "Thank God you're home."

"Where's Marion?"

Fannie heard the cold tone of his voice and immediately sat up on the sofa. "Oh, she's upstairs in her room," she replied with an easy wave of her hand, trying to defuse his anger. "It's cooler up there."

He walked over to the television and turned it off. Then, putting his hand on its top, he ground out, "It's burning hot. I told you I didn't want you watching television all day with Marion."

"It's hotter than hell out there," she fired back in defense. "In here, too. You've got to do something before we burn up. Can't you get an air conditioner?"

"I told you, not now. I just spent all the extra cash for the flight pen."

"Damn that flight pen. Damn the birds. Everything always goes to them. It's always the same with you. Nothing's changed, not in all the years I've known you." She slapped her hand to her chest. "What about us?"

"There are two air conditioners in the house, go in one of those rooms! This hot spell has to break soon."

"I can't bring the TV in there."

"So, don't watch so much TV!"

"There's nothing else to do in this godforsaken place," she shouted back, rising from the sofa to square off in front of him. She bounced around on the balls of her feet like a bantam. "I've been here for six weeks and I'm going out of my frigging mind."

"You knew what it was like. You begged me to let you stay. And it's not like you don't have anything to do. There are lots of things you're supposed to be doing that aren't getting done. Things that I count on you to do."

"Like what? Laundry? Oh, great. I can hardly wait. And digging a garden? Playing Chutes and Ladders? Cooking? Man alive, I never knew such a thrill."

"Are you done?" he said, trying to hold his temper.

"No, I'm not done! I'm just getting started."

Harris pinched the bridge of his nose. They seemed to fight all the time now. She wasn't happy about anything or anybody. They slept in separate bedrooms and ate in silence.

"I don't suppose you cooked dinner tonight?"

She began rubbing her arms as though she were scratching. "It's too damned hot to cook. I thought we'd order a pizza."

"We did that last night."

"So do it again tonight!" she shouted back at him. She raked her hair with her fingers, then reached over to the table to grab a clasp and pin her hair back. Harris noticed that her hands were shaky.

"Are you okay?" he asked, searching her face. "Is it too much for you, Fannie?"

Fannie heard the concern in his voice and stopped pacing to look at him, her face frazzled and tear-stained. "I'm trying, Harris. Really, I am. It's just so hard." She began rubbing her arms, gaining steam. "I can't keep up. Every time I turn around, the kid needs something. And I'm bored! Maybe if I had a break. I just need some time to myself. I need some fun."

He sighed heavily, feeling the heat and fatigue weigh his heart to his shoes.

Sensing the change in mood, she came close and wrapped her arms around his neck. "I don't want to fight no more," she said against his ear. "I didn't come home for that. I miss you, Harris. You haven't come to my bed. How do you think that makes me feel? Maybe if we were, you know, together, I'd feel more like I belong here." She pressed herself against him, rubbing her hips seductively.

He put his hands on her hips and held her there, tight. All the anger that had roiled inside of him switched like quicksilver to passion.

"Come on, honey. Make me feel like I belong here."

He brought his lips down over hers in a crushing embrace that had more to do with release than love. Fannie stretched against him, seemingly climbing him, hungry and demanding.

He moved his hands along her back, her rear, up and down, feeling her softness against him as a million memories from years past assailed him. When he moved his hand across her hips, a sharp plastic edge scraped his palm and a package slipped from her pocket into his hand.

He looked down for a second to toss whatever it was onto the table when something jogged his mind. He tore his lips away to blink and focus at it.

Fannie was kissing his neck when she noticed he'd stopped moving. In fact, he was standing rock still. She dragged her lips from his neck to look at his face, then followed his stern gaze down to his palm. She froze.

"Where did you get this?" he asked, flattening his palm.

Fannie dropped her arms and took a step back. She didn't reply.

Harris held up the small plastic container of pills. Several pockets had been popped open. "How much of this did you take? This stuff can tranquilize an elephant."

"None! I didn't take none of it."

"Don't lie to me, Fannie." He tore back the plastic covering and found one cut in half. Rage whipped through him and he had to hold himself still, squeezing the pills in his fists, or he'd lash out dangerously. He knew the medicine just as he knew she had to have stolen it from the clinic. He remembered thinking it odd to find her there the other day. When he'd asked her about it, she'd just laughed nervously and said she was curious to see it. His instincts had shot up a red flag but he'd ignored them, telling himself he wasn't being fair to her, that he shouldn't be so suspicious. When coherent thought returned to him, he glared back at her menacingly.

Fannie shrank back, twisting on one heel. "Well, okay. Maybe a little. I was just fooling around. Harris, I was so bored! I didn't hurt no one!"

Hurt... He had a sudden thought that shot straight to his heart, causing it to pound in panic. He cursed and rammed the tranquilizer into his pocket. "Marion!" he called out, racing up the narrow stairs, two at a time.

He found her lying on her bed, propped against the pillows reading a book. He slumped against the door a minute, just soaking in the sight as relief surged through him.

She looked up at him and smiled weakly. "Hi, Daddy."

Harris smiled and swallowed hard. When his heartbeat slowed to normal, he walked across the room, past Gaudy Lulu lying discarded on the floor, to sit on the bed beside her. The narrow mattress sank with his weight, and he stretched out an arm along the feminine white-wood headboard.

"Whatchya reading?"

"Goodnight Moon," she replied, leaning her head listlessly against his chest. "Ella used to read me this story."

Alert to the sadness in her voice, he asked, "Are you okay, honey?"

"I miss Ella."

He felt his heart crack. "Do you? I do, too."

"Is she coming back?"

"I don't think so."

"Is she downstairs? Can you tell her to come up and read me a story?"

A warning signal went off in his head and he said, "You know she's not here, honey." He bent to kiss her head. "What's that perfume I smell?"

"I don't know," she replied, missing the usual cue. She sat up suddenly and began climbing from the bed. "I'm going to get Ella," she said, and started walking toward the stairs. "She likes this story."

Harris knew another moment's panic. She was clearly disoriented. He rushed from the bed to hold her shoulders and look at her face. She seemed flushed, and, pulling her closer, her breath smelled fruity.

"Does your head hurt?"

She nodded. "I don't feel so good, Daddy. And I'm thirsty."

Harris carried her to the bed as his heart began pounding again. "It's okay, honey. You stay right there. Daddy's going to get your test kit. I'll be right back." Before he turned, he caught sight of the empty juice carton by the bed. Worry swirled in his chest as he pounded down the narrow stairs and raced through the living room; past Fannie, who stood wringing her hands nervously.

"What's wrong?" she called after him, following him to the bathroom.

"When was the last time you checked her blood?" he demanded, grabbing the test kit from the medicine cabinet.

She put a shaky hand to her forehead. "Uh, let me think! Not long ago. Shit, I can't remember. Didn't I write it down?"

"No," he snapped, pushing past her on his way to the stairs. According to the chart, Marion had missed her last dose. Maybe two. He cursed himself for trusting Fannie, for believing he could save her, save their marriage, save their family. All he'd done was risk his daughter's life. Well, no more.

He turned on his heel before going up the stairs and, jabbing an index finger in Fannie's face, roared, "Get your stuff packed up. I want you out of here by morning."

Marion was listless but cooperative as he reached for her finger and quickly completed the stick test. She didn't even peep when he administered the shot. When he finished, he gathered her in his arms and held her close against his chest. In a minute, he'd call the doctor, he told himself. But for now, he needed to hold her close while the insulin did its work.

"Your daddy's here," he said with urgency as he sat on the bed, rocking her back and forth and making a hundred and one vows about things he was going to do, to change, to make his daughter safe. "You're going to be all right. Everything's going to be all right."

Sentinel Species. Birds of prey are a sentinel species. As predators, raptors are at the top of the food chain. By the time a raptor becomes ill or dies from a toxic chemical, the toxin has already worked its way along the food chain from plants to herbivores to carnivores. It may be a million times more concentrated than when first applied to the environment. One in eight of all bird species have a real risk of becoming extinct in the next hundred years—fifty times the historical rate.

23

THE MORNING SUN FOUND HARRIS ALREADY sitting at the table, dressed and with a mug of coffee in his hands. He'd spent most of the night sitting by Marion's bedside, afraid to leave lest she call for him and, not finding him near, be afraid. The doctor assured him many times that the crisis had been averted, that Marion was just fine. But Harris had relived the horror of that night in December when he'd stood in Wal-Mart and watched helplessly as his daughter convulsed. He could not be drawn away from Marion's side while the night terrors still hovered.

The pink light of dawn chased away the irrational fears of the dark, however, and he began to see things more clearly. In a dispassionate manner that was oddly comforting, he could see the patterns of his life and choices spread out before him as though on a game board. Looking at it now he realized that no matter how he'd thrown the dice, he'd made the same wrong choices over and over again. He had always believed that he could heal those he loved. If he tried harder, worked longer, if he didn't quit trying, he believed he could save them.

Unlike with the raptors, he had not been able to recognize when it was time to let go.

He looked at his wristwatch, keenly aware of the time. It was just after six o'clock. Months ago, he'd scheduled a flight demonstration for eight o'clock that morning for a group of corporate executives interested in supporting the center. He'd insisted on the early hour because of the heat. The birds would be sorely tested if flown when the weather sweltered. It was too important a fundraiser to cancel, and he'd had to do some juggling with Maggie late the night before to make the event work.

Picking up the phone, he dialed Maggie's number. Despite the early hour, she answered on the second ring.

"Don't worry, I'll be there," she told him upon answering.

He half smiled. "Just checking. I don't want to leave Marion alone with Fannie."

"I'll be there by seven-thirty."

He hung up the phone, aware that Fannie was standing at the hall door, dressed and dragging her duffel bag. She'd heard what he had said to Maggie.

"I'm sorry, Harris." Her voice was contrite. "I'd never do anything on purpose to hurt Marion. I love her. I tried my best."

"I know." He didn't feel anger toward her any longer. He didn't feel anything for Fannie at all except, perhaps, pity. He wearily moved his hand toward a chair. "Sit down. Do you want some coffee?"

"Don't get up. I'll get it."

She dropped the bag on the floor and went to the kitchen, coming back a few minutes later with a mug of coffee in her hands. She looked thin and drawn, with dark circles under her puffy eyes. She'd lost the bloom that she had regained when she'd first arrived. That was because Ella had been taking care of her, he realized. Fannie was like another child. She couldn't hold it together on her own.

She stared down at her coffee, her fingers tight around the mug, and said in a small voice, "You sure you won't give me another chance?"

He leaned back in his chair, unable to believe she could ask that, after all that had happened. They looked at each other for a moment, holding on to each other's gaze with a burning look.

"I guess not," she said, looking back at her hands.

"Fannie, I want a divorce."

Her head shot up and her eyes were wide with disbelief. "A *divorce?*"

"It's way overdue, don't you think?"

"No, I don't think!"

"Lower your voice. Marion's asleep."

"I don't want a divorce," she said, leaning far forward over the table, straining her whisper.

"I do."

She looked back at him, her eyes intense. "I won't give you one," she replied, frantically shaking her head.

"The law is on my side, Fannie," he said tolerantly. "I've got desertion, endangerment, neglect." He had moved his hand as he spoke, but now placed it flat on the table. "And I want full custody."

Fannie paled as she registered that, this time, Harris was serious. "It's that Ella, ain't it?"

He shook his head. "It's you. And me and Marion. It's for the best."

She lifted her chin, leaned back in her chair and rested her elbow on the table. Cocking her head she said in a smug tone, "Oh, yeah? You think you're so smart? I know a few things, too, Mr. Harris Henderson. I don't think them lawyers are going to like that you shacked up with your girlfriend."

"It won't matter. I'm getting the divorce, Fannie."

"Well, just you remember, I'm still your wife and I get half of everything you own. That includes this place. Everything you've worked for. Divorce me and I'll shut you down."

He shrugged and opened his palms. "Then that's what will happen."

She stared at him, unable to reply.

They sat for a few more moments, looking at each other. Each of them had just spoken—and heard—the threats that they'd most feared, yet had never dared utter, during the seven years of their marriage.

I want a divorce.

I'll shut you down.

And having spoken them, the reality wasn't as horrible as they'd thought it would be. When they spoke again, it was tentatively.

"Fannie, I don't want to hurt you," he said slowly, feeling his way over new ground. "I want more out of life. I want to be happy." He shrugged. "Besides, I don't know why you want to hang on to this sorry excuse for a marriage."

"Because I love you. I love Marion."

The statement hung in the air, sounding false in both their ears.

"We both know that's the pat answer. Marion and I, we're

tired of being the cushion for your crash landing. When you really love someone, you make the tough choice to put his or her needs over your own," he said, thinking of Ella, loving her more in that instant than he ever had before. "The only thing you love is your addiction. You always choose it over me, over Marion, even over your own well-being. Why, Fannie? Why?"

She licked her lips, appearing haunted, and said honestly... softly, "I don't know."

"Let me help you," he said, leaning forward. He picked up a piece of paper from the table. It was a list of things that he'd wanted to get done. Harris had written the list during the early morning hours and number one was to ask his wife for a divorce. "I've looked into it and found a rehab center in Charleston. Let me take you there."

"No way," she said, backing against the chair and shaking her head.

"You need help, Fannie. Not just with the drugs. You still haven't dealt with all that happened to you when you were young."

Agitated, she shook her hand in front of her, as though dispelling the words in the air before they got too close. "Look, Harris, forget it. I'm not going to one of those places. Rehab's your thing, not mine."

"I should have done this years ago."

"Haven't you figured it out yet?" she screamed, her eyes small flames scorching his. "Are you blind, deaf and dumb? You did try! And every time you tried, I left. Face it, Harris. You can't save me. I don't want to be saved!"

She pushed back the chair with a loud scrape and disappeared into the kitchen.

At seven-thirty, Harris was pacing on the front porch, frequently checking his watch. He'd already given Marion her injection and now she was happily playing a game with Fannie in front of the television.

At seven-forty he went into the house and called Maggie's number again. Her husband, Bob, told him that she'd left a while ago, ought to be pulling up any second.

He looked at his watch and pursed his lips.

"Oh, for heaven's sake. Go!" Fannie said from the floor. She sat playing cards with Marion and was looking up at him with sober eyes. "I've taken good care of her for weeks. I think I can watch her for another five minutes."

He hesitated.

"Harris, we're sitting here in front of the television playing Old Maid. What can happen?"

Harris put his hands on his hips and thought it through. He was just going over to the flying field down the road. Five minutes there, five minutes back, plus a half-hour demonstration. He'd be back in less than an hour. And Maggie was due any second.

"All right," he said, uncomfortable with his decision. He went over to kiss Marion's forehead. "I'll be right back."

"Bye, Daddy," she said, not looking up from her cards.

"Fannie," he said, stopping in front of her. Again their eyes met and held. "Think about what I said. I'd like to take you to that rehab center."

Fannie didn't reply. She only lifted her hand once more to wave, wiggling her fingers the way a child would.

Fifteen minutes later, Maggie still had not shown up. Fannie was rifling through Harris's drawers and closets, trying to find anything of value.

"Adios, amigo," she muttered as she dug through Harris's pants pockets. "I'm out of here. No way I'm going to a rehab center. Go ahead and get your divorce. I'll send you a post-card letting you know where to send the money."

She came back into the living room, looking at her palm and scowling. "Two dollars and thirty-two cents," she said "Not even a decent watch to pawn. Sheesh. Did you know your daddy was dirt poor?"

Marion looked up from the television and frowned, shaking her head. "No, he's not! Daddy always says he's the richest man in the world."

Fannie let loose a short laugh, then, seeing her daughter's hurt expression, softened. A faint smile fluttered across her face. "Does he, now?" she said with a change of voice. "Well, precious, you know what? I think he might just be right."

She stuffed the few dollars and coins in her pocket and stuck out her hand to Marion. "Let's you and me go on that walk you wanted."

"Okay!" she exclaimed with surprise, scrambling to her feet.

"Let's play spies. We're on a secret mission, okay? We have to find something but we can't let anyone find us. Quiet now. Remember, we're spies."

Hand in hand they sneaked across the yard toward the clinic. They slunk along the med pens, peeking in. There she spotted Lijah cleaning out Santee's pen. He didn't see them as they hurried past, hands over their mouths, giggling. No one was in the weighing room or the clinic, either. Maggie was scheduled for the first shift and Brady and the other volunteers wouldn't arrive until nine. Only the two vultures watched them from inside their wire enclosure as Fannie lifted Marion up to the lower branch of a longleaf pine tree that grew tall and proud beside the rear of the clinic.

"Hi, Mama!" Marion called down to her from the tree branch. She always was happy in a tree.

"Shh! We're spies, remember? See that window there? The top of it is open. Do you think you could climb inside?"

Marion scooted along the branch that lay like an arm right in front of the double-hung window. "I can't. There's a screen."

"That ol' thing? Just kick it, honey. It'll fall right out."

Marion frowned in worry. "I don't think I oughta. Daddy might get mad."

"You just do it. You can tell him I told you to. Go on, now."

Marion scooted to her bottom, held on to the branch and kicked the screen. She wobbled a bit but hung on.

"Good girl! Now climb on in. There's a desk right under the window you can step on."

She watched as Marion easily slipped from the branch and shimmied down over the window onto the desktop. She looked through the window at her mother, questioning what to do next.

"Open the door. Hurry now!"

As soon as Fannie got into the clinic, she went directly to the back room where the small cabinet held the clinic's drugs. It was already after eight o'clock and she was running out of time. She rattled the cabinet door handle, cursing when she found it locked.

"What are we looking for?" Marion wanted to know.

"Something fun." She guided Marion back into the office and pulled down a plastic bin of pretzels and opened them for her. "You just sit in here and stay out of trouble," she said, shoving the bin of pretzels into her arms.

"I don't think we should be here."

"Hush now," Fannie warned.

She went into the main treatment room and opened the glass cabinets where the daily medicines were stored. She shoved aside dozens of small tubes and pill containers, mostly antibiotics and antifungals, desperation licking at her heels. She grew more careless, knocking items from the narrow shelves and sending them crashing to the floor.

Then she saw it. Ether.

She laughed when she pulled it from the cabinet and looked at the can in her hand. Not the drug of choice, but it would do in a pinch. She'd never tried it before, but she'd heard people talk about the high. She thought about it for just a minute, then twisted off the cap and sprinkled some on a small cotton towel, guessing at how much she'd need. There was a heady smell and for a moment she hesitated. "Oh, what the hell," she muttered, and placed the towel under her nose. She tentatively sniffed a little, then waited. She didn't feel much. She sprinkled more on the towel and tried it again, this time with a lusty sniff. Then, rolling her eyes back, she waited to feel the effects.

"Mama? What are you doing?"

"Just playing around, honey," she said with a giggle, tossing the towel into the trash can. She already felt light-headed, sort of like she was drunk. She wiggled her fingers and toes. Yeah, they were feeling kind of numb, too. She tried to walk toward Marion, but her knees felt watery. "Whoa," she said, holding on to the counter. "That sure packed a punch. You go in the other room, sugar. I don't want you smelling this stuff."

Her legs were starting to feel like jelly so she slipped down to the floor, stretching them straight out in front of her like she did as a child, laughing at her feet, which suddenly looked very funny to her. What time was it, she wondered, looking at the clock? Even squinting, she couldn't see the numbers through her blurry eyes, then found she really didn't care what time it was, anyway. This stuff was really beginning to kick in. Okay, no panic, she told herself, leaning back. She had enough time to wait until the stuff wore off.

She felt herself letting go. Everything around her seemed shrouded by an impenetrable haze and she felt safe. One snug little bug in a rug, she thought with a short laugh. She sighed deeply and let the drug flow through her system. Oh, how she'd needed this. Craved it with a physical ache that was all-consuming. Harris had said that she loved her addiction more than him. More than her daughter. And though she'd shaken her head no, she knew in her heart that it was true. It pained her to recognize this flaw in herself. She hated this need.

Fannie closed her eyes and let her head fall back against the wall. She'd had to turn away from the bruising intensity of Harris's gaze this morning when he'd asked her why she always chose drugs over him or Marion. She always managed to hurt him, she thought, and that made her sad. Sad, sad, sad.

I don't know, she'd replied. But that was a lie, told to him with love. He'd find her heartless if she'd told him the truth. Though he'd named it—she loved her addiction—he could never understand why. How could she tell him, how could a man like him understand that the only intimacy she'd known in her life was with drugs?

She shook her head woozily. It was the ol' moth to the flame, she thought, and laughed again as she groped for her purse. Now, where were her cigarettes? Talk about addictions… She felt groggy as she tugged one out from the pack in her pocket, fumbling with her numb fingers. After a few misses, she finally was able to light up. It was so weird, she thought, because her lips felt a little numb, too. She giggled and waved the flame out, then tossed the match into the trash.

The *whump* of a plume of fire stunned her. Fannie could only sit on the floor and stare as the fire hissed outward, flying like dozens of golden and orange birds to alight on bits of paper, curtains, towels, anything it could devour.

"Mama!"

The scream penetrated her stupor. Marion. Her baby! Maternal instinct pushed her to her knees and she half crawled, half dragged herself to the small office across the hall where Marion huddled under the desk.

Lijah heard the birds screaming in alarm. He ran out from the med pens to see the glow of orange flames and plumes of black smoke spiraling from the clinic.

"Lord have mercy," he muttered. He sprinted to the door of the treatment room but the flames were already blocking the entrance. A window burst to his left and he ducked, putting his arms up to cover his face from glass that flew like shrapnel. Coughing, he backed away, studying the building for a way in. He could readily see the way it would be. The grass and leaves were so dry and brittle the fire could spread to the other pens like greased lightning. Another window burst from the treatment room and he knew there was nothing he could do for the few birds in the intensive-care kennels. He turned and ran for the med pens.

Brady came running from the parking lot. He was late coming in because he'd found Maggie on the side of the road with her car hood open. The car had to be towed and he'd waited with her, then drove them both to the birds of prey center. They saw the thin streak of smoke rising from over the trees when they pulled up. Brady took off for the clinic while Maggie headed straight for Harris's house.

"I've got to check on Marion. I'll call the fire department," she cried as she ran.

Across the yard, Brady spotted Lijah coming out from the med pens with Santee in his arms. It looked to him like the old man was talking to the bird. The large eagle's eyes were more yellow and fierce than the glow of the fire. She jerked her wings in his arms, restless to be off.

Maggie ran up to Brady's side, breathless. "What's he doing? Is he letting her go?"

"Let him be," Brady told her, holding her back. "He knows what he's doing."

Lijah turned to face the wind, his white head tilted upward. He lifted his long arms and, with a firm lift, spread them open in release.

The eagle stretched out her mighty wings, slicing the air with powerful strokes, her proud, massive white head arched forward in determination.

Brady held his breath and Maggie's grip tightened on his arm, knowing that the eagle had not yet tested its wings for any real distance. Santee cut through the air with aggressive purpose, lifting higher and higher till she caught the wind at last and flew a slanted path high into the sky. Soaring, she banked once, then turned in a stately manner. The last they saw of her was the flash of white on her tail.

"Lijah!"

He heard the shout over the roar of the fire and saw Brady running toward him with Maggie right behind.

"Where's Marion?" Maggie said, her eyes wild with worry. "She's not at the house!"

"Don't know. Reckon she's with her mother. She be all

right." Lijah looked back at the flames engulfing the treatment room. "We can't save the birds in there. That wood so dry it going up like tinder."

"Oh, my God," cried Maggie.

"The wind's blowing toward the med units," Lijah said, coughing as the stale stench of smoke stretched toward them. He waved his hand as he turned toward the wood building. "Let's go! We have to hurry and save those birds first."

From the corner of his eye he caught sight of the two vultures in the wire pen, not fifty feet from the burning clinic. They hunkered together in the far corner, mute with fear. Lijah detoured toward the pen, waving away thick black smoke that billowed from the clinic.

"Come on, you two," he said as he undid the latch and opened the gate wide. "Go on, git. You ain't children no more. It's up to you to find a safe place. Go on, now."

He shuffled inside the pen, waving his arms and shooing the Tweedles out to freedom. Lijah didn't wait to see where they were headed. That fire was some devil-beast belching hellfire—and it was hungry. Lijah shook his fist at it and trotted across the field to the med pens, damned determined not to let the beast devour any more of his birds.

Harris was standing in the middle of the flying field with Cinnamon relaxed and perched on his glove. Eighteen men and women, all corporate rollers with a keen interest in conservation, clustered around him, listening avidly. This was the kind of group he felt excited to talk to. Interested people who, once shown that they could make a difference for their families and the world they left behind, became dedicated men and women of action. As he was talking, Cinnamon suddenly opened her wings, flared her head and tail feathers and hissed defensively.

Harris saw a large black shadow cross the field and, looking up, caught his breath as an eagle flew directly overhead. He was stunned by its unexpectedness and his heart expanded as it always did when he witnessed the eagle's majesty of motion. All around him he heard the "ahs" of wonder and thought with a soft chuckle that the eagle's timing couldn't have been better.

Then the eagle banked and circled again, a rare treat, calling out in its high-pitched cry. All eyes were focused on the massive, long-winged bird as it led their gazes to the smudge of billowing gray smoke against the azure sky.

Santee.

With a sudden bolt of clarity, Harris knew. His face drained of color.

He handed the hawk to his assistant. "Bring her home," he shouted, then grabbed the shoulder of Adam Pearlman, the man who'd organized the day's presentation. "Can you drive me back to the center? Now!"

"Marion, honey, listen to me. You've got to climb out!"

"No, Mama!" The child clutched her mother, burying her head in her neck, trembling.

They were huddled under the desk in the office, unable to leave because of the flames behind the door that blocked the hall. The heat was oppressive and smoke began billowing under the door into the room, burning their eyes and choking their lungs.

"Marion," Fannie said, shaking the child loose. "You can do this. You're Mama's big girl. All you have to do is climb out that window the same way you came in." The child whimpered and shook her head no. "We're spies, remember?"

"You come, too," she cried in terror.

"'Course I will. Come on. Now hurry!" Fannie dragged herself to her feet, the numbness in her legs making her movements clumsy. The fire was like a living thing, sucking up the air from the open window, licking its flames toward them. Fannie felt a terror that broke through the fog of ether and she clawed her way through the thick, rancid smoke, feeling with her hands the hard wood of the furniture. She dragged her daughter up from under the desk. Marion coughed and spit, but Fannie urged her to climb up onto the desk. She leaned forward, pounding against the frame to open the window so that they could climb out. The old, swollen wood wouldn't budge. She felt her strength ebbing, but her brain kept screaming, This is my baby. I have to save my child!

"The top," she cried, gathering her strength. "Climb out the top!"

Fannie cursed her numbness, then took a breath of the fetid air. She pushed Marion forward with all her might as she did her best to guide her useless hands to shove Marion's bottom up and out the top half of the window. The sweat poured down from her face and she grunted with the effort. She felt Marion wiggle, then the sudden lift and shift of weight as Marion grabbed hold of the tree limb.

"Climb, Marion!" Fannie screamed breathlessly. She inhaled the smoke and coughed, spitting out the foul taste. "Get away and call for help!"

Fannie's last sight of her daughter was of her scrambling up the tree like a little monkey. She choked a cry in relief and said a prayer of thanks. She didn't know if God listened to sinful women like her, but she prayed, anyway. Then she gripped the edge of the desk and tried to lift her leaden legs and climb up on it. The black smoke swirled in the room, swallowing up the oxygen and burning her eyes. She commenced coughing again and her legs weakened, dropping her to the floor. The smoke was less down here so she flattened herself till her lungs could catch some air. Behind her, she heard the sound of sizzling, like bacon frying on the griddle. She looked over her shoulder. Through the foggy haze, it looked like the room was blossoming into one enormous, yellow bird, its wings outstretched, wide and shuddering, tipped with brilliant orange feathers. It was a hissing, heartless, ravenous beast with black, fathomless eyes.

And it was staring directly at her.

They swerved and skidded up the gravel road as Adam accelerated the car toward the center. Harris could hear the sirens of fire engines right behind him. He clutched the handle of the door, muttering, "Come on, come on, come on," and leapt out as soon as the car careened to a stop.

All was mayhem and he had to stand for a second to take in what he was seeing. Flames were shooting from the windows of the clinic and Lijah was standing not far away with the hose pouring water through the windows. Brady was running like some wild football quarterback across the field with buckets that Maggie was filling from the other hose near the med pens, dumping them one by one in a pathetic effort against the mounting flames. Soot blackened their faces and perspiration drenched their hair flat against their heads.

He ran straight to Maggie, calling her name. She looked up and gasped with relief, dropping the hose and running frantically toward him, meeting him midfield.

"Harris!"

"Maggie, where's Marion?"

"I don't know!" she screamed, her eyes pools of despair. "She must be with Fannie, but we haven't seen them."

Harris paled and jerked his head toward the burning clinic while a wild, mad fear howled inside of him. The howl burst from his lips, a deep guttural roar that seemed rent from the scorching furnace in his chest. "No-o-o-o!" She was in there. His baby was in that hellfire. He *knew* it. He'd thought he had faced the worst in the emergency room. Then again last night when Marion was ill. But he was wrong. He'd committed the fatal error; he'd left Marion with Fannie. He couldn't lose her to another bad decision.

Harris felt a sudden shift, as though he were detached from his body, watching in a dispassionate manner the actions of a desperate, determined man. The noises of the world seemed to muffle around him and he saw everything through tunnel vision. Releasing his grip on Maggie, he ran directly to the clinic, pushing aside Brady when he tried to keep him back. He couldn't feel his feet as they hit the earth, couldn't feel the heat of the fire as he circled the building, looking for a way inside. He was vaguely aware of the fire engines roaring to the site as he turned the corner to the back of the building, calling Marion's name.

One voice penetrated his focus. It sounded like a bird calling from somewhere high in a tree.

"Mama! Mama! Mama!"

His gaze flew to the mature longleaf pine at the rear of the clinic. It stood close to the building where smoke poured from the open window. Following the tree's skyward path, he found Marion clinging tight to a high branch with one arm. The other was outstretched toward the office as she screamed hysterically for her mother.

He mounted the tree and watched himself move his hands, one over the other, past the plumes of smoke, higher up the tree, climbing steadily toward his daughter. When he reached her at last he spoke to her in a low, calm voice, gentling her as he wrenched her rigid fingers from the branch and guided her trembling arms to cling, instead, around his neck. He took it limb by limb, hampered by the smoke and Marion's hysterical trembling and crying.

"Where's Fannie?" he asked her.

Marion's eyes were round balls of terror. He couldn't get through to her. When they reached the lowest branch of the tree she reached out with one arm toward the open window and screamed, "Mama! Mama!"

"It's okay, honey," he replied, and understood with the same cool detachment what it was he had to do.

Lijah miraculously called up from below the limbs of the tree.

Harris looked into the face of the old man. "Take care of her," he shouted as he lowered his daughter from the tree into Lijah's waiting arms.

Firemen came running around the corner, calling out to him to stay put. Harris waited until he saw Lijah carry Marion to safety, then turned and leapt through the window into the burning building.

He found Fannie lying on the floor near the window, struggling to breathe in the few inches of air. He crawled beside her and gathered her in his arms, alarmed by the streaks of black smoke across her face. Her eyes fluttered open and he knew the moment she recognized him through the haze of smoke because she shrank back with a hoarse whimper.

"Don't be afraid, Fannie," he told her. "I'm here."

She moved her cracked, parched lips, but Harris couldn't hear what she was saying against the roar of the fire. He tilted his ear close to her mouth.

"Marion?" she rasped from her ravaged throat.

He met her gaze. "She got out. She's okay."

Fannie's eyes were consumed with relief, then she closed her lids.

An explosion in the next room rocked the house, as though the beast had risen and roared in fury. The power of its fiery breath rattled the rafters, shaking loose chunks of ceiling and shattering glass as beams collapsed around them. Harris felt the foul plumes of heat hiss past him, sucking the air from his lungs and singeing the hairs on his body.

Fannie clutched his shirt and choked out a scream.

Harris put his back to the flames that were lapping the walls and, crouching to shield her from the heat, lifted Fannie into the black smoke. "Hold on," he shouted.

He never would remember how he managed to carry her through the wall of murky smoke to the window. Firemen in yellow-and-black coats swarmed like worker bees at a hive, cutting out the shards of glass and wood from the window while shouting out instructions. As he lowered Fannie into their arms, she looked back at him with red-rimmed eyes. He froze, transported back in time. In those eyes he saw again the same amalgamation of raw fear, deep-seated sorrow and haunting regret that he'd seen in the eyes of the eleven-year-old girl who had come to his house many years before, seeking a safe haven.

The house shuddered and wailed once more. Then all was blackness.

Survival. Because birds of prey are numerous and conspicuous, many people are unaware of their struggle to survive. They all have many natural predators, yet their defensive behavior is highly variable. Some fly away at a threat while others defend their nest aggressively. The beautiful plumage of most raptors acts as camouflage in their natural environment. Still, disease, lack of food, human threats and, most of all, the loss of their habitat make each day a challenge to survive.

24

ELLA SAT AT THE NURSES' STATION LOOKING out the front plate window at another sultry summer day. There'd been a long string of steamy days this July and she'd been looking to the sky for signs of clouds and rain that would break this monotonous hot spell—like everyone else in Charleston.

A bittersweet smile eased across her face as she sunk her chin into her palm. She really shouldn't complain. Warmth was what she'd come south for...

She dropped her palm and adjusted her position in her chair. Any thoughts that drifted to the past still had the power to stab with pain. Though it was much better now, she'd learned to steer clear of that line of thinking and to keep busy.

She was a nurse again. This meant a great deal. Her profession gave her life purpose, and her dealings with patients gave it meaning. But she wasn't the same nurse she'd been before. Her time at the birds of prey center had changed her life forever. She likened herself to a bird that had been rehabilitated, a trauma case restored to her former healthy state and condition, and then released. Now she was expected to establish herself in her new territory and to flourish.

Well, she'd done her best. After leaving Awendaw she'd returned to Charleston and accepted a nursing position at the Medical University Hospital. At the beginning it was all she could do just to get up every morning, get dressed and go to work. She'd never known such heartache, such raw pain. But each day she thought of him a little less, and each night before falling asleep she told herself that tomorrow would be easier. Finally one day she found herself laughing once again. And she knew then that she could continue on without him, that she would be just fine.

Ella smoothed her uniform, trying to ignore the resistant pain that still lurked in the deep recesses of her heart. She wasn't over him yet. She still loved Harris. She probably always would. Even though she knew she shouldn't love him, because he belonged to another, she felt no shame for her love. It was the purest, most true thing she'd ever known. The past few weeks since she'd left him had been the most painful in her life, but her love for him had brought her her great moments of joy. She wouldn't trade her experience at the center for anything.

And she'd learned from her experiences working with the birds of prey. From Harris she'd learned to keep her voice low and pleasant, to minimize her patients' stress and to always treat them with respect, even when they were snapping and attacking. She'd learned from Lijah to open her mind and heart and to take the time to listen to what her patients were telling her. And most of all, he'd taught her to watch. To observe. To pay attention to the telling details.

She needed to hope that her love for Harris had made her stronger, like metal forged by fire. After all, this hope and her memories were all she had left.

Ella turned from the window when a limping young girl was ushered into the emergency room by a cadre of friends. The girl wore skimpy clothes and heavy makeup, but Ella's experienced eye marked her as a fifteen-year-old. Grateful for the distraction, Ella hurried to her feet to meet the girl across the floor and put her arm around the girl's trembling shoulders. The girl burst into tears and Ella thought to herself how all pretenses collapsed in the emergency room.

"Girls, you have to wait out here," she told the cluster of worried friends when she escorted the patient into the treatment room.

The girl's toe was sliced open from a seashell and, medically, all she needed were a few stitches. Looking at her ashen face, the quivering lip and tear-filled eyes, however, Ella knew the girl needed something more. She reached out to take her hand.

"Carrie," she said in a calming voice. "I'm going to clean the wound, then the doctor's going to stitch you up. Everything is going to be okay."

The girl looked into Ella's steady gaze and her fear diminished. She nodded, sniffing. "I guess I should've been more careful."

"You didn't do anything wrong. Everyone likes to run on the beach."

"Yeah?" She wiped her eyes. "I wouldn't know. It's the first time I ever saw the ocean. I'm on vacation with my family. We're from Ohio. You're lucky to live here."

Ella chuckled and rose to prepare the tray for the attending physician. "What would you say if I told you I've never even been to the ocean?"

"Really? But it's right there. You can go any time you want."

Ella felt the twinge of pain inside her heart again and was glad she had her back to the patient. Harris had promised he would take her and Marion for an outing at the beach this summer. She couldn't yet bring herself to go alone.

The door to the treatment room swung open and a fellow nurse poked her head in. Ella could see the faces of the girl's three worried friends peeking in behind her.

"Ella? We just got a call from the paramedics. They're bringing in two burn victims."

Ella nodded in understanding. "The doctor will be right in. And don't worry. You'll be fine," she said to the young girl with a pat on her hand.

She hurried into the hall, pausing only to tell the girls that their friend was going to be okay. Adrenaline was pumping in her veins. Burn victims were some of the most difficult to treat. Each second was critical.

"What do we know?" Ella asked Liz when she came to the front desk.

Liz was a middle-aged woman who'd seen it all. It took a lot to get her excited. She was as wide as she was tall and had to hold her breath in order to reach far over the desk to grab the sheet of paper and draw it near. "Here it is. This says there was a fire over in Awendaw," she said, reading. "Up at that birds of prey center. They're bringing in two burn victims."

Ella stood frozen in shock while the attendant continued reading the rest of the report. She couldn't hear the words against the rushing of blood in her ears. Over and over she replayed only the words *Fire… Birds of prey center… Two victims*. And all she could think was, who?

"Ella? Are you all right?"

She became aware that Liz's blue eyes were looking at her with concern, and that she'd been standing there, like a stone figure, not answering her questions.

"Who are the victims?" she blurted out.

Liz leaned back in her chair, stunned by the frantic tone of Ella's voice. She ducked her head and scanned the report again. She shook her head and raised her eyes, almost apologetically. "It doesn't give names. It only says they're bringing in a woman and a man."

"A woman?" Ella jumped on this. "Not a child? A little girl?"

She shook her head, frowning with suspicion. "That's all it says."

Ella spun from the desk and ran to the triage room, her heels pounding the polished floors. En route she called out to make certain that the burn specialist had been called down to the E.R. She gathered together the supplies that would be needed for treatment, muttering to herself as she worked at a fevered pace. "It won't be Marion. Of course it won't be her. What would she be doing at the clinic, anyway?" Her mind would not even allow her to contemplate the *man* being brought in.

Ella had learned over the years not to pray to God for anything specific in the emergency room. A woman could lose her faith pretty quickly if she did. Instead, as she laid out the bandages and equipment with hands that were remarkably steady and efficient, Ella prayed that she'd have the strength to do her best in the next few hours. And that she would be able to understand and accept and live with whatever came through those doors.

She didn't have to wait long. Twenty minutes later the emergency room doors slammed open and the first gurney was rushed inside. Ella ran to it, gripping its sides and peering down at the patient.

She was ashamed of the relief she felt when she recognized Fannie. *Not Marion...* Fannie's face was blackened with soot, her eyes were closed and her muscles slack. Ella knew immediately that she was dead.

She released the gurney and let it pass, then turned to face the second gurney that was now being pushed through the doors. She stood motionless, unable to move, waiting for what seemed an interminable amount of time while the paramedics navigated through the double doors. Her eyes traveled wildly across the man's body as the gurney wheeled closer. His dirt-stained work boots peeked out from the edge of the blanket. The cuffs of his pants were blackened and torn. His hands, his beautiful long fingers, lay still, scraped, and his nails were embedded with soot. Then, when she could hold back no longer, she slowly raised her gaze to his face.

Even as she saw the wicked, raw-red burn slash on his cheek and the bandage across his eyes, even as she stared at the ravaged shoulder, her heart surged with rapture at seeing the face that she loved more than all others—alive! She gripped the sides of the gurney and ran alongside as they raced to the treatment room.

"What happened?" she asked the paramedic.

"This guy's some kind of hero," he replied. "He brought out his daughter."

Ella's breath hitched. "Is the child all right?"

"Yeah. They're bringing her in just to make sure. She's shook up, though. She was inside the building with her mother when the fire broke out." He jerked his head toward the other gurney where the medics were covering Fannie's head. "Had to be tough for the kid."

"What happened to him?"

"After he brought down the kid, he went into the building after the mother. They tried to stop him. Some guys, they just don't listen. The firemen came running but he'd already jumped in. I have to hand it to him, though. He found the lady and got her out. But he got a bad break. The roof fell as he was climbing out the window. Lucky for him that the firemen were there to pull him free." He shook his head. "It's too bad, you know? But the fact is, he shouldn't have gone in. It was too late to save her."

Ella looked down at the burned and unconscious man on the gurney while tears welled in her eyes. "He couldn't have made any other choice," she said softly. "It's who he is."

"I don't know about that," the paramedic replied in his brusque manner. "I've seen this kind of thing over and over again, where some guy rushes in to save someone. And I always wonder. Does the man make the choice? Or does the choice make the man?"

They wheeled him into the treatment room where the burn specialist was waiting. The team moved quickly, tearing off his clothes, inserting IVs and treating the burns that she knew would scar his left cheek and shoulder. She was sad to see his handsome face marred, but what did that matter, really? It only mattered that he healed and got well. She worried most when they removed the bandage covering his eyes. Harris fluttered open his eyelids, then gazed out blankly. He didn't blink under the bright lights.

Ella shared an ominous glance with the doctor.

Harris raised his hand and groped into the air with fear. She quickly grabbed it and held tight.

"Harris, it's me."

His eyes searched but were unseeing, and his lips, cracked and dry, opened. "Ella?" he rasped.

"Yes, I'm here."

He squeezed her hand in his and closed his eyes tight. "Don't leave me."

Ella held on to his hand, firm and steadfast, yet her heart took off. She felt as though she were a hawk, flying high above the emergency room, circling round and round with her wings outstretched, crying out a piercing, plaintive call. With her binocular vision, she brought forth images from her past, narrowing her focus, resolving the images with remarkable clarity: Bobby's hand relaxing and his heart monitor flattening, Buh Rooster staring back at her from the loblolly pine, Brady and Clarice laughing together with shining eyes, Marion's downy head resting against her breast, the whispered wing beats of an owl against her cheek, Lijah standing beside the cabin smoking his pipe, Harris's arms reaching out for her under a dimly lit tarp, in the tangled sheets of a narrow bed, drawing her into safety, closer to his heart, bringing her home.

Like the hawk to the lure, Ella grabbed hold, never to let go. Her heart lifted her higher, higher than she'd ever dreamed possible. And smiling down at him, she was soaring.

__Migration.__ In the fall, when the seasons and sunlight change and food availability grows scarce, raptors adapt by changing geographic location. They migrate from their breeding range, soaring great distances in thermals. The gathering of hundreds, sometimes thousands of birds swirling and crisscrossing overhead in spirals is called a boil or kettle. No one can witness the spectacle and not be filled with awe and hope.

Epilogue

HARRIS STOOD ALONE IN THE CENTER OF THE flying field. He turned slowly in a circle, breathing in the fragrant air that was as yet balmy but held the hint of cooler nights to come. The grass beneath his feet was browning, deciduous leaves were tipped in gold and scarlet and, beyond, the wetlands were in the process of changing costume for Halloween. The wind gusted and he heard a frenzied calling. Lifting his chin, he saw the sky filled with birds with wings flapping, chattering, weaving in and out of exuberant flight patterns overhead.

Songbirds had been migrating through the Lowcountry for weeks and clustered noisily in the trees and along power lines. The hawks were passing through, as well, but they traveled at such high altitudes most people didn't see them. Kestrels, ospreys and falcons were among them, soaring southward along the coast. Some would survive the long journey and return again come spring. Others would not.

Such was the way of nature, he realized. He could not save them all.

Harris brought his hands to his hips and looked around once again at the Coastal Carolina Center for Birds of Prey. His legs felt rooted to the soil and he knew with a soul-stirring satisfaction that he would not be journeying to a new location. This was his home. He was staying put.

Summer had been too long and too filled with burning issues and heated passions. He was tired and looked forward to the shortening of sunlight hours and long nights around the fire, nestled close beside his loved ones. Fall was a time of change; winter an introspective season. He had much to reflect upon, he thought. Much to be grateful for.

He turned again to look past the field toward the fifty or so people who had congregated for a good, old-fashioned barn-raising. Donations had poured in after the news stations reported the disastrous fire that had destroyed the clinic building. People had shown they cared and they'd collected enough not only to construct a new clinic, but to complete the flight pens, as well. It had been gratifying for him to see the outpouring of support from the community he served. The new clinic building was better equipped and the number of volunteers continued to swell. Harris was renewed with hope.

He squinted and made out the form of Ella in the group of people milling about the new clinic. She was laughing, and her long braid was flopping against her back as she served plates of barbecue to the guests. His heart swelled at the sight of his wife. Ella was the heart of the place; he knew that without a flinch of envy. She had the ability to give and give, then give a little more.

He didn't even want to think about what his life would have been like if she hadn't come back and agreed to marry him. He'd likely be some grouchy, crippled coot, old before his time, and Marion might have been traumatized for life. They were a sorry pair after the fire, but Ella wouldn't give up on either of them. She gently, firmly, coaxed them back to health. They'd both bear scars for life—his physical and Marion's mental. That couldn't be helped. But Ella made them easier to bear. She had been his eyes when he could not see, and now that the bandages had been removed and his sight restored, she was his heart. He thought again of how much he had to be grateful for. Not many men had a second chance in life.

He spotted Marion running across the field with Maggie's daughter, Annie, in hot pursuit of the springer spaniel puppy he'd brought home with him when he returned from the hospital. His injured eyes were as yet sensitive to the light, but that wasn't the reason they'd filled with tears when he saw Marion's first smile since the fire. That had been in August, and she'd started school a few weeks later. Since then, Marion had made lots of new friends. A bittersweet smile crossed his lips as he realized that his little girl was a "brancher," climbing farther and farther out on the limb, away from the nest. His smile broadened as he thought of the small coterie that walked her down the dirt road to the highway to catch the bus for school each morning: himself walking the puppy, Cinnamon, following in the trees, and the Tweedles.

He shook his head and his smile burst into a chuckle at the memory of those crazy vultures waddling down the road behind them. Even a fire couldn't convince them that they were better off in the wild. As soon as the ashes had cooled, those two birds walked in their rollicking gait to the back door of the house and roosted. The Tweedles were his failure, he had to admit. Just as he had to admit that he liked the silly birds almost as much as Maggie did. They were residents now and being trained in education programs.

Brady's voice calling his name broke through his reverie. Looking up, he saw the group of people advancing toward him across the field. Brady was in the forefront carrying a hooded bald eagle in his heavy gloves. Lijah had been right about the young man, he thought, watching with admiration the confidence in his straight-backed stride. Brady was a natural-born falconer. While Harris was recuperating, Brady had come to the hospital to visit and told him the truth about that fateful Christmas Eve when Santee had been shot. Harris had not been entirely surprised. He'd known that one gun had been a rifle and the other a shotgun. And Roy Simmons's reputation as a marksman was well known. Still, Brady's honesty brought them one step closer as mentor and student.

Lijah had set the example, and Harris would try to be a wise and giving teacher to Brady. In this way, he would leave his mark on the future, as Harris felt the old man had left his mark on him. Like Lijah said, That the finest mark a man can leave behind.

Lijah... The old man was sorely missed. Soon after the fire, he'd disappeared, leaving only an eagle's feather on the pillow in the cabin. A lone eagle's feather was believed to hold great power, and they liked to think he left part of himself behind. He'd always told them that he'd leave when Santee did, but his unannounced departure caught them all off guard, nonetheless. Marion had claimed the feather as her own and it replaced Gaudy Lulu as her favorite item. She wore the feather on a strip of leather around her neck.

Ella missed Lijah most of all. For the few months after the fire, Ella never lost hope that she'd see him again. She'd stop short whenever she spied a slim black man walking along the road or standing in a crowd. Her breath would hitch when she thought she'd spotted him in an open field, or in the forest, or standing along the shoreline. It was never Lijah. But every time they saw an eagle soar overhead they'd turn to each other and smile as they thought about The Watcher who'd come to a remote outpost in the middle of nowhere to help injured creatures heal.

Brady drew near and his tension from carrying the powerful bird was palpable. Their eyes met—student and teacher—and Harris nodded his readiness. Then he reached out to carefully secure the eagle's powerful feet into his gloved hands. The eagle flinched at the transition, stretching out its immense talons and jerking back its gleaming wings. Harris maintained a firm hold and soon brought the massive bird under control. He remained still, gentling the bird, waiting until the cluster of people spread out to form a circle around him.

When the group settled and quiet was restored, he signaled Brady. The boy stepped closer to reach out and remove the leather hood from the eagle's head. Instantly, the bald eagle reared back against his chest. Her yellow eyes shone from the ponderous white head like fierce beacons over her mighty yellow beak. She'd come to the clinic near death and covered with maggots, the victim of barbiturate poisoning. They'd worked long hours with her and she was one of their successes. Now look at her, he thought, his own eyes shining. Her black feathers were gleaming over a substantial body. She was a fine specimen, strong and fierce. She was able and eager to fly, to fight the good fight once again.

Looking at her, Harris felt again the old, familiar urge to blend spirits with the bird in these final few moments before flight. For so long he'd despaired of ever making the link. The dark, murky shadows of his past had impaired his vision, allowing him limited sight of himself and the world around him. He'd believed that only a rare shaman held the secret to a true connection with birds of prey.

It was Lijah who had taught him that all living creatures were connected. There wasn't some great secret to divine, no mystery to ferret out. The lesson was not learned cognitively but intuitively. It wasn't reasoned with the brain, but felt in the heart. The Garden of Eden was here on earth if only we might open our eyes to see. Harris had tried to communicate only with the birds, but Lijah taught him that he couldn't separate one creature from another. To communicate with birds was to communicate with all other animals, plants and, most especially, humans. We were all in this together.

Only when he understood this did he open himself at last to love—and compassion, humility, understanding and forgiveness. And ultimately to the sweetest joy and contentment he'd ever known.

A brisk breeze whistled through the trees, bending the tall grasses. Ella turned the collar up along her neck. Brady reached out to smooth back the hair that whisked to his face. Marion grabbed hold of the eagle feather that lifted in the wind. The eagle lifted her snowy head, catching the scent of freedom in the air. Harris breathed deep the communal air and felt the soul-stirring connection.

It was time to send her home.

An expectant hush settled on the group. Harris turned to face the wind. The air was crisp, gusting, challenging. The eagle tensed in his arms, her eyes fierce.

"Godspeed," he murmured.

Then, with a mighty lift, he opened his arms.

The eagle arched her head forward, stretched out her long, massive wings and sliced the opposing air with the finesse and strength of a master swordsman. Onward, upward, she traveled on her slanted path to freedom. When at last she caught a thermal, the eagle held her black wings in a uniformly straight line. Neither drooping nor flapping, she seemed to defy gravity. Harris's throat tightened and his chest rose in exhilaration as his spirit flew with her. Together, they soared.

Harris stepped back from the center to join the circle. He wrapped one arm around his wife, the other around his daughter, and holding them close, he lifted his face and kept his eyes skyward.

★ ★ ★ ★ ★

Author's Note

How many of us have looked into a brilliant sky and felt our emotions stir at the sight of a hawk, falcon or eagle riding a thermal? Yet few of us know much about them. Birds of prey are found everywhere on earth and have evolved to adapt to a wide range of environments. It is their sensitivity to the environment, however, that makes them the most vulnerable of all bird species. Human interference through loss of habitat, toxins and trauma is by far the greatest cause of their death.

Rehabilitation centers seek to restore injured birds of prey to the wild. Experienced volunteers transport injured or threatened birds to rehabilitation centers where licensed staff members and volunteers work miracles, acting as surgeons, technicians, dietitians, therapists and cleanup committees. The goal of rehabilitation is to heal, then release raptors to the natural environment. Not all of them make it, but those that do will hopefully flourish and breed future generations.

Education and rehabilitation work hand in hand. Grassroots efforts across the country—and the world—are working to preserve habitats and to compensate for the damage done to birds of prey and all wildlife. If you're interested in supporting these efforts with either your time or a donation, there are rehabilitation centers located in states throughout the country. Or you can contact the SCCBOP at the address below. Your support is greatly appreciated!

South Carolina Center for Birds of Prey
P.O. Box 1247
Awendaw, SC 29402

Acknowledgments

During the writing of SKYWARD I met many devoted, impressive individuals and groups that work tirelessly for the protection and care of our important and threatened natural resource—birds of prey. I am indebted to all. In particular, I would like to thank:

James Elliott, founder and director of the Center for Birds of Prey and indefatigable teacher to us all, and to Franci Krawcke, Grace Gaspar, Stacey Hughes, and Laura Buchta, and Stephen Schabel. A special thank-you to my dear friend Mary Pringle, for serving as my mentor at the center and for sharing countless duties, including the dread mute scrubbing.

I am indebted to Marquetta Goodwine, "Queen Quet," of the Gullah/Geechee Nation, for graciously offering consultation regarding the Gullah culture and the character Lijah.

The character of Lijah in this story was inspired by the Gullah tradition of the African-American oral historians (griots). The Gullah language is as rich and complex as the culture, and I was fortunate to have the guidance of Queen Quet of the Gullah/Geechee Nation in writing Lijah's dialogue. However, I have taken the liberty of making substitutions so that the reader will more readily understand the text. Thus, while the dialogue is not pure Gullah, I've done my best to convey the unique qualities and rhythm of this significant Lowcountry language.

Several outstanding nurses shared their expertise. I'm grateful to Janet Grossman, Gail Stuart, Therese Killeen, Alexandra Koch, and Eileen Dreyer. Thank you also to Dr. Timothy Assey and Vanessa Ward for assistance with the issue of diabetes. I am well aware of the advances made in juvenile diabetes, and hope the reader takes into account the date of when the book was written and the circumstances of the characters. I made my choices carefully with the assistance of medical professionals.

Heartfelt thanks to SC poet laureate Marjory Wentworth, for allowing me to use her magnificent poem, *Contretemps,* and to bestselling author and fellow osprey lover, Anne Rivers Siddons, for her endorsement. A big thank you to Angela May for her editing.

New York Times
bestselling author

Mary Alice Monroe

They are the Season sisters, bound by
blood, driven apart by a tragedy. Now they
are about to embark on a bittersweet journey
into the unknown—an odyssey of promise
and forgiveness, of loss and rediscovery.

Jillian, Beatrice and Rose have gathered for the
funeral of their younger sister, Meredith. Her
death, and the legacy she leaves them, will trigger
a cross-country journey in search of a stranger with
the power to mend their shattered lives. As they
search for the girls they once were, they find what
they really lost—the women they were meant to be.

The **FOUR** Seasons

Available now wherever books are sold.

NEW YORK TIMES BESTSELLING AUTHOR

Mary Alice
MONROE

On the surface, it is a monthly book club.
But for five women, it is so much more.

For Eve Porter the club is a place of sanctuary. For Annie Blake it
is the chance to finally let down her guard and dream of other
possibilities. For Doris Bridges it is her support group as she
acknowledges her dying marriage. For Gabriella Rivera it is a sense
of community. And for Midge Kirsch it is a haven of acceptance.

They are five women from different walks of life, embracing
the challenge of change. And as they share their hopes and
fears and triumphs, they will hold fast to the true magic of
the book club—friendship.

The Book Club

"Monroe offers up believable characters in a well-crafted story."
—*Publishers Weekly*

Available now wherever books are sold.

MMAM2708TRR

A beloved novel by *New York Times* bestselling author

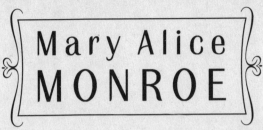

Mary Alice MONROE

Caretta Rutledge thought she'd left her Southern roots and troubled family far behind. But an unusual request from her mother—coming just as her own life is spinning out of control—has Cara heading back to the scenic Low Country of her childhood summers. Before long, the rhythms of the island open her heart in wonderful ways as she repairs the family beach house, becomes a bona fide "turtle lady" and renews old acquaintances long thought lost. But it is in reconnecting with her mother that she will learn life's most precious lessons—true love involves sacrifice, family is forever and the mistakes of the past can be forgiven.

The Beach House

"Mary Alice Monroe is helping to redefine the beauty and magic of the Carolina Low Country. Every book she has written has felt like a homecoming to me…"—Pat Conroy

Available now wherever books are sold.

MIRA®